I0741906

animal magnet

gary anderson

ISBN: 978-0-692-68928-8
© Gary Anderson, 2011
Revised Edition, 2016
Run Amok Books

ANIMAL

MAGNET

Believing, with Max Weber, that man is an animal
in webs of significance he himself has spun,
I take culture to be those webs.

-Clifford
Geertz-

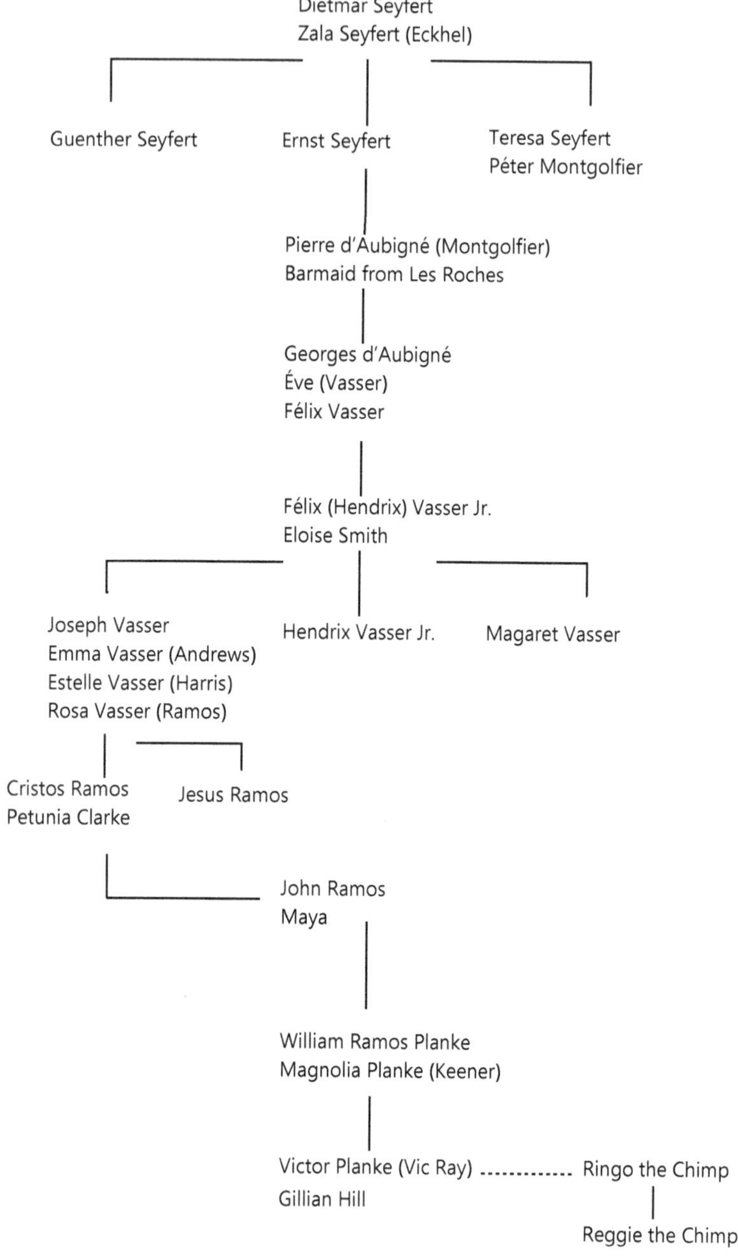

Dietmar Seyfert
Zala Seyfert (Eckhel)

Guenther Seyfert
Ernst Seyfert
Teresa Seyfert
Péter Montgolfier

Pierre d'Aubigné (Montgolfier)
Barmaid from Les Roches

Georges d'Aubigné
Éve (Vasser)
Félix Vasser

Félix (Hendrix) Vasser Jr.
Eloise Smith

Joseph Vasser
Emma Vasser (Andrews)
Estelle Vasser (Harris)
Rosa Vasser (Ramos)
Hendrix Vasser Jr.
Magaret Vasser

Cristos Ramos
Petunia Clarke
Jesus Ramos

John Ramos
Maya

William Ramos Planke
Magnolia Planke (Keener)

Victor Planke (Vic Ray)
Gillian Hill
Ringo the Chimp

Reggie the Chimp

Preface

Excerpted from *Mind Games: The Life and (Good) Times of an Amazonian Toad Licker* by William Ramos Planke (Grove: 1963, 263-64)

My father and I transitioned in two opposite directions: He from the civilized to the savage and I from the savage to the civilized. He from the bed to the hammock and I from the hammock to the bed. Father had no intention of taking me back to civilization—ever; he desired only that I stay with him in the wilds of the Amazonian rainforest. For what he had come to realize, with an immiscible clarity unattainable in unaltered states, is that civilization is an artificial system superimposed upon the natural world. Nothing more than a semblance of order forced upon nebular chaos. By extension, the taxonomic system, with which we divide, classify, and ultimately judge all of creation, is also artificial and contrived. Speciation is an idea, a grand myth. The evolutionary tree— moving down from one age to the next; from one phylum to two classes, to three orders, to four families, to five genii, to a thousand species, to a million sub-species—is a contrivance meant to separate humans from the rest of the natural world and to establish primacy. My toad-licking father saw through the chimera of taxonomy, past the hubris of the Linnaean system. He believed that life—all life—should be viewed, not vertically, or hierarchically; but horizontally, equally: "The spectrum of life," he called it.

Despite my father's objections concerning speciation, one cannot help but think vertically where families are concerned: father to son, mother to daughter, and so on and so forth. That I was destined to escape the clutches of my drug-crazed father was made certain by my mother. And having been literally handed over to my adoptive parents, I spent much of my youth wondering about the verticality of my own biological progenitors. So that when I reached the age of majority, I set out to discover who they were, only to uncover a shameful parade of bastards, miscreants, and foolhardy eccentrics. It quickly became a search that no longer interested me. Even the sickly pale runt-of-a-life that I had sired in my youth no longer interested me. (For, I reasoned, would he not also be some freakish patchwork of my ancestral parts and passions?)

Genetic goo trickles down the boughs of the family tree like a slow moving sap, combining and re-combining, inventing and reinventing.

And therein is evolution at its most fundamental. A microcosm stripped bare of human politics, stripped bare of pretense. There is no way of changing who you are or where you have come from (unfortunately, some would say). I am my drug-addled father and my Karubo mother, recombined and re-invented, just as the snake is its father and mother, the jackal its father and mother, and the whale its father and mother. There is no other distinction to be made. They, too, are stuck with their genetic past. And if this is indeed true, then there is no meaningful distinction to be made between us and them: humans and animals. This my father understood, and this was his conviction.

So he lingered among the *caceteiros*. He longed for their natural state. He longed to take his place in the natural world, not as Homo sapiens but simply as a living creature. He blocked out the civilized Jekyll in himself by licking the cane toad, until only his natural self remained. Even so, as a boy, I recall not fully understanding the two people my father seemed to be. Nor could I reconcile them. The stark difference was jarring, sometimes terrifying. For he could not lick the toad day in, day out (not for lack of trying), and the civilized man would inevitably resurface in him. He simply could not keep that version of himself forever at bay.

There was something about the civilized man that I was drawn to, a tenderness, perhaps, which was absent in the natural man. It was at those times that I would clutch his hand or climb upon his back for a spirited piggy-back ride through the village, which would invariably end with us falling into heaps of tearful laughter.

Mother once told me that my father cried when I was born. I have always wondered who he was then, at that moment, and I sometimes imagine the event. My mother screeching in agony inside the birthing hut. My father fidgeting with the bore tusks dangling around his neck. He is anxious, speaking nervous gibberish to everyone around him. When the shaman exits the hut and delivers to him an infant son, father cuts the foreskin on the edge of his teeth. Then he holds me up, gently, and the entire forest falls silent as he utters the words: "My son, my son."

A Short Accounting of the Very Short Life & Times of Ernst Wilhelm Seyfert, with a Fervent Plea for Assistance

From that remarkable day forward, his most honorable and worthy name would ne'er again cross my lips, but he would be known to me only as MASTER. Even now, as the dark symmetry & whetted verdict of the fallbeil propose to set my wretched soul free, he remains so: MASTER. I, Ernst Seyfert, you will by now know, am slated to be one head less than reputable in one week less a day. And the most worthy MASTER of whom I speak is—I shall recite it here once, Gentle Sir, then nev'rmore—Franz Anton Mesmer. MASTER! Oh remarkable day! Fateful day! When first his landau did lope to the Manor house of my Master—that being the Master of my employ—Baron Horeczky de Hôrka. And what, Kind Sir, does my most worthy MASTER—whose name shall ne'ermore be utt'r'd— have to do with my present circumstance? Nothing & everything. 'Tis no jocosity! I should rather feed at the tail of a flatulent swine than be so presumptuous as to pose riddles to you.

But let me begin at the beginning, as they say, which ere long will lead to the crux of the matter. And 'tis a crux, Sir, to be sure! For what hapless young man of twenty & one finds himself shackled with a week less a day to delight in the undiminish't ensemble of his body corporeal? Oh, to find a more symbolic salvation than the one heretofore offer'd me by the fallbeil! Oh, inhumane contraption! Oh, that my days stretch't out before me as Time's long-spun highway in the stead of my youthful neck, which in a nigh-coming day will be stretch't o'er the chopping block! 'Tis to this end that I give account of my short life, Gentle Sir, in hopes that you may take pity on me and assist me in my humble quest to keep body & soul together.

'Tis a matter of public record that I was christen'd Ernst Helmut Seyfert in the year of our Lord, seventeen-hundred & fifty-first—second son to Dietmar Seyfert, third child of Zala Eckhel Seyfert and last to navigate the fertile canal of her womanhood, only to thereupon breech the blessed aperture. Sir, 'tis not my intent to here offend ears polite; for this final detail was made known to me only by my Uncle's lowly explanation—due, no doubt, to his Stableman's station in life—that had I been a donkey, he would have "grab'd the tail of that ass and yank't it forcefully into this despicable & disastrous world." Perhaps just such a rash & violent act would have saved my poor departed Mother, as leading with my rear end, I put an untimely end to her life & times. According to Uncle Manfred Eckhel—yes, Kind Sir, 'tis the same whose plight as a lowly Stableman taints all that he is bound to utt'r—nor have I stop'd leading arsy-versy since that day. I should have heels under toes for all the leading I do in that astern & hindermost direction, says he.

Yet, for all his seeming unkindness, I know Uncle Manfred is fond of me and holds me blameless in his Sister's unhappy passing into the great & marvelous beyond. For his fondness was rehearsed to me by my elder Sister and eldest sibling, Theresa, who was witness to those festive occasions when he would take me, a shabby toddler, on his knee and bounce me in a frightfully spirited fashion. In fact, the slight ringing in my left ear may be attributed, I believe, to one such session, when so exuberant was his bouncing that he bounced me thusly onto the hardened clay of our cottage floor.

Forgive my wearisome intromission, I beg you, as my wandering account bumbles forev'r forward. It is my tedious habit, as my friend and Tutor, Péter, has ofttimes told me. In my own defense, let me here say that he is not without blame, for it was he who once encouraged me to aspire to a level of perfect eloquence befitting a Master's Footman—my life's design!

As I have already so indelicately explained, my dear departed Mother died at my hand—or at my rear, to be precise. My Father, it turned out, was an equally star-cross't soul, although my rear had no part in his untimely demise. One morning he lay down for forty winks in the hay—he being Stablemaster and Uncle Manfred his underling Stableman—as he was often apt to do, and ne'er awaken'd. Had he lived to hoist open his eyes a last time on that sullen spring morning, he would have found himself flatten'd flatter 'n' beam's end beneath old Virgil, the mottled stallion whose studded past has caught up to him, and—as Uncle Manfred is apt to make a point of—has left him swinging so low that he routinely knocks about his swollen pills, despite a most cautious gait. Virgil, being Uncle Manfred's unspoken but not unwitting drinking mate, after snorting a hogshead of ale commandeer'd by Uncle Manfred and roll'd twelve furlong from the village rectory, had flopp'd down drunk on my napping Father. The old horse may have died himself had Uncle Manfred, upon discovering the where-abouts of his unfortunate in-law, not try'd to rouse the screw'd beast with a battery of assorted blows & abuse. Sadly, 'twas to no avail. My Father, Dietmar Seyfert, was from then on crassly refer'd to about the village as the stud Virgil's "last lay."

And that, Gentle Sir, is how I came to be the orphan Ernst Seyfert before I'd bid farewell to the tender years of my childhood; and how, too, Uncle Manfred came to be Stablemaster and head of our humble cottage home here among the scattered Ash trees on the edge of my Master's— Baron Horeczky de Hôrka—Manor.

Not so long ago, I took great comfort in the knowledge that my MASTER—he whose name shall nev'rmore be utt'r'd—although not an orphan, was pluck't for greatness from a fallow field of commoners. His Father—a gamekeeper—was not so very different from my own Father. His Mother press't him towards the priesthood, but the young MASTER had no predilection for stale reveries concerning GOD and HIS nature; instead he revel'd in the Heavens above—the Earth & Moon, the Planets and their occult derivations—perhaps under-standing even then, at that early age, the connectedness of all things in Heaven & Earth; and how the Universe is a tingly vat of warm current and we are all submerged in it; for a magnetic fluid infuses ALL—every tree, every stone, every beast, every man. 'Tis the KOSMIC umbilical cord that ties us each to the other. But I digress. As I said, I once took great consolation in this, but now as a young man not long for this world my chances of achieving even the most meager portion of my MASTER'S greatness appears to me as thin as the arse of a tinker's breeches.

As a boy nigh eight years of age, with my Father but a year's time away from being lay'd by Virgil into a final resting place, I took my place on the bottom rung of the Manor hierarchy, working as a Stableboy's boy. To my great & abounding chagrin, the Stableboy who lorded o'er me was none other than my elder Brother Guenther, whom, I now believe, was muddle-headed as to the true stature of his Stableboy position—his logic, could it fairly be called such, ran as follows: "Take a maid's maid for instance . . . would n't't mean that said maid's got her own maid to wait on her hand & foot?" He clearly believed it to be true. By extension, he concluded, "Since you're a Stableboy's boy, an' I'm said Stableboy, then you must sure as shadflies be MY boy." This is where the confusion began for Guenther and ended for me. My Father, being a goodly sort, and not one to dabble in the affairs of others, raised no objection to my Brother's despotic hold o'er me; for soon Father, too, would be on to the Great Beyond and himself sure to be some boy's boy in that Kosmic hierarchy. And so it went for me for much of my childhood: The Stableboy's boy.

But then, as with all stories worth a straw, the unexpected happened—unexpected but not unwelcom'd. In hindsight, perhaps it might be attributed to the grueling hours of pitching hay, or cartful upon cartful of horse trágya shovel'd; whate'er the cause, I grew suddenly aloft with dizzying speed, to the plain height of a sizeable pikestaff; I was topmast, that is to say, my elder Brother Guenther was low mast; I had outgrown him, my master, the Stableboy.

The tragedy & irony in this, my Brother's unfavorable lot, cannot be overstated. The tragedy, of course, stems from the well-known fact that the Baron's Footmen are always the tallest and sturdiest young fellows from among the rank & file: 'Tis a time-honored tradition that a Nobleman's Footman be a young man of stature—physical & otherwise. But forgive me, Gentle Sir, as you yourself are surely quite aware of this hallow'd tradition. Thus it seem'd, that in the contest to attain the post of Footman, I had surpass't my Brother Guenther, a cruel twist of fate, to be sure, Gentle Sir; yet if the tragedy be cruel, then the irony is pitiless. Even so, as tragedies go, it is undeniably amusing—or as the Baroness & her clutch of hens would surely say after the manner of the fashionable French, "'Tis a delicious morsel of *moira.*"

Not long into the reign of his absolute rule o'er me, Guenther expanded my duties to include a daily ritual which entail'd rigging him with ropes to old Virgil and his slightly more youthful companion old Horace. How assiduously I loop'd a trusty & versatile bowline about each ankle & wrist, then fasten'd the opposite end to the tack of either stud with an always secure buntline hitch. In the case that it may interest you, Kind Sir, in the months before his passing, my goodly Father put me through a rigorous regimen of knot tying, one which was carried on, and to some degree undone, by Uncle Manfred, who, with several draughts of ale under his belt, could undertake nothing more complicated than a booby knot.

With the rigging in place, Guenther inhaled & exhaled thrice deeply before huffing a bellow'd command, "Stretch, beasts! Stretch for yer lives!" And stretch they would, until Virgil & Horace show'd signs of broken wind, at which time they would drop their hind quarters to the ground and sit panting like two drowsy Vizslas in the honey'd-light of

June. Despite his efforts to stretch the bounds of Nature, my Brother the Stableboy, if one were to believe the furry notches he had carved into the central beam of the stables, was diminishing in stature. Yes, Gentle Sir, he was shrinking.

'Twas around this time that Fortune smiled upon me. Having taken up the cause of self-improvement—perhaps another instance, Uncle Manfred would surely say, of me leading with my rear end—and wanting to learn the ins & outs of grooming, I began to eagerly assist the Stable Groom at his trade. Thinking that Virgil might suit my novice needs, the Groom left the old stud in my care. First mastering the curry-comb, I moved on to dandy-brush; the mane comb & hoof pick follow'd. By this time, old Virgil look't ready to reclaim those earlier hey-days of courting young & stylish mares; even Uncle Manfred was duly impress't with the transformation of his drinking mate, and in fact, the two of them had retired to the feed room to toast the old stud's new veneer when the Baron appear'd unexpectedly. Since I do not believe that your Excellency is acquainted with Baron Horeczky de Hôrka—at least, in the years of my employ, I did ne'er hear mention of your most honorable name, Kind Sir—allow me here to sketch an abbreviated history of the fine Master of my employ.

My Master's Baronry is one of the oldest in the empire, which may account for its hazy beginnings. What is known is that Baronry was granted to the Baron's ancestor, Ákos Horeczky, by the Great Ferdinand II, King of Bohemia & King of Hungary, for distinguishing himself on the battlefield; that is, for single-handedly slaughtering half a battalion of Frederick's Protestants in Bohemia. Gentle Sir, you will surely agree that no higher calling nor nobler undertaking exists in the eyes of God & Church than the brutal slaying of Heretics; thus duly, land & the castle Zvolen were given o'er to the brave Knight; however, when Zvolen fell into disrepair and suffer'd greatly at the hands of invading Turks, Ákos Horeczky's son, György, my Master's Grandfather, moved to the Manor House at Hôrka. 'Tis there, Kind Sir, that much of my story unfolds, although admittedly, my story, I own, has yet to unfold the lines of consternation that my twitter-twaddling has assuredly sculpted into the gentle slope of your fine, gentlemanly brow.

When my Master, Baron de Hôrka, tread a noble gait into the stables, 'twas a momentous occasion and the first e'er in which his magnanimous gaze fell upon me. Being stun'd as I was, words dribbled from me like cranch't meal; so, I dusted off my breeches and executed a most plain approximation of a specious & respectful bow, in the hope that such might divert his attentions away from my unintelligible babble. As it turned out, my approximation proved to be an effective one, as the Baron ask't me who I was and how I had come to be a Stableboy's boy in his Noble Stable's stables. To this I responded with but a modicum of hesitation, having now gather'd my wits about me: "Why Excellent Majesty's Nobleman, Sir, I am the humble outcome, issue & progeny of the Stablemaster Dietmar Seyfert, at your service." Even Uncle Manfred would here have to concede that for once in my life I had kept my rear end rearward and had led perfectly with the nub of my nose.

Not long after this auspicious occasion, I was hail'd to the Manor house where I was to take up my position as Hall boy, which, it turn'd out, was the Footman's boy's boy. Indeed, I own'd the added import of my promotion from Stableboy's boy to a Footman's boy's boy was well reflected in the seeming thriving nature of the title itself. Guenther clearly believed as much, as he was green'r than a toad's missing tail with envy. Before I pack't my belongings and made the short but symbolic trek to the Manor house, he beg'd me rig him up once more, vowing ne'er to cry for release 'til he reach't the honorable stature befitting a Footman. Feeling a twitch of remorse & an inkling of sympathy, I obliged my Brother this one final whimsy, although I own'd that old Virgil & old Horace would peter out to a well-deserved end before my Brother e'er found himself in the press't plush velvet britches of a Footman.

I took up quarters under the stairs in the back hall, which well explains why the Footman's boy's boy is often refer'd to as simply the Hall boy. A Footman's boy's boy, it turn'd out, was not so very different from a Stable boys' boy. In short, Kind Sir, I still found myself knee-deep in trágya, except that the trágya I now saw to slosh't about in copper chamber pots and, in truth, was so much the more vile for it. As Footman's boy's boy, the lion's share of my time was taken up by the collection & disposal of chamber pots. Each morning, I would gather and see to the chamber pots of the Footman; the Footman's boy; the Tutor, Péter; the Valet, or Butler's boy; the Butler, or Master's boy; the Master's actual boy, András; and the Master Baron de Hôrka himself, whom, I own, might rightly be regarded of as the King's boy.

And what, you may wonder, does trágya have to do with the price of tea in China? If, kind Sir, you will indulge me but a moment longer, I will do my utmost to explain the seemingly questionable relevance of trágya to this tragic tale. One day, several months after taking up my position as Footman's boy's boy, as I was collecting the previous night's trágya, I came across something very odd indeed: a gem in the Footman's pot. At the time, I had no knowledge of the precise ilk of that gem (I would later learn that the stone was an icy blue sapphire), only that 'twas a precious stone sparkling there like the morning star in a dysenteric sludge-fill'd sky. I immediately stole down to the kitchen to enlist the help of my elder Sister, Theresa, the scullery maid; there, I procured a sterling silver ladle with which to scoop up the gem. My first thought (in truth, more of a question than thought) was how does such a thing end up in a copper pot of trágya? My second thought was what shall I do with it now?

With all due respect, I wonder if your Excellency can appreciate how such a bit of unexpected good Fortune could turn a Footman's boy's boy's world around. The price that such a gem might fetch would, I own, be more than I could earn in five honest lifetimes. However, bless't with a level head, as I have been (Uncle Manfred deems it a curse, claiming that if my head were any more level, I could erect myself as a column for Basilica di San Pietro—sadly, he is neither a sober nor pious man), I quickly realized that such a find might be more likely to turn my world topsy-turvy than to turn my world around. Resolved to do as my dear departed Mother would have me do, that is to say, the right & Christian thing to do, I look't for an opportunity to present myself before my Master—Baron Horeczky de Hôrka—most expeditiously.

As luck would have it, that very morning, the Baron, determined to take advantage of the uncharacteristically calm weather, decided to hunt game among the rolling hills & flower'd meadows of his vast estate. As a Stable boy's boy, I had on occasion had the occasion to look on as my Excellent Master blasted a pheasant in the brush or annihilated a green neck't goose on a sylvan pond with a fowling piece; that is to say, I had first-hand knowledge of his first-favor'd hunting grounds. At dawn's gold'n crack, the hunting party departed from the Manor House, and I saddled up old Virgil and set out after them with the sapphire tuck't safely away in a leather pouch tied at my waist.

Fortune once again smiled upon me, for just ahead I spy'd the group standing at a stand-still, yet still mounted on their steaming steeds. One lone Soul, whom I recognized as the Baron himself, had dismounted and stood off to one side with only his boy András for a companion. I must admit that at that moment my heart went from lope to spirited gallop; for 'twas the opportunity I had been waiting for. I pointed Virgil directly at my Excellent Master and spur'd the old stud on. But as my earlier anecdotes clearly attest to, Virgil has a mind of his own; and on this particular occasion he had it in his mind to gallop cleanly by the Good Baron and mount the sensually swaying haunches of the Baroness's sorrel filly; all of this, I might add, despite my firm objection with reign & whip. Left with no alternative course of action, I bounded earth-wise from the old stud's back, rolling & tumbling like a rum-dumb Monk from his mountain monastery before coming to a halt at the Baron's excellent feet. To my great horror, Good & Noble Sir, I quickly learn'd that my Master was making water with the assistance of young András, who suspended the Master's riding breeches in one hand and his Noble *kakas* in the other.

Despite this awkward introduction (or re-introduction, as it were) my most Magnanimous Master greeted me with a kindly if startled greeting. Fighting the urge to scramble to my feet, I rose with all the calm & dignity that the infelicitous situation would allow. "Most Excellent Master & Good Baron, I, Ernst Helmut Seyfert, son to the late Stablemaster, Dietmar Karl Seyfert, and most recently having taken up the post of Footman's boy's boy in the most splendid Manor de Hôrka, do greet you, humbly & gratefully, on this grand & glorious morning in this the most favored land on God's Green Earth," said I.

The Good Baron affected a pink & spongy grin. The earlier salient stream of his Noble water had now drop'd to a Plebeian drizzle in the grass. "Yes, I do believe you're right . . ."

"Seyfert, Good Baron, Sir."

"Yes, Seyfert. 'Tis a grand & glorious morning," said he. András hiked up the Master's breeches. "Ah, yes. Now I recall your Father the Stablemaster. Such a pity. What was it?"

"Virgil's last lay, Good Baron."

"Yes, 'twas that. Crass, indeed."

Sensing that this awkward encounter may be nearing an abrupt end, I loosen'd the pouch, reach't in, and produced the gem I had retrieved from the Footman's pot earlier that morning.

"Good & Kind Baron, 'tis highly unusual, I know, yet I beseech you, Good Master, to give me audience and hear how this precious gem came into my lowly possession." I held out the stone; it caught a ray of sunlight and sat glowing in my palm. Honesty compels me to here say, I know not if 'twas my eloquent plea or the sight of his Excellency's missing sapphire that convinced the Baron to spare a moment of his Noble time—although I suspect the latter.

Be that as it may, I sit here now, Gentle Sir, a young man condemn'd to death, reflecting on the weight & folly of this world: I see now that there are few times in one's life when one knows he has made the right decision; that is, reach't a favorable resolution. Of course, one knows when he has chosen imprudently; that is, trod upon the wrong path, for these choices invariably end in dire circumstances, such as those I now find thrust upon my own self, and those for which I intrepidly & impudently seek your most merciful intervention. However, only once or twice in his life-time, I own, may the fortunate man know & appreciate that he has judged judiciously and made a wise decision. Why do I trifle with such platitudes, Gentle Sir? 'Tis only because it turn'd out that my decision to seek an audience with the Good Baron was one of those few times. That is to say, I knew that I had judged judiciously. Of this, there can be no doubt.

For so exulted was my Master with the return of his sapphire, that I was raised forthwith to the post of Footman. Yes, Gentle Sir, Footman! A shock to you no doubt: 'Twas doubly a shock to me. Then & there, at the tender age of eighteen years was my life's ambition fulfill'd—still wet behind the ears (as the English say) and with my scuff't shoes yet damp with the Baron's Noble water, I was a footman. My thoughts naturally turn'd to Guenther, and I could not help but wonder how he might react to the gladsome news. In that moment, I had a snap vision of him lying in the stables, reduced to a fleshy stump, limbless from the incessant stretching of old Virgil and old Horace. Yet, even this morbid excogitation fail'd to dampen my rhapsodic spirits, for I had done it, I had scaled the shaggy cliffs of social exclusion aided only by my ambition and had reach't the plateau of polite society, from whence, I could behold the summit of sublime social rank: NOBILITY. I had risen to my natural station in life; I was a Footman. At least, so was my thinking at the time, Good Sir.

Caught up, as I was, in the moment, it did not occur to me until later to wonder what had become of the former Footman, that I should find my young self set so fortuitously in his stead. And, in fact, 'twas only after I had stolen down to the kitchen to tell my Sister, Theresa, of this portentous tale that I learn'd of his unhappy fate. For news of the sapphire in the trágya had spread among the servants quicker than scabies on a berth deck. The Footman before me, Balogh, a long-trusted servant of the Baron, had been sack't (again, as the English say) that very morning, upon the Master's return to the Manor House. The sapphire, it turn'd out, was not the first of the Baron's gems to go missing, and, thanks to my recent discovery, it was now known that Balogh had been the culprit all along. He was in the habit of popping a diamond or ruby or emerald into his mouth and quaffing it with a goblet of wine; he would fetch the jewel from his bedpan before the Footman's boy's boy saw to the pots the next morning. However, this morning, Balogh had slept late, having tip'd one too many goblets of wine the previous night, and I, the new Footman's boy's boy, had discover'd the sapphire before he could retrieve it. Thus had I thwarted his plan.

With a light heart and a tune buzzing around in my head like the honey bee in a mead jar, I moved from my quarters under the stairs to a proper room in the main hall, next to the Valet's room and near to the Master's quarters. Scarcely had I done so, when the Valet himself knock't and enter'd my room. It quickly became apparent that I was now the Valet's boy, who was the Butler's boy & so on. He handed o'er a list of my duties, which involved a great deal of standing about & doing nothing. In the morning, I was to stand outside the Master's quarters until he had eaten, dress'd & emerged. Then I was to stand in the great hall and wait, in the event that the Valet or the Butler should need assistance in attending to the Master. If the Master should travel that day, I was to stand on the back of the coach and see to the Good Baron & Baroness's safe entrance & exit, to & from the carriage. At meals, I was to stand in the dining room and attend to whatever manner of chore & task the Butler should bid me do. At night, I was to stand again outside the Master's quarters until which time he slumber'd soundly. All in all, the Valet made it clear that I was to do precisely as he bid me do. And most of all, I must always look neat & seemly, for, said he, "The employment of a Footman is a symbol of status among those of rank."

I must admit, Gentle Sir, that this remark made perfect sense to me, as I own'd my duties were not real duties at all. In a word, I was simply an ostentatious show of wealth: from my gold braided waistcoat to my brass button'd knee breeches to my white silk stockings to my brass buckled shoes; I was an adornment & testament to my Master's great wealth. I beg you, Sir, to not think me ungrateful; I was terribly grateful. In fact, so grateful was I that then & there, I took it upon myself to be the best standing Footman that the Manor had e'er seen. I would stand the longest, the straightest, the most attentively. I would raise the task of standing to an Art, Sir.

And I am happy to report that I did do just that: raise the task of standing to an Art. Humbly, I proclaim in all humility, that I was the best Footman in the county. It fact, it soon became common knowledge among the servants of Noble households everywhere that Baron Horeczky de Hôrka had the best standing Footman in the county Spiš. Yet even as I recount this particular accolade, no doubt your patience wanes, and you wonder precisely when it was that my troubles began. But, Good Sir, fear not, for troubles are on the horizon, looming large, for the best standing Footman in the county Spiš.

As a boy, I was given o'er to the idea that only the poor suffer'd and that affliction was something unknown to those of social rank. If you recall the mishaps of my own youth, particularly regarding the untimely end of my poor departed Mother & Father, you may understand my mistaken notion. Not long after I had taken up my Footman's position, I became aware of a certain ailment that tormented my Good Master, Baron Horeczky de Hôrka, from time to time. When it struck, the Baron's throat swell'd and a manner of paralysis follow'd, rendering his speaking faculties speechless. For several days, he would remain in his chambers, flat on his back, feverish & unable to eat or drink. For her part, the Baroness paced about the Manor in these trying times, manifesting an extreme vexation of spirit, which led her to hiss like an adder at anything that moved; however, most of her worry & solicitude were directed at her esteem'd Physician, Miroslav Kvetnica, who was helpless in helping the Good Baron. In fact, the Baroness had caused such a fright in the old Physician that he finally refused to visit the Manor de Hôrka while the Master was afflicted thusly. Instead, he refer'd the Baron to a man of lesser renown & greater infamy: a Physician whose unorthodox treatment was not without its critics, nor its champions. Yes, Good Sir, you have undoubtedly guess't his identity; 'twas he, my MASTER, Franz Anton Mesmer, whose name I shall utt'r but one last time, then nevermore.

Given the high esteem with which I esteem him, you may be astonish't to learn that my most Excellent MASTER only e'er address'd me on but one occasion. 'Tis true, Kind Sir! And 'tis a testament to the potent almightiness of his puissance. The address in question was a simple phrase: "You there, Footman, hold this," said the MASTER, and he held out a silk stocking, his own silk stocking from his own blessed foot. Yet, Gentle Sir, I see now that this single line may not convey the true sense of his pre-eminence when rehearsed without the beneficial benefit of context.

That very day the MASTER arrived in a fine black & red landau pull'd by two fine bay stallions—of the Trakehner breed, no doubt—a more majestic sight would have been hard to imagine, Sir. Erect, he sat: a stately composure with a princely profile, in a fashionable beige & gray cutaway satin waistcoat; his periwig, club'd & powder'd, trail'd a white, scented plume of Orris root. As Footman, I dutifully awaited his arrival outside the Great Hall on this most auspicious Spring morning, although I had yet to fully grasp the import of what was about to transpire in the Manor de Hôrka.

Not being one to stand on ceremony, the MASTER refused my supererogatory assistance. Exiting the carriage, he tug'd at his waistcoat and strode to the Manor with the clack of his heels & the click of a rattan cane, as one for whom a pressing task awaits. Erstwhile keeping my gaze level'd on a distant prospect in the presence of social superiors (as every worthy Footman knows), I let my attention wander but a moment to the MASTER'S luminescent visage, where I found myself drawn to the magnetic force of his Prussian blue eyes. Noble Sir, my senses swoon'd, I swear it! 'Twas as if I were a blushing virgin in the bed chambers of Don Giovanni! For in that brief interlude, I found myself utterly under his control; I would have writhed and spat as a King Cobra before a Mongoose had he will'd me to do so. Thus was my first glimpse into the power of Animal Magnetism, a theory I study'd at length in the wake of my MASTER'S departure.

Of course, Kind & Gentle Sir, you may wonder what business a simple Footman has studying a theory roundly regarded by science as Charlatanry. With all due respect to you and to those of the Academy, allow me, here, a fleeting foray into the hyperbolic (yes, 'tis again inspired by Uncle Manfred, regrettably): If my MASTER, Franz Anton Mesmer, whose name shall nevermore be utt'r'd, is a Charlatan, then I am Papa Bonifacius Primitus, Secundus, Tertius, Quartus & Qunitus. For shame! I hear you, Pious Sir—to stoop to such heresy. But in this sully'd & disrespectful repàrtee, Noble Sir, lies the true extent of my certainty that the MASTER is no Charlatan. For I witness'd the might of his restorative powers with mine own eyes, Kind Sir. 'Tis no jocosity! I should rather sleep at the hooves of a peasant jackass inflicted with a sour gastric zephyr than be so idleheaded as to try to deceive you. As to the reason why I would study my MASTER'S theory of Animal Magnetism, I beg you forebear my circumlocution but a spell longer, when all will become clear as the conscience of Saint Stephen on Judgment Day.

The Manor was alight with news of the MASTER'S arrival, and the maids stole away from their duties long enough to catch a glimpse of the charming Physician with his charmingly ruddy complexion & full pale lips. As I have mentioned, his was a visage that commanded attention; there was something heraldic in it, it must be said. Soft & round, yet render'd masculine by a heavy jaw & exquisite chin. And he was sturdy, Kind Sir, displaying the air of an outdoors man, not the sickly positure of a scholar who takes his meals o'er a book, ne'er to venture beyond the pale of his musty library.

The Baroness awaited the arrival at the entrance of the Great Hall, attended by her lady-in-waiting & her chamber maid. (Of course, the Baron himself was laid up in his bed, unable to speak and sweltering with fever as a field o' fire.) Good Sir, you are undoubtedly aware of the Baroness's reputation as the beauty of all beauties; let me hear say, 'tis a well deserved reputation. Truly, she is a most comely creature. If I might be allow'd to employ a trope, Good Sir: her beauty is like wine—there are those for whom it is a sublime intoxication, and there are those for whom it is a bitter & lethal poison. (Exactly what this means, I am not entirely certain, for it was a trope borrow'd from Péter, who as the Baroness's nephew knows more of such things than I.)

On this day, Lady de Hôrka look't exotic as the Nile, with gold & jewel'd trinkets of adornment adorning every strut, beam, vault, & arch of her natural architecture. Her embroider'd bodice, which held snuggly to her regal bosom, eventually gave way to a cataract of lace and ribbon. Her head was bare and her ebony hair plaited. Perhaps thinking to make a favorable impression, the Baroness had set aside her usual disquietude and greeted the good Physician (of whom, it must be said, she was in no small way suspicious) with the offer of her Noble hand, which the MASTER swiftly peck't as the cockerel might peck at the comb & waddle of a henhouse competitor. I & the Valet follow'd behind, each on either side of the sizeable, leathern black case which I would later learn contain'd the MASTER'S glass armonica (no doubt, Kind Sir, you have yourself laid eyes on the *glasharfe* in the noble courts of Austria, for Péter informs me they are all the rage). Seeing it, and presuming it to be some large largess intended for her household, the Baroness let an uncharacteristic titter spill from her pursed lips. With her gratitude now unbound from its customary parsimonious constraints, she usher'd the Physician of dubious renown into the dining hall, where pots of tea & a fortress of stack't pastries awaited his assault. Despite this heartfelt welcome, the MASTER was eager to see the patient and so chose to forgo the hospitable gesture, instead making his masterful way up the winding staircase of the great hall to the Baron's chambers.

As Footman, 'twas my duty to take my dutiful place attending to the Baron; that is, standing statuesque outside his living quarters. Thus, seeing the MASTER striding purposefully for the staircase, I promptly took to his heels. Kind Sir, to walk in his glorious wake was nothing short of a delightful delight, a thrilling thrill. As Uncle Manfred would undoubtedly say of such a pleasure: 'Twas more pleasing than spying a fair maiden, denuded and *fokken* a battalion of the King's soldiers. Forgive me, Gentle Sir; how quickly I forget that the bywords & truisms of Uncle Manfred ring truest whilst utt'r'd in the horse barn.

I have already made a point (and perhaps belabor'd it) of mentioning my valued accomplishments as Footman. Yet, here I must admit to having stray'd from the dutiful path of my duty but for a moment. So great was my inquisitiveness & marvel where the MASTER was concern'd that I could scarcely keep myself from glancing 'round the corner of the Baron's chambers. The regal blue velvet curtains were drawn, allowing only the thinnest shiv of light to slice through the sickly milieu of the chamber. There the MASTER, dimly lit, now strip'd of his waistcoat, with sleeves roll'd & hoisted above the elbows, hover'd o'er the Baron, who appear'd barely conscious of his magnetic presence. The MASTER straighten'd upright and swish't through the leaden half-light to the toilette, where he removed a single modest band from his wedding finger and poured water into a silver basin.

Gentle Sir, you will no doubt agree that there is nothing peculiar, spectacular, or even noteworthy about this particular detail. In fact, 'tis probably something akin to standard practice in the daily negotiations of a Physician. Yet the MASTER did not then proceed to wash his hands, nor did he bathe the briny brow of the Baron. No, Kind Sir, he did neither of these things. The MASTER set the basin on the floor in close proximity to the foremost canopy post of the Baron's bed and, bracing himself with one hand there, he raised a leg (at which point bark't the boom of breaking wind) and pull'd his silk stocking from his right foot. Looking about, he spy'd me spying him and utt'r'd that unforgettable phrase, those first mystical words burn'd forever into my memory, as if inscribed by the fiery quill of St. John of the Cross: "You there, Footman, hold this." Of course, I hasten'd to him and relieved him of the stocking, giving utt'rance to my newly-found & deeply felt deference: "Yes, MASTER," said I, with a slight obeisance. The MASTER dip'd the big toe of his right foot in the water then grasp'd either of the Baron's thumbs in full grip, much the way a farmer grasps the teats of a stall'd dairy cow. The Baron stir'd, responded with a groan & snort that was reminiscent of the shocking array of sounds that usher forth from sundry orifices of old Virgil in a fitful sleep brought on by an excess of honey mead. Still, the MASTER persisted. And in that dim light, I swear I saw him glowing. A radiance of gold'n vapors radiating from him. 'Twas nothing short of miraculous—stupendous. I know now, Kind Sir, 'twas the Animal Magnetism emanating from him in a shimmering show of excited plasmatic particles.

By this time, the Baroness & her clutch of domestic ninnies had gather'd in the chambers (forgive my crassness, Good Sir, but the whir of the fallbeil outside my window, of late, stirs the madness in me), and, to the Baroness's great dismay, the Baron was now affecting the harrowing sound of a baying dog being ready'd for the spit. Still the MASTER clutch't his noble thumbs (wobbling slightly on one foot), sending a stream of magnetism coursing through the Baron. Then the MASTER swung his head my direction, so violently that his periwig came unstuck and sat aslant on his blessed head: "Music! We need music!" shouted he.

Gentle Sir, among my proud accomplishments as Footman, I must here say that handling a musical instrument is not one of them; not even with the strain'd finesse of a novice could I be counted on to play. The Tutor, Péter, whose social refinements admitted a violin sonatina or two, had left suddenly for Prešporok three days prior to bid farewell to his dying Father, and I knew no other capable individual.

"Footman!" said the MASTER, more emphatically than before. "We need music. Does no one in the Manor or on the Estate pluck the Gold'n Lyre of Orpheus?" Good Sir, self-school'd as I am (save for intermittent lessons with Péter), and having descended from the humble loins of a Stablemaster, I still doubted that the Gold'n Lyre of Orpheus was any-where to be found about the Manor de Hôrka, so I could only surmise that the MASTER'S reference to it had been nothing more than a clever trope. Yet, this recognition did nothing to assist me in my present quandary. But then it came to me, as in a vision, as with Saul on the road to Damascus: a way out of this present impasse.

Deciding to act decisively, I excused myself and sprinted from the room, returning minutes later with Uncle Manfred in tow and a Nicolò Amati violin, which the Baron had gifted to Péter, tuck't under arm. The room fell silent, save for a number of exaggerated exhalations, which I believed to be indubitably related to the fetid odor of horse trágya & stale spirits which, by no coincidence, arrived at precisely the same moment as Uncle Manfred. The Stablemaster bow'd to the Baroness (who wrinkled up her nose and stretch't her lips into a painful grimace) before propping the violin snug against a besmirch't armpit, where he began to saw mercilessly at the instrument, squawking out the Romani tune "Evening of Roses," a favor'd number from his pitiful repertoire. I must admit, Gentle Sir, that I had not heard Uncle Manfred fiddle since I was a small boy, and in those foggy recollections he was no virtuoso, to be sure. Yet, the reality was far worse than I had e'er imagined possible. 'Twas an assault on the senses and an affront to fine instrument on which he hack't away insensately. And I now fear'd that Uncle Manfred might raise up his feral voice in accompaniment to this cacophony. Thus was I prepared, should the need arise, to put the MASTER'S silk stocking to good use and bung the bunghole beneath my well-meaning Uncle's hook't beak.

Yet the MASTER took no notice of this contrapuntal crucifixion (although the Baroness, aghast, appear'd to be suffering from her own bout of speechlessness). The intensity of the MASTER'S gaze rested squarely on the Baron, who by this time had squeak't open his eyelids and was, I own, aware of the great Physician's presence. The MASTER released the patient's thumbs and placed a hand on either side of his neck, where he claim'd the affliction had block't the flow of Animal Magnetism. Leaning in close, he stared into the Baron's eyes, which were now flittering about in a trance, like starlings set greedily on a scattering of cake crumbs. 'Twas clear to me then that the Baron was MESMERIZED, as it had come to be known. Aware of his surroundings, but highly suggestible to the MASTER'S commands, the Baron lay still for the first time in days.

Had this been the end of it, Kind Sir, it could be said that it ended well. But this tranquil hiatus was destined to end. With renew'd determination, the MASTER seized the Baron's thumbs and, immersing his foot to full immersion in the silver basin, swung 'round to Uncle Manfred, charging him, "Play, man! Play, by God! Play like the Devil!" At this point, Gentle Sir, Bedlam was unloosed in a lunatic torrent upon the chambers. Uncle Manfred dug deep into his repertoire, and finding nothing but a dissonant void there, reprised "Evening of Roses" with demonic gusto. The Baron responded with a bawl & yowl, punctuated by sputtering guttural grunts. For her part in this fiasco, the Baroness swoon'd, finally collapsing into the clutches of her clutch of ninnies; together they went down much like a billowing tabernacle in a hail storm.

In the corner, the Baron's boy, András, cower'd in trepid suspense. Yet, I, Good Sir, I did nothing—stood stock still, a chicken with its head on the chopping block. For I, too, had been Mesmerized by the MASTER.

Meanwhile, the Baron reach't a climatic screech (the "crisis point," I would later learn) and quite suddenly went limp in his bed. With this, the room once again fell silent, for we were all anxiously weighing our part in what appear'd to be the Baron's untimely demise.

To my great horror & shame, 'twas Uncle Manfred who finally broke the silence. "Sweet creepin' sally! He's jump'd the twig 'n' turn'd up his toes!"

"Hold your peace, you old fool." The MASTER let the patient's thumbs slither from his grip. "He has neither jump'd the twig nor turn'd up his toes. He rests now. And we must leave him to it." With what can only be call'd deistic adoration, stood I, Kind Sir, adoring the curt eloquence of the MASTER. And from that moment forward he would remain to me, MASTER. Even well beyond his imminent departure, 'twould be a fair to say that I was an eager convert to Animal Magnetism and a proud disciple of my MASTER, whose name shall nevermore be utt'r'd. The significance of this can scarcely be understated, Kind Sir (although, admittedly, in your keen & noble mind the significance of this event may yet lie somewhere in the murky precincts of indifference).

Even now, as I sit in this börtön, condemn'd to have my Footman's stature lessen'd by a head, I recognize the moment as a point of juncture: a confluence of the many forces that propel us to our eventual end (albeit, in my case, 'tis an end-less eventual than the distant eventuality I had hoped for). Had I not, Kind Sir, so emphatically embraced the principle of Animal Magnetism, believing myself capable of harnessing its charged & particulate power, I might yet be standing stolidly outside the Baron's chambers, awaiting his beckon call and tending to his chamber pot.

By dusk, the Baron had recover'd. Well enough, was he, to take a meal in bed and express his deepest gratitude to the MASTER in low, unfaltering tones. Having taken up my position outside the Baron's chambers, I was privy to the private conversation that took place there. The MASTER was adamant that the treatment continue: "For," said he, "the cure has not been fully actualized." I roll'd my eyes to one side, to that strain'd point where peeping became a genuine possibility. The MASTER stood straight, his girth stretch't o'er the wide trunk of his upper body gave him an authoritative air; his feet together at the heels and slightly asunder at the toes recall'd the former discipline of a boy's school.

He inform'd the Baron & Baroness that a relapse was likely, and that a full cure for that which ail'd the Baron would require sessions much like that of today's for a further fortnight. To this, the Baron responded with a whimper, and the Baroness swoon'd again; both acts swollen with a reluctance whose finality would finally be given utt'rance by the Baron himself: "Good Sir & Gentle Physician," utt'r'd he. "I would that the cure were not worse than the malady, but 'tis so. Think me not ungrateful, but I fear I cannot bear another treatment. Please stay on at the Manor de Hôrka as long as you wish, and take your leave when best it suits you." With this, the Baron slump'd back into his goose down pillow and let his eyelids scrub o'er his boil'd eye-balls. Momentarily, he was snoring the bombilations of sleep—or as Uncle Manfred would put it: snorting like a stag sniffing out a hind in heat. The MASTER took it in stride, as they say, and I would later learn that 'twas not the first time he had been let go; that is to say, released from his Hippocratic duties. The next morning, he took his leave; the MASTER was gone, and my eyes would ne'er again behold the majesty of his magnetic visage.

Kind & Gentle Sir: everything and nothing (you will recall my enigmatic claim); the MASTER'S part in this tale. And although this may sound like the end of it, 'tis in truth, the beginning. For my glorious encounter with the MASTER prompted me to seek prompt erudition in the occult & mysterious precepts of Animal Magnetism. For this, I turn'd to the Manor Tutor, Péter, who furnish't me with two works by the MASTER: *De planetarum influxu in corpus humanum* & *Sendschreiben an einen auswärtigen Arzt über die Magnetkur* (both, as Péter inform'd me, having recently caused a stir within the noble courts), which I pour'd o'er in the months following his departure (of course, not without the good Tutor's assistance, especially where the MASTER'S thesis was concern'd). Undoubtedly, Sir, the question yet foremost in your otherwise pansophic mind is why Animal Magnetism would 'rouse such interest in the dull mind of a dullard Footman, and what a Valet's boy or a Butler's boy's boy could possibly hope to fathom from such *hókuszpókusz*. 'Tis a fair question, indeed, Sir—the answer to which is deceptively simple: 'Twas all done in a desperate bid to recover my Sister, Theresa; that is, to rescue her Soul from the inexplicable Evil that had so utterly & violently seized upon it. Yes, Gentle Sir, 'tis no surprise that a woman fills bladder & bleat- ing of this goat's song. 'Tis for a woman that I now pace, reluctantly, the Stygian shores, in search of some escape: Theresa, sibling of my heart. 'Tis all for her—in her name and for her honor.

Kind Sir, may I be so bold as to wonder if you have known the tender intimacies of one so angelic & peerless as I have? You will recall that my poor departed Mother's life & times were brought to an abrupt end by mine own end—rear end. And so 'twas upon Theresa's tidy bosom & barely budding breasts that Guenther & I were suckled, until the day of her sixteenth birthday, when she was call'd to take up her duties in the Manor scullery. 'Twas a sad & sorrowful day for Guenther & I, her being the only tender & matronly morsel in the otherwise gristle & rind of our peasant life. We watch't her disappear into the towering edifice, not oblivious to our youthful yearning to be nurtured by her. 'Twas Uncle Manfred who broke the spell: "Not a moment too soon, eh boys?" said he. "Bachelors now, the three of us." But his words fell like heavy raindrops in the Tisza Valley, fruitless & unheeded. We were alone, Kind Sir, so very alone.

But not long after this sorrowful day did we discover that our fair Sister was not lost to us; not entirely. Loitering outside the scullery, Guenther & I would steal a moment or two with our angelic Theresa when the clank and squawk of the shrunk'n door announced her arrival there, at which time she would spiritedly fling a bucketful of gray water into the dirt. Then would she flip the bucket end-for-end and drop down on it, digging into her apron to produce a handful of sweet bread or plums! Such are the happy memories of my dear Theresa, yet untarnished—*szûzi*—yet untouch't by the Evil waiting in the wings to despoil her.

The Evil of which I speak first manifested itself to me in the sniggle & smirk of a fledgling hysteria. 'Twas now my habit to visit Theresa nightly in the maids' quarters, and, Gentle Sir, 'twas my one delight, my one indulgence—to there let my eyes drink in her comely charms, lustily quaff a draught of her virginal bloom, gorge on the feast of her shimmering gold'n locks, which even the confinement of a coarse scullery bonnet could not conceal. With cheeks aglow, she would bid me read (her having not had the benefit of Péter's lessons, as I had), so I would open a ragged copy of the *Legend of Saint Margaret* and read: *In the Island of the Hares, in the island of the Blessed Mary, where the body of the holy lady Margaret reposes ...* When I grew tired of reading, I would rest my head in her lap, and she would recite stories and recollections of our dear departed Mother.

'Twas one of these most precious moments that I first beheld the stirrings of madness behind her eyes as green as the Aral Sea. Good Sir, I try'd desperately to ignore it; 'twas all I could do to put it from my mind.

But each time I call'd upon her, the tempest in her swell'd, manifesting itself in fits of lunatic laughter & untoward remarks. At times, she would chortle, spit, and pull at her hair. Good Sir, I hesitate to wallow in the details, but on one such occasion she lifted her black muslin dress, knickersless as she was, and made the most vulgar remark (let me just say that "amber puss" and "dickeybird" were mention'd in a context unbecoming the fair'r sex) then she squatted in the corner and made water, a puddle that hiss't & steam'd o'er the cold stone floor. 'Twas at this point, I thought it prudent to take Péter into my confidence, and seek his advice, for he was an educated young man who knew the ways & wiles of the world.

I am not unaware, Good Sir, that the Tutor Péter surfaces often in this story (although this is not a fair indication of his relative importance in its sluggishly thickening plot). If you will indulge me but a moment more, I will tell you something of him, Sir, only because 'twas he who was instrumental in bringing the matter of "amber puss" and "dickeybird" to the attention of the Baroness. Péter Montgolfièr is the Baron's distant relative. It was generally agreed that his Mother, the Baron's second cousin, marry'd below her station in life when she yoked herself to a Frenchman of low nobility—the second son in a family of chicken manu-facturers, whose recent pedigree & sizeable wealth had been squander'd on the invention of brothers twelve & fifteen (the usefulness of their muddleheaded contraption—*globe airostatique*—being limited to pleasure rides, and of no substantive monetary value, says Péter). However, it was from his inventor uncles (both less than a score of years his senior), whose invention has allotted them a small measure of renown, that Péter inherited his love for natural philosophy, which, as you are no doubt aware, Kind Sir, is now more commonly known as Natural Science. The young Montgolfier studied for a year at École d'Arts et Métiers before the family coffers ran dry, at which time, with little money and fewer prospects, Péter, not a day o'er eighteen years of age, accepted the Baron's offer to Tutor whatever little Barons the Baroness might in future produce. (Unfortunately, the Baroness has proven to be less than accommodating in this regard, for the Baron yet awaits the arrival of an heir.)

One day not long after the uncelebrated event of the new Tutor's arrival, Guenther and I were occupying ourselves with a spirited bout of stretching. Just as old Virgil dug in and began to huff & puff, and just as young Guenther began to groan & snap, Péter stroll'd around the corner of the stables with book in hand (*Aristotle's Poetics*, I distinctly recall). I think it no exaggeration to say that the young Parisian had ne'er before clap't eyes on a true stallion, having been a city dweller his entire life. Certainly, it seems safe to say that he had ne'er before clap't eyes on such a dipsomaniacal and world-weary beast as old Virgil; just as it is safe to say that he had ne'er before witness't a young man being voluntarily drawn to within inches of his life for the purpose of exaggerating his God-given stature. Despite whatever misgivings he may have had at the time, he immediately join'd in the sport (in fact, 'twas he who first suggested that the addition of old Horace would substantially increase the force of the pull) and, to make a long story short, Good Sir, before long we were fast friends, Péter and I.

'Twas Péter who suggested that the Baroness might be able to help my dear Theresa, after I'd recited to him (in somewhat vague terms) the incident involving the "amber puss" and "dickeybird." To my great astonishment, the Baroness saw fit to summon me to her quarters, where she grill'd me quite mercilessly about my Sister's condition. Clearly, Kind Sir, she had taken a personal interest in the person of my Sister, Theresa, and I was impress't & touch't by her concern. After I again hesitantly recapitulated the "amber puss" and "dickeybird" episode, additionally adding the making-of-water scene, she immediately summon'd Miroslav Kvetnica, stating (to no one in particular) that this kind of hysteria could spread like a plague throughout the rank & file of the servant women. I am sure I could not fathom her meaning, Good Sir, nor her intent; for hysteria, I had heard (yes, from Uncle Manfred), was the just deserts for the likes of strumpets and tarts, or as the French say, *la fille de joie*. But I assure you, Good Sir, that my beloved Sister was none of those things.

Upon his examination of Theresa, the Physician confirm'd the Baroness's suspicions, diagnosing hysteria resulting from moral turpitude. He spoke gravely, without a trace of compassion, all the while tugging at the grizzled cusp of his white beard. Admittedly, Sir, turpitude was not a word familiar to me, unlike moral; however, judging from the way the two mix't so disagreeably on the good Doctor's tongue, I easily surmised an approximate meaning. Oscillating betwixt outrage and disbelief, I found myself tongue tied; at which point Péter took his cue: "Surely, there is some mistake," said he. "The young woman's maidenhead cannot rightly be call'd into question because of one … questionable … comment."

"Questionable?" said the Baroness. "Opprobrious is more to the point."

"And what say you of the water making?" asked the Physician. "Was that also a questionable act?"

"Nothing more than an indiscretion," replied Péter. "Why, Sir, I have seen grown men in the alehouse do the same, not even possessing the wherewithal to drop their breeches beforehand. Do you say they too are all hysterical?"

Understandably, the Baroness took issue with the vulgar case-in-point pointed out by her relative (albeit distant and by marriage only). Yet, case-in-point it was, Gentle Sir, for I myself had been witness to such indiscretions and worse in the alehouse (mostly where Uncle Manfred was concerned and, more often than not, accompany'd by the unwelcom'd declaration: "I've shat me breeches again, boy").

"You are correct about one thing. There can be no question of her maidenhead," retorted the Physician. "For it is certain that she is no maiden! The *szûzhártya* is burst!" With this, Miroslav Kvetnica turn'd to the Baroness, letting his head bow slightly: "Forgive my coarseness, my Lady."

"There it is, then," said she. "Moral turpitude. And what is your recommendation, my wise friend and Physician?"

"Fool's Tower, my Lady."

Being a political luminary in Prešporok, Good Sir, it is almost certain that you know little of our fair Hôrka residing in the outer reaches of the Kingdom; although you must certainly have heard tell of the infamous Fool's Tower, which hunkers there in the green rolling hills that announce the nearby towering Tatry peaks. But then, perhaps I presume too much. Indulge me but a moment more, Indulgent Sir, in order that I might err on the side of caution and recite for you the tower's brief but colorful history. For it is there that the Baroness's Physician, Miroslav Kvetnica, took my angelic Sister on the morrow.

As local legend has it, Sir, the Archduchess Maria Magdalena, daughter of Leopold I & his third wife Eleonore-Magdalena of Neuburg, commission'd and oversaw the building of Fool's Tower. The Archduchess had a reputation for lunacy (sometimes refer'd to more tactfully as "diminishing capacity," Petér once inform'd me, especially where Royals are concern'd), particularly in her autumnal years, as the English say, when she was said to commonly forgo the company of humans for animals, mainly felines from Persia, rumor had it. Sensing a need for sanctuary where women of a like mind (& maidenhead) could take refuge from prying eyes and live in the company of their feline friends without persecution, the Archduchess commission'd the building of what would later come to be known as Feline Tower. Construction of the rotundly round tower took better than two years (the expense for which was, of course, paid for out of Royal coffers) and when it was completed, the Archduchess lived there among her cats and, as the story goes, a gaggle of other old maidens of the feline persuasion. As you undoubtedly know, Good Sir, Maria Magdalene was at one time close to her young niece, Maria Theresa (later to become the Holy Roman Empress). However, when Maria Theresa took the throne in 1741 (by then her conservatism & intolerance of the peculiar—which in her mind was embody'd in full by the most peculiar Jews—was legendary), in an attempt to put an end to the continuing shame & embarrassment that her aging aunt continued to bring upon the House of Hapsburg, she order'd bars install'd in the tower and lock't all the old maidens in, including her aunt Maria Magdalene; this, only after summarily executing each & every feline on the wheel and afterwards drowning the broke & bloody carcasses in a barrel. As you can imagine, Gentle Sir, the yowls & screeches that pierced the green hills near Hôrka were rumor'd to have been unearthly. (Some have astutely remark't that if the old maidens were not hysterical before the executions, they surely were afterwards.) In time, the imprison'd old maidens, too, died out, their gray & leathery corpses ground to dust on the stone floors under the merciless heel of Time's narrow boot. Not wanting a good & sturdy prison to go to waste, the Empress order'd hysterics & lunatics from o'er the span & breadth of Spiš to be asylum'd there among the malevolent feline phantoms and their ghostly maidens. In time, it became known as Fool's Tower, and 'twas to there, Gentle Sir, to that very tower of horror & shame, that they took my angelic Theresa.

In my desperation to help her, I acted desperately, rashly, Sir, and broke with decorum by addressing the Fine & Magnanimous Baron directly in his chambers. In truth, I was counting on the Good & Gracious Baron to recall how I had recover'd his prized sapphire from the chamber pot of my predecessor; that is, the Footman who proceed'd me. Unfortunately, the Master of my employ recall'd no such thing. In fact, he appear'd fluster'd & apprehensive of my presence in his chambers. Even his boy András, who work't to relieve the Baron's noble stress by rubbing and caressing his noble thighs & buttocks, look't nonplus't. I spoke quickly, while the opportunity yet presented itself.

"Most Excellent Master & Good Baron, I am Ernst Helmut Seyfert, son to the late Stablemaster, Dietmar Karl Seyfert, and have most recently taken up the post of Butler's boy's boy, or Valet's boy, in this most splendid Manor de Hôrka."

Unfortunately, this rattled not so much as a fistful of stones toward the landslide of remembrance I had hoped for. So, I try'd again: "Virgil's last lay, Good Baron."

The nobleman's noble eyes jump'd to me for the first time.

"Ah . . . yes. Pity, that. Seyfert, is it not?"

"Yes, Good Baron. 'Tis Seyfert. Ernst Seyfert. Day in and day out, I stand at your noble beckon call outside these chambers doors, sir. That is to say, your beckon call as it comes to me through the Butler and Valet, Good Baron."

"Outside these doors?" query'd he, albeit nobly. "I thought 'twere a statue outside these doors. Good Lord, Seyfert, you must twitch or fidget occasionally, even a sneeze will do, to make it known that you are a living creature and not a stone figure."

"Yes, Most Noble Baron. My deepest apologies. I will remember to do so in future."

"Now, what is it that you want, young Seyfert?"

"My Sister, Good Baron, Theresa, is a scullery maid in the Manor. She is to be taken to Fool's Tower on the morrow."

"Fools Tower? What ails her?"

"'Tis hysteria, as diagnosed by Miroslav Kvetnica, the Baroness's Physician. But it cannot be so, Good Baron."

"Ah, Miroslav Kvetnica … an imbecile among imbeciles," said the Baron. "He'll stick his thumb in your *arsch* and tell you your *scheissen* stinks. Thus accounts for the entirety of his skill as a Physician."

Admittedly, Good Sir, I was taken aback at this comment, for it sounded very much like one of Uncle Manfred's ribald verdicts.

"Of that, I know nothing, Good Baron. But I do know as sure as I stand humbly before you that moral turp … turp—"

"Turpitude."

"Yes, moral turpitude plays no part in her condition."

"On what does Miroslav Kvetnica base his accusation … this accusation of moral turpitude?"

Good Sir, I could not bear to utt'r it aloud again, so I lean'd in close and whisper'd dear Theresa's now infamous comment in the Good Baron's ear.

"Amber puss & dickeybird? There may be a kernel of truth to the moral turpitude charge, after all, Seyfert."

"But Good Baron, Sir, my Theresa has ne'er known a man before. Of this I am certain. How, then, can moral turpadude—"

"Turpitude."

"Yes, how then can that be the charge?"

"Seyfert … Seyfert. 'Twould not be the first time that a youth such as you are has been trick't into believing his Beloved has been constant."

"But, Noble Baron, she is my Sister, not my Beloved."

"It matters not," said he, with noble resignation. "For the principle is the same. You have been trick't, young Seyfert. And that is the simple truth."

Good Sir, my hopes lay dash't before mine eyes on the noble rocks of my Master Baron. There was nothing more to be done. I was dejected, downtrodden beneath his aristocratic boot heel.

On the morrow, I rose early from my bed, that I might bid my angelic Sister farewell. Being forced to abide a spell outside the maids' quarters with the scoundrel & imbecile Miroslav Kvetnica (whom I was now convinced was the pretender that he had accused the MASTER of being), I did my best to suffer his insufferable presence, Good Sir, as he paced on my periphery as a sizeable blob in a scholar's velvet frock.

"'Tis for the best," said he, pompously. "You shall see."

To this, Good Sir, I could only respond with a disgruntled grunt, which halfway through its utt'rance I decided should be somewhat more deferential, for I was, after all, still a Footman and he an esteem'd guest of the Baroness. Thus, Sir, 'twas an admittedly odd sound that both gush't & squeak't from my larynx, one that seem'd more to puzzle than to offend the old Physician.

At long last, dear Theresa emerged carrying in her one hand a small embroider'd bag that I recognized as our dear departed Mother's (for Theresa herself had reveal'd this detail to me on one of our strolls along the Manor brook), while the other gather'd the folds of her wool'n scullery skirt. Her head was obscured by a bonnet (as it always was within the Manor) and her hair, gather'd tautly, disappear'd somewhere beneath its churlish design. There was nothing mischievous in her eye today; nothing of the impish grin that she'd worn on our previous meeting, which, to my chagrin, had now become the talk of the Manor. Her smile was sincere, Sir, almost tragic in its simplicity. A tear fix't like a diamond in her lashes finally let go and slid gemlike down her delicate cheek to the creased corner of her mouth. I was about to address her when the Physician step'd betwixt us.

"Off we go, then," bluster'd he. With this he clutch't her arm and swept her down the dim hallway, which grew more unbearably abject with each departing step my comely Sister took. Good Sir, I was helpless but to follow, in the hope that I might utt'r a fleeting word to dear Theresa as the Physician escorted her from the Manor to the awaiting carriage set to transport her to the prison that was Fool's Tower.

The Baroness & her lady-in-waiting stood waiting in the Great Hall, along with a representative collection of the house staff, whose only reason for being present, I own'd, was to mock & sneer at my hapless Sister. The Baroness, who, for her part, did nothing to stem the torrent of tacit ridicule, look't on, unmoved and characteristically stern. As one who has been yoked with an unpleasant yet necessary task, she presided callously. Dropping my eyes in deference, I march't by her and exited the Manor House to resume my role of Footman.

Holding open the door of the carriage and maintaining a slight Footman's bow, I was helpless but to watch, Kind Sir, as the Physician Miroslav Kvetnica thrust my dear Sister to a seat directly facing him. I let my eyes wander up to the green irises fleck't with plashes of silver that I had so often gazed into, and paused to speak one last time to dear Theresa. But, Gentle Sir, the words lodged in my throat like a barb'd hook in the mouth of a stun'd sea bass. I felt the shame of ten traitors sweltering in my cheeks. My dear Sister must have noticed as much, for she smiled weakly for but a moment before fading back into a muted shade of subjugation. At length, I gave the driver a dutiful if doleful nod and bow'd deeply as the carriage lurch't forward and set out down the drive, trailing a plume of yellow dust. 'Twas only then, Good Sir, that my attention turn'd to the two lone figures among the distant Ash trees: one was leaning heavily there, prop'd on an outstrectch't arm (Guenther), and the other lay senseless in the grass with a porcelain jug solder'd in his fist (Uncle Manfred). Gentle Sir, 'twould be a lie to say that it did not right then occur to me that across that trim, pared & pruned garden of the Manor was all that remain'd of my starcross't family. One by one, the harsh hand of destiny had struck them down, if not in death, then in some equally appalling manner; that is, except for I, Good Sir, Ernst Seyfert, Footman to the Noble Baron Horeczky de Hôrka (but their collective demise was but a prelude & overture to the symphony of woe & affliction that awaited me, Gentle Sir, the same which, I own, will yet reverberate through bole & branch of the Seyfert family tree). Thus, at that moment, the fortuitous fate that had befall'n me alone matter'd less (as Uncle Manfred would put it) than a mouse *torde* in a meal of *muk*. With the sorrow of a Judas, I ground my heel into the dirt and spun as on a trundle back to the Manor, there to face a bleak prospect of a future without my dear, angelic Theresa.

Admittedly, in the days that follow'd, my reputation as the best Foot-man in all of Spiš may have suffer'd, due to a lackluster performance in the discharge of my duties. Untrue to the promise I had promised the Good Baron, I stood lifeless as a marble statue outside my Master's quarters. My impuissance acted upon me as a narcotic; stuporous & numb stood I, paralyzed by my own guilt.

'Twas during one of these moments of ossification, Good & Gentle Sir, that it quite suddenly became clear to me how I must proceed. On the occasion in question, the Baron's boy András was perch't before the *toilette* pouring water, with which to lave the Baron's *nemzõszervek*, into a basin. As I stood stock still, the sound of water plashing was nothing short of Mesmerizing; 'twas beyond an enchantment, Good Sir, for it seem'd to fill my very soul with rapturous current. I knew at that moment what I must do. That very eve, I visited Péter in his quarters and beseech't him tell me all that he knew about Animal Magnetism, that I might learn its secrets, its esoteric conjurations & occult incantations. Then, Kind Sir, as was my plan, I would go to my dear Sister and cure her, just as I'd seen the Great MASTER do for the Baron. Surely, you will agree, 'twas a simple but worthy plan, and at the heart of it was the pure & true yearning to be reunited with my angelic Theresa.

From the MASTER'S writings, I learn'd that charged streams of Kosmic particles infuse the whole of the Universe. By deduction, Good Sir, one can deduce that such streams flow through all of Nature: each & every tree, stone & creature. 'Tis, in short, the power & force that vivifies all. Gentle Sir, I am not so fill'd with hauteur as to demand any further explanation or evidence than this; I am not one of those detractors who taunts the MASTER with such vagaries as "What accounts for the existence of such a force?" or "What is the source of this Magnetism?" 'Tis evidence enough to know that it exists, Sir, for I have seen its magnitude & manifestation manifested within the ailing body corporeal of my Master, the Baron Horeczky de Hôrka.

As both aperture & vortex of the magnetic streams, the MASTER focuses a shaft of magnetic energy into the patient and obliterates the blockage that is there within. Sickness, he makes it clear, occurs when the flow of Animal Magnetism is obstructed. Once the natural flow has been fully restored, the patient is cured. Of course, reaching this "crisis point," as the MASTER calls it, when the flow is set to be restored, can be accompany'd by a period of discomfort for some, as was the case with the Good Baron. This discomfort, I own, often dissuades the patient from continuing with the treatment; and this alone explains the occasional, yet too well known, failures of Mesmerism.

Gentle Sir, I beg you forgive my endless meanderings, for my point is this: although Animal Magnetism flows through us all, not all of us have been bless't with the MASTER'S ability to focus and direct its force. Thus, having educated myself regarding the nature of it, I had next to discern whether I was one of those who could control it. And so I ask't myself: Might I be an aperture through which the force of Animal Magnetism might flow? And so, to that end, I undertook a series of experiments, beginning with insensate life (stones & trees) and eventually working up to sensate life (small mammals & birds), in which I would do as I had seen the MASTER do and stand with a bare foot in water and a raised & pointed finger stabbing like a Saber into the unseen forces of the Universe. In truth, Good Sir, I observed nothing in the stones & trees; they sat and stood motionless as stones & trees are apt to do. However, I believe I register'd some success in Mesmerizing an anxious ground squirrel; in fact, after I had lured it with acorns to within ten paces of me and directed a stream at it with my eager finger, it stood so high & still on its tiny haunches that a Goshawk struck like lightning from out of the blue sky and with a bloody shriek swept the little fellow away, leaving in its wake nothing more than a small heap of crack't shell shucks. Encouraged by this successful if unfortunate episode, I went on to successfully Mesmerize a flock of the Baron's carrier pigeons. So successful was I in this attempt that the unruly brood bob'd behind my every footfall in the days that follow'd. For three days and nights they flutter'd & coo'd about the front doors of the Manor, awaiting my appearance (as if I were their beak't & feather'd Messiah), until the Valet was forced to drive them off with a blast of the Baron's blunderbuss. With success seemingly looming close, it occurred to me then, Good Sir, to try my hand at Mesmerizing a human being. Since, I wish't to conceal my experiments from the prurient minds & ways of those servants of the Manor, I decided to enlist outside help, which meant Guenther would be my willing volunteer, my reasoning being, of course, that anyone who would willingly allow himself to be drawn to within inches of his life by two cast-off studs would not object to being shot betwixt the eyes with the vivifying force of the Universe. Unfortunately, Guenther, in his typical muddleheaded fashion, did not see it that way; he was neither willing nor would he be my volunteer. This led to the even more desperate, if not dire, measure of enlisting the help of Uncle Manfred.

Having lived a great portion of my life in the closest proximity to my Good Uncle, I realized that timing rather than stealth would be the key to my success. For I knew if I were to time the Mesmerism to coincide with his fourth draught of ale, there would be no need for stealth at all. The MASTER makes no mention of what may become of the man who is Mesmerized while deep into his cups, so, admittedly, Gentle Sir, I was not prepared for Uncle Manfred's uncommon reaction. On the night in question, I waited several hours upon his return from the alehouse before, growing impatient, I set out for that destination myself. My determination was such that I would Mesmerize him from the pulpit of the Sistine Chapel if needs be. Fortunately, there would be no needs be, for he was slump'd still on a table in the alehouse when I arrived.

Seeing that he was nearing a near insensate state, I knew I had to act quickly, and that improvisation was going to play no small role in this extemporaneous production. Slipping my foot from its brass-buckled Footman's shoe and white silk Footman's stocking, I wedged it into Uncle's leathern tankard, where my biggest toe just reach't the malted froth. Then with the conviction of Sancta Fides, I clutch't my Uncle's thumbs and opened myself up to the force of Animal Magnetism, an act that can only be liken'd unto throwing open the terrestrial shutters to a Kosmic celestial sunrise. Good and Gentle Sir, 'twas a near miraculous moment. A jolt shot through me. Like a cold singe of ice, it brazed down my arms and tweak't Uncle Manfred's thumbs. He gave a sudden start, a slight jump, Good Sir, and then he was sitting upright. In that charged moment his eyes sparkled as if two silver denarii in a sparkling stream. Before I could restrain him, he was up and running for the door, where, braying like a hinny, he rush't out into the night and set out galloping through the trees. By now, a small crowd had gather'd outside the grogshop, just in time to witness Uncle Manfred hasten his sodden self headlong into the bole of an enormous Beech tree. In that moment, as Uncle Manfred timber'd momentously to the forest floor, now insensate, to be sure, I knew that I had the touch, Good Sir: I was indeed & after all one of the chosen few who could control the forces of the Universe.

And so it was that with little more than a thimble-full of confidence, I set out the very next day for Fool's Tower that I might cure dear Theresa's hysteria and return her to her rightful place in the Manor de Hôrka. 'Twas a gold'n summer's day, not ten months ago now, that I sat upon the notch't & sway'd back of old Virgil, plodding on towards a not-so-distant hill, where Fool's Tower rose in the misted shadows of

Vysoké Tatry. How, Gentle Sir, could I have known what awaited me there? Who would have believed that that fateful trip would end here, in this börtön of Prešporok, where the sun yet taunts me with its inconstancy, falling in false gold'n bars upon this cold cinder floor? I am no philosopher, Sir, to this you may by now fairly attest. I can only wonder at the malice with which Fate has struck me & mine down, and console myself in the fact that some Soul somewhere knows but why; surely, a noble mind more nimble than mine own (such as your own, Sir) has uncover'd the answer for which I seek, unearth'd the truth of it all. For how to live without such a consolation? Without such a hope, Gentle Sir? That is the real question. For who can live a life so unavailing? A life, Good Sir, that has no more worth than the dust upon one's heels, no more meaning than the gray water slosh't from a scullery bucket?

I reach't the tower before the sun had fully retreated into night. In the half-light, it resembled a colossal stack of dull copper coins set down in the hills of Spiš by a Hapsburg giant. A standard bearing the familiar banner of a red lion under a regal blue crown hung limp & tatter'd o'er a solid oak door, the only visible entrance (this I learn'd only after circling the tower aimlessly, as if myself a lost lunatic). Locating a watering trough for old Virgil, I let the well-hung stud drink his fill before setting him loose in a nearby field of wild oats, an act not devoid of a cruel and symbolic significance, it must be said.

Although the austere look of the tower seem'd to suggest that gaining entrance might prove difficult, the oak door swung effortlessly open and no attending person or personage rush't to impede my ingress there. Having said this, Gentle Sir, the otherworldly sounds of tortured Souls and a foul odor of the long unwashed were, as I own'd it then, cause to beat a hasty retreat. Yet, thoughts of my dear Theresa in that infernal Hades steady'd my nerves, tempering my resolve to press forward and find my angelic Sister, that I might cure her with the charged & pulsing finger of Animal Magnetism. Annexing a nearby lantern, I shuffled o'er the smooth stone to the center, the very core of this dank abomination, and, turning my gaze upward, counted nine floors, each connected to the other by a staircase that wound like a serpent's spine up the structure. Gentle Sir, 'tis difficult for one of genteel spirit, such as you are, to cast your refined mind to contrive such a place; for there I stood at the unholy heart of that loathsome sepulcher, the sights, sounds & smells of the damn'd filtering down in a confluence of wail & squelch, a maelstrom swirling down into its turbulent marrow of all that is ungodly & indecent.

I placed my unsteady feet each before the other and mounted the sweating staircase. Gaining the first floor, I paused long enough to peer into the gray light swirling behind the bars, where two lunatics spouted gibberish: *tempus edax rerum*, gibber'd the one, and *mens sola loco non exulat*, gibber'd the other. Next to them, a fair-skin'd Persian with a fine & delicate nose sat plucking at the hair of his chin. Upon closer inspection, I was startled to find that 'twas in actual fact an old bearded woman with a crook't & black't-out smile, save for a single tooth top & bottom—and she busily weaved a coarse carpet from the dull strands of her abounding beard. A quick scan of the place reveal'd that dear Theresa was nowhere to be found there, so I once again took to the stairs. On the second floor, a portly Friar held his fellow inmates hostage with a booming flatus that billow'd as a pungent gale beneath his frock. With a sleeve press't to my nose, I search't again, but again found no sign of my angelic Sister.

Good Sir, I will spare you the unsavory details of all the sights I beheld, sounds I heard & smells I smell'd; instead, let me simply say that 'twas a lurid & uncouth scene that predominated my visit to Fool's Tower. On the third floor, a drunk'n attendant lay curl'd up on the floor, an arpeggio of snorts & growls usher'd from his wolf-like snout. As I was about to rouse him, a fat, naked & pink-skin'd man spoke from the darkness in a high-squealing pitch. "Touch not, the attendant," said he. "The inflamed eyes of his Morphean stupor will shred thee for pleasure, 'tis certain." Good Sir, what could I do but heed the fat man's words? So I ask't him if he knew of my angelic Sister, a fair maiden & scullery maid that may sometimes hoist her scullery gown to make water. "She doth here reside," said he. "The seventh floor, but take heed, young stranger—" With great haste, took I to the stairs, taking them two at a time: past the fourth floor, past the fifth (where I paused long enough to witness an attendant pouring briny water down the throat of a poor wretch strap'd to an iron cot), on to the sixth, until finally I arrived at the seventh floor in this Fool's Tower. There I began my search in earnest, where the iron bars span'd from floor to ceiling, exposing all. Yet oily shadows crept from the corners and oozed from the nooks, obscuring that which lay in their path, setting down doubts and calling in to question what one might actually observe and what one might merely imagine to have observed. Be that as it may, Gentle Sir, there could be no doubt that an orgy of the unnatural raged in this seventh circle of Hell. As one raised in the stables of the Manor de Hôrka, I am no stranger to randy & rutting animals in the throes of romping coitus (as Uncle Manfred would put it: "'Tis all in a good night's dream for old

John Le Fuck"); yet, scenes of the exotic and extravagant modes of mating to which I was reluctant witness will go with me to the grave, I assure you, Sir (a time that is all too quickly advancing, you will recall). In the murky shadows, men lay with men; women with women, men with boys; women with boys; boys with small animals, men with bleating animals, women with braying animals, and the list goes unhappily on, Sir. Navigating the sin & filth, I continued my search, scouring the darkness. Then, wafting on the foul breeze that sluiced through the crannies, I heard it; 'twas unmistakable: the song of Saint Margaret in a high tittering voice. *In the Island of the Hares, in the island of the Blessed Mary, where the body of the holy lady Margaret reposes …*

It could be no other, Good Sir—'twas my dear, forsaken Theresa.

I rush't to the sound of her voice, its breathy timbre beckoning me to come quickly. Good and Magnanimous Sir, 'twas the moment that seal'd my fate: the same that would send me to the gallows and the same that will surely damn my Soul for all eternity. Every night, huddled in the perfectly sharp corner of this *börtön*, the vision comes to me again, washes o'er me, Sir, until I sink as a stone to the bottom of that bottomless sea. The glazed bare back; the rippling buttocks in & out of blackness like a lunar Moon dipping in and out of the frothy tide for what seem'd a full epoch of meanwhile. All the while, my dear Theresa lay with her dress hiked high and legs open to the intruder, singing the song of her favorite Saint Margaret. 'Twas a perversion so debauch't & base that I can scarcely give utt'rance to it here. Something that was once alive in me wilted and died in that moment, Sir. The fresh wound of my heart, suddenly a dry'd scab, hard & senseless. But then, from somewhere deep in my bowels it rose: a seed of anger, rage, hatred—a destroying seed that took bloom and flower'd fearfully in the steaming *faszság* of my gut. Sir, there is no other explanation, except to say that at that moment I was Death's minion. 'Twas to that infernal moment that the whole of my life had been leading me, I now own. I could no more have avoided it than a star avoids the darkness or a tree avoids the rushing wind.

With all the might that I possess'd, and more, I throttled the fornicator who, there before my horrified eyes, despoil'd my sweet Theresa. Pressing a knee against the fiend's spine, I wrap't ten malicious fingers about his throat and squeezed until my knuckles crack't in their joints. The demon struggled to his feet in a comic dance of death. With his *pizzle* prick pointed Heavenward, I would send him to Hell. A jolt shot through him and a curdle of his seed plash't to the stone floor. Then a jolt shot through me, a charged stream that pulsed up my limbs and spread as molt'n metal to my feet. His last breath still hung in the sickly sweet air, as I let the serpent's lifeless body, now a cold shell, slither to the floor.

I hasten'd to my Sister's side and folded her into my arms. With her every breath, the whines of a wounded animal escaped from somewhere deep within. Pulling her head to the cradle of my shoulder, I brush't a dull gold'n lock from her eyes and bid her be still, for all was well. But of course, Kind & Gentle Sir, as you know, all was not well. In truth, all was far from well. For just then I follow'd the line of dear Theresa's terrify'd gaze to the blank stare of the dead man on the floor and his muddy features look't all too familiar. Convinced that the shadows now trick't me, play'd me for a fool, I rub'd my eyes and squinted hard again into the darkness. There could be no doubt, Sir; sprawl'd there on the floor, dead at my hands, was my own flesh & blood: my own Brother Guenther.

There are no words to describe the legion of emotions that then overthrew me; 'twas as if some vile hag's potion churn'd in the boiling waters of my Soul. A fratricide, the most despicable of all murders. My own Brother, Sir, the devourer of maidens, nay sisters; and I the murderer of men, the Cane that killed Abel. In the muddle that was my thoughts, I wallow'd but a minute. Had I not still believed that dear Theresa could be saved, I would have given myself o'er to the Sheriff forthwith. For how, wonder'd I, could I save my angelic Sister from behind gaol walls? I could not, and I knew I could not. (My present circumstance is clear testament to such an obvious answer, is it not?) To erase this monumental blunder was the only answer, or so I own'd it at the time. So, with some effort, I situated Guenther's half-naked body on my shoulder and ready'd myself to take a silent & stealthy leave of the place. For her part, dear Theresa sat numbly in her corner, yet chiming the soft song of Saint Margaret. Promising her I would return on the morrow (a vow utt'r'd to no one, for her mind had retreated to some distant realm), I spiral'd down the staircase, a descent into darkness, from which I knew I would ne'er return.

The world outside had been alter'd somehow: bleaker & more abject, certainly; but also clearer in a most remarkable manner. 'Twas as if I were the only stationary thing in this world, in the Kosmos; everything around me now moved in relation to the precise point where I then stood. Orbiting, spinning, shifting on its axis, revolving. Some things moved closer, some farther away, but all in relation to me, as if to bring all sharply into focus—my focus. Good Sir, forgive my nebulous abstractions. They fall short of explaining my thoughts & mind at the time. Allow me to make one simple observation: in that single moment, not a single question linger'd in the air, as to the nature of the Universe. 'Twas not, I own, that the answers danced in some Kosmic dance before my eyes, but that the Kosmos seem'd to unravel in one long single strand, one long line, unbroken by the splice of question and answer. Taking a man's life will change you, they say. Sir, I know now that they speak the truth.

Disposing of Guenther's body was the task that now faced me. No one would miss an addlebrain'd Stableboy—this I realized—provided that the body was ne'er unearth'd. The one hitch, Sir, as it occur'd to me then, was Uncle Manfred. Of course, even in his perpetually befuddled state, the Stablemaster would notice the absence of his Stableboy. I decid-ed then that I would reveal all to Uncle Manfred, make him a confederate & fellow conspirator. There was, I own'd, no other way to proceed.

I left Guenther's limp body prop'd against a tree, so as to appear as one poor besotted fool who had wander'd into the forest, only to find himself lost & losing consciousness. Good Sir, I say limp, yet his *kakas* was anything but limp. There in the silted moonlight I attempted to force the stiff obelisk to a position more subdued, but 'twas to no avail. I must admit that the possibility of hacking off the offending member occur'd to me then, and I search't about in vain for a farmer's scythe or a timber-man's axe. In the end, I settled for a dry clump of grass, which strategic-ally placed, obscured the proud monolith, yet itself would be somewhat of a puzzlement to any who might have the misfortune to stumble upon the curious scene.

Gentle Sir, perhaps you wonder at the unlikely predicament into which I had so unwittingly stumbled. 'Tis a natural reaction; for, even now, I too wonder at the senseless tragedy. Slouch't alone in this börtön of Prešporok, I often recall a phrase from one of good Péter's tutoring sessions: *reductio ad absurdum*. At the time, it seem'd only a stale dictum; now its truth rings out and drops with the finality of the fallbeil.

I found Uncle Manfred sleeping off the previous night's revelry with old Horace in the stables. He and the hoary stallion were sprawl'd out in a like manner, both rumbling with the grumbles of Vesuvius. Uncle Manfred's grip was still wrap'd around its tankard. A silver crown was all that remain'd of his once frightful shock of hair, for it now tangled about his head as a smash't laurel wreath. The Mesmerism of two nights prior yet manifested itself in a blue & yellow sunset dropping below a swollen brow. Lying there, he look't frail & aged; 'twas something I had not noticed before; indeed, I was ill-prepared for such a revelation.

I realized then that I was exhausted. The urgency that had press't me on through the night now waned into sleepy conviction. My eyes, I own'd, were weighted with the weight of Sleep's teeming sandbags. And so it was that old Virgil and I lay'd down beside Uncle Manfred and his equine companion and drifted into sleep.

I was awaken'd several hours later by a cooing chorus of the Baron's carrier pigeons, who had gather'd around me, a throng of yet Mesmerized disciples. I sat upright in the straw and with a vigorous flap of my arms set the pigeons aflight. A vivid memory of the previous night came flooding into my head, as if the blind I had unconsciously drawn to shroud those unhappy events had right then been thrown open. Extreme measures were needed, and taken (in the way of a hurl'd pail of water), in order to 'rouse Uncle Manfred from a Bacchanalian torpor. He cursed God and all His creation in a most vile manner before rising unsteadily onto two bony wooden shanks; at which time, I beg'd him make haste, for the life of our dear Theresa depended on it. While he laved at the horse trough, I hitch't old Virgil to a wagon. Presently, we were traveling at the uneven pace of Virgil's lopsided lope for the green slopes of Spiš. With Uncle Manfred reclined stern side, I reveal'd all—from beginning to end—Guenther's end, to be precise. His response was predictable if opprobrious and I shall recite it here now, Good Sir (however, not without some hesitation): "May the rakish reptile have his fundament reamed by Belial's woolly haunches," croaked he.

The plan, as I sketch't it to him then, was bare in its simplicity: we would remove the body of my Brother and bear it home to be buried in an unmark't grave. As for Theresa, I would treat her with the healing force of Animal Magnetism, and, once she had convinced Miroslav Kvetnica that her soundness of mind was once again sound, she would be return'd to the scullery in the Manor de Hôrka (and I would again take up my Footman's post). In a word, all would be return'd to normal—at least, as normal as these most peculiar circumstances would allow.

You may wonder at the seeming callousness of my scheming, Good and Gentle Sir, for had I not twenty-four hours earlier strangled the last breath of life from my own Brother's throat with a rapt & delirious claw? 'Twas true, I had. In my own defense, I can only say that the unspeakable event had transform'd me in some way; now, I clearly saw what stood betwixt me & my angelic Sister. For, Sir, hers was the last remaining remnant of Goodness in my life, the vestigial vestige of virginal Grace. I could no more turn away from her than the Moon can turn its pale countenance away from wanton Earth. 'Twas written in the Stars long ago. But, yes, most Generous Sir, I feel the gentle tug of your reproachful refutation! For perhaps my present circumstance, too, was written in the Stars. Perhaps, yes! Perhaps to have my garret lop't offward was decreed before Time e'er was a tick or tock. Such a question is for Philosophers & wise men, Sir. Suffice to say, that one whose pinnacle of power scrapes the belly of Heaven, such as yours does, is one who can change the very course of the Planets, and erase what may or may not be scrawl'd among the Stars. 'Tis only this that I ask of you, most Magnanimous Sir; this, and nothing more.

In daylight, Guenther appear'd much like one of the Baroness's white porcelain dolls from the Orient, sitting stiffly among the Ash & Pine trees. By stiffly, Sir, I mean the *zászlórúd* of his *kakas* had yet to slip to half-mast; this was made obvious by the meddling forest creature who sometime during the night had drag'd away the green sod intended to obscure it, and in doing so, made certain that the tool of my dead Brother's demise was at once visible to any who might venture near. Uncle Manfred guffaw'd at the sight of the proud *kakas*, a performance that quickly turn'd into a tragedy of whoops & retches. Finally, he roll'd from the wagon and slump't to the ground in a slumbering heap, exhausted by his own excesses. Unassisted, I lug'd Guenther to wagon and swathed him in straw.

By now, mid-afternoon was approaching, and 'twas prudence that convinced me wait for nightfall before storming Fool's Tower. I pass'd the time wandering through the forest, in search of some sentient creature to Mesmerize, finding only a bronze & oozing toad among the brambles; but I dared not touch it, for I own'd, 'twas among the noxious species of which Péter had once spoken. Upon my return to the wagon, I was relieved to discover that Uncle Manfred had roll'd the rock from before his tomb, so to speak, and was busily suckling at a wineskin like a piglet to its teat.

When the Sun was no more than a sizzling ember in the Occident, we stole up the staircase of the Tower to the seventh floor (as you can well imagine, Sir, my companion was swooning & near prostrate in the grips of his dyspnoea). Uncle Manfred hoisted his glazed globe long enough to witness a dwarf spit a squawking hen onto its drawn flesh *kard*. Scrambling to his feet, Uncle cursed the puffing poppet and took another draught from his wineskin. 'Twas then that I heard it again, aloft in the sour air, the sweet song of Saint Margaret. I knew well 'twas a call to make haste; thus, towing Uncle Manfred along, I follow'd the frail & simple melody to its resplendent source—resplendent, I say, despite it being smother'd in oily shadows. Gentle Sir, there we found dear Theresa, my angelic Sister, alive, yes, but not well. For even in the darkness, 'twas clear that her legs were asunder once more and her dress drawn up into two clench't fists. There in the valley of her maidenhead was another head, bury'd & bobbing as a sow in its scrap bucket. A stab of pain pierced my temples, gnaw'd the morsel of gristle that now was my weakly bleating heart. 'Twas my final defeat, Sir, my unwilling surrender. And I laid down my sword at the feet of infidels, just as Balian of Ibelin had done.

In this shadow of defeat, before I could utter a word, Uncle Manfred charged the cunnilingus, knocking him to the floor (in the process, halting the cunnilingue) and pounced on him with the force of a younger, more forceful man. Only when Uncle Manfred had the cunnilingus by the throat did it became clear that 'twas not a him at all, but a her. It took a shake or two of my head to recognize her. 'Twas none other than the Baroness, Good Sir. I swear on my Mother's blessed aperture 'twas so: 'twas the Baroness with the sweet scourge of twat yet dribbling down her chin.

As Uncle Manfred cinch't his grip on the tensed sinews of her neck, the Baroness carved out desperate figure-eights in the air about his ears. Dumfounded as I was, there was little else to do, but stand by and watch this impossible performance wind down to its regrettable *dénouement*. *Reductio ad absurdum.* When it look't as if the final curtain was soon to drop on this true passion play (Sir, even at Death's door, the Baroness's noble eyelids flutter'd as the wings of a most delicate finch), a strange & peculiar thought sprouted between my ears in the gray soil of my peasant's skull. Not a thought, so much as an inclination & incitation; perhaps 'twas the Footman's bounden duty that then seized me and bid me act. Procuring a piss pot, whose dull copper sheen reveal'd a sizeable & previous pate -shaped dint, I thump'd it forcefully upon Uncle Manfred's seat of thought, an assault to which he responded forthwith by slumping onto the Baroness's noble bosom. The gasps that escaped the Noble Woman's tremulous lips, and the groans that issued forth from deep in Uncle's *folyószűkület* proffer'd a scene of salacious intrigue, to be sure. And 'twas at this unfortunate moment that Miroslav Kvetnica chose to come pattering up the stone steps along with the Sheriff of Spiš, who promptly arrested both Uncle & I (Good Sir, I would later learn that the old Physician had earlier spy'd us in the forest and had gone in search of the Sheriff, who was, not surprisingly, a friend & ally to Baron Horeczky de Hôrka). When they roll'd Uncle Manfred from atop the Baroness, he spoke the last words I was e'er to hear him utt'r on God's Green Earth: *"Te hülye!"* said he. "All these years, and still you lead arsy-versy."

As the old Physician help'd the Baroness to her feet, pulling the jute hood of a peasant's smock o'er her pale visage, and hastily conducting her from this indelicate scene, his complicity became clear: clearly he had known of the Baroness's Sapphic bent, just as, clearly, he had known the source of dear Theresa's hysteria—that is to say, he had known half the source; the other half had been Guenther, for whose murder, even now, although sadden'd by it, I cannot summon even the slightest inkling of remorse. Wicked Guenther! May the rakish reptile have his fundament reamed by Belial's woolly haunches.

Kind and Gentle Sir, the rest is history, as they say. You no doubt heard tell of the legal mischance that follow'd, for the rumor of it sat like a lead'n storm cloud o'er the whole of the Kingdom. My accusations of Sapphic libertinism against the Baroness were dismiss't as the grumblings of disaffected servants, at best, and the poisonous sibilance of ludicrous flimflam, at worst. Today, the Baroness goes about her noble business as usual, saved by my hand, an act of no avail to me, as is clearly attested to by my present circumstance. And the Baron has chosen to look the other way, on both her count & mine; equally, of no avail to me.

Uncle Manfred was gaol'd in Vienna for the attempted murder of a Noble Woman, where soon after, he choked on the fist of walloping French-man who'd become enraged upon discovering that Uncle had been secretly imbibing in his secret hoard of wine. Poor, wretched Uncle Manfred, gone to join his dear departed Sister.

As you are well aware, Good Sir, I await my own untimely & ignomin-ious end for my part in bringing the piteous life of my Brother Guenther to an untimely & ignominious end. Only the hope of your magnanimous intercession keeps me from stretching my own neck from the very bars that hold me captive. Even now, Good Sir, as I near the end of this lamentable tale and hope that it finds you in time and with a heart teeming with humanity & compassion, I have my doubts. For the fallbeil awaits— all too eagerly, I fear. Perhaps, then, it was written in the Stars, after all. Perhaps life for some is unavailing: worth no more than the dust upon one's heels, meaning little more than the gray water slosh't from a scullery bucket into the dirt.

My dear, angelic Theresa remains a prisoner of hysteria in Fool's Tower. She is said to there have befriended a dwarf and yet sings the song of Saint Margaret. Sometimes, in this lonely börtön of Prešporok, I prop an ear toward the outside world and imagine I hear her simple, sad refrain. *In the Island of the Hares, in the island of the Blessed Mary, where the body of the holy lady Margaret reposes …*

Yes, there it is again, Kind Sir; I hear it, light as a feather on the breeze. A breathy melody to remind me I am yet alive.

Legitimizing Georges

Beneath an oily halo of lamplight, a young man with tousled hair—made older by the wedges of fine whiskers that creep down either side of an obscured jaw line—scratches feverishly into a folio with a steel dip pen. He stops, tears away the wire-rimmed spectacles perched oblongly on his nose and rubs his eyes with two balled fists. He lets his hands drop to the heavy, burnished table top, and he exhales, as if to announce the end of le *manuscrit* over which he has been toiling. He sits for a moment, staring at nothing.

Gaunt and pale, his face lacks the mathematical symmetry of which Euclid and the Greek aesthetes wrote: with a nose running slightly askance below a delicate brow, and eyes, clouded by obsession, seemingly having drifted too far apart. He wears a collarless shirt with open sleeves rolled to his elbows and loose fitting *pantalon noir* of the working class. Yet something in the manner of Georges d'Aubigné betrays a *bourgeois lignée*.

The room, a gray plaster box in *une pension* on Rue Mouffetard, boasts a single stained-glass window overlooking Quartier Latin. It is arranged around a squat brick mantelpiece centered on the front wall. A small bookshelf weighed down by Greek and Latin texts stands perceptibly splayed against a back wall. In the corner: *un pot de chambre* and *une cuvette en porcelaine*.

He watches two fist-sized rats scamper across the floor. They roll into a tangle of filthy fur until the larger of the two mounts the other, pumping its rodent caudal with impressive zeal.

—*Elle baise bien, non, M. Rat?* says Georges. You have more *rapports sexuels* than a Russian tsar. Which reminds me, it is a night for *célébration*. Twenty-three years in *ce monde ignoble* is quite enough, is it not, M. Rat?

In a *réponse impolie*, the rat *manoeuvres son postérieur* into the young man's line of vision and whips its tail back and forth, finally lifting the dorsal appendage upright, revealing *un petit cul rosé*.

—That's how it is then, non? *Allez au diable Vauvert!*

Georges fastens an Ascot collar and ties a deep-brown *cravate* loosely then slips into a tan gilet and matching redingote that hangs to his knees. He snugs a black felt d'Orsay onto his head until the brim rests just above his eyebrows. Then with great haste, he sweeps le *manuscrit* into his arms and drops it into the dying embers of the fireplace. He waits just long enough to see the first threads of smoke curl around the corners of the folio. When he extinguishes the lamp and closes the door, M. Rat is still about his *affaire obscène* and *le manuscrit* is in flames.

On the narrow stairway, Georges squeezes by a wine-soaked tenant, whom he acknowledges with a clipped bow of head and shoulders; at the bottom, *la propriétaire* awaits.

—M. d'Aubigné. Can I assume that some tragedy has befallen you, since your rent payment is three weeks past due? says Mme. Legard [*in a manner approximating concern*].

—*Non*, Madame. No tragedy, but a fable, *oui*. A fable has befallen me.

The landlady, who is carrying a silver serving tray, wrinkles her nose as if some foul odor has accompanied the young man down the stairs.

—Georges d'Aubigné! Speak plainly! says she. [*vexed*]

—The play, Madame—it is a fable, not a tragedy. Please excuse my simple witticism.

—The play! *L'enfance de l'art*, Georges! A waste of *études supérieures*! So what, then, is the name of this play which has so preoccupied your mind that you cannot make your rent payment?

—Well, Madame, that is a matter still under consideration. Perhaps *Le Royaume des Porcs* will do, says Georges [*stepping around la propriétaire*]. But I must bid you adieu, for a night of *célébration* awaits. [*swinging the door open*]

—A night of *célébration*. *Ça me fait une belle jambe*, says Mme. Legard. [*muttering to herself*]

Georges exits *la pension* and turns up Rue Mouffetard in the direction of Saint-Germain-des-Prés. The air is a vile broth of human and animal filth. The Seine River is close enough that he can detect its polluted presence with at least two, perhaps three, of his five senses. He checks his pocket watch—11:03. The cafés are lit up with spirits, wine, and the loud chatter of *le prolétariat*, all spilling out into the narrow street. In the gray heat, a snapping cur mounts a bitch, humps with canine zeal.

—*Ah, elle baise bien, M. Chien?* It is a night for love, *non*?

The mutt growls and snaps at the bitch's ears, tearing away a morsel of pink flesh.

—That's how it is then, *non*?

Georges continues down Rue Mouffetard, stepping and bounding over and around green glistening globs of *crottes de cheval*. Presently, he slips under a green awning and enters a café through a door with cross-hatched windows. He is hit with a blast of air heavy with tobacco smoke and bitter coffee; a hint of anis snakes into his nostrils like *un enchantment exotique*. He spies someone he knows: a young man with a long face and prominent proboscis; markedly unhandsome. The man's front teeth protrude like the barkless nubs of a stripped-bare branch as he sets a demitasse to his lips. His eyes, two wet and fuzzy disks, rise to meet the arrival. Georges drops down into a chair.

—*Chartreuse, fais vite*! he says. [*calling out to no one in particular*] It is a night for *célébration*, my friend.

—*Chartreuse*? How have you come into money? Do you spend your tuition funds? Or perhaps you've at last robbed your rich relatives, *les doctrinaires*? says Armand Bagot.

—Armand, you promised, *non*? There will be no talk of those matters.

—Those matters! What do those matters matter? They care nothing for you . . . *bâtard de la bourgeoisie*. You are a mangy cur in the shadows to them. Just like the one who haunts Rue Moufettard.

—Ah, but M. Chien is taking his bitch from behind as we speak, *non*? Perhaps, then, there is still hope for me.

—Who cannot find a bitch to take from behind? It's francs you want. When will you take what is rightfully yours? How can you number yourself among *les républicains* while *la bourgeoisie* buys your silence?

—Tonight your *cynisme abondant* buys my silence, *mon ami*. I ignore you because tonight is a night for *célébration*.

—What is so special about tonight that I must bite my tongue? What is it that makes you so oblivious to my usual gripes?

—Tonight marks twenty-three years *dans ce monde, mon ami*, Armand.

—Ah, twenty-three years. Almost a lifetime since first *ton grand-père* took his lunatic bitch from behind, *non*? *La putain hongroise*?

—*Non, mon ami*. [*sighing*] Hungarian, *oui*. But she was no whore . . . *la domestique*. Why must you bring this up? Why now?

—It is no fault of mine. Perhaps now you regret revealing your past to me. *Totalement étrangers l'un à l'autre*, we were when first we entered La Sorbonne.

—It was foolish of me, *oui*. But how could I resist your charm? It was *destinée, non? Moi et toi . . . les amis*. [*makes to embrace his companion*]

—Enough! Sentimental slop! Let us drink, then, and celebrate *ton existence misérable*!

Georges pours Chartreuse into two glasses. The two young men drink. The café swirls around them: clinking glasses, bursts of laughter, bawdy rapport.

—Speaking of whores . . . where is *ta putain*? says Armand. [*vulgarly licking the inside of his glass with a mollusc-like tongue*]

—Why must you always resort to things *bas*? My Éve awaits my call this very night.

—*La bourgeoisie* have a wife with child at home and a whore in *le bordel*. But you, Georges, you have only a whore *de la rue*. You are no self-respecting member of *la bourgeoisie*.

—Non, Armand, I am not, say Georges. [*with thoughtful resignation*]

—But you wish to be.

—*Non*. It is too late for that, *mon ami*. Perhaps in my youth. Perhaps to save *mon père et ma mère* from *une existence malheureuse*. But they are gone. And now it is too late.

—I will weep for you another day, *mon orphelin*.

A third young man appears as if out of thin air, drops down into a chair. Most noticeably, his flaxen hair is thin, balding from the crown of his head in a radiance of oily flesh, yet inexplicably aging him little. His features are soft and round, pleasant if not quite striking: a long, straight nose, plump pink lips, eyes as green as the liqueur that sits before him.

—I passed *ta pension*, says Félix Vasser. *La propriétaire* says your rent payment is overdue.

—Ah, the mystery of unaccountable wealth solved, says Armand.

—She also says you've finished your play.

—Mme. Legard is not one for secrets, says Georges [*with a crooked smirk*]. Not a week ago she told me her husband was plotting a fresh *Bourbon démolir*.

—Ha! Plotting! Sounds as if she is plotting to rid herself of that scoundrel husband of hers.

—But the play is no secret, says Félix. [*almost in earnest*] You've been toiling over it *sans cesse*.

—There is truth! The only secret is what this play, this *pièce de théâtre*, is about. I beg you tell me it is more than simply an artistic fart in the wind.

—All in good time, *mes amis*. First, we wet our gullets with the elixir of monks, *non*?

The three young men raise their glasses with an eager *salut!* and drink them back. The latest arrival, Félix, suddenly turns sullen, as if no longer able to bear the weight of the bad news that is threatening to drown him, despite the abounding good cheer sloshing all about. His two companions are not oblivious to this abrupt change in mood.

—*Donner sa langue au chat*, Félix! What is it?

—I won't be returning to *mes études*. It's my father . . . he's had a bad turn and I must stay and run the business.

—So now you make nails and spikes with which the railroad will crucify this country from one end to the other? said Armand. [*slapping the table with an open hand, emphatic yet mirthful*]

—But why, *mon ami*? What has happened to your father?

—A carriage horse kicked and struck a glancing blow to his knee as he passed by on Rue du Bac. *Un accident peu probable*. It seems the horse was spooked by *deux chats* tangled in *une soirée érotique* under its gray-chipped hooves.

A knowing look passes between Georges and Armand that leaves little doubt as to its meaning. What they both realize is all of Paris has of late been besieged by copulating animals. Something *dans l'air* stirring the loins of quadrupeds *grands et petits*.

—Ah, *baisant aux rues*! What has become of our Paris?

—Not an hour ago, I watched M. Rat *baiser* Mlle. Rat across my floor in ways *pas anatomique*. Likewise, M. Chien and his quivering bitch.

—It portends evil, says Félix.

—Too Biblical for my tastes, says Armand. I prefer something more *politique*. Perhaps another *révolution* simmers just beneath the Bourbon calm, and Charles shivers and shakes under silken bed sheets.

—A toast to that! says Georges. [*raising a glass*]

—You must be mindful of where you are when you say such things, Armand. Take heed! The walls have ears.

—What? Ultras here? *Conneries! Ultras manges la merde!*

A man at the next table pricks up his ears, turns to see who has uttered the foolish if bold declaration. He skids his chair over. An unholy nimbus of stench passes with him—a sweet rot reminiscent of death that announces his trade as *un boucher*. *L'intrus* is double the age of the young men who now eye him suspiciously beneath youthfully wrinkled brows. His dress is lowly: loose pantaloons; an open-collared, gray-wool shirt, beneath which bubbles a cheap froth of white hair; and a wide-brimmed peasant's hat pulled tightly down to his eyes. The whole ensemble looks to have been freely drizzled with *vin de province*.

—What is this I hear, *mes frères d'armes*?

—Something about Ultras and *merde*, says Georges. [*twisting his head toward Armand, shooting him a look that is at once angry and playful*]

—May they flare like a dry stool in *les toilettes d'Hades*, says Armand.

—[*laughing boisterously from the black hole under his craggy nose*] L'homme speaks plainly, says *l'intrus*. And poetically. Let us drink to that, *non*?

He extends his glass, hoping for a taste of something better than the poison he has been draining into his rancid gullet. Georges and Armand hesitate. Finally, Félix palms the bottle of Chartreuse and tips it to the man's waiting glass. *L'intrus* blurts out a salutation then, not waiting for the others, drains the glass. He raps it on the table, waiting for another. Félix makes to comply, but Armand stays his hand.

—First, a quick and honest answer. Then we drink again. Who are you, *Monsieur*?

—Is it not plain as *le Démon à l'église*? I am a fellow enemy of the Ultras, *bien sûr*.

— *Bien sûr*, says Georges. [*in a gently mocking tone*]

—But Monsieur, I have not seen you before. I know all *les républicains* in Quartier Latin.

—*Je suis le boucher*. My shop is beyond the stench of Paris proper, or should I say beyond the proper stench of proper Paris? [*leaning in*] *La chien* that rolls in its own *merde* cannot smell the *merde* on others, *non*? [*he winks a hollow gray eye*]

—Now who speaks poetically? says Georges.

—And unintelligibly, says Armand. Away with you, *boucher*! *Vous êtes l'imposteur certainement*. [*dismissing l'intrus with a flippant wave of his hand*]

—[*Félix jerks the bottle and sloshes Chartreuse into the glass of l'intrus*] Drink up first, *Monsieur*. [*in a jittery voice*]

—*Oui, oui*. By all means, *Monsieur*. Drink up. Then away with you! [*with clear disdain*]

The man stretches two besmirched lips tightly over a menagerie of repugnant, blackened teeth; the smile is forced but not strained. He appears eerily calm, composed. And suddenly much more robust than he had at first seemed to be. Wrapping the glass in his grubby grip, he pours it into his gullet, raps it soundly onto the table then wipes his mouth on an already soiled sleeve. The young men watch as the man's fist trembles around the glass; one by one, his knuckles crack and turn pale. Yet his gaze is one of detachment, almost tranquil. A chink of glass snaps off and rattles across the table. *L'intrus* relaxes his grip, picks up the shard, places it on his tongue, and begins to chew. The sound of glass grinding in his teeth is nauseating, and the three young men wince in unison. Finally, with only the slightest grimace, *l'intrus* swallows with an audible gulp.

A long silence follows, one pregnant with disbelief, awe, and trepidation. Finally, intrepid Armand breaks the spell.

—[*clapping*] Bravo, Monsieur! Bravo! Parlor tricks, as the English say, *non*? Now away with you, scoundrel!

The man rises slowly, turns on his heels, and strides for the door with a crooked gait, one which inexplicably announces itself as a battle wound from some former revolt or uprising. He exits quietly amid the now steadily rising din of *le café*, yet the three young men clearly hear the uneven drumbeat of his march. Their eyes follow l'intrus until he disappears into a dark recess of night.

—*Très affreux*, says Félix.

—*Très redoutable*, says Georges.

—*Très, très, très*, says Armand. [*disgusted*] *Conneries!*

With this, they try to return to their former mood and manner. Their collective gaze converges on the broken glass, where inside two flies lay one atop the other, motionless, save for the almost imperceptible twitching of the topmost abdomen.

—*Wouaou! Plus baisant!* says Armand. It is a crazy night, *non*? All of Paris *baisent!* Let us drink, *mes amis*. [*pouring*]

—*À votre santé*, says Georges.

— *À votre santé*, says Félix.

The three young men drink: one, two, three toasts. As if to fill the void with the sound of their clinking glasses. What each of them is thinking but does not say is that the *l'intrus* has soured *la célébration* with his unwelcome political overture. Georges, in particular, has forgotten why he is here. But well-intentioned Félix attempts to revive merry spirits.

—Georges, now that you have finished your play, you must tell us something of it.

—Yes, George. *Cracher le morceau!* You have kept us in suspense long enough, non?

—But it is best that you read it for yourself. There will be time for that later. But tonight we drink.

Even as he hoists an eager glass to his mouth, Georges knows this is a lie, for le *manuscrit* is now nothing more than a heap of ashes. And he has no intention of re-writing it. For it was decided some time ago—years ago—by him, that tonight was the night—his twenty-third birthday—that he would end his own life. The burning of le *manuscrit* was a more recent improvisation, although still a planned act that defies the seemingly spontaneous nature of such indelible deeds. It begs the question why twenty-three? What was the deciding factor in Georges d'Aubigné's morbid timetable? The answer is simple: Twenty-three was the age of his own mother and father when they passed from *ce monde misérable.*

Georges was a boy at the time. His father, a *Fusilier* in Napoleon's *Grande Armée,* did not survive the Battle of Maloyaroslavets. He yet recalls standing between his father's legs, tugging at a brass button and teasing the red-plumed feather of a black-brimmed shako. The grand uniform of *La Grande Armée.* It is his final memory, the last time he would see his father alive.

The grief had been too much for his mother to bear, and she threw herself into Rivière Loire near their home at Aubigné-sur-Layon. Young Georges followed her that day, weeping as she wept, wailing as she wailed, and watched her step off the bridge, plunge without hesitation into the murky current of her own swirling grief. That memory would stay in his mind like an unsigned masterpiece—macabre, forever vivid, centered on the front wall of his subconscious. Sometimes in those gray and transitory moments between wakefulness and sleep, he still hears the flap of her dress like a torn flag or sail, fluttering in his ears as she drops and drops and drops.

—*Mon ami,* you must tell us about *ta pièce de théâtre. [Armand confiscates the Chartreuse as if to hold it for ransom]* A drink for a story, *non?*

—*Bon d'accord.* I will do my best. [*George leans back in his chair, runs a hand through his hair, and sighs*] As you know, it is a fable, in which *le protagoniste* is a pig . . . a king pig.

—*Le protagoniste est un porc? Un roi porc?* How can this be?

—It is a fable, *non?* says Félix. It is possible, a king pig.

—What, then, is the king pig's kingdom? A pig pen?

—*Exactement!* says Georges. The king pig is king of the pig pen.

—The pigs in this kingdom, they are talking pigs, *non?*

—*Exactement!* They are talking pigs. That is why it is a fable, *mon ami.*

—*Oui, oui.* What, then, makes this king pig king? And why is the pig pen not *la république?*

—Armand! Let him tell the story, says Félix. [*rescuing the Chartreuse, he pours*]

—It is not *la république* because there has been no uprising. And the king is king because he is pure pink in color, except for his tail, which is black. In this kingdom all *les descendants royaux* are pure pink with a black tail. It is the mark of their *lignée. Le cardinal* and *l'évêque,* are pure pink, as are all other *aristocrates.*

— *Attends un peu!* The pig pen has a church and *une aristocratie?* How can this be?

—Armand! *Arrête!*

—*Oui,* the pig pen has a church and *une aristocratie.*

—Then it must also have corruption and taxes, non?

—*Oui, bien sûr,* Armand, corruption and taxes. [*with mild exasperation*] Now, if you please, I will tell you of the king's *situation difficile.*

—*Oui, oui,* tell us.

—The king's name is *Charles le Porc.* He is not favored by the people. He is a weak king, one who looks to his own well-being before the well-being of his royal subjects. *Charles le Porc* fears the wolves and has been known to sacrifice one or two brown or black pigs to the wolves in order to *sauver sa peau,* and his kingdom, too.

—Why the brown or black pigs?

— Because clearly they are not pink. Pink is the most delightsome and desirable color in the kingdom. As I said, the king is pure pink, but for his tail, which is the noble marque de distinction. And all of the *aristocrates* are pure pink. The brown and black pigs are the most *indésirables* in the kingdom. They are the lowest classes. *Les paysans.*

—Ah, but what then of the mottled pig? Brown and pink? Or black and pink?

—They must lie somewhere between, then. The middle classes, non? says Félix.

—*C'est ça.*

—What of *la bourgeoisie?* asks Armand. What is their *marque de distinction?*

—*La bourgeoisie* are pure pink but for a black spot around one eye, which they cannot see on themselves.

— Ah, so they do not see their own black spots . . . they know nothing of their own *noirceur, non?*

— *Exactement!* They believe themselves to be *l'aristocratie,* yet they are not pure pink.

—Who, then, are the wolves that terrorize the kingdom? asks Félix.

—But that is simple, says Armand. *Réfléchis bien.* The king's name is *Charles le Porc* and he appeases the wolves with the blood of peasants.

—*Tiens ta langue,* Armand, says Georges. It will all become clear, in time.

—*Oui, oui.* Continue. [*leaning back and lighting a pipe*]

—*Charles le Porc* has no *héritier présomptif* by his queen, *La Reine des Porcs*. But he does have *un enfant illégitime*.

—*Un bâtard*, says Armand. [*delighted*] *Merveilleux!*

—*Oui, un bâtard.*

—And does *ce bâtard* have a name, *mon ami*?

—*Oui*, his name is simply *le Bâtard*. [*the young men all laugh together*]

—And does *Charles le Porc* favor *le Bâtard*?

—*Oui, bien sûr. L'intrigue* of the play centers on the efforts of *Charles le Porc* to legitimize *le Bâtard* in the eyes of *l'aristocratie*.

—Who opposes *Charles le Porc*, that he should not legitimize *le Bâtard*?

— *Cardinal le Porc, bien sûr.*

—*Bien sûr.*

—*Ce Bâtard* . . . does he bear the black tail *de la royauté*?

—Ah . . . a most pertinent question. *Oui, le Bâtard* bears the black tail *de la royauté.*

— *Merveilleux!*

—On what grounds, then, does *Cardinal le Porc* oppose the legitimizing of *le Bâtard*?

—Ah . . . *oui* . . . but you see . . . *le Bâtard* also has a single black spot on his fore leg. Although he bears the black tail *de la royauté,* he is not otherwise pure pink.

—*Oui, c'est un problème complexe!*

— *Continuer, Georges! Continuer!*

—*Charles le Porc* pursues *des tactiques variées*, that he might present *le Bâtard* in a favorable light *à l' aristocratie*, but in particular, *au Cardinal le Porc.*

—*Cardinal le Porc*, then, is a moral man, *non*?

—*Non*, Félix, *Cardinal le Porc* is not a moral man . . . *il aime* . . . *enculer les porcelets.*

— *Tous les prêtres* . . . *tous les mêmes*, says Armand. *Les enculés!*

—*Le Cardinal le Porc* objects to legitimizing *le Bâtard* because he wishes to control the kingdom.

—*Le salaud!* [*Armand slams his fist on the table*]

—To legitimize *le Bâtard* is to weaken his own position *stratégique.*

—*Charles le Porc* is defeated then, *non*? says Félix. And the story ends?

—*Non*, Félix, *pas encore. Charles le Porc* has one final *stratégie.* He will legitimize *le Bâtard* at the annual *Bal des Cochons.*

— *Continuer!*

—Before the ball takes place, Charles le Porc has the foreleg of *le Bâtard* amputated. *Bien sûr*, this solves the problem of the black spot. At least, so thinks *Charles le Porc*.

—Now *le Bâtard* is pure pink, but for his black tail.

—*Exactement!* The day of the ball finally arrives, and *Charles le Porc* publicly presents his *fils illégitime à l'aristocratie. Le Bâtard* hobbles in on three legs and bows before the pure pink crowd. [*George lights his pipe*]

—And? The plan works, *non? Le Bâtard* is legitimized.

—*Non*, Félix. The plan does not work. The crowd roars with laughter. They say they have never seen such a thing . . . such an *absurde* thing. And from that time forward *le Bâtard* is known as le Bâtard à trois jambes.

—Ah . . . but Georges. The three-legged bastard! *C'est tragique!*

—It is not over, *pas encore.*

—*Continuer!*

—*Charles le Porc* is so humiliated. Everywhere he goes he hears about *le Bâtard à trois jambes.* It turns out that the young *bâtard* has become somewhat of novelty among *l'aristocratie.* But *Charles le Porc* is humiliated, for he knows that they are laughing at him. Always laughing. And he stews about it for week after week, wondering how to *sauver la face.* Finally, it comes to him.

—*Oui*, what is it? What does he do?

—He has no choice but to makes *le Bâtard à trois jambes* go away.

—Go away? What is this 'go away'?

—Disappear.

—How, Georges? How does he make *le Bâtard à trois jambes* disappear?

—Can you not guess, *mes amis?*

—Ah . . . of course, says Armand. [*he pauses to revive his smoldering pipe*] *Charles le Porc* sacrifices his *fils illégitime* to the wolves. That is how he makes him disappear.

—*Exactement*, Armand!

—Surely that is not the end? says Félix. *Le Bâtard à trois jambes* finds favor with the wolves, and they spare his life, *non?* Then he returns seeking revenge on *Charles le Porc,* non?

—*Non*, Félix. *Le Bâtard à trois jambes* is eaten by the wolves. That is the end of the story.

—But what then is the moral? Fables have a moral, non? There is no moral to your tale.

—Ah, but there is, says Armand. '*L'aristocratie* is not impressed by *une partie du corps.*' [*snorting at his own remark*] Or 'once *le bâtard* always *le bâtard.*'

—*Pas amusant*, Armand.

—Here, then, is your moral, Félix, says Georges: 'Class is only skin-deep when *le bâtard* is who you are.'

—*Non, non.* It is not right.

—Félix, why do you take *cette pièce de théâtre* so personally? It is Georges' story, non? If it is to be taken personally, it is only by him. Is he not himself *le Bâtard* in his own silly tale?

—Armand, you are drunk. Why must you always say these things when you are drunk? says Félix.

—La Chartreuse *est le sérum de vérité.* [*speaking softly*] I think the title of *la pièce* is actually *Legitimizing Georges, non?*

Georges rises from his chair, realizing now that recounting the story of his fable to Armand was a mistake. He digs two silver franks from a pouch and places them on the table one at time. There is an undeniable gravity in this gesture.

—Have another, *mes amis.*

—Georges, stay a while yet. Armand is sorry. You know he is not himself when he is in the clutches of spirits.

—*Oui,* Georges, *oui. Je suis l'âne.* Sit down, please.

—*Non, non.* It is late and time is short. My Ève awaits.

—But what is this 'time is short?' The night is young. Stay awhile yet.

—*Adieu, mes amis.*

George turns and cuts a narrow swath through the crowded café. He exits without a glance back at his two young friends, despite the secret knowledge that he will not see them again on this godforsaken green plain. For a crudely fashioned noose awaits his return to *la pension* on Rue Mouffetard. Earlier today, he coiled the six loops of a hangman's noose to squeeze the last breaths from his lungs. It lies beneath his bed, a reluctant promise waiting to be fulfilled, a shadowy sin to be coaxed out into the light of day.

Continuing on his way to Saint-Germain-des-Prés, Georges maintains a solid gait, seemingly unaffected by the halo of fog that has settled like a blanket of gray ash in his head. Thoughts of Ève push him on. Up ahead, a parked brougham rocks and rattles in the street. Upon overtaking the carriage, Georges witnesses the peculiar sight of a fine white Carthusian mounting a mare half its size and relentlessly working its haunches as if a battering ram at the gates of the city, much to the detriment of the attached brougham.

—Ah . . . *elle baise bien, M. Étalon?*

The Carthusian responds with a gushing snort and the clatter of iron hooves on cobblestone.

—*Oui, M. Étalon,* it is a night for love. I myself run to the arms of *ma maîtresse.*

The night sky is dull and flat, starless. The moon has been snuffed out by a heavy blanket of low-slung clouds. Georges cannot help but feel that it is all for him, and somehow fitting—the obscured heavens. As always, he is alone on this dismal planet, abandoned even by God's empyrean mantle.

But then *le lupanar* glows as a lone star ahead. He steps up his pace. He longs for *les effluves agréables, le chuchotement du désir, la poire en dentelle de la lingerie.* Georges enters *le lupanar* and takes the stairs two-at-a-time. The lights in the parlor flicker waxy and low, and the wink of crystal meets his gaze at every turn. Two men wait with hats in hand; one lounges with *une jeune lorette* sitting in his lap. Ève is conspicuously absent. Georges pauses but a moment then strides for the next flight of stairs. Before he can mount the first step, a brutish hulk of a man with cloves of garlic on his breath and sprigs of parsley wedged in his teeth blocks his passage.

—M. d'Aubigné . . . you know *le règlement.* No one goes upstairs *sans être accompagné.*

—Pascal, *espèce d'imbécile!* You know me. I am here often, non? I must see my Éve!

—*Non, Monsieur. Elle est malade.*

—*Malade?* How can it be? I saw her not two nights ago. *Elle était en parfaite santé.* I must see her!

Georges shifts his weight, makes to step around the man he knows only as Pascal. He is stopped short by a pudgy palm laid flat on his chest. When he struggles, the man Pascal sends him tumbling to the floor in a dandyish heap. A man in the shadows huffs a leaky chuckle. Georges gets to his feet, retrieves his d'Orsay hat, brushes the collar of his redingote. He is about to resort to the ungentlemanly tactic of catapulting his boot into Pascal's undoubtedly sizable groin when he hears his Éve call out from the top of the stairs.

—Georges, *non!* Pascal, let him up. Please. [*a trace of hesitant tenderness*]

The big man stands aside with the dull look of a grazing ox that has moved from one green oasis of grass to the next. Georges brushes by him and ascends the stairs. Reaching the top, he opens his arms to his Éve. Her high-sloping forehead is only slightly obscured by two dark looping curls with the shape and effect of some pleasing punctuation that never failed to give George pause. Her almond-shaped eyes with their deep nut-brown hue give her a perpetual air of mystery. A gently cusped nose complements two full yet delicate lips. For Georges, the slight gap between her front teeth is *le défaut* that transforms her beauty into something *véritable*, just this side of perfect, something forgivably less than Platonic.

He gathers her in his arms and drops a hand to the curve of her hip. He squeezes it gently. Éve clasps the hand and twirls, somehow twirling about face while at the same time winding herself snugly into his side. She leads him to *sa chambre.*

—*Tu es malade?*

—*Non, non.* You needn't worry, *mon amour.*

Georges sets his hat on la commode then flops down onto the bed, kicks off his boots, and removes his redingote one sleeve at a time by rolling first this way then that. He loosens the *cravate* around his neck and unbuttons his gilet. Éve unfastens her *robe de chambre* and lets it fall to the ground, unveiling a tautly molded, corseted figure. George feels his stomach tighten and his loins stir.

—Ah, *ma fleur de lys.* It is this that I have waited for, consumed by thoughts of you every minute of every hour this day, from the very moment *le coq* did crow.

—*L'encens!* What makes this day one for such flattery?

—This day . . . every day. They are the same. I am consumed by you *éternellement.* [*smiling foolishly*]

—But this day is a special day, is it not? [*unlacing her corset, letting her breasts drop naturally within her linen chemise*]

—Special, *ma fleur?* [*slightly apprehensive, aware that this is indeed a 'special' day*]

— Allumeur! *C'est ton anniversaire!*

—*Ah, oui. C'est ça.* And we must celebrate. Come straddle me and ride for the sunrise with the might and zeal of *un cavalier romain.*

—Georges! [*playfully aghast*] We shall see. [*coyly*] But first you must declare *à moi ton amour éternel.*

—Such an easy task. Hardly worth performing! [*teasingly*]

—Georges, please!

—*Bien!* [*rising*] I love you with the boldness of haughty *Mont Blanc,* with the frothing passion of mysterious Moskstraumen, with the tenderness of the flowing fields of Normandie, and with the sadness of solitary *Île Plate*. [*dropping to one knee, gazing up at her*]

An almost undetectable gasp catches in the young woman's throat. Right then her likeness to the vision of his mother forever falling occurs to him. The resemblance is momentarily startling. Georges wonders how he could not have noticed it before. Until he realizes it is not an exact pictorial resemblance, so much as a substantial resemblance. *Un doppelganger de l'âme.* A part of him wants to tell her this, but he is uncertain how one goes about saying such a thing.

Éve knows little of his past, and nothing about his mother. Georges has told her nothing about who he really is. His trip from *Aubigné-sur-Layon* to Paris—a young orphan in search of a paternal grandfather—remains a secret to be kept from her. How could he tell her that d'Aubigné is not his rightful name? Or that his father was the bastard son of a low nobleman and a lunatic scullery maid? What difference would it make to her to know that the blood of a Montgolfier coursed through his veins? Yet even as he wonders, Georges knows it would make a difference. For it had made a difference to him.

Although the tale had but once been vaguely recounted to him when he was a boy, its toll reverberated over the hills and valleys of his youth, staying with him even now like the faint melody of a distant nursery rhyme. The story of how his grandfather, a tutor in a noble manor, had saved a scullery maid from a lunatic asylum and thereafter had fallen in love with her was nothing short of heroic. In time, their unbounded love brought forth a child who would bear its father's Christian name—Péter—but never family name. For the father was never to wed the scullery maid. Being betrothed to one of social status, he was obliged to cultivate the strategic alliances that amounted to an incremental advance in the weight which his family name both bore and wielded.

The boy Péter was nurtured and raised solely by his mother, of whom it was said was never again to return to her former lunatic state (aside from momentary lapses when she would hike up her skirt and urinate in the corner). She did, however, finally succumb to consumption, or as the locals would have it, she was hag-ridden—turned into a horse by night and ostensibly ridden to death by malevolent hags attending their heathen orgies and Sabbats. After his mother's death, the young man traveled from his home in the northeastern hills of the Kingdom of Hungary to *Maine-et-Loire* in France. There he worked in the flax fields near *Aubigné-*

sur-Layon by day and by night dreamed of traveling to Paris to meet his long-lost father. Living in close proximity to the Montgolfiers, it seemed, was more comfort than agony to the young man. At seventeen years of age, he enlisted in *La Grande Armée,* under the name Pierre d'Aubigné, having never made the trip into Paris to claim his true birthright.

He married a barmaid from the nearby village of Les Roches. At eighteen years old, she was decidedly ripe for nuptials, at least, so it was said by villagers of Les Roches. Pierre d'Aubigné met her on his first day of leave and married her on the next. He was also eighteen. Before he turned nineteen, she had borne him a son.

After his father was slain on the point of a Russian bayonet and his mother walked off a bridge over the Rivière Loire, Georges d'Aubigné was kindly taken in by the villagers of Les Roches. Some years later, he made the trip that his father never had: he traveled to Paris. To his great sadness and dismay, his grandfather, Péter Montgolfier, has passed away almost a decade earlier. However, the old man, suffering from years of guilt and remorse over the affair, had made provisions, in the event that someone should one day come looking for him, claiming to be an illegitimate line of the Montgolfier family. That person was to be "met with open arms, ushered into the family, and taken care of as one of our own." Of course, in legal terms, the warm approximations of such well-intended clauses mean little. Especially when twisted beyond recognition by an able-minded barrister. In the end, the Montgolfier family sent Georges on his way with a modest stipend, with which he was meant to live modestly and secure a proper education. This he had done.

   —*Embarque maintenant,* says Georges. [*hoisting his cock like a main mast*]

   —*Oui, mon amour! Oui!*

   —*Lève l'ancre!*

   —*Oui, anchors aweigh!*

Éve dispatches what remains of her undergarments and eases herself down onto her lover's member, the lips of her labia stuttering along his hard, dry shaft. Yet in a moment's time, all is silk and shine, glistening and thermal. The gay gurgle of her secret cavity floods the bed with sound and scent. Éve drops her head back: puffs, whines, and whinnies (a sound that distracts Georges, given the spectacle he'd earlier been witness to). He reaches up and cups two breasts that are dipping and bobbing in time to the passionate, yet somehow mechanically cyclic, rhythm of their lovemaking.

Suddenly Éve props two hands on his chest and rises; his cock egresses. She rolls onto her back, legs akimbo. Georges flips over like a fish in the bottom of a boat, and is presently inserting himself into the interstice of her womanhood. In and out, in and out, he moves, his buttocks pumping. He feels the thunderheads gathering, gathering for the climactic electric boom brewing just over the horizon. Yet the sudden realization that this will be their last night together fleetingly sullens him, and he stumbles in his slow-metered march towards climax. Perhaps sensing the storm's premature dissipation, Éve clutches his ears.

—*Baise-moi*, Georges! *Baise-moi!* she screams.

—*Oui, je te baise, je te baise*, he pants.

Newly invigorated, he steps up the pace—marching, marching. The storm clouds, now thick and black, rumble in his gut. The air snaps and sizzles with electric glee. Georges grits his teeth and thrusts one final thrust just as the storm breaks loose. Éve screams loudly. A bolt of lightning shoots from his cock and strikes ground. Éve shudders and vibrates as a current of high-seed voltage pulses through her. Every hair on her body stands on end, twitching; every cell floods with ebullient bliss. They collapse together, entangled, glazed with sweat. Then comes the pitter-patter of rain, quiet and reassuring. Showers and showers of rain. Cool rain. Georges and *sa fleur de lys* soak it in.

Finally, he extricates himself, stretches across her and retrieves his pipe from a pocket.

—Why is it that Pascal hates me so?

—Oh, Georges. You imagine it. It is not hate so much as annoyance.

—*Non, non. C'est de la haine.* Every time I arrive, he acts as if he's never set eyes on me before. And he refuses to let me up.

—You've only been coming here three nights a week for the past year. [*spoken playfully*]

—*Exactement!* Is it that he hates me, or does he have a secret desire for you?

—*Un béguin? Nigaud!* [*spoken more playfully*] And what if he did? What would you do?

—I would bend him over and stick *des plumes d'autruche* in his *trou du cul* . . . pointed end first.

—But he may find it *tres agréable.*

—Ha! *Oui, c'est ça.* [*pausing to smoke his pipe*] Why does Mme. Tremaine allow him to treat gentlemen in that manner?

—Ah, so you count yourself among them . . . gentlemen. But you always rail against gentlemen of *la bourgeoisie.* What is it you call them? 'Fondlers of fortunes.'

—*Oui,* fortunes they do not deserve.

—But Georges, what are you if not one of them, *la bourgeoisie? Tu es instruit, non?* Certainly, you are no *paysan.* [*placing a finger on his chin*]

—What? Only peasants can rail against *la bourgeoisie?* That I am *instruit* is nothing more than *un coup de chance.*

—Ah, *la bourse mystérieuse.* As long as I've known you, and I still don't know you. You hide behind secrets.

—*Non,* it is no secret. A stipend from a distant relative. There is no more to tell. Why, *ma fleur,* you are beginning to sound like Armand.

—*Aïe!* Then I shall die and say no more. You know my feelings toward Armand. Félix, however, is *une agréable compagnie.*

—Ah, another secret desire. But this time, you on him, *non?*

—Non, Georges. It's only that I find him to be *un homme de bonne volonté.*

—Ha, that he is, *certainement.* [*setting his pipe on la table de chevet*] He intends to end his studies at La Sorbonne.

—Non, Georges. [*shocked*] *Pourquoi?*

—His father has been injured, and he must take over *l'entreprise.*

— Poor Félix. Such a shame, *non?*

—*Oui,* a shame. Business is not for him. He loathes it.

—Armand seems much more suited for business.

—Armand *le Républicain?* [*chuckling*] An honorary member of *la petite bourgeoisie? Inconcevable!*

—His lack of conscience makes him so.

—*Ma fleur,* it is not that he lacks conscience, simply that it fails him *de temps en temps.*

—Georges, you make excuses for *ce fumier.*

—Excuses, *oui.* [*becoming thoughtful*] He is *mon frère, après tout.*

—*Pourquoi,* Georges? [*almost pleadingly*] You are not like him, yet he has such a hold on you. His hatred for others . . . for *la bourgeoisie* . . . is only la continuation of his *haine envers lui-même.* He hates the world only because he is in it. And one day soon the world will hate him back.

—Ah, *ma fleur et mon philosophe.* Enough of Armand.

Realizing that the conversation has come to an end, Éve reaches beneath the bed, producing a brown paper package. She sets it by him as an offering of sorts.

—*Qu'est-ce que c'est?*

—It is a gift, *naturellement!*

—Ah, but *ma fleur.* My love-making was *spectaculaire, oui . . .* but a gift is not expected.

—Tu es ridicule. C'est un cadeau d'anniversaire.

—Open it now, *oui?*

—Oui, oui, Georges! [*growing excited*] Open it now. I can bear it no longer. [*now fully excited*]

—Perhaps a toast first, *non?* A birthday toast?

—Georges d'Aubigné! Why must you torment me so?

—As you wish, *ma fleur.*

Georges tears away the brown paper. The box is large, too large, he thinks. He opens it and peers in. Reaching deep inside, he removes a pair of tiny knit boots. The arching of his brow looks like a tawny caterpillar caught in a morning shower.

—But they are *trop petites, ma fleur.* [*pulling one boot over his big toe*]

—Georges, *nigaud!* Don't you see what this means?

—It could only mean that you have taken up a new *passe-temps.*

—Regarde, says Éve.

She takes his hand and places it on her belly. Georges drops down onto one elbow to survey it in profile, one eye squeezed tightly shut. There is a slight protrusion, swelling out from the tangled mat at her pubis and receding just beneath two pink-tipped breasts. He lets his hand roll over it, circling lightly, gliding over downy, colorless hairs. In all the months of their lovemaking, this is the most intimate touch ever to pass between them. Not a touch to simply tickle and arouse but to divine what lay beneath.

The thoughts that begin to flood his head do not form an anxious tide of questions, as one might think would be the case. How did this happen? Is it mine? What to do next? It is only one thought that keeps surfacing again and again, only to burst ecstatically in his brain as a simple conviction: *Mon fils, voici mon fils.*

The long silence may have made Éve anxious had it not been for the expression on his face. She thinks it is one of equal parts delight and awe, with a hint of longing. The anxiety she has felt at the coming of this moment dissipates. For it lay lodged in the gurgling stream of her thoughts for two days prior, since first she found out. Yet, as the scene replayed itself over and over in her head, it was never clear to her how Georges would react. She knows Georges is an honorable man. He is not like the others that come to her in those darkest hours of night, sick with desire. He may not be a proper gentleman in title, she thinks, but he is more gentleman than the whole lot of *petit-maître* on the *rive droite.*

She recalls how they met shortly after her arrival in Paris. A young woman, Éve left her home on the *Massif Central* of Auvergne province, where the boredom and drudgery of being a dairy maid seemed more unappealing than the untold perils of Paris. In the capital, she walked the street of Les Halles, working for cabbage, carrots, and the occasional *centimes*, until Georges took her in. Within six months, she had met Mme. Tremaine, who registered her, trained her, and set her up in *une maison de tolérance*. Although she had a steady stream of gentlemen lovers—mostly married men of *la bourgeoisie*—Georges, with his Greek and Latin flourishes, was the one she loved. The one she still loves.

—Georges, you must say something, please.

—But there is nothing to say. [*pausing to stroke her belly*] What can words say of such a thing as this? Words are a mere pittance. The hard speckled seeds of an expansive possibility, *un potentiel merveilleux*. Words create ideas and ideas words. But words cannot create this, only *le réel* can, *ma fleur*, the actual. *La chair et le sang*.

—*Mon amour et mon philosophe*. But what are we to do?

—What are we to do? But that is simple. We are to marry, and we are to have a child *ensemble*.

—But are you sure?

—*Oui, ma fleur*. We will marry on the morrow. Summon *le père* to *l'église*. By nightfall, we shall be man and wife.

—Oh, Georges! [*tears welling in her eyes*]

—I shall take up the post of tutor, as *mon grand-père* before me. A happy life awaits us, you shall see. The three of us together.

—*Je n'ai aucun doute*. But are there no dreams you forsake? Have you no *ambitions élevées*? What of *le dramaturge* in you?

—*Que des plans stupides.* [*growing serious*] I came here tonight to set you free and to bid you *adieu*.

—*Non, mon amour!* [*collapsing into his arms*] Do not say such things.

—But everything has changed. I see it all now *clairement*. This has changed everything. [*placing a hand on her belly*]

—*Oui*, this has changed everything. [*she leans in close and presses her lips to his*]

For Georges, the pregnancy is a revelation. It seems as if all his life he has been trying to read a book in a language that is foreign to him. Page after page, he has searched for a shred of meaning, a word that makes sense, a phrase that rings true. Now, suddenly, he understands perfectly, every word, every sentence, every nuance. Something has changed, not in the book itself, but in him. No longer does his life seem all for naught. The nihilism that he flirted with in the past, now strikes him as hollow infatuation. For there is something where there once was nothing, something that has taken root in him and grows even as he sits contemplating it.

—Tomorrow we are to wed. So, there is much to do. [*springing from the bed, he gathers his clothes into a heap*] I must find Armand and Félix. Perhaps at the café still. I must rouse *le père*. And you must ready yourself, *ma fleur*.

—*Oui*, I must find a dress to wear. Perhaps I shall borrow one.

—Yes, do that. And I shall return before midday. [*fully dressed now, he bends to peck her on the cheek*] Am I not now the happiest man in Paris? Until tomorrow, then, *ma fleur*.

The emotions swirling within him concoct an unholy broth as he flies down the stairs and out into the street. He is elated, ashamed, nervous, enthralled, and remorseful all at the same time. The news of his impending fatherhood has made the night seem brighter, the air crisper, and the boulevards less depraved. Yet a sense of urgency drives him on, fueled by a desire to return to *la pension* and destroy the stiff noose beneath his bed. Cast it into the fire, where it belongs. As if this act alone will exorcize the dark inclinations that had first prompted him to devise such a lurid plan. Naturally, the thought of going through with it has not occurred to him since learning of the child that slumbers in the belly of his Éve.

Georges is stepping lively over the cobblestone, strides that are long and smooth. He checks his pocket watch: 2:07. The white Carthusian and the mare are nowhere in sight. He decides to stop in at the café, in the hope that Armand and Félix have not yet left. Who better to share the wonderful news with? Stopping to gaze up at the sky, he sees a broken constellation shining through the clouds. A good omen, thinks Georges d'Aubigné.

At le café, the crowd has thinned out. The table where he earlier sat with his two friends is empty. When he asks *le serveur*, he learns nothing, so he leaves. Outside, he makes his way down Rue Mouffetard. The oil streetlamps flicker like golden tongues, lapping up puddles of darkness of the bare boulevard.

Up ahead, he sees M. Chien and his bitch. The two dogs have their heads buried in a quagmire of muck and filth; they are gnawing at something. Georges greets the dogs cheerfully. Only when he peers over the mongrel's spiked ears, does he notice the human hand. Georges halts abruptly, and a chill sparks and fizzles up his spine. Thinking that perhaps his eyes deceive him, he steps closer. M. Chien and the bitch growl and snap greedily at his approach. There can be no doubt: with sharp carnassials, they scissor fibrous sinews; and with rumbling molars, they grind the bones of each digit to a red powdery paste.

Georges' stomach churns. He fights the urge to vomit. He wants to turn and run. But his curiosity holds him captive there, draws him closer. Inching forward, he sees a sight most horrific, one that makes him stumble backwards and pitch into the street. His hat drops with a soft thud onto the cobblestones. Georges d'Aubigné begins to tremble uncontrollably. From the shadows, stares the head of Armand, with dull and inanimate eyes, tipped onto its side, as if a toppled bag of pears. He notices the deafening hum of flies that now fills the air. His feels his hands are wet. Scanning the ground around him, he sees that he has fallen into a curdled rivulet of blood. A scream wells in his chest and bursts into the night.

Then from out of *la ruelle* steps a figure who Georges immediately recognizes. *L'intrus* from the café. *Le boucher* says nothing. Only the sepulchral pits of his eyes speak — scream *meurtre!* Georges is transfixed by this sinister expression. He wants to ask 'why?' but the word comes out as a whimper. There is a sudden movement, a lightning-quick slash through the air. He does not see, or even feel, the blurred silver flash that slits his throat.

Onward Christian Soldier

Joseph Vasser wondered how he had got here. Not that his memory had prematurely begun to fail him. He was, after all, only twenty-two years of age. Hardly headed for the grave, at least he hoped as much were true. He knew how he got here—this place, this one-room, shiplapped jail. He had been hauled away by the ragtag scrum of dairy farmers that comprise the Vermont Militia. No, his memory was fine. The here he wondered about was the unscripted imbroglio heretofore known as his life. How could it have taken such an unexpected turn? Had it not been for one innocent little snake bite, he might still be lazing among the golden crowns of nodding wheat, dreaming of his sweetheart Emma, and gazing longingly towards the muted heavens.

As it turned out, the snake bite wasn't entirely innocent.

Four years earlier, he had been rooting around the woodpile outback of his Father's farmhouse in southern Vermont when it happened. A timber rattler struck him on the hand, right on Father Abraham's bum, as his own father used to call it (although Joseph never understood why)—that meaty gully between thumb and index finger. After that everything changed. He woke up from a syrupy sleep a fortnight later talking like the Ten Commandments, babbling like a brook full of Bible. The doctor had attributed the glottological anomaly to a fever of the soul, brought on by the several raps he had recently sounded on death's foreboding door. Joseph's family, however, had settled on a less generous aetiology: they thought he'd gone mad.

"What's wrong with you?" his younger sister Margaret had asked, as if indeed Joseph knew precisely what was wrong with him.

"I know not, child," said he. "Except that mine is an affliction like unto Job's. God has willed it so."

It was only after several months of this kind of lopsided discourse that Joseph recalled the voice that had spoken to him while he was struggling for his life. The voice had said, "Go thee unto the hill and dig, that thou may'st know my will and my ways." It occurred to Joseph then that his own voice was merely a mortal version of the voice in his vision. But that wasn't what worried him; there were more pressing problems. The most pressing being that the hills in southern Vermont are legion, and the will and ways of God could be anywhere.

June 12, 1871

Dear Matilda,

Thank you for your most recent and delightful correspondence. As always, it was a pleasure to receive your letter. (Wherever did you find such lovely stationary? Who would have ever guessed that temperance could be so flowery!) Yes, I still have plans to address your woman's group. As you yourself have so eloquently put it, "the story of Joseph Vasser is a remarkable one." It is a story that begs to be told. And that is the story I intend to tell.

You mention the excitement that this much-anticipated event has already generated. That is truly wonderful news, although I cannot personally take any of the credit for it. My better half is responsible for that, I am sure. For were he not already matrimonially mine, I myself would swoon at the sight of him. No prophet of the Great Almighty should look that good, don't you agree?

Yes, I will be sure to recount the story of my first meeting with the prophet, although he was not then a prophet but a flaxen-haired dreamer with a mind enfeebled by fancy and romance. You will surely be amused to know that even the sight of my finely freckled bosom could not capture his undivided attention, so enraptured was he with "exalted" ideas! Such a reader he was; of course, a reader of the Good Book only. As you may know, his critics and enemies use this as fodder against him. They proclaim his own writings to be a mere imitation of the Bible. Such a misguided charge! I say (in truth, he says), how can God be accused of imitating Himself? You must certainly sense my frustration, so I leave that topic to bearded men in smoke-filled halls, where such things are crossly debated.

No, I feel certain that I have never before made your acquaintance, as I have never ventured as far as Boston and so have never had the pleasure of attending one of your meetings. I must admit that I am looking forward to seeing some of the sights beyond our little Vasserean paradise here in Vermont. A break from my duties as chief scribe and editor-in-chief will serve me well, although my prophet husband may have to eat manna from heaven in my absence, as he is hopeless in the kitchen.

Joseph has forbidden me from sending an excerpt from the "Book of Vasser" (or as it is affectionately known among his followers, the "Bible 2"). As I have previously mentioned, my husband has toiled over it for nearly three years (with my humble assistance). Now that it nears completion and we are looking for a publisher, he feels it best to keep the manuscript "under wraps." What I will send along, however, (warts and all) is an early (and clearly clumsy) attempt made by the fledgling prophet (and yours truly, for I was both scribe and editor of the manuscript) at generating scripture. But allow me a line or two to put that chapter of his life into context.

Before he became prophet and founder of the Vasserean faith, the prophet-to-be, Joseph Vasser, endured a time of trial and tribulation. Indeed, the prophet himself now refers to that time as his "pitiless year of Job." Although there was nothing as unsavory as seeping boils or bursting carbuncles, it was nonetheless a time during which the almighty tested the faith of our young (and handsome) prophet-to-be.

You have no doubt heard tell of the occasion on which the voice of God came to Joseph while convalescing from a snake bite (or as the prophet now refers to the incident, his "wrestle with Satan"). God commanded him to find His will and ways among the hills and vales of southern Vermont. Being a quick-witted and intelligent young man, Joseph suspected he might find some ancient artifact (secretly, the young romantic was hoping for the Holy Grail, no doubt) to turn the then-occurring religious revival on its ear (which persists to this day, albeit with somewhat less intensity). However, a year went by and he had found nothing. To make matters worse, God had not spoken to him since his wrestle with Satan. Out of frustration, and perhaps boredom, too, our prophet-to-be wrote the three books of Elihi and one book of Olihi, all transparent attempts at penning a family history in Biblical fashion. In hindsight, he views it as an unremarkable rehearsal for what was to come later. A novice's prelude to a Maestro's masterpiece, if you like.

Of course, as you will learn when I address your women's group, God finally did reveal the whereabouts of His will and ways to Joseph, which turned out to be an ancient artifact, as suspected: a record of an ancient American people written on plates of gold. From this ancient record, he began to translate the "Book of Vasser" (the "Bible 2"), his masterpiece (I should say His masterpiece). But more on that latter. I shall save the best parts of the story for my talk.

Hoping this letter finds you well and happy. And, yes, I too am eager to meet you in person.

Fond Regards,

Emma Vasser (née Andrews)

Writings of ~~FELIX ELIXFI~~ Elihi:
Book One

1 I, ~~Felix Jr. Elixfi~~ Elihi, being born of a ~~whore prostitute~~ sinful woman and a ~~murdered~~ slain man in the second year of the ~~rain rein~~ reign of King ~~Charles Charlekiah~~ Zedekiah, have seen ~~rogues, villains and miscreants eating the bowels of this city through its anus~~ the wages of sin consume this city.

2 ~~Yeah,~~ Yea, nevertheless, I was raised up in the ways of ~~the Republic~~ God by ~~a man of the petty bourgeoisie~~ goodly and righteous man, a man once well loved by my ~~butchered~~ slain father.

3 ~~For, it happened~~ came to pass that in the first year of the ~~rain rein~~ reign of ~~Charles Charlekiah~~ Zedekiah, my father was ~~butchered~~ slain by a ~~miscreant and thug a sour-smelling butcher and spy for the Ultras~~ Babylonian soldier ~~on the cobblestones of Paris~~ in Jerusalem.

4 And the ~~miscreant and thug~~ Babylonian soldier, seeing the ~~blood and carnage~~ sin that he had ~~unleashed~~ committed against an innocent man, ~~fled~~ did flee into the country, where ~~peasants found him out and slaughtered him and fed his testicles to the tusks of snorting swine~~ God did smite him down in his wickedness.

5 The ~~butchered~~ slain man, my father, had ~~slept with poked the beard of womanhood~~ lain with the ~~whore~~ sinful woman, and so ~~yeah~~ yea verily, she was ~~in the straw parturient pregnant heavy~~ big with child.

6 And ~~it happened~~ came to pass that in the second year of the ~~rain rein~~ reign of ~~Charles Charlehiah~~ Zedekiah, the ~~whore prostitute~~ sinful woman

~~hatched~~ ~~gave birth to~~ did bring forth ~~a baby boy~~ male child.

7 And so ~~yeah~~ verily, ~~Felix sr. Elihi Sr.~~ Eli, the man who was ~~friend to~~ well-loved by my ~~butchered~~ slain father, ~~took~~ did take pity on the ~~whore prostitute~~ sinful woman and her ~~bastard~~ son of no lineage, ~~and went~~ did go to her and was secretly ~~married~~ bound to her in marriage in the third year of the ~~rain rein~~ reign of ~~Charles Charlehiah~~ Zedekiah.

8 And I, ~~Felix Jr. Elifi~~ Elihi, being that ~~bastard~~ son of no lineage grew strong in the ways of the ~~Republic~~ God, under the guidance of ~~Felix Sr. Elihi Sr.~~ Eli, ~~who was like a father to me so I took his name~~ became the father of my heart and blessed me with his name.

9 And ~~Felix sr. Elihi Sr.~~ Eli ~~became a moneyed man made bags of money~~ did prosper in ~~Paris~~ the Kingdom of Jerusalem, which was ~~hotter than a Hades bonfire in constant political upheaval~~ plagued by sin and disobedience to God's word.

10 And in the ~~sixth~~ eleventh year of the ~~rain rein~~ reign of ~~Charles Charlekiah~~ Zedikiah, ~~the people Nebacanezer~~ Nebuchadnezzar ~~rose up in the July Revolution and kicked his shite-stained-arse out of Paris~~ and laid siege to Jerusalem, and conquered it.

11 So ~~Yeah~~ verily, King ~~Charles Charlekiah~~ Zedekiah was ~~ploughed, plucked, and undone overthrown~~ brought down by ~~Louis-Philippe~~ the hand of ~~Nebacanezer~~ Nebuchadnezzar.

12 And ~~the July Monarchy~~ darkness did ~~ruled the French~~ land.

END of Book 1

The search for God's will and ways was a long and grueling one. Every night for almost a year, Joseph picked a new spot on a new hill and dug until the first rays of sunlight peered through the frosty peaks of *les verts monts*. It may have been a better organized search, had he not been awaiting further instructions from someone who was a little more omniscient than himself. His younger brother Hendrix Jr., who Joseph had managed to conscript into the service of the Almighty, made no attempt to conceal his annoyance.

"How long are we going to do this, Joseph?" The scruffy teen stood raking his square chin, where a prochronistic stubble marked the advent of early manhood; this in clear contrast to Joseph's velveteen complexion and his abiding boyish features.

"It has been decreed by God in heaven above. I surely don't know the will of God, Hendrix Jr., only that he bid me dig. So that's exactly what I'm doing . . . digging." At this point, the Biblical brogue that had a year earlier commandeered Joseph's regional vernacular was beginning to fade—as had the distinct glow of a cosmological sunburn—leaving in its wake an uneasy polyglot of the two incommensurable linguistic systems.

"You mean that's what we're doing . . . digging. Why don't you just drop down onto your knees and ask Him where this . . . this . . . whatever it is we're looking for is?" There could be no mistake: this had been uttered with an uncontrollable gush of derision.

"Hendrix Jr., why dost thou tempt God? A bolt of lightning could snap from the sky and lightest up thine arse like a July brush fire. How wouldst thou likest that?"

Joseph couldn't really blame his younger sibling. In moments of weakness, he too felt strangled by the fat fingers of frustration. But he wouldn't allow himself to believe that his vision (otherwise known to his family as "the sickness," or alternately, "the coma") had been nothing more than a feverish dream. Still, the day he had awoken, he knew he was destined for greatness—he knew that God had something important in store for him. This had been made abundantly clear to him when his Father, Hendrix Sr. (who thinking to anglicize his name had changed it from Felix Jr. to Hendrix Sr. upon his arrival in America) had clasped his hand, pressing the hard keratin bulbs of a snake rattle into his palm. At the time, Joseph felt the sting of glory and in that instant saw his destiny in a blinding flash. Even saw his life and death. Finally, he raised himself onto his elbow and spoke.

"And the LORD God said unto the serpent, because thou hast done this, thou art cursed above all cattle, and above every beast of the field; upon thy belly shalt thou go, and dust shalt thou eat all the days of thy life."

"You can say that again," said Hendrix Sr. with a wink.

November 8, 1872

Dearest Joseph,

Oh loving husband and prophet, what a city is Boston! I have never seen so many people in one place: trolleys, markets, squares, and gardens. Pleasantly crowded, is the only fair description of this venerable old town. And such a learned town, too, Joseph. The men all speak Greek and Latin (although I feel certain they don't speak with the Almighty), and the women of the temperance group are equally accomplished; they are like women I have never known before, so confident and assured in their fight to bring temperance to this state. (Perhaps this is something to think upon, don't you agree?)

Matilda has been such a gracious host. She strikes me as a lady of the finest stock. And intelligence is her strong suit, dear husband. She has opinions on everything, from politics to home remedies to the latest scientific theories. She has even read, from cover to cover, *On the Origin of Species by Means of Natural Selection, or the Preservation of Favored Races in the Struggle for Life*. What a title! What a theory! What an imagination has this Darwin! (Although, Matilda's jocular husband John has suggested that one of our former presidents—initials A.L.—was fair proof of such mad science.) God will certainly hold no warm and cozy place for that horrible monkey-loving Englishman upon his return to the great hereafter.

Tomorrow is the day of my address. I must admit to having a case of the jitters. The women are all so curious about you, dear prophet. It seems that everyone awaits the hour when they will learn more about one Joseph Vasser and the

Vasserean Bible. Perhaps it is just the kind of recognition we need to secure funds for publication. Yes, dear prophet, I know you do not like to speak of such things yet (how superstitious you are); however, the book is now completed and we must move forward. If the opportunity arises, forgive my boldness, but I will make mention of "an investment into eternal life" to Matilda and her husband James. We shall see. I shall trust in God, as I know you would also do were you in my position.

I must go, dear husband and prophet. For tea awaits my arrival in the sitting room (such a wondrous thing, a sitting room; we must have one someday). I shall write again tomorrow, to tell you of my great success or resounding failure as a public speaker.

Your Loving Wife,
Emma

"Be still, and know that God forbids it. And there's no room back here, anyway." Joseph took two steps, turned on his heels, and paced two paces back in the same direction. A jute curtain partitioned him off from the rest of the cramped, single-room cabin. Emma sat at a table, his scribe and editor, scratching down his exact words and revising them as necessary, as he translated from the plates of gold.

"I just don't understand why I have to be out here. And why do we need this curtain?" protested Emma. "What purpose does it serve?"

"God hath commanded it. That's why."

"Even the tiniest glimpse of the plates would mean the world to me."

No one other than Joseph had seen the gold plates, which he'd extracted from a hillside two counties away, not even Hendrix Jr., who, in a somnambulist's trance, had missed it all. Joseph kept them locked away in the Brunswick-green, barrel-top trunk that had traveled with his father and mother through the Atlantic Ocean's icy March floes in the year of his birth. Lately, Emma couldn't help but wonder if the plates were real at all. It was all so recondite, so occult. But no sooner would she think such thoughts than the guilt would overcome her, and she would admonish herself with deep lacerations from the emotional lash that she kept on hand for just such occasions. After all, who was she to question her husband, the mouthpiece of God?

"Can't do it, Emma. For God wouldst smite thee and me down like a rabid dog in ditch water."

She jabbed the nib pen into its holder.

"I see. Well then, what about one of those new pens? The fountain pen, they call it. Surely some small consideration is in order, since I'm allowed to scratch down every word you utter but not allowed to see the plates from which you utter them."

"Dearest wife, Emma. Where wouldst we lay hold of such a thing? We live in Vermont, smack-dab in the middle of nowhere, a far-flung Hades if everest there was one."

"And when will you take the next step? Surely, you plan to gather a congregation. Perhaps organize a new order, a small church, something of the sort."

"I haven't a clue as to what thou meanest, for thou talkest out of the back of thine head," said Joseph.

"Joseph, what I mean is there are people who wish to follow you. Your vision from God is the talk of the town. Ever since we took our wedding vows, townspeople have been flocking to me, asking me when you will be preaching the "new Good Word.""

"Verily I say unto you, God hath not commanded it. And I'm in the very throes of this translation. Who canst know the will of God? I fear I cannot."

"But you can, dear husband! God talks to you. Who better than you to know His will? All I ask is that you give it a try. Is that too much for a wife to ask of her husband?"

"Nay, it is not. I will sleepeth on it."

And sleep on it he did. For the next fortnight Joseph slept on it. Being a prophet, it did occur to him to ask God about it—"the next step," as Emma had put it. And when the answer came, there was no doubt about it: Emma was right. And Joseph was ecstatic. He would start a church. It was no new fountain pen, to be sure, but it might just pass for a small consideration anyway.

December 10, 1872

My Dear Prophet and Husband Joseph,

You have no doubt been sick with worry over the past weeks, having heard news of the great fire here in Boston and wondering if I had perished in it. I assure you, dear Joseph, that I have survived, although I am not entirely well. Sweet Mattie tells me that I have been in and out of consciousness, mumbling then screaming verse then singing mournful hymns and reciting questionable limericks (I had no idea that I had ever committed a limerick to memory) for a seemingly interminable spell.

You'll recall from my last letter that I was set to speak before the women's temperance group on the very next day. The hall had been rented and banners unfurled (trumpeting worthy slogans such as "Temperance is God's Way" and "Liquor is a Losing Game"). There was milky tea and sweet biscuits, as well as punch and crackers laid out on a table at the rear of the hall. Dear prophet, the whole place was abuzz with anticipation, which I found unnerving and exhilarating, at the same time.

I had scarcely related my amusing opening anecdote (if I may toot my own horn), when I smelled a faint whiff of smoke. Thinking nothing of it, I segued seamlessly into the story of my youth (which leads nicely to the story of your youth), until I noticed a growing number of scrunched up noses among the ladies of the audience. There came the odd polite cough and sniffle from here and there—small distractions. However, by the time I got to the story of how we first met, the room was sputtering under a shroud of gray smoke. Clearly, dear husband, something was amiss. I did not realize just how amiss things were until I witnessed the ladies begin to clear out in a rather disorderly, distinctly unladylike manner. I continued with my address, despite the smoke and chaos, although at that point, dear husband, I was beginning to feel lightheaded, not realizing that I had already slumped to the stage floor and was sitting crossed legged (Indian style), reciting my address to no one.

Fortunately, God was watching over me, and Sweet Mattie, who had earlier escaped with the others, came bursting through the doors hacking and gagging, and in search of me. You'll recall my singing her praises in my previous letter. It is true, my prophet, she is a lady of the finest stock: sweet, intelligent, and, as I was soon to discover, inordinately sturdy. This fine lady of Boston's upper crust slung me over her bony shoulder like a County Kerry lad hoists a gunny sack of potatoes and shuttled me out of the building.

Outside, the city was ablaze. It was as if the sky were raining hot globs of glowing hail down upon it. Add to this, the black, choking menace of smoke and the deafening roar of buildings being consumed, as if the very timber itself did shriek in pain. Dear husband, I got to my feet and stumbled into the street to get a look at what the fires of hell must surely look like, when I was run down by the fire brigade. Yes, dearest prophet, I went under hoof and wheel of a charging wagon. As you can well imagine, I recall nothing after that. All went black. Were it not for the charitable ministrations of my guardian angel, sweet Mattie, my soul may not have returned to its broken and bruised body, nor to the charred remains of this city, at all. But I have returned, my dear. The doctor tells me I am healing nicely and should be on my feet before the fortnight turns. You need not worry yourself further, dear husband. And you need not jump aboard the next Boston-bound train. I am fine and will return to you in good time. You must keep your nose to the grindstone, as you are prone to say, for the work must move forward. I will see you again before the toll of the New Year's arrival. Until then, God bless and keep you, dear husband and prophet

Your Eternally Loving Wife,
Emma

From the very beginning, when first he'd uttered the first "And it came to pass," the problem had always been one of money. Joseph and Emma lived in a small cabin on a small piece of land that Hendrix Vasser Sr. had graciously if begrudgingly signed over to the newlyweds. Much to the senior Vasser's chagrin, the field had lain fallow for more than two seasons, so consumed was Joseph with his book. Finally, the fledgling prophet was forced to return to his earlier and occasional money-making practice of scrying—treasure hunting, as it was crudely called by the uninitiated locals—to make ends meet.

Emma's father, Blair "Bud" Andrews, mayor of the town, put Joseph in touch with a collector of Native American Indian artifacts, Henry Fielding Priestly, "like the author and the natural philosopher," he'd made a point of telling Joseph upon their first meeting. Priestly was an Englishman whose father had taken out a British patent on the spring-loaded clothespin and made a sizable fortune from it. As a coddled son of one of London's most famous *parvenu*, young Henry was witness to the Indian craze, once seeing an imitator of the Indian princess Pocahontas, and had developed an insatiable appetite for all things American, and all things American Indian, in particular. Eventually he pulled up stakes and moved to New York City, where he could properly pursue his life's passion. That's where Joseph Vasser, diviner and scryer, came into the picture.

As a young man, Joseph was known to be a crackerjack doodlebugger. The men about town used to say, "Spit in a drought and the young'un Joe Vasser'll witch it quick as a flash on the switch of a hickory stick." He later graduated to scrying with a cream-colored stovepipe hat and a glossy brown seer stone. The hat had been a gift from his future father-in-law, but the stone was plucked from the bowels of the earth. Joseph had found it some years back while he and Hendrix Jr. were digging a neighbour's well. Twenty feet underground, fixed in a lime-cemented wall of gravel, it flashed like the eye of a panther. He pried it loose and tucked it in his pocket. Not long after that, he began to see things in the stone—objects, trinkets, treasures. Cupping it in his hands, he would peer through the black crack between his thumbs. Then, at the bottom of the stovepipe hat, the seer stone came more clearly into focus. With his face buried in the hat, Joseph would read the ghostly glow of the stone like a treasure map, and later, the ancient scriptures that would become the Bible II.

His return to scrying did not meet with Emma's approval, who thought it a cheap imitation of prophesying. To make her point, the spirited Mrs. Vasser compared the prophet's return to scrying to a toddler's return to crawling. Be that as it may, there were bills to be paid, and Joseph could think of no noble way to lay hands on the ready cash he needed to keep writing his book.

Their first meeting with Joseph Fielding Priestly did nothing to change Emma's mind. The wildly eccentric Englishman arrived in a carriage, sitting stiffly, stoically, with a colorful Indian headdress propped on his head, twitching in the breeze, and a long wooden tobacco pipe clenched in his teeth, belching smoke rings that were promptly flattened and carried by a breeze to a nearby grove of cottonwoods.

Over the course of the next few days, Joseph scoured the hills with hat and seer stone in search of Mohawk and Abenaki "antiquities," as Priestly liked to call them. But the arrowhead that Joseph unearthed, along with the two shells that may or may not have been part of a wampum, seemed to interest the collector less than tell of the gold plates which Joseph had discovered not two years earlier. Before returning to New York, Joseph Fielding Priestly had "invested" two hundred dollars into the prophet Joseph's translation of the gold plates. "Call it an investment into my future," said he. Priestly scooped up the shells and the arrowhead, dropped them into a pouch, and was gone by first light of the following day.

Writings of ~~FELIX ELIXH~~ Elihi:
Book Two

[1]And it ~~happened~~ came to pass that ~~in the third~~ first year of the ~~rain rein reign of King Louis-Philippe~~ after the fall of King Zedekiah, ~~my father Felix Sr. and the Republicans were suppressed by Louis Philipe the lying, two-faced shyster, who spit in the face of the very people who had put him on the throne and wiped his feet on the flag of their freedom~~ Nebuzaraddan was sent by Nebuchadnezzar to destroy Jerusalem and the temple of Solomon.

[2]~~Yeah,~~ Yea, so great was the ~~suppression~~ destruction that my father ~~Felix Sr. Elihi Sr.~~ Eli ~~went to wrack and ruin because of arse-kissing conservatives who clamored at the arse of Guizot~~ lost ~~much~~ all of his wealth to the fires of evil.

[3]~~So Yeah~~ verily, the people of Judah did flee into Egypt, and many years ~~past~~ passed ~~under the rule of Louis-Philippe~~ in the new land, and ~~I grew~~ did grow strong in the ways ~~of the Republic~~ God; and I ~~did~~ cared for my father, whose losses had ~~addled his wits rendered him berserk~~ brought the scourge of illness upon him, and my mother, who ~~seemed always melancholy and forlorn~~ was downtrodden and repentant ~~for her whoring~~ the sinful ways of her youth.

[4]And in the fifth year ~~of the rain rein of Louis-Philippe~~ after the fall of Zedekiah, my father ~~Felix Sr. Elihi Sr.~~ Eli ~~did~~ died ~~in Paris~~ the land of the Egyptians.

5And it ~~happened~~ came to pass that I, being only ten years of age, did greatly ~~mourned~~ mourn my father's passing; for ~~now the godless scum who call themselves loyalists had murdered both of my fathers~~ he was the father of my heart.

6And ~~as a result~~ yea, my mother ~~became dull as ditch water suffered bouts of hysteria~~ was sorely afflicted by the death of the father of my heart; ~~verily~~ verily, she ~~lay bedridden~~ took to her bed for ~~the space of many weeks~~ a growing season.

7And it ~~happened~~ came to pass that I ~~visited my mother~~ did go in to the bedside of my mother; and seeing that she ~~was on the verge of dying would soon give up the ghost~~ was about to shed this mortal coil, I did ~~asked her about my real father~~ the father of my flesh, who had been ~~butchered~~ slain by ~~a spy for the Ultras~~ Babylonian soldiers; for although young and inexperienced in the ways of the world, I sensed that ~~there was more to the story than I had been told~~ the story had not been revealed to me in its entirety.

8And ~~so~~ verily, the tears flowed from her, and ~~she wrenched out her hair by the fistful so overcome with grief was she~~ so wracked with the torments of hell was she that she confessed ~~her part in the untimely demise of my father~~ unto me a tale of untold woe and misery, thus did she reveal to me the part she had played in ~~my father's death~~ the death of the father of my flesh, whose name was called ~~George d'Aubigne~~ Oren.

9~~In the time~~ Before the fall of King ~~Charles Charlekiah~~ Zedekiah, my mother ~~who was still a prostitute whoring~~ laid with

~~George d'Aubigne~~ *Oren*, the father of my flesh many times, while laying also with many other men in her sinful way.

[10] And it ~~happened~~ *came to pass* that a young man, whose name was called ~~Armand Andarmay~~ *Armani,* did ~~visit~~ *also go to* her often and ~~had his way with her~~ *did force himself upon her,* and ~~punched her with steely fists and kicker her with tempered boots~~ *did beat her cruelly*.

[11] Yeah, ~~while George d'Aubigne was sexing her~~ *even as the father of my flesh knew her,* ~~so was the young man sexing her~~ *did the young man* ~~Armand Andarmay~~ *Armani* know her. But ~~no~~ *nay,* ~~she did not love them both equally~~ *they were not equal in her heart,* ~~for she loved the father of my flesh best~~ *was filled with righteous love for* ~~George d'Aubigne~~ *Oren, the father of my flesh.*

[12] And ~~so~~ *verily,* ~~Armand Andarmay became jealous of my father~~ *the seeds of jealousy took root in the young man Armani's heart,* and he ~~punched and kicked my mother often~~ *did beat my mother more for it,* and ~~then sexed her again and~~ *again lay with her often.*

[13] And it ~~happened~~ *came to pass* that she ~~contacted~~ *did call unto her* a man, a customer ~~who also partook of her favors~~ *whom she had lain with from time to time,* and who ~~was a cold-hearted killer~~ *knew only evil;* and she ~~paid~~ *did pay* the man five ~~francs~~ *gold pieces* to ~~butcher~~ *slay* the young man ~~Armand Andarmay~~ *Armani.*

[14] And ~~so it happened~~ *thus it came to pass* that ~~at the very moment that~~ *even as* the man ~~butchered~~ *did slay* the young man ~~Armand Andarmay~~ *Armani,* my father ~~George d'Aubigne~~ *Oren, the father*

of my flesh, ~~stumbled upon the grisly scene~~ came upon them; and
so yea verily, the man ~~butchered~~ did slay ~~my father~~ the
father of my flesh in the same ~~way~~ manner that he had ~~butchered~~
slain the young man ~~Armand Andarmay~~ Armani.

¹⁵Thus, when my mother ~~learned about~~ did learn of ~~my father's murder~~
the ill fate of the father of my flesh, she was filled with despair
and grief for the part she had played; and she ~~was consoled by~~ did fall
into the arms of ~~Felix Elixhi Sr.~~ Eli, who would become the father of
my heart, and she ~~married~~ did marry him and bore the ~~bastard~~ son, who
was I, and named him ~~Felix Jr Elixfi~~ Elihi.

¹⁶And it ~~happened~~ came to pass, that when my mother had finished her
~~tragic story~~ tale of woe, she ~~died~~ did pass from this life into
the next; where I pray that by virtue of her repentant ways, God will take
her into his embrace, just as he took ~~Felix Sr. Elihi Sr.~~ Eli, the father
of my heart, and my ~~butchered~~ slain father ~~George d'Aubigne~~
Oren, the father of my flesh.

END OF BOOK 2

When he first heard the sound of a wagon rattling up to the cabin, Joseph thought he might jump out of his skin and run for the hills. At twenty, he had, after all, only recently left his teenage years behind. What did he have to say in regards to the eternal salvation of a handful of teat-twisting dairy farmers from Vermont? Not to mention their frumpy, bonneted wives and cream-fattened children. He wished now that he hadn't listened to his wife. He wished he'd never asked God about this. He wasn't ready. There was still work to be done on his book; that is to say, His book.

"Oh Joseph, what have you done to your neck cloth?" Emma tugged a loose strand and the drooping bow came unfurled below the two stiff wings of a Grafton collar.

"Woman, why dost thou persecute me? Canst you not see-eth that I'm more nervous than a yearling on castration day?"

"Dear husband, there is no call for coarseness. Calm yourself. And remember it is they who wish to hear you. And you said yourself that God has commanded it."

"Yea, God hath commanded it. At least, I'm quite sure he hath. He camest to me in a dream. Well, He wast more liketh a blob of goodness and light than an actual personage. It wast so dark. I think it wast Him. But how canst I be sure? Oh, give me strength, Father! For here cometh the bleating masses."

An eager rap at the door indeed announced the arrival of the sheep God had commanded Joseph to herd from the grassy hills and vales of Vermont to the billowy heights of heaven. Emma swung the door open and ushered the faithful to a grove behind the cabin, where an odd assortment of makeshift benches (rough planks nailed to log stumps) teetered beneath a strung canvas tarpaulin that sagged between the trees. The Sabbath sun warmed the spring air, stirring the green scent of new-bristling pine needles.

Joseph waited in the cabin, pacing from wall to wall, still not sure what he would say to the congregation, to his congregation. And the fact that he knew all of them — had known them since he was a boy — did nothing to drive away his anxiety. Finally, he dropped to his knees and beseeched God to help him.

He emerged from the cabin and tread to the grove in a gait that was part march, part trot, part amble. Halting behind a waist high pulpit that Hendrix Jr. had gone to great pains to fashion from the trunk of a hundred-year-old oak, he placed a hand on either side and propped himself there. Joseph placed no page or book before him, but simply began to speak with an authority well beyond his years. "And it came to pass…"

February 22, 1873

Dear Joseph,

I hope by now you have noticed my absence, although it would not be from the cold impression I have left in our marriage bed (yes, I have heard the rumors, if rumors is indeed all they are). I have not returned to you because anger has stirred me to sinful thoughts, thoughts of you and a slow and harrowing death. Yes, you, dear Joseph! And that little tart who is the apple of your eye! Why? Why? Why, Joseph? Do our vows before God mean nothing to you? Or perhaps you have become puffed up in your own prophetness? I demand to read in your own hand just what it is that you have been doing while I have been here recovering from grievous injury, or I shall never return home. Not to you, no never! Is that clear, Joseph?

Mattie has been gracious enough to allow me to stay on here in Boston with her. No, it is not she who has been filling my head with nonsense. (I can almost hear you say such a thing.) She has been a great comfort to me, a pillar of womanly strength. I have decided to abstain from any act of vengeance (for vengeance is mine, not yours, sayeth the Lord), despite the fact that Mattie has encouraged me to visit you in your sleep with sheep shears and relieve you of your manhood. But I shall forbear, until I hear it from you. Then we shall see. As for now, I await your response (that is, your explanation).

Yours in Anger,
Emma

P.S. What wonderful winter weather we are having here in Boston!

P.P.S. Please water my blooming cactus from California.

Writings of ~~FELIX ELIXA~~ Elihi:
Book Three

1 And it ~~happened~~ came to pass that my mother repented of her ~~whoring and murdering~~ sinful ways and died without ~~sin~~ blemish, with a ~~clear conscience~~ as white as fleece.

2 And ~~so yeah,~~ it was with great sadness in my heart that i, ~~Felix Jr Elixa~~ Elihi, did bury her ~~beneath a mean metal cross in a pauper's graveyard~~ with mine own hands in a sepulcher of white stone, ~~alongside~~ next to the father of my heart and the father of my flesh.

3 And i, ~~Felix Jr Elixa~~ Elihi, being only eleven years old, ~~took~~ did take refuge among ~~the Republicans~~ those who were faithful to the memory of the father of my heart ~~and dedicated to pummeling the Royalists with their royal mace~~ descendants of Judah: and among them i did ~~learned~~ the secret ways of ~~destruction and revenge~~ usurpation, insurrection, and revolution.

4 And it ~~happened~~ came to pass that a space of ~~twelve~~ fifty years did pass, and great ~~political unrest~~ prosperity did ~~filled~~ the land: and when finally the ~~Republicans~~ Persian King, Cambyses, ~~rose~~ did rise up in ~~revolution~~ war against ~~Louis-Philippe~~ Egypt, i was ~~leading the pack~~ at the forefront of the charge.

5 Yeah, and ~~the~~ our enemies, ~~of the father of my heart~~ Persians were ~~strong~~ mighty, and they ~~took~~ did take strength in ~~his demise~~ the fall of Egypt: and learning that i was ~~Felix Jr Elixa~~ Elihi, a usurper of Psamtik, they did ~~track me down~~ seek me out, that they might

~~slit the throats of me and my fellow Republicans~~ slaughter me and my brothers of Judah.

6 And i was ~~more frightened than a yearling on castration day terrified~~ sore afraid, and i ~~fled did flee~~ from ~~Paris~~ Egypt ~~to England the isle of the English~~ into the wilderness with my ~~fellow Republicans~~ brothers of Judah.

7 And it ~~happened~~ came to pass that in ~~England the isle of the English~~ the wilderness, i, ~~Felix Jr. Elixfi~~ Elihi, ~~married~~ did marry a peasant girl ~~whose name was Eloise Smith~~ raised in the ways of God, and i ~~knew her in the flesh~~ did lay with her, and she became ~~fraught with pups pregnant~~ heavy with child.

8 And so ~~yeah~~ verily, with the help of God, we did build a ship, and we ~~sailed~~ did set sail across the ~~Atlantic~~ great waters to America, and God did ~~directed~~ us to a new land, which we called ~~our new home~~ the land of ~~Felix Jr. Elixfi~~ Elihi.

9 And it ~~happened~~ came to pass that ~~Eloise birthed a son~~ my wife did bear a male child in ~~America~~ the new land: and we ~~named~~ did name him ~~Joseph Osephji~~ Olihi.

10 And we did ~~break ground and till the land~~ build our homes and a temple unto God and did ~~called Vermont~~ this new land our home; and we ~~broke both arse and back~~ toiled happily ~~like common beasts of burden day and night in order to make ends meet~~ and peace and prosperity did attend us there.

END OF BOOK 3

The money from Henry Fielding Priestly turned out to be a godsend. The steadily growing take from the collection plate was also a great help. To Joseph's mind, there could be no doubt that the work was moving forward in leaps and bounds. All with His help, of course.

Over the past six months, he had gathered a small but devoted flock, and there was talk among them of constructing a church. On top of that, the Vasserean Bible was better than half done. In fact, the work was so happily and steadily moving forward that he'd been forced to enlist extra help, someone to look after church records, donations, and that sort of thing. Emma grew weary of being his scribe; her wrists often seized, locked up so tight that she had difficulty performing even the most mundane household chore. So Joseph had handpicked the young woman who'd so fetchingly caught his eye one bright Sunday morn in May; she would be his personal assistant.

He recalled the feeling he'd had that first day, watching her from behind his high oak pulpit (which he now thought a touch too phallus-like, leading him to avoid resting on it or even placing his hands upon it for too long). It was as if they were peg and saddle of some magnificent celestial instrument, the two of them, and the taut silver string between them had right then been plucked by the hand of an angel. The desire rang in his ears and echoed through a distant valley of blood-filled organs. After a brief, passing flush of guilt, he decided there was no use fighting it. He simply had to have her.

The young woman's name was Estelle Harris, Joseph later learned, and she was niece to Malcolm Harris, one of the first and staunchest members of the Vasserean congregation. Harris was the local merchant—that is, the one and only merchant in the locale—and, as such, he dealt in the currency of small-town trust and fellowship, an invaluable resource and bankable asset for Joseph. Harris's niece, Estelle, had come to him from the big city—Chicago. It turned out her mother felt a dose of the rustic life would add a slightly more rugged hue to the young woman's too patrician complexion. As it was, Joseph found that complexion, with its smooth kaolin planes rising almost imperceptibly over two tight-pored dumplings, to be nothing short of the very scheme and conceit of perfection.

Smitten is as smitten does—and Joseph hired her the very next week, making a prophetly house call to the Harris's to that end. Malcolm Harris was more than obliging. And the young woman Estelle was happy to get out from under the hawkish gaze of her uncle, if only for several hours a week.

For her part, Emma was grateful for the respite. She found the young woman pleasant company and often encouraged her to stay for the evening meal of meat pie and canned berries. When the table was cleared, Joseph would reach into his waistcoat and produce a pipe and tobacco pouch, and Emma would reach for her basket of yarn balls skewered by smooth wooden needles, while Estelle read aloud from a bulky book that belonged to her uncle, the Plays of William Shakespeare (whose stories Joseph found amusing although roguish and unenlightening). These were the happy times, simple times. These were times before Joseph began to take ungentlemanly liberties.

April 6, 1873

Dearest Mattie (May I still call you Mattie?),

As you will by now know, I have returned safely to the green rolling hills of Vermont. And to answer your question, yes, I am lost and lonely. And my heart is broken. But my heart has been broken by you, dear friend, not by my Joseph. I pray that one day you will understand why.

It is true I was angry to hear that my husband had taken a second wife (a spiritual wife) in my absence. And I was, as you say, a hornets' nest in a bodice. Yes, when I walked into my home, my haven, I was shocked to find another woman in my stead. Even after my angry letter, which Joseph clearly chose to ignore. And not another woman, but a girl, really! A girl that I had trusted and treated with utmost kindness. Yes I was outraged (to the point that I took after the prophet with knitting needles, thinking to gouge out his wandering eyes). Had we been in Boston, the shrieks would have roused the neighbors (not my shrieks but the young woman's with whom I now share my husband).

You ask about the conjugal arrangements. Yes, we share Joseph, equally—both being his wives in the eyes of God. After I had calmed down, my husband the prophet explained that God had commanded him to take another wife, and that all worthy Vasserean men should do the same (of course it would be up to God and Joseph to decide who was worthy and who was not). He pleaded with me to pray to God, and God would reveal the truth of it to me. Dearest Mattie, to make a long story short, I did and He did. He did! Like a whiff of spring in the dank chambers of my heart did the answer come to me. The work must move forward. And this is how.

You talk about moral outrage. I understand, my dear friend. I do. But the ways of God have never been the ways of man. For this reason, I must accept my fate as one called of God, chosen by God, to live as man and wife and wife. It is not so bad, really. There are extra hands to make the load lighter. And soon we shall have separate rooms (and I will no longer have to bear the animal grunts and groans of my husband rutting upon another; God forgive me for saying it, but it is true).

Oh, Mattie, try to see the great value, the worth of this new commandment. We are a small group. Think of the possibilities. A righteous man like Joseph siring twice or three times as many children as he would be able to with only one wife (and I have had my problems, as you know; you'll recall we once talked about them at length). It makes perfect sense, does it not?

Let me end by acknowledging the boundless debt of gratitude I owe to you, and you alone. If only you could understand me now. Forgive me, I beg you, if I have somehow wronged you in my actions. It was not my intent. But I must do this, for it is God's will.

Gratefully and Lovingly Yours,
Emma

P.S. Hugs and kisses to the little ones.
P.P.S. Shall I return the Kashmiri shawl you gifted me?

The modest church was completed around the same time as the Vasserean Bible. While faithful members of the flock were dabbing white paint at the sash windows of their new place of worship, Joseph was putting the finishing touches to his book. He had already done some preliminary legwork, and he was starting to have his doubts about finding a publisher. Joseph had taken Malcolm Harris with him to New York City in the hope that the town's only near-businessman could "talketh some sense into those Godless publishing types." To no avail, it turned out. The best they could find was a small printer of political tracts, who agreed to cover the one-time cost of typesetting, but Joseph would have to pay for the materials and binding, which put a price tag of about eight hundred dollars on his new book: well out his range; and well out the range of his congregation. Clearly, it was going to require a small miracle. But then that was an area in which Joseph, as prophet and confidante of the Almighty miracle-maker himself, was known to excel. Or at least, the historical precedence seemed to be in his favor.

He had made a point of calling on Henry Fielding Priestly while in the city. Priestly agreed to invest another three hundred dollars, on the promise that he would get a signed first edition from the author. Joseph wasn't entirely sure if the moneyed eccentric actually expected the John Hancock of God, but he agreed to the terms anyway. (He couldn't help but wonder if the First and the Last, the Alpha and Omega, would spill ink for a price.) That left three hundred dollars outstanding, and he felt certain he could depend on his faithful flock for only one or two hundred dollars; even then, he would have to wring it out of them. Thus was he about to dust off the seer stone for an encore bout of scrying, when a check came in the mail for two hundred dollars.

It was signed by Professor John Burns of Boston, husband of Mattie Burns. There was no explanation, just a brief note: *Temperance is God's way, is it not?* Joseph clicked his heels jubilantly then indulged in a happy little hallelujah dance. It was the miracle he'd been waiting for, and the printing could now go ahead. "Yeah verily, temperance is-eth God's way, sure as shooting it is," said Joseph to no one. For two hundred dollars, there could be no mistake about it: Temperance was indeed God's way. To prove it, he sat down that very moment and wrote next Sunday's sermon on the virtues of temperance and the evils of liquor. In fact, he decided that sometime between now and the Sabbath he would make a point of receiving revelation from God about that very thing. The more he thought about it, the more he liked the idea. What better way to keep the bodies and minds of the faithful occupied than to start them on a zealous campaign of self-prohibition? After all, he had to admit that for some of the simpler folk of the fold, the lofty idea of God, the Godhead, and life eternal was simply a bit beyond their cerebral grasp. Temperance, on the other hand was not. "Temperance," repeated Joseph. Yes, he liked it. He liked it a lot.

July 14, 1873

Dear Mattie,

I was delighted and, I must admit, surprised to receive your response to my last letter. At the time I wrote it, I had grave doubts as to whether I would ever hear from you again. Yes, I understand that you cannot condone my "marital circumstances," as you call it, but I am delighted that you still number me among your friends. (You do, don't you?)

I am relieved to hear that the re-building is ongoing there in your beautiful city. Sometimes I actually miss Boston, and I am envious of your life there. It was a thrilling town, indeed. So many intelligent and passionate individuals, you being first and foremost among them, dear Mattie. But I know that my place is here with Joseph and Estelle and the other Vassereans (no, her name was not penned with resentment, she is my sister in God, and my wifely partner).

Life here is simple, for we are simple folk. Simple but devoted to God. My dear husband has rallied us around the banner of righteousness, and we all look expectantly to a future of eternal life. The Vasserean Bible is completed now, and thanks to your great generosity is presently at the publishers (I hope when you learned of my "marital circumstances" you did not regret your sizable and timely donation to the cause.) Soon the word of God, as rendered by my prophet husband, will ring through the hills and vales of America. Joseph tells me he has seen a vision of the future, and the kingdom of God will be re-established here in America, a mighty kingdom, for which he has already laid the foundation. Isn't that wonderful, Mattie? Who better to manage otherworldly affairs than Americans? Look at what we've accomplished here in mere centuries, while the Old World has made a real mess of things. God no longer sees fit to visit the golden domes and steepled spires of their cathedrals. Instead, he now lights upon a cabin in the woods, a church house among golden fields of grain; that is where God lives now.

As far as the homefront goes, things couldn't be better. Really and truly. My initial response of rage and revenge has passed. I have always enjoyed the company of Estelle, and I continue to do so. We still work tirelessly as a team to move the cause forward. All that has really changed is that Joseph also enjoys her company, too, in a way that I do not, of course, and in a way he never did before. (Need I say more about that?)

I will sign off now. For it is late, and it is my turn to spend the night wrapped in the arms of my husband. I cherish your letters, dear Mattie. Thank you for extending the hand of friendship to me once again. I hope we will always remain friends.

Sincerely Yours,
Emma

It wasn't long after Estelle came to work for Joseph that he began to take what some would regard as rather ungentlemanly liberties with the young lady. He allowed his eyes to linger too long on the delicate protrusion of her clavicle. He let his pinky finger brush against hers. At times, he leaned too close and spoke too softly in her ear while she sat transcribing at the desk. It seemed that the kiss behind the cabin was inevitable; a quick brush of his hard lips against her soft ones, while Emma was inside, dozing off in the tilt of her imitation Shaker rocker. For her part, Estelle was quite taken with the tall, broad, yet oddly feminine, prophet of God. Who wouldn't be? He exuded self-confidence. There was a calm self-assurance in his every action. He spoke reservedly, yet with authority. What sixteen -year-old girl could resist that?

For his part, Joseph wasn't quite sure what to make of his desire. He could call it lust, but somehow that did no justice to the squelch and hiccup that happened in his chest every time he laid eyes on her. He could call it sinful, but that would do nothing to abate the feverish longing he felt. It was classic David and Bathsheba. He knew that, but it didn't help. He had to have her in the classic David and Bathsheba way.

And have her he would, with surprisingly little effort. A quick intra-specific tap dance to demonstrate his reproductive fitness and the deal was sealed. Of course, in the battle of sexual selection, it always helps to be able to say, "For God hath commanded it."

And the truth was Joseph had been wondering for some time how to conceptually frame the idea of having a sexual partner outside of marriage. *Infidelity* was an untidy substantive, a rather sloppy abstraction in the realm of ideas that needed some boundaries, a barrier to distinguish it from the much more despicable and damning *adultery* and *fornication*. As he'd been contemplating this very thing, Joseph stumbled onto the notion of a spiritual wife. For wasn't it Matthew who said, "What therefore God hath joined together, let not man put asunder"? And how seamlessly this segued into the whole "For God hath commanded it" supposition-cum-dictum! In the principle of spiritual wife, Joseph believed he had realized a most significant doctrinal triumph. It was sanctioned sin, theistically endorsed laxity. It was a stroke of genius.

Joseph married himself to his spiritual wife, Estelle, in a private ceremony—although ceremony may be overstating it—and consummated the marriage forthwith. That left only one potentially problematic obstacle standing between him and matrimonial bliss: Emma.

98

September 26, 1873

Dearest Mattie,

You ask how things are here. I must admit that all is not well. They have carried Joseph off to the local jailhouse, where he awaits trial on a trumped-up charge. The truth is they (by "they" I mean the local authorities) are blind to his vision and jealous of his power. To say that I am not worried would be an untruth. I am. However, I trust in God, just as my dear sister, Estelle does. His will shall be done, in any case.

Oh Mattie, the forces of evil are strong! This comes at a time when the Kingdom of God is beginning to roll forth in true Biblical fashion. The Vasserean Bible is selling well and the flock has grown to high triple digits (truly miraculous, isn't it?). The faithful among us cling to the hope that all will be resolved without bloodshed. Yes, bloodshed, dear Mattie, for the men who have orchestrated this farce are nothing more than the Devil's henchmen and Harris's thugs. Estelle is heartbroken over her uncle's part in this whole affair. He has stirred up the others to mobbery! Shameful brutality! Who are they to question the commandments of God? My Joseph speaks on the Almighty's behalf. How can they doubt it? Oh but I prattle on. Forgive me, dear Mattie. I don't know who else to turn to (except the great and good God of Heaven and Earth). I know it is a long way from our (troubled) little Eden to Massachusetts, but perhaps your John may know someone who has political sway in these parts? For some say the governor himself is behind this masquerade of justice. I know not what my dear Joseph has done to arouse the ire of such a man as Julius Converse.

By now, it is common knowledge that our beloved prophet has taken a second wife; yet, Estelle is a spiritual wife, not a legal wife. My Joseph abides by the laws of men (although the laws of God supersede all). Still the men of our county growl and snort like rutting bulls, all carrying on like scorned lovers. In truth, some have also taken issue with the arrival of the Bible 2, the inspired work that dear Joseph and myself (and more recently, Estelle) toiled over for years. They demand to see the plates of gold from which Joseph diligently translated the word of God. Ha! They "demand," dear Mattie, as if it is their place to demand anything from God and His prophet. It matters not, for Joseph is no longer in possession of the plates; he has secretly returned them to the place where he first unearthed them and is telling no one (myself included) where that might be. In doing so, he assures me, he protects the integrity of his endeavor and the sanctity of God's word. For there is no telling what the fools of men would do with such divine evidence.

I must sign off now, dear Mattie. For the biscuits and beans I have made for dear Joseph grow cold. The jailors haven't even the decency to feed my poor falsely-accused husband. I will write again when things here have simmered down. Until then, God bless.

Sincerely yours,
Emma

News that he had taken a spiritual wife was bound to get out. Joseph knew as much. So, he decided to announce it from the pulpit as a commandment. The truth was he hadn't really planned to, but it just came out that way. A commandment from the Almighty. "For God hath commanded it" just seemed to be the perfect send off for this particular non sequitur. Not that it was an untruth, exactly. He had mentioned the idea to God, in passing, just to test the waters, see what kind of response he would get. For now, he was assuming that no response amounted to tacit approval from above. And as far as non sequiturs go, this one was not a serious offender; nothing like some of the whoppers that the "scientific" community were floating these days. In a way, plural marriage did logically follow from righteous living. Joseph liked to think of it as incentive. God's way (pending formal approval) of rewarding rectitude among men. Only slightly ironic, he conceded, rewarding virtue with salaciousness. But there you had it: God was not without His seeming contradictions. Anyone who works closely with the Almighty must come to terms with this fact sooner or later. Joseph had.

A buzz set through the congregation like a short, snapping fuse, and when it finally reached Malcolm Harris, it exploded in a burst of blue expletives unbecoming the faithful. The local merchant who had stood steadfastly at Joseph's side from the beginning, who had been instrumental in getting the Bible II published, was now ready to throttle the last wisp of breath from God's squeaky mouthpiece. Had a number of the brothers not right then fell upon the unhinged Paddy, he may have done just that.

"You lecher . . . you seducer . . . you ruttin' daughter-fucker!" Harris punctuated each word with a discharge of sputum. "Why, yer nothin' more than a dick-wagglin' rake! Prophet . . . me droopin' arse."

"Now Malcolm, be still, for God hath commanded it . . . this. I shall usher your Estelle to the big and bright pearly gates of the Celestial Kingdom. At my side, she'll be none other than a goddess and a queen, ruling over all of creation. Thus sayeth the Lord."

"I'll send you to yer SEE-LESS-CHUL kingdom, you monkey-dong'd dust hole!" And so it went for the next fifteen interminable minutes, until Harris was forcibly removed from the church house.

For Joseph, it was cause for concern. A malcontent like Malcolm Harris could spread ill will like a festering plague through the rank-and-file Vassereans, which, it goes without saying, was the last thing he needed; especially now that membership was up and the Bible II was selling well. Yet at the same time, deep down Joseph knew that Malcolm Harris had a legitimate beef. He may've even been right. And it made Joseph think, really think, for the first time in a very long time, for the first time since the whole prophet thing had begun. In that insular and untouched part of his being that had not been caressed, felt, and fingered by the world and worldly things, he knew that he had strayed from the path he'd set himself upon as a young man in search of some crumb of truth. It wasn't about being a prophet or about knowing the will of God, it was simply about knowing what was right and wrong. He had betrayed a friend. He had taken advantage of a young woman who'd trusted him. He had deceived his wife and been unfaithful to her. These were not unforgivable crimes against God, nor were they heinous sins against nature; they were quite simply hurtful acts, wrong acts. What was worse, he knew it, the same as Malcolm Harris knew it.

Had Joseph been the man others believed him to be—prophet, seer, sage, and all of that—he would've admitted his mistake and redressed it at once. But he wasn't and he didn't. Instead, he reduced the lanterns in the church house to puffs of black stringy smoke and strolled home, vowing to think on it some more, while at the same time wondering which of his wives he would tickle with the finger of God this night.

Writings of Joseph ~~Oseph Ji~~ Olihi:
Book Four

1 And i ~~Joseph Oseph Ji~~ Olihi, ~~was born to Felix and Eloise~~ being born of goodly parent, who had crossed the ~~icy Atlantic~~ mighty sea ~~in the heart of winter~~ to start a new life in this the promised land of America.

2 And ~~so~~ verily, i was raised ~~to toil like a docile beast in the fields~~ in the ways of God, and was highly favored by Him, ~~and i clawed at the dust for a scrap of bread i all but starved to death in my youth so that~~ my days were made bright in the bounty of His blessings.

3 And it ~~happened~~ came to pass, that my mother ~~broadened the brood birthed another pup~~ did bear a second son whom my father named ~~Hendrix Endrixhi~~ Ilihi, after his own name; and ~~Hendrix Endrixhi~~ Ilihi ~~did not toil in the fields~~ was not favored of God, and was a ~~lazy and ungrateful arse~~ stiff-necked and rebellious son, who ~~would rather read a book on Newton than milk a cow~~ cursed my Father and his ~~goodly~~ Godly ways, and did ~~lived in an imaginary world of equations and numbers in his numbskulled head~~ sin and iniquity.

4 And so yeah, my father ~~whipped Hendrix Endrixhi ilihi with a switch or leather tack or anything else he could lay his hands on and~~ was steadfast in his desire to ~~make my brother work and not waste his life on fancy and foolishness~~ bring his stiff-necked son to the ways of God.

5 And it ~~happened~~ came to pass, that ~~Hendrix Endrixhi~~ Ilihi ~~worked for a spell but then returned to his books~~ did repent and did come

to God for a time, until his heart did harden and he did return to his iniquitous ways.

6 And I, ~~Joseph Osephti~~ Olihi, ~~had to cover for his sorry arse had to carry my lazy brother's share of the workload~~ did suffered much because of my brother, who did mocked ~~me and my father~~ the God of our fathers as we ~~toiled in the fields~~ followed His ways.

7 ~~And so it happened~~ Yeah verily, it came to pass that I ~~started scrying to search for buried treasure and as luck would have it I actually found some~~ began the history of our people on the plates of gold that God had directed me to, and ~~Hendrix Endrixhi~~ Ilihi, ~~thinking that it might somehow amount to a fortune changed his mocking tune~~ was touched by the ~~hand~~ finger of God, and he ~~suddenly wanted to help me~~ did again repent of his iniquitous ways and turned to God in righteousness, in the hope that he ~~too might be directed to some ancient things made of gold~~ might also please the Maker.

8 ~~So~~ Therefore, ~~I decided to~~ did God test ~~Hendrix Endrixhi~~ Ilihi, ~~by making him do the most unpleasant jobs especially those involving the outdoor lav~~ that he might know God's ways and become strong in them.

9 And ~~it turned out~~ yeah verily, ~~I believed he was sincere~~ God was pleased with ~~Hendrix Endrixhi~~ Ilihi ~~and I decided to let him be my second-in-command in building my empire~~ He did command him to assist me with the building of His kingdom ~~in America~~ the Promised Land.

[10]And so ~~it happened~~ came to pass, that ~~Hendrix Endrixhi~~ Ilihi did ~~proved~~ himself to be ~~very useful~~ one also favored by God; thus did we work side-by-side as brothers in God to build ~~our~~ His Kingdom ~~in America~~ on Earth.

END OF BOOK IV

Dec 12, 1873

Dearest Mattie

Forgive my long silence. I have been inconsolable for some months now. My heart is broken, dear friend, shattered into ragged shards like so much fine China in an earthquake, for they have murdered my husband, my sweet Joseph—companion, friend, and partner—my prophet. I take only the slightest consolation in knowing that he is with God in the Celestial Kingdom, and that there he awaits the designated day of my arrival into the afterlife. If it were not for Estelle, who has been a pillar of strength, despite her limited years, I would have crumbled into a contemptible heap of self-pity long ago.

The Judas Malcolm Harris is to blame. Yet he roams freely, as if no one were the wiser to his sinister deed. Everyone in the county knows the murderous mob that stormed the jailhouse was none other than Harris and his henchmen in black hoods (certainly they were drunken on the Devil's brew, too, Mattie). They are responsible for the murder of my Joseph. They have martyred the Vasserean prophet. Of this there can be no doubt. They shot my husband through the heart in the jailhouse that held him prisoner. Yet Governor Converse does nothing to bring these murderers to justice. It is the Wild West right here in Vermont, dear Mattie. God help us all!

To make matters worse, I have no body to grieve over. No cold white chest to lay my head upon and soak with tears. Only a tombstone driven like a stake into barren earth. For Harris and his men have secreted away the body of my beloved and have buried it in some unmarked grave. Left it to be ignominiously ravaged by wild animals. No better than savages, they are! I'm sure you can imagine that a funeral without a body is all the more sorrowful for it. So now my dear Joseph is but a memory that I will never bury. He will eternally haunt the empty chambers of my heart.

And what is to become of the Vassereans? It is shameful the way dear Joseph's friends and family carry on. Each claiming to be the rightful heir to the Kingdom of God on Earth. Perhaps I should throw my lot in with the rest of them and vie for leadership as well. For who knows better than I the toil and sacrifices made by dear Joseph in order to restore the Kingdom of God to Earth and to usher it forth to its rightful place here in America? A woman leader and prophet, now wouldn't that be a novelty, sweet Mattie? Could such a preposterous thing ever happen? No doubt, you believe it could, my dear friend. And that is why you are an inspiration to so many American ladies.

In all seriousness, though, trouble is brewing right here in our little Eden. There is a great deal of dissension among the Vassereans. Some wish to follow Joseph's right-hand man, William Curry, who talks of pulling up stakes and moving west to a promised land of milk and honey, while others believe Felix Jr. is the rightful heir to Vasserean authority—he, they say, should don the mantle of leadership.

As for me, I have not the heart for such squabbles. No other can fill the void left by my dear departed husband—that is the plain truth. Estelle and I will remain here to plant the fields that have too long lain fallow about this cabin. Perhaps some life slumbers there yet. We shall see.

And thus ends this chapter in my life, dearest Mattie. Perhaps our paths shall cross again in future. Perhaps. Yet something tells me they will not. For we serve different Masters, you and I—I, the God in Heaven (love and hope), and you, the God on Earth (justice and equity). But know that I shall always remember you and count you a dear friend. And know that I wish you well in your endeavors, for they are noble in their own right. Fare thee well, dearest Mattie. I shall never forget you.

Sincerely Yours,
Emma

The moon sat like an alabaster seabird in the craggy black cliffs of night, glowing overhead from its lofty midnight perch. Joseph paused to admire it, until the pressure in his bladder forced him onward to his eventual destination, the outdoor lav. He hummed a tune as he wend his way along the well-worn path, a ribald rendering of a favorite hymn he'd once heard sung by some of the more rambunctious boys in his congregation: Onward Christian soldiers, farting out-of-doors, with a soiled cheesecloth drooping in their drawers. He couldn't help but snigger.

His earlier love-making with Estelle had put him in a rapturous yet peculiar frame of mind, body, and spirit. She had been uncommonly active, a development that had brought him to a quick climax—too quick. But then, even a prophet of God can miscalculate in matters of copulation.

The lav door croaked open and Joseph shuffled into the stifling darkness. He hoisted his nightshirt and pissed a loud stream into the sulfurous pit. The fumes pricked at his nose hairs. When he breathed through his mouth, he thought he might suffocate in the acrid fog of the lav. A gag rose suddenly at the back of his throat, and he heaved dryly. In an attempt to regain gastric control, Joseph put mind over matter by turning to more pleasant thoughts. He pictured Estelle—the curving small of her back, her startled-white buttocks and the blond mound of its complement. He recalled the first time he had laid eyes on her glorious womanhood. Now there was a vision from God, thought he. Joseph felt his cock swell in his hand, until it was as thick and hard as an iron rod. The staff of Moses. He sniggered again. Perhaps all was not lost.

But just as he was about to further explore the possibility of onanism a sound distracted him, a sound from just beyond the cabin. The beating of hoofs. The muted echo of men boldly speaking of justice. The fizzle and snap of soaked carbon-oil torches probing the night air. Joseph felt himself go limp, first his member, then his whole body. He let his night shirt drop and sat down in the filth, waiting.

The Curious Case of the Man Who Loved the Bearded Lady and the Dog-Faced Boy Who Mourned Him

(Robert Hickson, Daily News – Cananea, Mexico) This small, insignificant border town first came into being in the 18th century when Jesuits discovered gold and silver in the humped hills of the Mexican state of Sonora. Today it is teeming —if that is the right word—with miners eking out a meager living in the pit and squandering it in one of two dilapidated cantinas in town.

Here, is a long, long way from New York, reading friends. It is also a long way from the Wild West you have read about in the very pages of this publication. There is no Buf falo Bill here. No Billy the Kid or Wild Bill Hickok. Wyatt Earp does not patrol the streets of this town.

Cananea has the dirt, grit, and grime of the Wild West; what it lacks is the luster of a gunfight, the buff of a bank robbery. In a word, it is dull here. Make no mistake, there is danger to be had; however, it is of the pedestrian ilk. Danger does not loom on a mountain pass with a Winchester leveled between one's eyes. It does not lurk around the next bend of the river, crouched and concealed atop an overhanging bough with a skinning blade flashing in its teeth. The danger here is not so grand: starvation, heat exhaustion, a tooth-rattling kick from a rogue billy goat. These are the dangers that Cananeans bravely (and gravely) face in their day-to-day existence.

It is here, in this nondescript Mexican aldea, that our story winds down to an ignominious end. It is an account too outlandish, too freakish, too outright incredulous, to be regarded as anything other than purely fictional.

But rest assured, reading friends, that this is no fiction. It is yet another quality story-series from the news people you have come to trust; in the newspaper you come to for news that goes beyond the pale, for news that tweaks the imagination and pricks up the ears. Yes, folks, it is the Daily News.

I arrived in Cananea in search of a scoop. Weeks earlier, I had heard tell of an outlaw—Deadeye Deacon Dick—who dipped south of the border in an attempt to lose the authorities hot on his trail and traveling with a hangin' judge, as they are apt to put it in these parts.

Of course, you can appreciate, my reading friends, that it was too good a story not to pursue. However, as it turned out, Deadeye Deacon Dick gave the authorities—and me—the slip by dying. Yes, dying. As rumor has it, his trusty steed was not as trusty as one might expect from the four-legged companion of an infamous outlaw and had thrown him (the ignominious death feared and abhorred by every true cowboy), which in and of it self is no guarantee that one will soon be on his way to meet his maker; however, landing in a breeding pit of vipers after being thrown from one's trusty steed is almost certain to result in a unexpected tête-à-tête with St. Peter just this side of the Pearly Gates.

And so, too, did my story die a quick and painful death at the hands —or more accurately, the fangs—of a thousand thrashing demons on the fiery hell-plains of this Mexican desert.

Seeking refreshment and a room with a bed, I looked for the nearest precinct of civilization, which, of course, was nowhere to be found. I settled for Cananea after eliminating a number of even less appealing options, most of which revolved around bullet-riddled villas crawling with Mexican banditos whose sour breath heavy with mescaline fumes and stolen horse meat stays with one for months, even years, after coming within breathing distance of them.

I settled into a coffin-sized room over a dingy cantina and set up office. That is to say, thinking to make the best of the situation and write a local color piece as some of my esteemed journalistic colleagues have recently done for Appalachia, I unpacked my Oliver #2 and my usual ten quire, or half ream, of typewriter paper.

Of course, reading friends, the most logical place to begin the enquiries from which I would develop my local color piece seemed quite clearly to be in the crumbling cantina over which I now found myself situated. With this in mind, I made my way into the dusty drinking hole, as always, trying to conceal any apparent journalistic airs under a mask of stupefied indifference. The story I had mentally rehearsed—which was intended to explain the presence of one *gringo sudoso*—had holes in it as big as the Grand Canyon. In a word, I doubted that anyone would take me for a professional breeder of exotic Mexican burros. However, strange as it may seem, it was this very yarn that led me to the story I am now following and indelibly setting down right here on these very pages.

After I had related my ill-imagined story to the barkeep, he snorted and with a char-grilled chuckle said in coarse English that if breeding exotic burros was my game, I should talk to the man in the corner. With this, he hoisted a loose-fleshed limb and pointed with a narrow, gnarled digit to the sternmost region of this too dark and dingy Dickensian hulk.

Jesus Ramos was seated face-down at a corner table, facing the wall. The somber slump of his shoulders was the kind of self-effacing gesture that one immediately recognizes as distinctly tribal or clannish in origin. Yet, the reason for his estrangement, indeed, his self-imposed exile, was not readily apparent to me. I say not readily, reading friends, because upon my approach it did become readily apparent, shockingly apparent!

Jesus Ramos peered out from behind a hackled, hirsute mask of hair. That is to say, there was no hairline per se, no beginning and certainly no end to the bramble-black mane that engulfed every contour, every phrenologic configuration of his camouflaged visage. The spectacle before me appeared wholly mythical. A thousand thoughts swirled through my swimming head! Foremost among them was the feckless musing that I had somehow stumbled upon the missing link between hominids and canines; that is to say a lycanthrope, the handiwork of a disgusted and disgruntled Zeus. Or in more common terms, a *werewolf.*

Jesus growled drunkenly in what I assumed was an attempt to scare me off, bearing a set of whalebone-white and surprisingly well-kept teeth. The chewed and crusted remnants of chili peppers, meat gristle, and *masa* clung to the hair high on his right cheekbone. I could not help but notice how, even in this dishev-eled state, the hair sprouting from his face parted neatly down the bridge of his nose. His eyes—two blank blue sparrow eggs, each in its own overwrought nest of hair—were at the same time wrathful and hopeful. It was then that I realized he was a young man, not an old man, as I had at first erroneously presumed.

He propped a pocked porcelain cup at his lips and took an oily, obligate slug of the blue agave brew. Perhaps sensing that I was not about to be intimidated by his canine-like yips and yowls, he finally spoke: "What do you want?"

Reading friends, I wonder if you can imagine the myriad of questions that right then percolated like peptic thoughts to the sparkling pink surface of my unsettled brain. And where to start was the most befuddling of them all. What do I want? he asked. Prosperity, fulfillment, happiness—the same as anyone else, I suppose. It sets one thinking, to be sure.

However, at that precise moment in time, it became clear to me that what I wanted more than anything else on this paint-box planet was to ask one deceptively simple, overarching and all-inclusive question: *What in the name of goodness glory happened to you?*

Of course, my journalistic sensibilities kept me from posing such a panderly (if only to my own morbid curiosity) question. If I have learned only one thing over the years it is this: A little delicacy and décorum go a long way in greasing the howling hinges that open mysterious doors into the past—closet doors, bedroom doors, cellar doors, even the door to one's subconscious. And so it was that I came at the question which burned within me from a more indirect, more oblique angle. "Have you ever been to the circus?" I asked.

My question, reading friends, turned out to be a perceptive one. For not only had Jesus Ramos been to the circus, he was born in a circus, and he was presently employed as a sideshow act—Jesus the Dog-faced Boy—in the famous Bartle & Bartle Circus. As luck would have it, Jesus was in town on family business, and the exact nature of that family business would be revealed to me in due time. For now, suffice it to say that Jesus Ramos's father was laid to rest here in Cananea not a week earlier. Another baleful grave on the bleak, sun-beaten landscape.

And so it was that I had stumbled upon the grieving son at the tail end of a one-man, tequila-fueled wake for his father.

Of course, reading friends, no journalist worth his salt would allow the story to end there, with unanswered questions hanging in the air like tantalizing, too-ripe golden apples bowing a bough on the tree of public knowledge.

I sat and joined Jesus in his tormented state of torpor. Midway through the second bottle of blue agave brew, the young man, Jesus the Dog-faced Boy, agreed to go on record in a one-on-one interview with yours truly, an exclusive for the *Daily News*.

And you, reading friends, can read all about it in the next edition of this new story-series. Trust me when I say that it is a story not to be missed! It is a story to amaze and astonish you! So, stay tuned! And keep your eye on the news!

The Curious Case of the Man Who Loved the Bearded Lady and the Dog-Faced Boy Who Mourned Him [Part II]

(Robert Hickson, Daily News – Cananea, Mexico) There is something about the scorching desert heat that convinces a man he is indeed comprised largely of water. Ten gallons to be exact. And that is about what I poured down my pulpy parched throat when I arose the following morning. My head felt like a ripe exotic melon that had puckered and popped in the heat, and I wondered at the point of that bacchanalian exercise. That is until I recalled that at some point in the muddle of tequila and *cerveza*, Jesus had agreed to a tell-all interview. A quick check of my notepad corroborated the recollection.

As I scanned the notepad—the stops and starts, the scratches and scribbles—it all began to come back to me: the story of Jesus Ramos, the weird and wonderful world of Jesus the Dog-Faced Boy. (And what a story it is, reading friends!) I sat down on the bed, and made myself as comfortable as the dual camel humps would allow. And then I set the notepad on my lap and began to read from the beginning. And this, reading friends, is where our story begins.

[*Late last night*]

DN: Jesus, I want to make something clear from the onset. So let me start out by asking you about your hair. Clearly, you have more of it than most people do. Can you tell us about that?

JR: Well, I have hair on pretty much every square inch of my body, including my face, as you can see for yourself. The only place I don't is on the soles of my feet and the palms of my hands. [*Holds up his hands*] I have this rare disease, you understand, a condition, the doctors like to call it, and it causes hair to grow all over my body.

DN: Just to be clear, the condition you're referring to is hypertrichosis, correct?

JR: Yes, that sounds about right.

DN: So let's be clear, you're not a werewolf, a wolf man.

JR: [*Laughter*] No, I'm not a werewolf, and I'm not a wolf man. I'm just the Dog-Faced Boy.

DN: You seem to take this all in stride. What I mean is it doesn't seem to bother you—this disease, as you call it, this condition, as the doctors call it. All the questions, all the looks: don't you ever feel angry or even resentful of normal people?

JR: Well, if I'm being completely honest, I'd have to say on occasion it bothers me to look the way I do. And that I have to groom myself to a degree that most people couldn't even imagine. Not the kind of quick job that most men are used to. It can't be done in five minutes with a comb and razor in front of a cracked mirror. So sometimes, yeah, I guess I do get angry, maybe even resentful, like anyone else would, I suppose. But most of my life, I've been tagging along one circus or another, you understand. So it's professional grooms that take care of me, by and large.

DN: You say you've always been around circuses. I imagine that circus people aren't shocked by much. But what is it like here in Cananea where no one knows you? They're not used to seeing you sitting in the cantina. Is it more difficult here?

JR: I won't lie to you. It's hard. As you say, people aren't used to my looks, and they know nothing about me, which makes things awkward at times. The way I see it, there's basically three kinds of folks. First, the folks who try to ignore me, act like they don't see me. These folks are trying so hard not to see me that they walk into posts or step in puddles or maybe they fall off chairs, or worse.

DN: So, then, those who are desperately trying to turn I blind eye.

JR: Yeah, that's right. Then there's the folks who act like it's real normal to see a kind of wolf man, like you say, walking down Main Street or sitting in the cantina.

DN: Okay, those people who are in denial. And last?

JR: That's the folks who just come right out with it; they say things like, "What in the name of all that's holy happened to you?" Or they'll whinny and heehaw as I pass by.

DN: Yes, of course: those of the disarmingly ingenuous ilk.

JR: Strange as it sounds, I guess I'm most comfortable with those kind of folks, the ingenious folks, like you say. Their reaction seems most honest to me.

DN: Interesting point. Just to be clear, there is no known cure for this disease. You'll be forced to live with it your entire life. Is that correct?

JR: It seems so. The doctors tell me there's no cure.

DN: Do you wish there was a cure?

JR: Well, I suppose I do. I mean, I'd be a rabid fool and a bald-faced liar to deny that. But it's like I said before, I've been this way since I was born. I'm not sure what I'd do if in the wink of an eye I was normal. Besides that, I'd be out of a job if there was a cure. [*Laughter*]

DN: Right. [*Laughter*] Far be it from me to argue with that kind of logic. [*Laughter*] And since you've brought it up, let's talk about the job, your job. What's a typical day like for you?

JR: Well, I'm not by nature an early riser, but when I'm on the road with Bartle & Bartle, I'm up with the cock's crow. If we're traveling to a new town, everyone is up, fussing over the details of moving on. The circus train is usually making steam by five and pulling out by six. So it's an early day. But if we're not moving on, I'm usually lazing around like a barnyard Tom until it's time for breakfast.

DN: Please tell me it's not table scraps or a raw beef shank. [*Laughter*]

JR: [*Laughter*] No, it's nothing like that. It's whatever the food tent is serving up that morning. Unless it's runny eggs. I shy away from the eggs. Try as I might, they always end up stuck to me somewhere. And once they're dried, they're the devil to comb out. Real painful, you understand.

DN: I would imagine so. And the grooms are likely not amused, either. [*Laughter*] So, what's next?

JR: After breakfast, I have some time to kill before grooming. So, I'll read, or if I'm feeling rambunctious, I'll wander around and watch some of the other acts rehearsing. I'm friendly with the high-wire fellas, so sometimes I might try my hand at walking the wire. Not without a net, you understand.

DN: Of course not. But I think you mean try your foot at walking the high wire, don't you? [*Laughter*] I wouldn't have taken you for a reader. What sort of books do you like to read?

JR: Well, most anything, really. I read what other folks are good enough to give me on loan. Dexter, the lion tamer, gives me true crime books and pulp magazines. I've been known to flip through those. Julian, one of the flying trapeze fellas—he's always giving me big heavy novels. He calls them Victorian novels, although beats me why, I've never come across a Victoria in a single one of them yet. Anyway, I find those novels long and boring.

DN: Well, I have to say you're not alone in that honest if bleak appraisal. [*Laughter*] What else do you read?

JR: Philippe, my friend the high-wire walker, he loans me old dime novels about the Wild West. Those are my favorite.

DN: You appear to enjoy a good rapport with your colleagues, that is, the other acts. Is there anyone with whom you are not really on friendly terms?

JR: Well, it's like this: we travel together three hundred and twenty-five days a year, so there's bound to be flare-ups. It's only natural, you under-stand. But I get on well with most all the circus folks. Sometimes the clowns can be, what's the word, *galling*, I suppose, particularly when they're kicking back the homemade hooch, which is real regular. The only other person I haven't never taken a shining to, and neither's no one else, for that matter, is Bartle & Bartle's new elephant act, Peter Stuckey. He's what you call a prima donna, I suppose, real arrogant like. He won't lower himself to associate with the other circus folks. The clowns are always poking fun at him. "Stuckey's got a stick stuck up his behind," they always say, except they don't actually say "behind" but something much worse, if you know what I mean. [*Laughter*]

DN: [*Laughter*] Wow, I would never have imagined that clowns could be so caustic. Aren't they supposed to be playful and fun-loving?

JR: It goes against expectation, I admit. But there's some of them can be real sour beggars, particularly on day three of a three-day drunk.

DN: Hence, the opposing masks of Thalia and Melpomène. [*Laughter*] Okay, let's get back to your routine. Let's talk about your act. It's a very popular act, isn't it? You've got a devoted following. Am I right?

JR: Well, yes, I suppose that's true. I get a fair draw. But most of those folks don't come special to see me. They come to see the big cats and the ponies and now the elephant, too. And those folks that do come special to see me are quiet,

you understand, solemn as sinners in church. They sit and stare. Not cheering, not clapping, nothing such as that.

DN: Okay. Quite a subdued crowd, then. Not exactly perched on the edge of their seats, as they are wont to say in theatre circles.

JR: Not exactly, no. They sit and stare at me, for hours. Not really at me, I suppose. More like at what they think they see. Like I'm proof of something they suspected all along but was never able to prove. And now the proof is sitting right there big-as-life before their eyes. It's curious, in a way. And a bit rattling at times the way folks stare at me.

DN: Yes, I imagine it would be unnerving, to say the least. So, are you in a cage for your entire act? And, if so, what are you doing the whole time?

JR: Uh, yes, that's right. I'm in a cage. I don't care much for that part of it, but I understand that it's all for the act—it's what folks expect. They want to see the Dog-Faced Boy locked behind bars for their own protection, you understand. Most times, I just squat there on all fours, like a dog waiting on a bone. When folks come in, I growl at them, at first anyhow. After they've been staring for a while, I ease off on the growling. You'd be surprised how something like that can take it out of you—growling. If you don't believe me, just try sitting and growling for twelve hours straight.

DN: Good point. Although some of our more pious readers might suggest that attending successive Christmas Masses is a similar such growling occasion. [*Laughter*]

JR: [*Laughter*] Yes, I suppose.

DN: So, you have to be selective about your growling. Is that a fair assessment?

JR: Yes, that's fair enough. I have to pick and choose when I'm going to growl. If someone comes too near my cage, I growl real fierce like, that's a certainty. And I lunge at them, snapping and barking. But on slow days, I might read one of my books in the back corner of the cage. Only when no one's around, you understand. When some customer comes in, I bookmark my page and start up with the snarling and growling. I've gotten myself into a few rows with Rico the ticket-taker because I've been too slow to close up my book and some customer maybe seen me reading in the corner. He says it destroys the—what's the word he uses—*artifice* of the act.

DN: Yes, I suppose it does do damage to the artificially conjured semblance of the Dog-Faced Boy. Do you ever speak? Words, I mean?

JR: Not as a rule, no. There's times I might bark in such a way that makes folks think that maybe I could speak, if I were trained right or taught to. I want them believing I have all the physical, uh, machinery, I suppose, necessary for speaking, but myself, being raised by wolves, was never taught to speak, you understand. Sometimes it's fun to watch the reactions on folk's faces when I do that. I'll bark out a word or part of a nursery rhyme or maybe a name, like, oh, say Santa Ana, and they'll look at me real curious like, wondering if they really heard what they thought they just heard.

DN: Yes, I imagine the disparity between what they see and what they right then hear is somewhat difficult to reconcile. But, I'm curious to know if you ever try anything more phonetically challenging than Santa Ana, something like, *onomatopoeia* or maybe even *sesquipedalianism*?

JR: [*Pause*] [*Confused laughter*]

DN: [*Laughter*] Excuse my waggish witticism. Can you tell us more about your bark-speaking, if I may call it that? A specific occasion, perhaps?

JR: I remember a time when a nice old lady walked into the tent and stood staring at me the way they're apt to do. While she stood there, a little street imp stole up beside her and thieved some money from her handbag, right under her nose. She was so occupied with looking at the Dog-Faced Boy that she took no notice of the thieving. But I did. I saw the whole thing, you understand. And the little imp saw that I saw the whole thing. But to his way of thinking, I was just the Dog-Faced Boy, a wild animal who can't say a word. So he starts making off with the money, backing away and all. Well, now, I'm at a bit of a loss, you understand. To my way of thinking, there's only one thing to do. So I start barking pick-pocket, pick-pocket! The old lady looks at me real curious like, as if she just then understood what I said. But she's so busy wondering if she heard what she thought she just heard that the little devil is getting away. So I bark again. Pick-pocket, pickpocket! Finally, it dawns on her that I'm trying to tell her something. She turns and sees the street imp with a fistful of her money and cries out, "Pickpocket, pick-pocket!" Of course, Rico hears her and reaches out with a rough hand to nab the little thief. [*Laughter*] And that's how the story ends. But not before getting a few more curious looks from that nice old lady. [*More laughter*]

DN: [*Laughter*] Jesus the Dog-Faced Boy saves the day! Terrific story! But can you demonstrate? How about barking something out for me right now? I'll try to guess what you're saying.

JR: Well, I guess I could do that. [*Makes barking sounds*]

DN: Hmm. I going to guess and say, "We come with cannons at Easter." Was that it?

JR: Not quite. Try again. [*Makes barking sound*]

DN: "Well shunned can can eat her." Was that it?

JR: I said, "Welcome to Cananea."

DN: Oh? Can you do it one more time?

JR: [*Makes barking sounds*]

DN: Yes, I hear it now. That is a strange effect, to be sure. But aren't there times when you're tempted to say something to someone in plain language just to shock or surprise them, maybe jar them from their comfort-able existence as a walking, talking, thinking member of Kingdom Animalia nobility?

JR: Well, I've been tempted. But, no, I never have said anything to a paying customer in plain language like that.

DN: [*Laughter*] This may seem like a somewhat fatuous question, although no more fatuous than any of the others I've asked: How do you address your personal expurgation needs while you're essentially incarcerated?

JR: You mean how do I answer the call of nature? How do I relieve myself in my cage?

DN: Right, how do you address your personal expurgation needs?

JR: [*Laughter*] It's simple, really. When I have to go, I do like a dog and raise a leg or squat in the corner.

DN: Are you're saying that you urinate and defecate in your cage? Wow! I have to admit to being a little surprised, even shocked, by this revelation.

JR: It's all part of the act, you understand. It was a hard thing to do at first, but I suppose you just grow accustomed to it. To my way of thinking, it's a natural thing, so I don't feel strange about doing my business in front of folks anymore.

DN: So, then, you do your business, as you put it, in public, without even the meager provision of a brass pot or scrap of newsprint?

JR: [*Laughter*] That's right. No pot, no newspaper. And that's not all: I take care of the whole mess myself after the show. How's that for shocking? The Dog-Faced Boy, raised in the wild by wolves, shoveling the dung from his own cage! Imagine if a paying customer were ever to see that. [*Laughter*]

DN: That is shocking! But let me get this straight, you have no scruples about doing your business before a crowd. Okay. But it occurs to me that you manage the small feat of unfastening and dropping your trousers, only to thereafter lift a leg or squat while relieving yourself, as you put it. Don't the two actions seem rather incongruous?

JR: In-what? [*Laughter*] Jesus the Dog-faced boy doesn't wear trousers. That wouldn't fit with the Dog-Faced Boy act at all. I'm a wild animal who just happens to be a boy, a human. I'm in a natural state, you understand. "Untarnished by civilization" is what Rico hollers out to the crowds. [*Laughter*]

DN: Truer words have never been spoken, I'm afraid. [*Laughter*] I don't want to delve too deeply into the details of your personal lavatory care, but this is so intriguing that I feel compelled to pursue it a moment longer. By your own admission, you eschew the wearing of trousers. Is it safe to assume, then, that ample natural coverage occurs in the areas in question?

JR: Natural coverage?

DN: Hair.

JR: You mean, do I have lots of hair down there?

DN: Exactly, yes.

JR: Let me just say that you can't see much of anything down there other than hair and more hair.

DN: Okay, I'm going to take your word for that. But something occurs to me, and I want to back up a few steps. You have ample natural coverage, which allows you to forgo clothing, particularly trousers, and facilitates a seemingly seamless answer to the call of nature, as you put it. But is it in actuality a seamless response? That is my question.

JR: I'm sorry, but I don't follow exactly what you're getting at.

DN: What I'm asking is do you find that on occasion, the discharge of, well, dung, as you call it, is impeded by your natural coverage and therefore becomes embroiled in an unpleasant excrementitious tangle?

DN: [*Pause*] You mean does dung get caught in my hair?

JR: Yes, that's what I'm asking. And if so, how do you undertake the necessary lavatory ablutions and paperwork, so to speak?

JR: Well, you might be surprised to learn that this is a serious matter for the Dog-Faced Boy. Yes, dung does get caught in my hair from time to time. Since I'm thought to be a wild animal, I can't clean myself up like most people would. I suppose it's just a matter of how bad it is, the unpleasant *excre-some-thing-or-other* tangle, as you say. If it's just a small clump of dung hanging there in my hair, I'll just leave it hang until it dries, and hope it falls off on its own. The problem is the dung can be bad, downright awful, truth be told, circus food being what it is and all. [*Laughter*] But as I said before, it's all part of the act.

DN: Fair enough. But what happens in the event that it is no small clump, as you put it, but a rather significant clump?

JR: If there's a good load of dung stuck and hanging there then I'm going to have to do something about it, as it makes sitting messy and uncomfortable, you understand. So, being the Dog-Faced Boy, I just do as a dog would do. I drop my

rear end onto the ground and drag myself along with my hands. It usually gets a lot of giggles from the youngsters in the crowd and a lot of embarrassed looks from their red-faced folks.

DN: You don't really, do you? You actually drop-and-drag on the spot, with the crowd looking on?

JR: God strike me dead if I'm lying. I'm an animal, so I do as an animal does. You must've come a-cross a dog doing the same at one time or another.

DN: Unfortunately, yes I have. But typically, it's some scab-riddled street mongrel in an alleyway. Let's change directions just a bit. Do you have female admirers? Many men in the entertainment business enjoy countless hordes of adoring female fans. What's it like for you?

JR: Well, I don't want to come across as all big-headed. I'm no cock -of-the-walk, you understand, but I have my fair share of female companionship.

DN: So, what is it about the Dog-Faced Boy that attracts these women? Is it your—what shall we call it—notoriety? Or is it your pure animal magnetism? Perhaps they find a man with a preponderance of hair attractive. Or maybe they simply find a man who does the drop-and-drag refreshing in some incomprehensible way. What do you think it is?

JR: Well, some of the ladies are plain curious. That's for certain. But most of them, to my way of thinking, are drawn to me by some kind of, I don't know, female instinct, I suppose. They want to try taming the wildness in me, or what they think is the wildness in me. Maybe that doesn't make much sense to you.

DN: More than you might think, actually.

JR: There's also a small number of female fans, I suppose you'd call them, who just want to experience, uh, mating in the wild. Plain old mating without all the love, you understand. Two snapping and growling dogs tussling in the bushes. The real McCoy, I suppose you could say.

DN: Wow, the real McCoy. Now that is truly an interesting perspective you've just delineated. And since I've just opened that can of worms, so to speak, can you give us an example, an anecdote? I'm profoundly curious to learn who such female admirers might be.

[Editor's Warning: In the interest of a full and accurate depiction of Jesus the Dog-Faced Boy, the following remarks have been left fully intact and have not been bowdlerized in any way.]

JR: Well, I suppose the most peculiar experience I ever had was with a congressman's wife down in Guanajuato.

DN: Wow! Please do tell us about it.

JR: She came in on a Wednesday afternoon. It was quiet, and I was reading a story about Billy the Kid. So I closed up the book and hid it in a pile of straw, as I'm in the habit of doing, and started pacing back and forth at the front of the cage, growling only half-heartedly. I remember she sat staring for maybe an hour, stock-still, just staring.

For all her staring, she was nothing much to look at herself, really, nothing special, you understand. Mid-forties, I suppose, more than twice my age, and a bit on the large side. She had a real heavy bosom that was a stirring sight to see, I recall. Pretty blonde hair and perfect nails, too.

I didn't know who she was at the time. After she'd left, Rico told me. But I didn't think too much more about it till she come back right about closing time. She waited for me and, well, to make a long story short, we ended in a rented room above a nearby cantina much like this one.

DN: Intriguing! And was she intent on encountering the real McCoy, as you put it?

JR: Not exactly. She stripped down bare and I was expecting the same such thing as always, you understand, the snapping and growling, the real McCoy, all that. But that's not what she had in mind. No sir. Next thing I know, I'm gobbling table scraps from the freckled canyon of her big white behind.

DN: Goodness glory! Can it be? You mean to say the stimulus for her sexual arousal lay in this queer comestibles fetish?

JR: [*Laughter*] Queer what? All I know is all night, I'm gobbling and she's carrying on, making all kinds of noises, some wild and some, I don't know, not wild, I suppose. [*Laughter*] By the time she's finished, I'm stuffed, you understand. I can't even fathom eating another bite. [*Laughter*]

DN: I have to say that at this juncture I really am at a complete loss for words.

JR: But there's more. She had this pint-sized dog, a barking rat, and she called it Kiki. Kiki was yipping and yapping at me the whole time. I'm still not sure if it was on account of my eating all of Kiki's table scraps or on account of my doing something that was normally Kiki's job. [*More laughter*]

DN: That is truly disturbing. Wow! Baffling! It turns out that the life of Jesus the Dog-Faced Boy is anything but run-of- the-mill.

JR: Yes, I suppose it would be fair to say that. [*Laughter and more laughter*]

[*End of interview, part I*]

Truer words have never been spoken, reading friends! "It would be fair to say that," indeed. But that will have to wait, as it was here in my notes that our first interview ended. And the call of nature, as Jesus put it, was upon me. On top of that, my camel-humped bed in a room above a cantina in the desert town of town of Cananea had put a miserly kink in my lower back. So I rose for a morning stroll to the common toilet before the stifling heat of the day fully took hold and, giving rise to a formidable sewage stench, made the facility utterly unapproachable.

And so it is, reading friends, that this most fascinating and, yes, truly bizarre story draws to a close for now. However, fear not! For in the final installment, I reveal my second and last interview with Jesus the Dog-faced Boy. So look for it—Part III—in next week's edition. Stay tuned! And keep your eye on the news!

The Curious Case of the Man Who Loved the Bearded Lady and the Dog-Faced Boy Who Mourned Him [Part III]

(Robert Hickson, Daily News – Cananea, Mexico) The person I discovered while interviewing Jesus Ramos was not the individual I had expected to find. There was the Dog-Faced Boy, yes. And there was the young man maligned by fate. But there was also a sensitive human being looking for ready answers to his own ontological investigations, answers most likely to be found obscured and even unrecognizable as such somewhere in his past. Yes, it is a past almost as outlandish, nearly as preposterous as all things present tense in the life of Jesus Ramos. And that, reading friends, is precisely where we now pick up with this installment of our exclusive one-on-one: the past.

[The following day]

DN: I know it is a difficult time for you, with the recent passing of your father. But can you tell us something about him. He was American, was he not?

JR: Yes, he was American. But I don't know much about him, you understand. The little I do know was told to me by gran. For myself, personally, all I know about my father is he left when I was just a pip-squeak and never came back. Most everything else was told to me secondhand.

DN: By your grandmother, or your gran, as you call her?

JR: Mostly by gran, yes.

DN: So, your father left home when you were very young. I understand he abandoned you and your family. Is that right?

JR: Yes, that's right.

DN: Is that why you didn't take you father's family name?

JR: I guess so, yes. I never really gave it a lot of thought, you understand. He wasn't a part of my life. So it wasn't really a matter of choosing or not choosing. It just seemed natural to me.

DN: Can you tell us the name of your father?

JR: I think it best if I don't.

DN: Fair enough. What do you think drove your father to abandon his family?

JR: Well, by mother's telling, it was to bill and coo with a posse of fat-bottomed prostitutes in the brothels of San Francisco. *[Chuckles]*

DN: The oldest story for the oldest profession—another man falls victim to the sirens' song of tart and strumpet.

DN: [*Confused pause*] Gran says it was because he wasn't thinking straight, plain and simple. The bottle, I suppose. It can make a man do crazy things.

DN: Yes, well, we certainly discovered the truth of that particular platitude last night, didn't we? But why do you think your father turned to the bottle in the first place? Do you think it had anything to do with you?

JR: You mean did it have anything to do with siring the Dog-Faced Boy? I can tell you I've asked myself that very question dozens upon dozens of times over the years. Personally, for myself, you understand, I know it would affect me in a bad way if I came home to find that my wife had birthed something looking like it'd been swept up off Van Doon's Barbershop floor. But gran, she said there were things in father's past, things I suppose he'd just as soon forget. That's why he turned to the bottle.

DN: Since you've brought it up, let's talk about the past, your father's, in particular, or at least what little you know of it.

JR: OK. My father was born back East somewhere. In one of those eastern states. New Hampshire or Vermont or maybe Maine. I'm not exactly sure which. He was raised in a religious home, I do know that. Although I don't know much about his youth. But I under-

stand he became a country preacher or reverend, whatever it is they call it up there. But he made some powerful enemies along the way, and he was finally arrested on a false charge of some sort or the other.

DN: Do you know what the nature of that charge was?

JR: No, I don't. All I know is he was arrested for something he never done, at least, that's how gran saw it. And even mother agreed on that account. He was jailed for the charge, and while he was waiting for a judge to arrive, a mob of men stormed the jail. They broke in and shot him point-blank, left him blowing bubbles of his own spit and blood. Or so they thought, anyhow.

DN: But he wasn't dead, correct? Or I wouldn't be sitting here talking to you now.

JR: No, he wasn't dead. Not even properly wounded, you understand. He escaped then headed west to California. There was a mini-gold rush going on there in '76.

DN: From preacher to gold miner. That's an interesting transition. From man of God to man of gold. The two seem at odds, don't you agree?

JR: Well, by gran's telling, the so-called near-death experience turned him bitter against God. I suppose he felt he'd been abandoned by the Almighty and left to die in his time of need. Who wouldn't? It was about that time that he first took up the bottle.

DN: Let's back up a little. How did he escape death?

JR: Well, like I said, they left him for dead in the jail, but he wasn't dead. He was saved by a good-sized gooseberry garnet he kept tucked away in his vest pocket. Busted it clean in two.

DN: The sanctity of life guarded by a common gemstone. The irony is thick indeed, don't you agree? [*Silence*] Did your gran tell you about the gemstone?

JR: More than that. Got it right here. [*Pulls a gold chain from inside his shirt and displays half of the translucent green stone*] It's the only thing I ever got from my father, a chunk of that stone.

DN: [*Pause*] I'm intrigued by the story of your father. How did he find his way out West to Cal-ifornia? And what did he do there?

JR: I'm told that he hid out in the back of a covered wagon for much of the way. He got to Bodie, Cal-ifornia in 1878. But he found that he'd all but missed the gold rush al- together. I suppose the only thing left of it was a handful of grizzled prospectors drinking up what was left of the gold from their dried-up claims. So he worked on the telegraph line between Bodie and Bridgeport for a time.

DN: And how old would he have been then?

JR: Not very. Mid-twenties.

DN: What did he do next?

JR: Next he headed to San Fran-cisco. It was there he met mother.

DN: Tell us something about your mother.

JR: My mother was born in Vict-oria de Durango in 1862.

DN: And she has the same rare disease that you do. Correct?

JR: Yeah, that's right.

DN: Does she also have hair on her entire body?

JR: Yeah, she does. She has hair pretty much everywhere, same as me.

DN: Can you tell us about your mother's past?

JR: Well, she was second born. Her older sister was normal. By that I mean she didn't have the dis-ease. When mother was born, gran quit having kids. She thought moth-er was a curse from God. Like Cain after he killed Abel—God cursed his seed with a dark skin. Gran could never figure out exactly what she'd done to raise God's ire in such a way, but she felt 'specially certain that if she were to keep birthing kids they'd come out furry, feather-ed, or horned, or some such thing—some mark of sin, you understand.

DN: Yes, well, in my admitted-ly limited experience, God's ire can be raised by even the smallest of trans-gressions. [*Laughter*] And searching for the cause proves a lifetime en-deavor for most. [*More laughter*]

JR: [*Laughter*] I suppose so.

DN: So how did this sins-of-the-father obsession, or sins-of-the-mother, in this case, play out?

JR: Play out?

DN: What kind of treatment did your mother receive at home?

JR: Gran kept her locked up at home until she was a near grown woman. She always said she was protecting mother from other folks and their prying eyes, her exact words. It wasn't till I was older, and working as the Dog-Faced Boy, that I began to question that.

DN: You mean whether or not it was actually to protect your mother? You think your gran may've been ashamed or embarrassed by her prodigiously hairy daughter?

JR: That's what I started to wonder. And I still don't know for certain, one way or the other.

DN: So then, your mother never left the house until she'd reached adulthood. Did she get any kind of schooling? Did she have any kind of social life? Friends?

JR: She got no schooling in the proper way, except what gran felt compelled to teach her at home. As far as I know, that wasn't much, at least it didn't go beyond regular female learning, you understand, about running a good Christian household. And to my understanding, she didn't have any what you'd call genuine friends.

DN: So then, what was it that first prompted your gran to allow your mother to venture into the outside world?

JR: The attempt, I suppose.

DN: The attempt?

JR: That's what gran called it when mother tried to, well, kill herself, I guess.

DN: I see. A suicide attempt. Wow! The plot suddenly takes a decidedly Shakespearean turn. Can you talk about the suicide attempt?

JR: Not much to tell. Gran half expected that mother might try some such thing. She'd been down in the mouth for so long. Never smiled, hardly a word to anyone. Gran locked her in the tallboy when it seemed like mother might try to do herself harm.

DN: Locked her in a tallboy? Goodbye Shakespeare, hello Dickens. [*Laughter*]

JR: [*Silence*]

DN: My apologies. Do continue please.

JR: One time gran opened the tallboy door and found mother hanging there. She'd spun a noose from her own hair.

DN: Goodness glory! That's terrible! I mean, brilliantly poetic on one level, but simply terrible on another. [*Pause*] And that, I presume, was the turning point?

JR: Yes, gran let mother leave *la casa* for the first time in her life.

DN: And what did your mother do first with her newly found freedom?

JR: I can't say for certain if she did it first, but not long after mother went to the circus, a small one out of Mexico City, you understand, *Circo Los Limón Hermanos* . And not only did she go to the circus, she joined it. I guess there she found a group of misfits who made her feel like less of a misfit herself. She left home that day as Rosa Ramos and returned as Rosa the Bearded Lady. She packed her bags that night and left the next day. By gran's telling, she never saw mother again until after I was born.

DN: And that brings us nicely round to you. You said your mother had an older sister. Do you have siblings?

JR: I have an older brother. His name is Cristos.

DN: Really? Jesus and Cristos? Wow! That's priceless. We'll come back to that. So how, then, did your father meet your mother?

JR: In San Francisco, father drank up what he'd earned working on the telegraph line. He was foul and desperate for money, and he took whatever odd jobs came his way. Well, one day he heard *Los Limón Hermanos Circo* was coming to town and looking for day laborers. So he got there sober and on time and they put him to work driving in stakes for the big top. It was hard work, tedious work, you understand, but that was just what he needed to keep him off the drink for a day

or two. The men who raised the big top were also guaranteed two more days work tearing it down. All they had to do was be there, willing to work, when the teardown started. My father didn't want to miss it, so he decided to stay at the circus for its three-day run. He bought a fifth of sour mash and slept with the animals in the stable. And it was during that time that he first laid eyes on my mother. By gran's telling, at first sight, he mistook her for a monkey wearing a dress—one of those big ones that's part of the clowns' act, I suppose. [*Laughter*]

DN: [*Laughter*] I've had precisely ly the same experience on the streets of Manhattan. [*Laughter*]

JR: [Laughter]

DN: Please go on.

JR: When father finally figured out mother was a hairy women and not a monkey, after all, he was shocked. And fascinated, too. And, well, aroused is the only way I can think to put it.

DN: Wow! I just have to cut in here long enough to say, wow! It's disturbing to hear you say that. In so many ways and on so many levels, it's disturbing. I'm almost afraid to ask, but why do you think your father was aroused, as you put it, by your mother hairiness?

JR: Well, by gran's telling, father had some odd appetites, I suppose you could say. He liked things that were different, or as gran was apt to put it, he liked exotic and wild things.

DN: Exotic! Wild! So he was not so different than some of the women who pursue Jesus the Dog-faced boy.

JR: I suppose not. [*Chuckles softly*] Mother, well, she just got into his nut and stuck there, you understand. Heated up father's already over-active imagination is how gran put it.

DN: So, how did things proceed from there?

JR: As I said, father slept in the stables for a spell. By gran's telling, that was probably where he first got his taste for animals.

DN: You mean to say he actually consumed — ate — the animals in the stable?

JR: No, no. I mean he got a taste for animals, in a physical way, you understand. [*Thrusts hips*]

DN: [*Long pause*] My goodness glory! Sweet heavenly hosts! Are you suggesting what I think you're suggesting? His sexual appetites had a bestial bent?

JR: If by bestial you mean animals then, yes, I'm afraid that would be true.

DN: My word, no! Go no further down that road! Although it is particularly illuminating where your father's character is concerned. Let's keep with the story, for the moment anyway.

JR: Well, after the big top came

down, father stayed on with the circus. He worked on the grounds crew, setting up and tearing down. And he worked repairs on the steam engine and shoveled coal into the coal car. In between times, he watched mother. He never missed a performance of Rosa the Bearded Lady.

DN: And what would a typical performance of Rosa the Bearded Lady be like?

JR: Oh, her act was worlds apart from mine, like night and day. I'm a wild animal, so I sit on my haunches and yowl and scratch at fleas and do my business in the corner, you understand.

DN: Yes, we have certainly established that fact.

JR: But mother, she was the bearded lady. She dressed in velvet gowns with ribbon collars and frilled sleeves. She wore carved shell cameos from places with names like Torre del Greco, and she sang opera — arias, they call them — or in plain language just songs. People took a real liking to Rosa the Bearded Lady.

DN: Yes, I can see the attraction. The marriage of contrasting elements must have enthralled audiences.

JR: Well, it certainly did my father, enthrall him, as you say. Her exotic looks, you understand, her hairy body and her angelic voice, taken together, they were like a slug of strong drink to him, a stiff shot of bathtub hooch. He was hypnotized by her, I suppose, at just the sight of her. At night, he played high Chicago with the clowns, drinking hard and talking non-stop about the bearded lady. That is until the clowns got tired of it and tossed him out on his ear. He'd stumble over to the groom to see if he could steal a glimpse of mother being combed before bed. Through a crack in the door, he watched, aroused and somehow lost, too, as the fine metal curry -comb ran from the nape of her neck to the small of her back. One long stroke of shimmering black hair. Over and over, up and down, over and over, until he could no longer stand to watch. He would stagger through the dust and grass back to his bed of straw in the stables and drop as if he were dead.

DN: It sounds as if your father's affections never went beyond the peeping-Tom stage. So how, then, did they finally meet?

JR: The ringmaster saw to a formal meeting between the two of them. He was also from back East somewhere and for some unknown reason took a shining to father.

DN: The ringmaster. Suitably appropriate. And what happened?

JR: They went on a picnic. The way gran tells it, father was nervous as a beehive in a hurricane, mostly because he stayed sober that day, I suppose. They sat there on a checkered blanket in Balboa Park eating pickles and bratwurst and rye bread, saying nothing more than "delicious" and "good" to each other. Finally, father plucked up his courage and reached out a trembling hand and stroked mother's hair. It was something he'd wanted to do since he first laid eyes on her.

DN: Do you mean to say he stroked her hair as one might stroke their favorite Pekingese puppy?

JR: I couldn't say for certain. This is all by gran's telling and she never said one way or the other about the details, you understand. But I imagine he stroked her head in a real romantic way, like in those Victorian novels. But now that you mention it, I don't know. Maybe he did scratch her under the chin! [*Laughter*]

DN: [*Laughter*] Right! And she jumped into his lap and licked his face. [*More laughter*]

JR: Anyhow, that was where it all started. From that moment on, they were inseparable. Father even put the bottle aside for the first time since arriving out in the West. Seven months later, they were married in a steepleless church in a small border town during a week-long break from *Los Limón Hermanos Circo*. My older brother, Cristos, was born ten months later. And I was born fourteen months after that.

DN: Let's talk about your brother. Does he have the same disease as you and your mother?

JR: Not exactly. He has half the disease. He's hairy only on the bottom half.

DN: You mean to say he resembles Pan?

JR: Pan?

DN: Pan, half goat, half man. Plays a flute.

JR: I don't know of any pan that plays the flute.

DN: Tell me more about your brother. Are the two of you close in the fraternal sense?

JR: Fraternal sense? I can't say for certain about that. But we're not close the way brothers ought to be. Critstos has taken after father, you understand—he drinks 'specially heavy. We only ever see him when he wants more money for drink.

DN: Is it safe to say that he has no wife? No kids? No job?

JR: I suppose it would be safe to say that. He would have to be sober for more than day for that to happen. By mother's telling, he used to be an orange picker for some rich fellow in Orange County. But that didn't last long, you understand. He got himself fired. Now I don't know for certain what he's doing.

DN: So let's talk about you, Jesus Ramos, Jesus the Dog-Faced Boy. We haven't really touched on you and your life much. Can you tell us something about your childhood? Was it similar to your mother's experience?

JR: If you're asking was I locked up at home, the answer is no. My mother never saw me as anything more than a blessing from God, her special child, you understand. Not like gran. Mother never read anything into my being born, as far as sin and such goes. So my childhood was nothing like hers. Mother pushed me to get out and make friends.

DN: And did you?

JR: Not really, no. Kids my own age were afraid of me, you understand. And the older kids picked on me, bullied me. If there was ever any chances at making friends, well, they were ruined by my disease.

DN: Can you give us a specific anecdote to illustrate the point? Something which conveys the pathos of what it was like to grow up as the Dog-Faced Boy?

JR: Well, yes, I suppose I could do that. I was eight years old at the time, and it was at Darío Mendoza's ninth birthday party. Darío's grandfather was the only judge in Victoria de Durango, and his father was one of two lawyers. So, they were a well-to-do and influential family in town, you understand. Darío had four older brothers and they were all liked well enough by the other kids. They—the Mendozas— were a pillar of society, I suppose you'd say. Anyway, Darío sent me a fancy invitation to his birthday party. It was to be some production, and his parents had spared no expense. You can imagine I was excited by the idea of attending, and maybe even making a friend or two. And mother had bought a carved wooden soldier painted with the red, green, and white uniform of the Mexican Army about the time of Independence. She combed my head and back, licked her hand and plastered a stubborn cowlick to my face, as I recall. It was a wonderful party, in the beginning. There was cake and a piñata and then games and horseback riding. The horseback riding is where everything went wrong. Not because I was afraid of horses, you understand. We had an old *mula* that Cristos and I rode double to school, so I knew how to ride. I suppose it was just a spot of bad luck is all. As we were riding along, one beside the other, Darío and me, I'm swarmed by cowbirds real suddenly. They're swooping in and fluttering around me, looking to pick bugs and critters off me. I remember Darío, who wasn't a 'specially cruel boy, I remember him laughing and laughing, till he almost fell off his horse. And when I finally got off, those birds still swarmed me, wouldn't leave me alone, you understand. It's like they thought I was some straight-up-walking longhorn or some such thing. Finally, I had to leave the party because the birds were getting disruptive and all, and messing on the food and the others. After that party, I never tried again. And after that, friends were just something I knew I was never going to have.

DN: Wow! That is a somber tale, to say the least. No friends at all, then. [*Pause*] So you were you teased and bullied as a boy, then.

JR: Yes. Our school was small, two rooms, one for the little ones and one for the older ones. So there was no hiding from the big boys, the bullies. I mean, I took a lot of beatings at school, you understand. And the big boys would scare me with matches. I had a fear of fire because when I was just a youngster, maybe five or six years, I was warming myself in front of the fireplace and an ember popped and landed on my foot. In a flash, the better part of the hair on my body went up in a puff of brown smoke. I was like a haystack going up in a drought, you understand.

DN: Goodness glory! You must have been a sight to terrify Vulcan himself. [*Laughter*]

JR: I still recall the smell. It was like burnt shoe polish or some such thing. To this day, I'm terrified of flames large and small. The bullies knew about my fear and they'd chase me around with matches almost every day.

DN: Where was your brother when all of this was taking place? Did he do nothing to help you?

JR: Cristos? He was skulking under his desk, hoping they wouldn't turn their attention to him. Since he looked normal, at least from the waist up, he used to tell everyone that we come from different fathers, that his father was a rich *Americano* who built motor cars in Cleveland or some such place. I don't know if anyone believed him, but they seemed to leave him alone well enough.

DN: Let's shift our focus to the here and now. You are here in this border town, Cananea, on family business, important but unfortunate family business, as I understand it. Would you strongly object to addressing the circumstances that have brought you here?

JR: Well, not strongly. It's like I said before, I wasn't close to my father and although his passing saddens me, I suppose it really doesn't change much for me personally, you understand.

DN: Allow me to sketch in the barest of details. Your father, who shall remain nameless, has lived here in Cananea for nearly a decade, is that correct?

JR: Yes, I suppose it is. But, you understand, until a few weeks ago, before we got the telegram and I came here myself, I had no notion of where he was or what he was doing.

DN: It is my understanding that he was not doing a great deal of anything in Cananea, that is, aside

from drinking. He took the odd job here and there, just enough to finance his next alcoholic binge. Does that sound about right?

JR: I suppose it does. You know, there's some folks that liquor, well, it just turns them inside out. Shows up everything–who they are, where they've been, what they've seen, but mostly it shows who they can be and how badly they can be that person. I suppose there's just some things can't stand the light of day. And so the drink kills something inside them. Something important. I'm not so educated, not like you, but I've seen plenty of what liquor can do to a man.

DN: That was a very enlightened observation, Jesus, educated or not. So, your father was essentially going from one drunken episode to another. Where was your mother?

JR: She quit *Los Limón Hermanos Circo* after she had me. Then after father left, right around my fourth birthday, she returned to Victoria de Durango, where we lived with gran. She's been there ever since.

DN: Let me just inject a bit more context here for the readers. Victoria de Durango is located in central-west Mexico, and Cananea is a northern border town, no more than twenty miles from the Arizona border. Now, according to my research, which was really nothing more than jawing with the locals, as they put it in these parts, your father was routinely in and out of the town lock-up for public intoxication. But aside from that, there were no ser- ious charges. So what, then, hap- pened to him? Can you pick it up from that point?

JR: Well, for the last, I don't know, year or so, I suppose, he'd wrote letters to mother. Long letters, rambling and romantic letters smudged with drink and tears, telling her how much he missed her and how he wanted to come home. After all these years and he decides he wants to come home, out of the blue. Judging from the letters, it seemed certain he was on the brink of self-destruction.

DN: How did your mother react to the letters?

JR: Well, she read them. I suppose she wasn't unmoved by them, if that's what you mean. She did love the man once after all. But I don't really think she gave them serious consideration, 'specially the part about coming home. The remorseful drunk is someone mother knows too well, you understand. And gran was always warning her against it, too, saying he'd just return to his drinking ways. Truth is it wouldn't have really mattered much to me, one way or the other, personally. I'm on the road fourteen weeks out of every fifteen doing my Dog-Faced Boy act. And Cristos is somewhere in California living

from drink to drink, just like our father.

DN: So why, then, if it really didn't matter one way or the other to you did you decide to come here to Cananea? Can you fill in some details for us?

JR: Well, the letters from father soon enough slowed to a trickle, and finally stopped, just like gran said they would. "Ignore him and he'll just go away," she said. Then one day out of the blue mother got a telegram from the Sheriff here in Cananea. Well, in a word, it said that father got himself arrested and jailed, not just for the night, not just to sleep one off, but jailed for real. For a real crime. Of course, it wasn't put in quite those words, you had to read between the lines, you understand. But that was the gist of the telegram. There was no special mention of the crime he'd committed, so mother begged me to come here and find out what happened. She didn't want to come herself, I suppose, and gran was behind her in that decision. So I came. When I sent her a telegram telling her the crime he committed, mother swore by God she'd never set eyes on father again in her lifetime. And she never did.

DN: I have to say that at this juncture I am shamelessly intrigued. What was that crime? Please, do tell.

JR: Well, as I said before, father had picked up a taste for animals somewhere along the line. Here in Cananea, he was working on and off as a hired hand for the local stables. During that time, he was charged with, well, I don't quite know how say this in a fitting manner for the decent folks who might read this, but he was in jail for having his way with a burro, sexually speaking, you understand.

DN: My great goodness glory! My word! I had not the slightest inkling that this was all leading to the ignominious charge of bestiality, which, by the way, is what the act is properly known as.

JR: Yes, that is what the judge called it, bestiality.

DN: My, my, my word! I'm speechless. [*Awkward pause #1*] You mean to say that your father had sexual relations with a burro? He was gratified by a common beast of burden? Impossible to comprehend! [*Awkward pause #2*] This just keeps getting worse. [*Awkward pause #3*] What did your father have to say for himself? How did he answer to the shocking charge that was brought against him?
[*Editor's warning: The Daily News extends its sincere apologies to our readers of the fairer sex for including the following segment of the interview. It is uncensored but integral to the story.*]

JR: I visited him at the jail to see if it were true or not. His side of the story was somewhat different than what the Sheriff had told me. As I said before, Father was missing mother bad, thinking about her from sun-up till sundown, wondering how he could get back with her. One 'specially bad night, he got himself drunk as a wheelbarrow in this very cantina. Half crazed, he was, according to witnesses. But somehow, he managed to crawl back to the stables. As he approached the barn, there in the darkness, a small burro was slumbering upright, snoring lightly. Father said in his muddled state of mind the rounded and hirsute haunches of that jenny ass bore a striking resemblance to the furry bottom of his wife, the same wife he'd been pining after for months, Rosa Ramos, Rosa the Bearded Lady. He could still picture her standing so straight, so stately, and proud, an arm resting on the piano, singing something or other in Italian. By father's telling, before he knew what he was doing, he was rocking to and fro on an oats bucket with his trousers at his ankles, having his way with that jenny ass, all the while, imagining in his fevered brain that he was with his wife, even as the burro hawed and snorted and his belt buckle rattled its alarm in the night.

DN: Great goodness on high! [*Long awkward pause #1*] I don't quite know how to respond to that disturbingly poetic picture you've just painted. [*Long awkward pause #2*]

But it does beg the question, what happened next? How was your father caught?

JR: It was just a case of bad timing, I suppose you could say, bad luck, too. As father was having his way with the burro, the owner of the stables stepped out of his house to smoke a pipe of tobacco. There in the leaden light of the moon, the old man saw the most unnatural, the most God-awful and God-wrong sight he ever saw before and would ever see again. He charged father and knocked him to the ground, knocked him out cold. Father never moved a muscle, just lay there so still the old man figured he'd killed him, and in his own mind that would've been for the best, I suppose. But father wasn't dead. When he woke the next morning, the Sheriff was stooped over him hee-hawing like an ass that's taken to the whip.

DN: And the outcome?

JR: He was convicted by a county judge and sentenced to death by firing squad. It's a serious crime in Mexico, you understand, and has been since the colonial period, when the Spanish Military used to get liquored up and ravage the locals and their livestock.

DN: My word! It defies reason! There must be something in the water down here. Why must the livestock come into it?

JR: There was no real defense in father's case. To my way of thinking, being drunk only made the crime more ridiculous. So he was destined to die. [*Thoughtful pause*] The last thing father said to me before they took him away was this: "I dodged a bullet once, but I don't think I'll be so lucky this time." And he wasn't.

DN: No one else from the family was there at the end? Just you?

JR: Just me. The Sheriff told me I could watch if I wanted to. Crazy don't you think? I sat here, where we're sitting now, drinking blue agave tequila. But I heard the shots. Not a dull thud echoing over the sand, like you might imagine. It was more of a crack, like a cracking stick, or maybe a pane of glass splitting from heaven to earth. Then nothing, just silence. And from now on that's what it'll be, silence. You see, there's nothing else left. Just silence

The Curious Case of the Man Who Loved the Bearded Lady and the Dog-Faced Boy Who Mourned Him [Epilogue]

(Robert Hickson, Daily News – Cananea, Mexico) So there, reading friends, you have it. A most peculiar tragedy. I left Cananea the following day, somehow feeling that a part of my soul had been torn from me over the course of my long conversation with Jesus Ramos. I shook his hand, looked him squarely in the eye, and conveyed my sincerest sympathies. At that moment I was sorry—truly sorry. Sorry for the death of his father, yes. But for all the rest of it, too; for everything. The indignities, the pain. For a preacher-turned-alcoholic father; for an uncaring brother, for flocks of swarming cowbirds, for schoolhouse bullies; for the Lime Brothers Circus; for Bartle & Bartle Circus; for the Dog-faced Boy; for the women collectors who wanted to take a piece of him away with them like unholy relics; for the braying jenny ass; for the small-minded Sheriff; for the Judge who legitimized that small mind; for the men who took his father's life. For all of it. There was nothing else to say or do but feel sorry.

I caught a train north to Tucson to Santa Fe to Kansas City and so on, reaching my home in the Big Apple a week later. I never looked back. And I doubt that I will ever go back that way again. It is a land unto itself, to be sure. But one thing is certain: I will never look at another burro the same way again (not that, in my travels, I am prone to consort with them often). Neither will I look at a sideshow freak in quite the same way (not that I am prone to consort with them either). For who knows what lies just beyond the shock, the disgust, the horror? Who can say what lies on the other side? Behind the bars, beneath the skin, within the man— within the wolf man. Grief, maybe; pain, perhaps; but sadness, certainly. For it was precisely these things which I discovered beneath the hirsute exterior of Jesus Ramos, the Dog-faced Boy.

[Editor's postscript: For reasons unknown to us at the Daily News, Jesus Ramos never left Cananea following the execution of his father. Sadly, three months subsequent to the publication of this interview, he took his own life with a gunshot to the head, sitting naked and cross-legged in the corner of a room above the cantina.

The fact that he used a single silver bullet to end his days seems telling enough. His mother, Rosa Ramos, formerly known as the Bearded Lady, could not be reached for comment. The Sheriff of Cananea, on the other hand, was rather more forthcoming. Upon discovering the body, he was said to have uttered the following: "Don't know whether to drop 'im in a grave or skin 'im out back." Unconfirmed reports have it that a new fur rug has mysteriously appeared in front of the Sheriff's fireplace.]

Heart of Larkness

Planke drops down into the chair harder than intended; his neck pops loudly. A single expletive shoots from his mouth (a habit picked up while traipsing through the jungles of Borneo). The man across from him, slumped eruditely behind as enormous oak desk, raises a disapproving eye. Planke grimaces, smiles apologetically. This is precisely the kind of meeting that sets him on edge, and Arthur Hendry, PhD, is precisely the kind of highfalutin academic that has prompted him take a field rather than classroom position at the college. But how is he to explain this to his aunt, who daily harangues him on the merits of being an educator (even the way she says the word grates on his nerves; a precise, syllabic enunciation dripping with praise and adoration). His daily rebuttal that a researcher is an educator, of sorts, falls on deaf ears. "Of sorts," repeats Aunt Flo, frowning and clicking her tongue.

When his application for a research grant was finally approved last year, he thought it might help to ease the tension between them. Yet even as he bid her farewell (half-heartedly as it was) and set out for Malaysia to study *Rafflesia arnoldii*—the corpse flower, he told her with some relish—she harangued him. And now that he has returned to northern California with no further prospects on the horizon, the harangues have started again, in spades. So much so, that he is driven to meetings such as this one in a desperate bid to escape his septuagenarian millstone.

Arthur Hendry, PhD, sets his pen down, leans back, and kneads his hands together over the small tight mound of his belly. Planke allows his gaze to wander until finally letting it settle on a framed photo of Colonel Theodore Roosevelt in profile, complete with mashed hat, ridiculous round spectacles, and moustache—no doubt wilted by his scandalous horseradish breath. Planke does not have a high opinion of Theodore Roosevelt. Nor is he enamored with Teddy's cousin, Franklin D., the current commander-in-chief. Exactly why, he can't say. But then, Planke has always had issues—authority issues.

"Were you surprised to receive my phone call, Tom?"

Planke hesitates, partly because he can't shake the feeling that he has just been addressed by Teddy Roosevelt, and partly because no one calls him Tom. As long as he can remember, it's been Planke. Not Tom, not Tom Planke, just Planke.

"Yes sir, I must admit that I was a bit taken aback."

"I understand that your research in Southeast Asia was top notch."

"Thank you, sir. I'd like to think the project was a success."

"And you are still adverse to an instructor's post?"

"Yes, sir. I'm afraid that is also true." Planke fights the feeling that Aunt Flo is about to fly out the closet and murderously charge him with an impossibly dull butcher knife.

"Well, then, we shall have to find something else to keep you busy. And, in fact, that something else may have just come up. Have you ever heard tell of Professor John Ramos? He's one of our own, although slightly before your time. Fully tenured here at Chico State."

The name is familiar, but Planke can't quite put a face to it. Arthur Hendry, PhD, slides a plump manila folder across the desk toward him. "Everything you need to know about him is in this file." Planke tips open the folder. There is a photograph at the top. "It's the most current we have."

He inspects the photo. The man Ramos is youngish, perhaps approaching his mid-thirties. Not a great deal older than Planke himself. The photo is clearly a candid one, as Ramos is looking away from the eye of the camera, busily engaged in some important task just out of view. Wiry hair pokes from his head, stiff and tall, looking to be the work of some crazed taxidermist. Planke thinks he sees a glint in the professor's eye, the mercurial flash of one who is brilliant, impulsive, and maybe a touch mad.

"As far as we know, John Ramos is somewhere near Tres Fronteras, an area near the borders of—"

"Brazil, Peru, and Colombia. Yes, I'm familiar with it." In truth, Planke isn't familiar with it. But he has studied the books of men who are.

"John left to do field work in the Amazon Basin five years ago. And he hasn't been heard from in nearly three."

"I'm sorry. I'm not following you. Where do I come into it?"

"John Ramos was a distinguished toxicologist. He traveled to the Amazon on a much-deserved grant from Chico State in '35. His research was to last only eighteen months. At first, his correspondence was regular and intelligible. But then it started to become sporadic and, well, odd—unintelligible gibberish. There were rumors, a lot of rumors. Rumors that he was alive. Rumors about, well, cult-like activities. We ignored them in the hope that Professor Ramos might one day rejoin us here in the hallowed halls of academe. But now our hope has run out, not to mention our patience and our funding."

"And you want me to go find him and bring him back."

"Find him, yes. Bring him back, no. We want you to retrieve his field notes. For all the money this institution has sunk into his research, we must have something to show for it."

"That's it, then?"

"Not quite. Tell Professor Ramos that his tenure has been terminated. He's fired."

Outside the train window, a stand of ponderosa pine slides by. Planke finds himself pleasantly surprised by the scenery of southern Arizona. It's not what he expected at all. Not like Zane Grey described it. Planke sips tonic water as he pores over the file that Professor Hendry has entrusted him with. He expects the train will arrive in Houston by early morning. There, he'll take a ship to Macapá, Brazil, which will give him four or five days to learn everything he can about John Ramos. Before departing Chico, he checked out Ramos's books—*Toxicology and You*, and *How to Slay Friends and Poison People*—from the college library. That it is highly improbable he will be able to return the book before the due date in two weeks does not bother Planke. The way he looks at it, the college owes him. The only reason he's taken the assignment is to put some miles between him and Aunt Flo. Although he has to admit to being somewhat intrigued by John Ramos. Here's a guy who's really stuck it to the college, left them high and dry, thinks Planke. He wishes he had the courage to do the same.

Planke pulls out a progress report from the file. It's signed by Ramos and dated November, 1935. He skims it, looking for clues: clues as to what has happened to the esteemed toxicologist; clues as to what possesses a brilliant and accomplished professor and researcher to abandon all—his livelihood, his home, his family. And according to the file, there was a family—or a wife, at least, named Rebecca. Planke notes that both books are dedicated to her. But there are few other clues, clues that tell him why. Why had Ramos slugged his way deep into the heart of the Amazon, never to return? Planke lets his gaze drift to the bottom of the page; he reads the last lines of the letter.

All is well. Research moves forward slowly but surely. Patience is the key to our endeavor here in this harsh Eden. For who can rid the world of sickness and disease in a month, or a year, or even one hundred years? And who can know what cure lurks beneath this rock and that, or infuses this plant and that? That is the task that I am about, Arthur, and that is the challenge we face. Keep the faith.

Something Arthur Hendry, PhD, had said to Planke comes to him right then: cult-like activities. That the old fellow had been purposely vague was clear at the time. But only now does Planke stop to wonder why. He digs deeper in to the file. There are letters of all kinds: letters of recommendation and commendation; course outlines and evaluations; an FBI file on Ramos; even minutes from a meeting of the Disciplinary Actions Board. From what Planke can gather, Ramos was called to give testimony—damning testimony, it would seem—concerning a colleague in the biology department. Planke eases back into his chair and digs in to the document.

Board Member Bloom: Distinguished members of this board, the charge against Professor Fichen is that of sexual deviance. He has been accused by a number of his students of lecturing at the front of his classroom with an erect penis.

Board Member Fish: Why, exactly, would one want to lecture using an erect penis?

Board Member Jameson: Why, indeed. It's not as if it were a class in anatomy, now, is it?

Board Member Brooks: More to the point, how does one lecture using an erect penis?

Board Member Ransom: And where does one even lay his hands on —if you'll excuse the expression—an erect penis?

Board Member Bloom: Please, please, esteemed colleagues. Allow me to clarify. The erect penis was his own, and it was in his pants at the time.

Board Member Brooks: Is there not some law against such a lewd act?

Board Member Bloom: Well, yes, there is if the penis is exposed. But since his penis was clothed, it is a big gray area, legally speaking.

Board Member Jameson: Practically speaking, how is it possible that he lectured with an erection for an entire fifty-minute class?

Board Member Ransom: Precisely! Ten minutes—perhaps such can be done. But fifty? Impossible! Impossible!

Board Member Bloom: That is why we have asked Professor John Ramos, a toxicologist from our own biology department, to give testimony here today. To find out if such a thing is possible. Professor Ramos, thank you for being here today.

Professor John Ramos: Glad to help.

Board Member Bloom: You've heard the charges. You've also heard the questions. Could there actually be any truth to the charge? Is it at all conceivable that Professor Fichen could lecture for just short of an hour with an erect penis?

Professor John Ramos: It is conceivable, yes. Large doses of maca root, an herbaceous perennial found in the Andes of Bolivia and Peru, would do it. *Epimedium grandiflorum*, a perennial commonly known as horny goat weed and found in southern China, could also conceivably cause one to maintain an erection for hours.

Board Member Bloom: You are personally acquainted with Professor Fichen, are you not? I mean, he is a friend of yours.

Professor John Ramos: Yes, I would say that is true.

Board Member Bloom: Is it not also true that Professor Fichen has recently returned from conducting research in the southern province of Guangdong in the Republic of China?

Professor John Ramos: Yes, that is true.

Board Member Bloom: Is it possible that he obtained this horny goat weed while there and is now using it to produce protracted erection times?

Professor John Ramos: I suppose it's possible, yes.

Board Member Bloom: Prior to his research in China, had you ever known Professor Fichen to have an erection for an hour or more at a time?

Professor John Ramos: No, I have no knowledge of any such erections.

Board Member Bloom: There you have it, esteemed board members. Not only is it possible that Professor Fichen was lecturing with an erection, it seems probable that he was lecturing with an erection.

Planke sets the page aside, unable to read any further. He pulls another of the professor's progress reports from deeper in the pile and reads it.

The work goes slowly, as the perils of the rainforest are many. Our guide, Amaro, has been bitten by some unknown arachnid and totters on the brink of the grave. The others grow weary and grumble of returning to civilization. They say, "Although we search for the elixir of life, we find only the bitter dregs of death." They may be right, but I am determined to continue the search. Perhaps I shall be forced to go on alone. We shall see.

He slides a cigarette from its pack, taps it on the table, and lights it. The phosphorescent blaze illuminates his face in the opaque window, where Planke gazes at the last strands of sunlight streaming from behind Mogollon Rim. He twists in his seat and, catching the waiter's eye, orders another tonic water. Then he returns to the file and locates the final progress report. It's dated April 1937.

I have found it, Arthur! Finally! Chaang! Amrita! Soma! Ambrosia! Served on the back of Hēbē herself to heal the world of its maladies and ailments. I have found it! It is alpha and omega, the beginning and the end, the start and finish. It is in and out, shake it all about; it is up and down, do the hokey pokey and you turn yourself around. Nectar of Bufo, god among the cane, killer of the unworthy disciple. Kali dancing drunk on the bloody slain. This ain't no Popsicle stand, that's for dang sure. This is for real, the real thing, Arthur. Get yer ass down here, now!

John

Presumably, this is where the cult-like activities come in to play, thinks Planke. He flips the file closed, drains his glass, and shuffles down the aisle of the bar car. Back in his passenger's compartment, he sits across from an elderly couple snoring in unison. Planke lets his eyes slide closed and tries to get some sleep. A song loops in his head, somewhere in that shadowy no-man's-land between consciousness and unconsciousness: *You put your right foot in; you put your right foot out . . .*

The ship is called *USNS Bounteous Bole*, which makes not a scrap of sense to Planke unless it is some obscure reference to the dugout canoes of the Pacific Northwest. He finds his berth and deposits his bag before heading up on deck. Merchant marines are everywhere, which makes perfect sense since the ship is the part of the U.S. Merchant Marine fleet. Once out to sea, he settles into his berth and digs into the FBI file for Ramos. There are birth certificates and xerographic passport pages. John César Ramos was the only son of Cristos Carlos Ramos and Petunia Fay Clarke. And Cristos Ramos was the first son of Joseph Vasser and Rosa Ramos. According to the file, the second son, Jesus, committed suicide at twenty-two.

The file also includes fingerprint charts and police records. Joseph Vasser, the paternal grandfather, in particular, has a small police library dedicated to him. There are charges of bigamy in Vermont. And a multiple -page list of alcohol-related charges in Mexico. The final charge, "committing a lewd and lascivious act," jumps out at Planke. He wonders what exactly that might entail. There is a handwritten note scribbled beside the charge: Public execution, August 1904. Cristos Ramos, it turns out, also has a lengthy police record of alcohol-related charges. Apple doesn't fall far from the tree, thinks Planke. A real messed up family, this one.

Petunia Clarke is the daughter of Matthew Clarke, the largest citrus producer in Orange County. The maternal line of the family looks to be scandal free. Scrubbed clean with money, no doubt. How opposites like Cristos Ramos and Petunia Clarke come together, matrimonially speaking, is not explained, although Planke doubts it's any real mystery. He guesses it's the same old story—the spoiled, rebellious daughter out to infuriate the largely absent yet still somehow overbearing father. It begins as innocent flirtations with the hired help and ends in a steamy secret rendezvous. The girl finds herself pregnant and the hired help, fearing for his life, flees the scene of the crime. Or maybe the hired help intends to do the respectable thing but is forcefully dissuaded by daddy money-bags. Sounds about right, thinks Planke. So the bastard child, John Ramos, is raised believing that his father died a war hero in the trenches of some scarred field in France. And Cristos Ramos, the actual flesh-and-blood father, is paid off, made to disappear. Planke pulls out a death certificate for Cristos Ramos. Cause of death: acute cirrhosis of the liver. Presumably, he lived in a gutter somewhere and drank himself into an early grave.

The file has xerographic degrees for John Ramos from the University of Chicago (BSc and MSc) and Harvard (PhD). Planke also finds a letter from Harvard offering Ramos a postdoctoral research position. It seems he turned down Harvard, instead taking a position at Chico State College in 1930. Why he would walk away from Harvard is a mystery. But Planke believes he has the answer when he finds a wrinkled report from a private investigator, Harry Reidman of Reidman Investigations, Los Angeles. The report reveals the location of one Cristos Ramos. It turns out he was indeed drinking himself to death—in the Fillmore District of San Francisco. As proof of this, the report includes a photo of the senior Ramos lying unconscious in the doorway of Jack's Tavern on Sutter Street. The best Planke can figure, John Ramos turned down the position at Harvard in order to return to California to find his besotted father. A bank statement with circled transactions—$400 every month—appears to be proof positive that Ramos supported his father for years, until he died a classic drunkard's death. Somewhere along the way, thinks Planke, the story about the Great War war-hero-father must not have rung true to young John Ramos.

Planke decides to stretch his legs up top. Finding his way on deck, he leans on the gunwale and scans the horizon. There is nothing but an undifferentiated mass of blue in all directions: sea and sky. He pulls the photo of John Ramos from his shirt pocket and wonders what Ramos said to his father when he finally found him in San Francisco. "Nice to see you," or "where've you been," or maybe "let me buy you a drink." Planke suppresses a painful childhood memory of his own father hanging from a shower head in the asylum at Camarillo. He hadn't witnessed the scene himself but stole a peak at the photos in the police file left unattended on the investigating officer's desk. He is still horrified that his father would hang himself with a pair of state-issued Y-front briefs, a detail Planke has always been ashamed of. Why not a belt or shoelace? Why did it have to be a filthy pair of threadbare underwear? But he knows the answer. His father spent the last years of his life in the asylum, disfigured and insane from a particularly nasty case of syphilis he'd picked up while in the Foreign Legion in Northern Africa. As part of an elite squad of "dangerous" nuts and lunatics, the asylum did not issue him a belt or shoelaces, for security reasons. However, this did not deter Planke's father. Someone desperate to die will always find a way it turns out.

Planke never visited his father. And his mother died when he was young in a freak household accident—slipped in the bathroom and bashed her head on the toilet—leaving only him and Aunt Flo. And Aunt Flo refused to let him set foot in the asylum. It was as if she believed the senior Planke's madness to be somehow contagious. Perhaps she feared that her nephew might return home scratching at imaginary fleas and sniffing his own behind, or carrying on long philosophical conversations with a pitcher of homogenized milk, as his father used to do.

Planke heads below deck and stretches out his 6'3'' frame as best he can in the cramped berth. He allows himself to wonder about Aunt Flo for a fleeting moment before he drifts off to sleep.

When the *USNS Bounteous Bole* drops anchor in the Port of Macapá three days later, Planke disembarks and goes in search of accommodations. His plan is to stay two nights in Macapá, during which time he will hire a local guide and procure the necessary supplies, and then start his journey up river on the third day. He finds a suitable hotel built in mission revival style and named *Hotel Cadela no Cio*, which again, does not make a scrap of sense to him. Once settled in to his room, he asks the *velha* at the front desk where he might find a local *taberna*. He waits for the afternoon deluge to conclude before venturing out into the city.

The wet heat makes Planke feel as if he's shriveling into nothing, and the world glistening with rainwater pricks at his eyes. The *taberna* looks like the younger, retarded brother of *Hotel Cadela no Cio*: slightly askance with broken panes of blue-bubbled glass. Planke enters it through a torn screen door. To his surprise, the place is full of black flies and brown-skinned men, pardos with loose-hanging shirts and pocket-less shorts. He checks his watch: 4:00. At the bar, he orders a *cerveja* and asks the barkeep about hiring a guide.

Planke approaches the corner where four men are gathered around a game of mumble-peg. A squat, stocky pardo flings a pocketknife at the floor, where it sticks cleanly near a squatter, stockier pardo's bare big toe. Laughter and backslapping is followed by long pulls from bottles of *cerveja*. The stockier pardo wipes his mouth, retrieves the knife, and palms it confidently. It is at this inopportune moment that Planke decides to speak. "I'm looking for Luís Moreno." All heads turn, just as the knife makes its miscalculated flight and lodges itself in the flesh between the first and second metatarsal bones of the stocky pardo's foot, making a sickening thud as it does. The injured man screeches, stares at his maimed extremity in disbelief, as if the knife might dislodge itself if he looks at it long enough and bellows loud enough. The stockier pardo slaps his stocky opponent with a sweaty palm. "You moved, *idiota!*" He turns to Planke. "I am Luís Moreno. What is it you want?"

Planke finds himself slightly shaken up by the game of mumble-peg that has turned out badly for one competitor. Finally he speaks: "Shouldn't he see a doctor? Or at least pull the knife out?"

"He's fine, *amigo*. Once he calms down, I'll pull it out. A bit of a . . . what is it you say . . . cry-baby."

"You know him?"

"Know him? Ha! That *tolo* is my brother-in-law. And that is only because my sister is *um patinho feio* . . . how to say . . . an ugly duckling. So what is it that you want from me?"

A decrepit-looking steamer with *Começo e Final* painted by hand across its stern chugs laboriously away from the docks of Macapá on the northernmost bend at the mouth of the Amazon River. Luís Moreno is at the helm, both literally and figuratively. He yells out commands in Portuguese that have the crew—his brother-in-law, Mateus, and the four other pardos from the *taberna*—scrambling. Luís is a *caboclo* who is proud of his Portuguese heritage. Planke knows this because Luís has made a point of telling him about his great grandfather, a wealthy Portuguese rubber plantation owner in Manaus, who after ten years alone in the Amazon rainforest decided to wed a local native woman that went on to bear him three daughters and one son. That son, Chico, Luís's grandfather, eventually took over the rubber plantation. But when the rubber boom of the nineteenth century waned, Chico Moreno abandoned his family and was never heard from again. Luís grumbles that had it not been for "the damned Englishman Wickham," he would be a rich plantation owner. Planke knows something of Sir Henry Alexander Wickham. The English explorer stole seeds from a Pará rubber tree on his trip to the Amazon in 1876, and these seeds were later dispatched to Malaysia and Africa, essentially dooming the rubber boom in Brazil.

Planke lights a cigarette and stares out into the dense foliage of the rainforest. He tries to imagine John Ramos, five years earlier, gazing out into this same jungle of tangled vegetation. He drops his eyes to the slow-moving brown current, under which he imagines colossal serpents, whale-sized caimans, and boiling schools of razor-teethed piranhas. Planke sops the sweat from his brow with a blue checkered handkerchief (the impressive multi-colored set was last year's Christmas gift from Aunt Flo). As the *Começo e Final* pushes farther up the river, the world becomes perceptibly darker. Not that the sun has disappeared from the sky; more that the bright light of civilization has been snuffed out by a kind of prehistoric eclipse, or perhaps some modern-age extinction event. He cannot help but wonder why Ramos would want to remain in such a place, in such a state. Planke spent a year in the rainforest of Borneo, and that was more than enough. He wouldn't have stayed another day if you held a gun to his head. It occurs to him then that he and Ramos are not cut from the same cloth. Ramos has the adventurous spark that makes men do the most incredulous things. Perhaps he really has found what he set out to find, Planke thinks—some miraculous elixir dripping from the teat of Mother Nature out here in the middle of nowhere. He stops to ponder the implications of this.

But Planke's impromptu reverie is interrupted by a choleric outburst of Portuguese expletives. Luís Moreno is pointing to a plume of steam hissing from a pipe's cracked seal. Mateus jumps to attention and locates a massive pipe wrench that standing on end reaches his waist. A struggle between him, the wrench, and the pipe ensues, but finally Mateus manages to stem the breach. A proud grin overtakes his now ruddy mug, as he gives his brother-in-law an eager thumbs-up. But Luís Moreno is too busy twisting knobs and tapping gauges to notice.

When nightfall sets in, the crew drop down and slumber on the deck. Only the captain of the vessel remains upright and alert at the helm. Planke has brought a proper sleeping bag but decides to dispense with it for the time being. He slouches down onto the deck and, tipping his head back, examines the wildly sparkling Amazonian sky. The forest all around is still but not quiet. Planke knows that half the species in a rainforest come alive after sunset—the nightshift coming on, so to speak. A long hollow growl echoes off in the distance, a sound which grows perceptibly louder as they move up river. Planke has never encountered such a booming, primitive sound before, not even in Borneo. He tries to get the captain's attention by lighting another cigarette. The match fizzles into his fingertips.

"What's that?" he finally asks,

"What, amigo?" replies Luís Moreno.

"You know—that. The sound."

"Oh, that. Howlers."

"Howlers?"

"Monkeys. Don't worry, amigo. They're *inofensivo* . . . how you say . . . harmless. They stay high in the trees. They don't come down."

Planke extinguishes his cigarette and decides to get some sleep, but the collective snore of the crew conspires against him. It finally occurs to him that the reason he can now hear the somnambular sounds of the crew with such great clarity is that the howlers have stopped, which leads him to believe that the boat has passed the *inofensivo* monkeys.

He begins to drift off, just as a loud splat hits the deck near his feet. Planke leaps up and assumes a ready position. In the dim deck light, the offending splat looks to be something brown, flat, and probably dead. By now, the rest of the crew are also on their feet, mumbling and cursing. Another splat punctuates the silence and one of the crew screams: "*Merda!*"

Suddenly, the whole ship is under attack. Splats are hitting everywhere, dropping like fist-sized balls of hail. "*Merda! Merda!*" cry the men. Before he knows what is happening, Planke is hit in the chest and knocked off his feet. Only when the fowl stench overtakes him does he realize that the ship is being bombarded with monkey shit. "*Merda de macaco! Merda de macaco!*" bellows Luís Moreno. "Take cover!"

Planke scurries for cover behind a forty-five gallon drum, just as a gunshot rips through the mayhem. He peers out long enough to get a glimpse of Mateus swinging a rifle and firing indiscriminately at the night sky. "*Filho da puta!*" A deluge of shredded leaves rains down on the boat. Above the splats and gunshots, Planke can hear Luís Moreno bellowing at his *imbecil* brother-in-law to stop shooting. But it is to no avail. And when a brown glob hits Mateus square in the face all hell breaks loose.

"*Meus olhos! Meus olhos!*" Mateus drops the rifle, which fires on impact. A loud clang rings in Planke's ears, as a bullet ricochets off the steel drum. He peers from behind it, just in time to witness Mateus dropping to his knees, clutching at his chest. "*Puta macacos!*" The first mate topples face-first onto the deck. And for a moment all is silent. Planke can only assume that the shots have scattered the howlers. Slowly, the other pardos gather around the dead man, staring, mouths agape. Luís Moreno pushes a lever and releases the clutch, letting the engine free wheel, then shuffles over to his brother-in-law. The captain of the *Começo e Final* turns the dead man over with the toe of a worn gray canvas shoe.

"Ah, Mateus. So finally it happens," says he, matter-of-factly, without a trace of sadness. "He had the fear of monkeys. They were after him . . . out to get him." Luís Moreno turns to walk away, and then calls over his shoulder. "Throw him overboard."

Planke thinks this beyond callous. "What? That's it?"

"What would you have us do? Build him a casket? Or maybe flay him and hack him up into steaks? We are not *bárbaros, senhor* Planke, but it is best to throw him overboard."

"What about some kind of . . . I don't know . . . funeral service or something of the sort?"

Luís Moreno swings furiously about-face, as if expecting this resistance. "Ha! Mateus was a godless *imbecil*! No funeral is going to change that. What god would want him, anyway?" The captain smiles as if joking, but Planke suspects he's not. "Throw him overboard. It is better for everyone. Trust me."

Signs of civilization appear as they near Manaus. Day four on the Amazon River and the crew have only been ashore once. The captain decides to stop for provisions and minor repairs. Although Planke is outwardly opposed to stopping now, part of him thinks it might be prudent to let the men run amok on shore for a spell. Last night, he heard what sounded like the grunts and groans of rutting animals on board the ship.

Luís Moreno still has family in Manaus, and he persuades Planke to accompany him to the home of his youngest sister, Anitia. Only as they approach the village does it occur to Planke that he may have been recruited to help break the sad news to Anitia that she has been recently widowed.

The house is little more than a rickety shack. *Ramshackle* is the word that springs to Planke's mind. Anitia is pegging laundry to a length of jute twine strung between two bulletwood trees. Luís Moreno takes her in his arms and holds her close in what seems an interminable show of affection. Planke is beginning to feel uncomfortable when finally Anitia breaks free.

"Dear sister, this is *senhor* Planke. I am taking him to Tres Fronteras."

Anitia greets him with an even white smile. At that moment, Planke re- alizes that Luís Moreno has lied—if his sister ever was an ugly duckling, she is not now. Quite the opposite, in fact. Try as he might, Planke cannot wrap his head around the idea of Anitia and the *imbecil* Mateus together, matrimonially speaking.

"I have some bad news for you, *irmãzinha*. It's Mateus. The monkeys finally got him. We had to throw his body overboard. I am sorry."

Anitia says nothing, closes her eyes and traces a cross in the air. A tear gathers and stutters down the side of her perfectly slender nose.

"Do not worry. We will find you another. Men like Mateus are *às dúzias*."

Planke feels the captain's gaze shift to him.

"Now get us something cold to drink, *irmã menor*.

Anitia disappears into the shack.

"You said your sister was an ugly duckling," says Planke.

Luís Moreno half guffaws, half snorts. "Ha! That is my little joke. Ugly ducking . . . get it?"

Planke shakes his head.

"It's . . . how you say . . .?"

"Ironic," says Planke.

"Ah, *amigo*. So you do get it."

"No, Luís, I don't get it."

That night they drink a jug of sour, sticky wine made from jabuticaba berries. In no time, Planke's head feels like a gas giant, complete with baffling rings. He finds an empty cot and there gives into a black-sludge sleep that sucks him down to torpid depths.

He is not quite asleep when a hotly whispered word scorches his cheek: "*Desperte, senhor Planke. Desperte.*" In the darkness, Planke shrugs it off, attributes it to auditory hallucinations brought on by an abundance of alcohol. Until he feels a cool breeze blowing over his privates. And something cold and hard pressed there. Suddenly, Planke is wide awake and staring at a straight razor poised to lop off his flaccid member. Anitia looks crazy in the moonlight. A stunning lunatic, Planke thinks. She strokes him until his traitorous prick stands hard against the bristling edge of the razor.

"Where is my husband?" she asks.

"Mateus?"

"Yes, Mateus. What did Luís do to him?"

"Luís? Nothing. Nothing at all." Planke gulps hard.

"Are you sure? Was it really the monkeys? Did the monkeys get him?"

"Well . . . yes, I . . . yes they did. The monkeys got him."

Anitia sighs and releases the hostage. "The monkeys again."

"Again?"

"Mateus was my third husband. The other two . . . the monkeys got them."

"What? That's insane. Monkeys got all three of your husbands."

"Insane, *senhor*? Yes, insane but true. The monkeys got them all. It is a curse upon the Moreno women. The monkeys get their husbands. Mateus was terrified. He believed in the curse, the others didn't."

"He believed in the curse, and he still married you?"

"Well . . . yes, *senhor*," Anitia flutters her eyelids in the moonlight. "Look at me."

"Right. Good point," says Planke.

She drops her gaze. "Still *ereto*."

Planke is not sure whether he's embarrassed or excited by the remark. "Yes, it seems so."

Anitia slips the thin nightdress from off her shoulders and lets it fall noiselessly to the floor. She straddles him, taking him in with a slight gasp. Planke bucks, jolts his head back, and ejaculates.

"Whoops."

Anitia smiles. "Just like my Mateus."

Planke is not sure he likes being told he fucks like a dead man. "Give me five minutes . . . I can do better."

A day west of Manaus, *Começo e Final* turns south, entering the Purus River, a major tributary of the Amazon. Although Planke hasn't asked, Luís Moreno explains that it is the longest of all tributaries—twisting and serpentine, yet relatively mild, especially when compared to Madeira River, a spirited and dangerous tributary renowned for its treacherous falls. The Purus runs deep into the Amazon Basin, deep into the damp and tropical heart of the rainforest. A green tangle of vines, bushes, and overhanging trees hems the river in, encroaches on its silent pilgrimage to the sea. Planke has the feeling they are sailing into the open maw of some mythic beast that's about to snap its jaws shut at any moment, trapping them forever in the bowels of this prehistoric world.

"Tell me about the monkey curse on the Moreno women."

Luís Moreno's turns in surprise. "You know about that, *senhor* Planke?"

"Your sister mentioned it to me."

"Ah... while she was fixed on your *pau gordo* , no doubt."

Planke protests: "Now hold on—"

"My mother . . . wife of Afonso Moreno . . . was about to give birth to her first child and only son, me, Luís. But there was a problem. I was turned the wrong way, with my *bunda* . . . how you say . . . ass first. A shaman was called to save me. The old woman took one look at my mother and knew just what to do. She poured a handful of ground jaguar bones into a bowl. Then she slit mother's hand with a knife and drew blood, which she mixed with the white powder into a pink paste. Next, from out of her pouch she pulled the shriveled black hand of a monkey, which, I am told, looked like a stiff rubber glove. She dipped each finger of the monkey hand into the paste. Then she said a prayer to the Earth Goddess in a shaky voice and threw the hand into the fire. Heavy smoke filled the room, and before it cleared the old shaman had cut me out of my mother's womb and was cradling me in her bony arms." Luís Moreno paused to light his pipe.

"Did your mother die?" asks Planke, digging a cigarette from a badly crumpled pack.

"No. *Minha mãe* was fine."

"So, what about the curse then?"

"When you or someone in your family is healed by a shaman, it is tradition to make an offering to the shaman. Whatever it is they ask of you, that is what you give. They may ask for a dozen chickens, or two goats, or even your gold watch. You give it to them. So, my father labored up the mountain to see the old shaman in order to learn what offering he should make her. The old woman said she wanted a monkey hand like the one she threw into the fire."

"Seems reasonable enough," says Planke. "And did your father get her this monkey hand?"

"No, *senhor*. Monkeys are not so hard to catch, and people in the forest kill them often—eat them and keep the hands, heads, and other parts. But my father is *desatento* . . . how you say . . . muddleheaded . . . and he forgets about the monkey hand. So, the years went by, and my mother had three daughters. These daughters, my sisters, grew up and got married, but they all lost their husbands to the monkeys. It became clear to my father that someone had put a curse on the Moreno daughters. But who? That was the question"

"The shaman?"

"Yes. Father visited the old woman. She was near a century old by then. He asked her who has put a curse on his daughters, and the old shaman told him the truth . . . that she had cursed the Moreno women and he had brought the curse on his daughters because he refused to make an offering to her."

Planke blows a gray plume of smoke skyward. "So what did your father do next?"

"Nothing. He left. But not long after that day, the old woman died suddenly and violently."

"Your father?"

"No one knows for sure, but the old woman had a monkey hand stuffed into her mouth, so my guess, *senhor*—it was him. He finally got the old shaman her monkey hand."

Planke flicks his cigarette into the river. He is at a loss. It's not even disbelief so much as simply speechlessness. How does one react to such a revelation? he wonders. The ship's captain has just told him his father murdered a centenarian shaman with a monkey's hand. Planke says nothing. Then he shakes his head and makes to walk away.

"But wait, here's the best part," says Luís Moreno. "Now that you have *conhecimento carnal* of my sister the curse may be upon your head."

"What? No. Not possible. I don't subscribe to that superstitious mummery." Planke realizes that in this declaration, he has just admitted to having *conhecimento carnal* of Luís Moreno's sister.

"Still, a word to the wise, *senhor* Planke… beware the monkeys."

Two days later, the *Começo e Final* drops anchor at a small village Luís Moreno calls Tapauá. The crew lowers a flat-bottomed boat over the side and prepares to row ashore. It is then that Planke notices a group of naked young men—*índios*, the crew call them—lining the west bank of the river.

"Why are we stopping?" asks Planke. "What's here that we need further delay our trip up river?"

"Fresh meat," says the captain.

Planke is uncertain as to whether Luís Moreno is referring to the youths on the river bank or actual fresh meat, something they haven't had for some time, but he decides not to ask. The captain tugs on a big black knob in the center of the control panel, cutting the engine, and slips past Planke. "You coming? Or do you want to stay out here alone on the river?"

Once ashore, they are mobbed by the young men, who, Planke can't help noticing, have various gewgaws of ornamentation dangling from their pierced foreskins and scrotums. The young *índios* squeal with delight at seeing the ship's crew, leading Planke to assume that this is not the first time the *Começo e Final* has dropped anchor at Tapauá.

The rest of the village seems equally delighted to see them. Had Planke not spent a year among the indigenous peoples of Borneo, he may have been shocked by the appearance of the Brazilian *índios*. The men, also with a dangling assortment of penile paraphernalia, sport half-shorn heads and painted faces. Long sharp quills pierce their noses, lips, and cheeks. The women are painted and bare-breasted with small garments hanging from their shapeless hips. Luís Moreno talks to one of the men, who responds by leading them to a large communal hut. Following several minutes of discussion and lively debate, the captain tells him it has been decided that a traditional hunt will be held in their honor on the following day.

"But that would mean staying the night ashore," says Planke. "It is unacceptable. I can't allow it."

"Just one night, *senhor* Planke," says Luís Moreno. "This John Ramos you seek is not going anywhere, I assure you. He is either dead or *tornou se nativo* . . . how you say . . . gone native . . . a forest dweller. I have seen this kind of thing before."

"That's not the point—"

"Besides, we will never get the crew back aboard the ship."

Only then, at the mention of the crew, does Planke notice that the men of the *Começo e Final* have disappeared into the forest with the clutch of squealing young men. "What are they doing?" he asks.

"Who knows?" replies Luís Moreno. "They *fodem jovens homossexuais*. The folds of a woman are not for every man, *senhor* Planke."

"So it seems."

"But relax. It is only for one day. Besides, you might enjoy the hunt. It *descarga de adrenalina* . . . how you say . . . gets the adrenaline flowing."

With dawn sifting through the trees, Planke half-heartedly creeps over the forest floor, a long narrow spear in hand. The shaft seems flimsy to him, and he wonders if it would actually stop a charging animal. He consoles himself with the fact that he has—without giving offense—avoided donning a loin cloth, unlike Luís Moreno, who seems to be thoroughly enjoying the near exposure of his scantily wrapped genitalia.

"What exactly are we looking for?"

"Anything, *senhor* Planke."

"Anything?"

"Anything that's big enough to jab on a spit. These *índios* will eat a stone if it has four legs and tail." Luís Moreno kicks a round stone demonstratively. "The key is *dissimulação* . . . how you say . . . stealth."

From somewhere nearby comes the unmistakable whoop and holler of bloodlust, that timeworn battle cry of the perpetually predacious. Luís Moreno breaks into a trot and disappears into the bush. Planke plods on with spear upright in hand, as if it were his walking stick, waiting for the sound of a deathblow. He hears a high-pitched squeal, sees a rustle in the bushes. By the time he notices the creature charging him through a thicket of heavy shrubs it's too late to move. A fuzzy piglet-sized rodent nearly knocks him off his feet. Planke narrowly sidesteps the frenzied creature.

But it is a strange barking noise above him that really has Planke's attention. When he tips his head skyward to search for the source of the sound, he finds himself suddenly smothered in brown fur. Planke tries to free himself from the clutches of this forest evil that has befallen him but is unable to break the diabolical beast's grip. The struggle that ensues leaves him fighting for air. Planke wobbles on two shaky legs and claws at the world around him. But it is to no avail. Then, just as the black bubbles of unconsciousness begin to burst before his eyes, the malodorous assailant goes limp and drops to the forest floor with a dull thud, leaving Planke bent at the waist, arms akimbo, gasping for air. It is a timely deliverance, to be sure. But Planke soon realizes that all is not well when a sharp pain tweaks his thigh, burning like the fiery tooth of a raptor. He looks down at the feathered dart sticking there. Before he can give voice to his present disbelief, Planke is again overcome by the black bubbles of unconsciousness, floating in a large, ominous cloud this time. And when that cloud bursts, Planke feels himself pitch forward and tumble toward earth in a sloppy free fall.

When he finally comes to, Planke sits up and asks for water. He feels as if he's been feeding at the edge of a cold fire pit and his brain is a meringue of soot and ash. The events of the past day—or days, he's not sure which— remain submerged in a black tar pit of mystery, preserved, and awaiting discovery in some future eon.

"How long have I been out?" he asks.

Luís Moreno, as always, is perched with an air of authority behind the control panel of the ship. "Not counting the first day, when we thought you were dead, three days."

"What? Sweet Jesus! What happened back there?"

"I warned you, *senhor* Planke, beware the monkeys."

"You're trying to tell me a monkey shot me with a dart gun?" This sudden recollection surprises Planke. And Louis Moreno.

"Oh, you remember that? No, the monkey did not shoot you. You see, a brown spider monkey made an *ataque de emboscada* . . . how you say . . . a sneak attack. The first dart missed the monkey, but the second killed the little *desgraçado*."

"Okay. But who shot me with the dart?" demanded Planke.

"*Senhor*, what does it matter? It was a mistake. And that second dart saved you from the monkey."

"You shot me with a poison dart, didn't you?"

"You can't fire me, *senhor*. We have a deal. Besides, now you are protected."

"What do you mean—protected?"

Luís Moreno points. Planke follows the trajectory of the captain's finger to the shriveled black pouch hanging around his neck. He fights the urge to rip the pouch off and throw it overboard. "What is it?" Planke asks.

"It is . . . *colhões de macaco*," says Luís Moreno with a grin. "How you say . . . monkey balls."

Planke believes he has discovered the first signs of John Ramos near the village of Pauini. According to the locals, *um pajé branco*—a white shaman—once lived in the forest near their village, but he left abruptly a year earlier. Planke's gut tells him the white shaman and John Ramos are one and the same person. There are also rumors of *um porco branco*—a white hog—who lives with a small group of *caceteiros*, "men with clubs," farther up the river, north of Boca do Acre. But no one seems to know if *o pajé branco* is also *o porco branco*. Planke wonders if *um porco branco* could be Ramos. In all the photos he has seen, Ramos is as tall and lanky as a lamppost—hardly a hog.

A man with two black holes where his ears should be and half a nose leads them to the abandoned shack of *o porco branco* in the forest. The guide's disfigurement is jarring at first. Just as Planke is getting used to it, he notices that the man is also missing several fingers and toes. The ravages of leprosy, he guesses.

"This is Albert," says Luís Moreno.

"His name is Albert?"

"Well . . . no . . . it's *um nome ridículo* . . . how you say . . . a ridiculous *índio* name that no one can say. So let's just call him Albert."

"Oh."

"You're wondering what happened to Albert?"

"No."

"Yes you are, *senhor*. I can see it. You think . . . some horrible illness . . . maybe lepra— . . . how you say . . . "

"Leprosy," says Planke. "And no, I wasn't thinking that."

"But it is not leprosy, *senhor*. Albert is *um amputado* . . . how you say . . . "

"An amputee? My God! What kind of barbarians would do such a thing to another human being?"

"Oh no, *senhor* Planke," says Luís Moreno. "You misunderstand me. Albert *amputou* his own ears and nose and fingers and toes."

"Why in God's name would he do such a thing?"

"You mean you don't know? For money, of course."

"People pay to see him lop off parts of his body?"

"Of course, *senhor*. Why else would he lop off parts of his body, as you say?"

Inside the white shaman's shack, wilted bouquets of leaves, roots, and flowers dangle from a string looped over the dilapidated structure's single window. A porcelain mortar and pestle, a crucible, a Bunsen burner and tongs all lie scattered on the counter. Broken test tubes and beakers crunch beneath the soles of his feet. To Planke's delight, a sizable stash of field notes slump undisturbed in a makeshift bookcase. "Eureka," cries he. A quick glance at the books tells him that *o pajé branco*, as suspected, was indeed John Ramos. Planke thumbs through them. The early notes are ordered, thorough—just as one would expect from a scientist such as Ramos. This in stark contrast to the later notes, which are sporadic and obtuse, at best. The final book of notes is full of gibberish and cartoonesque drawings. In one, a man with an exaggerated penis licks himself with an exaggerated tongue; under it, a caption reads: "Lollipop, lollipop where is thy sting?" A closer look at the lollipop reveals that it is not your garden-variety lollipop. This lollipop is a toad on a stick. Planke flips to the final page. There is a drawing of another toad lollipop. Scribbled all around it is the word *Hēbē*.

Planke digs into his satchel and pulls out the last progress report Ramos sent to Arthur Hendry. His eye zooms in one line: *Served on the back of Hēbē herself to heal the world of its maladies and ailments.* From his undergraduate days, Planke recalls that Hēbē was the daughter of Zeus and the cupbearer for the gods and goddesses on Mount Olympus, serving goblets of ambrosia. Exactly what she had to do with Ramos's research, he couldn't say. Equally puzzling was why Ramos associated her with the toad lollipops in his cartoonesque drawings. Planke squints, puckers his lips at the mystery of it all.

Taken as a whole, the field notes clearly chronicle the mental decline of a genius to a sophomoric knucklehead. But on the bright side, the field notes are exactly what he has been sent to find by Arthur Hendry and his Chico State cronies. These eight bound notebooks contain five years' worth of research. Planke knows he can turn around right now and return to

California if he so desires. But he also knows that John Ramos has gotten under his skin, and he can no more turn around and walk away than he can return to Chico State and take a lecturing position. Ramos clearly believed he had found something important. *I have found it, Arthur! Finally! Chaang! Amrita! Soma! Ambrosia!* the professor wrote to Hendry. And Planke now finds himself curious—more than curious. He is almost desperate to learn just what it is Ramos has discovered, a sudden revelation that Planke finds somewhat surprising. With no more than three or four days travel between him and Tres Fronteras, he is simply too close to turn back now.

"Is this what you are looking for, *senhor* Planke?" says Luís Moreno.

"Well, yes and no."

"Does this mean our voyage is *concluída* . . . finished?"

"No. We go on to Boca do Acre to find *o pajé branco*."

"But *senhor*, why do you believe *o pajé branco* is this John Ramos you search for? There are many *norte-americanos* down here . . . all looking to make *dinheiro fácil* . . . how you say . . . easy money."

"It's just a feeling I have," says Planke. "Besides, Captain Moreno, have you forgotten that the deal was to take me to Tres Fronteras?"

"No, *senhor*, I have not forgotten. I will gather the men before they find something with *um cu firme*."

Ten miles from Boca do Acre, the forest becomes noticeably still. Planke, half expecting to be bombarded with fist-sized grenades of monkey shit, keeps one eye on the branches overhead, while scanning the riverbanks with binoculars for signs of human life. Something there catches his eye: he focuses in on a plank of plywood nailed to a tree. Squinting hard, he discerns a single English word scrawled in red paint: *HELP!!!*

Luís Moreno, who believes it to be a trap, drops anchor only after much protestation. The crew lower the flat-bottomed boat over the edge of the ship but refuse to row Planke ashore. "*Caceteiros, caceteiros,*" they keep repeating. Planke is well aware of what *caceteiro* means, yet he is also aware that the white hog is rumored to be living among the men with clubs. And if the white hog is indeed a bloated John Ramos, then the mysterious cry for help could be his. In which case, Planke feels both professionally and personally obliged to take appropriate action and assist the professor in any way possible.

Luís Moreno stops rowing long enough to pat his brow with a soiled shirttail, the same which hails from the same sleeveless cotton T-shirt he has been wearing day and night since the voyage began. Planke, pleased and relieved that the captain has reluctantly agreed to accompany him, spells Luís Moreno off, manually propelling the craft through the brown waters of the Purus toward shore.

They ground the boat on a sandbar and start inland with a kind of cautious haste. A yellow-throated toucan announces their arrival with a series of emphatic squawks, seemingly unaware of the emerald tree boa biding its time not five feet away in an invisible green clump. A copper-colored centipede scampers across the trail in front of Planke.

"Be careful of that one," says Luís Moreno. "Giant Amazon centipede. *Venenosa* . . . how you say . . . poisonous sting. Very painful. You know what we always say—there are a thousand and one ways to die in the Amazon, a thousand of them painful."

Planke bites: "And what is the one way to die that's not painful?"

"What?"

"You said there are a thousand and one ways to die in the Amazon, a thousand of them painful. So what's the one way to die that is not painful?"

"Oh, that," said Luís Moreno. "Heart attack. But not to worry, *senhor* Planke. I have lived in the Amazon my whole life. I know her like a lover knows the moles on his beloved's back."

Planke pulls up mid-stride and turns to consider his companion in a new light. "Very poetic, Captain Moreno. Bordering on romantic, even."

"Oh, yes. She will take you into her *lombos verdes* . . . how you say—her green loins, oh yes. But she will not let you go. She will rip off your *pau* . . . how you say . . . *pau*, ah yes—prick."

A mile later, they come across a hut with its roof blown off. The flagging door looks like to have been hacked from the same sheet of plywood as the sign Planke saw earlier. There are no windows, to speak of, just sizeable gaps in the structure's construction. Luís Moreno presses a finger to his lips then picks up a stone and tosses it over the front wall. A woolly opossum squeezes under a crack at the foundation and scuttles away into the bush. Assuming the coast is clear, the captain of the *Começo e Final* pushes the door open and steps into the hut.

"*Meu Deus!*" says Luís Moreno.

"What is it?" Planke shuffles by. Slumped in the corner is a human skeleton, not a stitch of clothing or a scrap of flesh left on it.

"I think there is your John Ramos."

Planke steps into the hut. An unfamiliar tightness cinches up around his chest, squeezing, making breathing difficult. He can't believe it, doesn't want to believe it. How can the great John Ramos, the same whose greatness Planke has unconsciously blown up to heroic proportions, even to Herculean heights, come to such an ignominious end? It is not possible, thinks Planke.

Luís Moreno squats by the skeleton and swabs his brow with his shirttail. "Look at this, *senhor.*"

"What?"

"A hole in the skull. This man was killed by a club. Looks like *os caceteiros* got to him."

Planke examines the hole. It's almost big enough to fit his fist through. It strikes him then, at that moment—the indignity of death. There really is no good death. Nobody looks good, together, or composed when they are dead. It always seems a bit foolish—dying, thinks Planke. Almost as if the deceased should have somehow known better or done something differently so as not to end up in such a compromising position. And make no mistake, there is no position more compromising than sitting skeletally bare in the middle of a rainforest. The thought makes him uneasy about crowding in and leaning over the dead man, looking for a cause of death as if he were looking under the hood of his Plymouth motorcar and wonder ing why it refused to turn over.

"*Dentes robustus,*" says Luís Moreno. "A man who dies with all his teeth dies too young . . . or maybe he just hasn't lived enough." The captain grins, exposing a well-experienced smile: a front gold crown, a chipped canine, two missing incisors, top and bottom, and a sizeable black hole left by an absent molar. The sight of it causes Planke to recall something significant. He pulls out a handful of photos from his satchel and flips through them. "Yes, yes, yes!"

"Yes what, *senhor* Planke?"

"In every one of these photos, beginning as far back as Harvard, John Ramos is smoking a pipe."

"And?"

"And, do you know what years of pipe-smoking will do to a man's front teeth?"

"Of course, yes," says Luís Moreno, opening his foul maw once again.

Planke snaps open the jaw of the skeleton and points dramatically, as if an attorney who has just introduced exonerating evidence.

"These teeth look good as new. This man couldn't have smoked a pipe. So—"

"This is not John Ramos," says Luís Moreno.

"Exactly! Which means we keep looking."

"I was afraid you were going to say that, *senhor*," says Luís Moreno, snapping his own jaw shut.

With sunset huffing down the deciduous neck of the forest's billowy canopy, they decide to stay the night in the hut and resume their search in the morning. Luís Moreno has his back propped against the wall; a rifle stands upright between his legs. The firelight animates his already slightly clownish features.

"You know . . . my sister . . . she likes you. And you know she's got no husband now."

Planke looks up from the field notes he has been thumbing through. "I know. I was there when Mateus was killed. Remember?" He returns to the book, adding: "She hardly knows me."

"Oh yes, but she is a good judge of *caráter.* . . how you say . . ."

"I know, character," Planke interjects. "With three husbands, I guess she's had a bit of practice." Only as he utters it, does Planke realize that it is a somehow a sore point for him. And perhaps Luís Moreno, too.

"But the monkeys got them. They were not my sister's fault, *senhor.*"

"Yes, I know. I didn't mean to suggest that it was her fault . . . any of it."

"But you . . . you have survived the monkey curse . . . you might be the one who doesn't die. You might be the one to make her happy."

A heavy morning mist obscures the trail ahead, as the sun tracks them from a distant slant. Luís Moreno seems oblivious to this almost daily occurrence. Moisture sticks to Planke's face, bare arms, and legs. They sweep through the fog, heading further inland with no clear destination in mind. But the path they tread upon is well worn, a detail which convinces Planke they are heading in the right direction. Surely, it leads somewhere, he thinks. Then it's simply a matter of asking the locals about *o porco branco.*

The light is dim yet somehow alive and teeming with vitality. In that moment, Planke imagines how Ramos must have felt. Life, with its seemingly infinite number of permutations, exists here. It's as if evolution has simply passed the rainforest by, as if Darwin could never have conceived of such a place. Unimaginable creatures thus far untouched, unsorted and ignored by natural selection—they all exist here in abundance, side by side. Evolutionary fitness, it would seem, runs rampant in this rainforest. Flora and fauna that have no business in a modern age, all mad experiments in genotypes, abound here, burgeoning with the secrets of the universe. Planke decides that this is what Ramos must have so keenly felt, being here, and Planke himself cannot help but sense the same, traipsing over the forest floor. Everything humans can ever hope to learn about themselves, about their world, is right here—extant, animate, demonstrative, effusive. Man the animal, top of the food chain, and every other chain. Yet still somehow managing to sit dumb, blind, and deaf in that precarious if privileged position.

This reverie is interrupted by the sudden realization that they are being followed. Planke rotates his head forty-five degrees and there in his peripheral vision stands a figure. Not one figure, he quickly surmises, perhaps two. Or maybe three. Stopping abruptly, he turns on his heels and comes face-to-face with a half dozen *caceteiros*. He knows this because large clubs of burnished wood dangle loosely in their fists.

"Luís, we have company."

Captain Moreno swings around, props the rifle against his shoulder, and squints down the barrel. "*Não movam, desgraçados!*" One of the *caceteiros* snickers a response, causing the others to join in. Before long, they are all chortling loudly.

"They don't look like they mean to do us any harm," says Planke.

"Leave this to me, *senhor*."

"But look at them. They can hardly stand from laughing. And they're dressed like, I don't know, mice or something." Planke points out the blackened noses, the quill whiskers, and the little rounded ears fashioned out of dried roots and pale green shoots.

Luís Moreno stops squinting and assesses the situation with both eyes open. "I think you are right." He lowers his weapon. "There's something wrong with them. I think they are *muito bêbados* . . . how you say . . . blind drunk."

"I have to agree with you there. Say something to them."

"What, *senhor*? They will not understand me."

"Ask them about the white hog . . . *o porco branco*."

This provokes an immediate reaction. The *caceteiros* collapse to the ground, prostrate and mumbling incantations to *o porco branco*. Another word also jumps out at Planke.

"*Hēbē, Hēbē* . . . is that what you're saying?" The sound of the word causes the *caceteiros* to redouble their incantatory efforts. He turns to Luís Moreno. "Do you know what this means?"

"No, *senhor*."

"Look at how they react to the mere mention of *o porco branco*."

"Yes, perhaps *o porco branco* is here somewhere. But how do you know it the John Ramos you search for?"

"Listen. Do you hear that? *Hēbē*, they're saying. Ramos wrote of *Hēbē* to Arthur Hendry. *Served on the back of Hēbē herself* . . . he wrote in his last letter. He's here—I know it. Tell them to take us to the white hog."

Luís Moreno turns to the prostrate *caceteiros* and bellows: "*Guia-nos para o porco branco!*"

The *caceteiros* lead them down the trail for another thirty minutes, Planke guesses. They arrive at a village that is suspended above ground, in the trees, save for a single communal structure, much like the longhouse of American Indians in the North Pacific region, notes Planke. Bare-breasted women chatter around a pot stewing languidly over an open fire. When they spy the intruders, they scamper up dangling green vines with their nimble arms in a way that makes Planke think of primates. They peer from their shelters as if they have never seen another human before, as if they themselves were not quite human.

Only a young boy remains on the ground, naked, taunting a mongrel dog, oblivious to the outsiders' presence. Planke guesses the child to be three or four years old. The little fellow giggles as he tugs on the tail of the mutt, which responds with a ferocious-sounding but otherwise harmless growl. The *caceteiros* take great delight in the child's amusing antic and their collective disposition again turns mirthful. Snorts and giggles erupt in small pockets among them. Planke can't help but wonder at the *caceteiros'* reputation for ferocity and savagery. So far, he can detect no trace of it. Before long, the boy and his mutt have the men in stitches. Luís Moreno gives Planke a sidelong glance, as if to say this is all *muito estranho* . . . how you say . . . very strange.

Suddenly the laughter stops and the men drop to a prostrate position, reprising their earlier incantations. Planke turns to see who or what has instigated the present bout of worshipful adulation, only to behold a massive man covered in white paint and wearing nothing but a loin cloth and a shriveled pig's nose. Two large boar tusks hang around his neck on a hide string. This can be none other than the white hog, thinks Planke. There is only the vaguest remnant of shocked hair that Planke recalls from the photographs, and the face seems bloated and stretched out of proportion—as is the midriff—but clearly this is John Ramos, or at least some loony three-hundred-pound version of him.

Planke is unsure what to say, or where to even start. Now face-to-face with the great John Ramos, he realizes that the professor is not bigger-than-life, although he is certainly bigger than a lot of other things. Could this be the highly regarded professor whose life he has feverishly studied down to the minutest detail? Or the young genius who once turned down a position at Harvard, instead traveling to California and to a no-name college in order to be near to—to care for—his alcoholic father? Is this the passionate researcher who sought to rid the world of sickness and disease? No, this is a lunatic, a man clearly insane. This is the white hog. *O porco branco.*

"Professor Ramos, my name is Planke, Tom Planke. You're a hard man to find."

Ramos appears visibly shaken and a long pause follows. Planke attributes the reaction to his being addressed as "Professor Ramos" in his mother tongue. After a lengthy pause, *o porco branco* responds. "Perhaps I did not wish to be found."

"Well, for what it's worth, I considered that possibility. It's just that there's a group of uptight college bureaucrats back at Chico State who want to know what happened to the research you were doing down here. Do you know how long it's been? I mean, do you have any idea how long it's been since anyone back in civilization has heard from you?"

"Civilization," he spits the word as if a rind of gristle unworthy of mastication. "What have I to do with civilization?"

"What about the elixir of life, the cure for sickness and disease. That's what brought you here in the first place."

"Ah, yes, that." He pops off the pig's nose as if he were a clown who suddenly wished to be taken seriously. "I have found the elixir of life, but it's not the cure-all that you—that *they*—expect."

"I don't understand," says Planke.

"There is time to talk later. But now it is time to eat. Join us for a modest meal." He turns to the young boy, who is now riding bareback atop the mongrel mutt. "Willy, come." The young boy dismounts and skips over to the white hog. "This is my son, William—Willy."

Planke bends to shake the boy's hand, noting that, unlike the women, he has no fear of outsiders. Willy smiles pleasantly and says something in the native tongue of the *caceteiro*—a primitive sounding language, all glottal and palatal.

Ramos twists his tumultuous weight and barks orders. The women respond by descending from the trees and dishing up steaming bowls from the pot.

"And this is Willy's mother Maya." She smiles. Planke can't help but notice Luís Moreno shamelessly eyeing her jiggling breasts. She holds out a bowl. The stew smells appetizing—a broth with meat and vegetables. It's been days since Planke has had a hot meal.

The three men retire to the longhouse. The white hog lowers his considerable girth onto a tall wooden stool covered in jaguar hide and adorned with spiky antlers and smooth horns, and digs in to the stew. Clearly, *o porco branco's* stool is a throne, of sorts, as the others are nothing more than bare, squat stumps. Planke follows the professor's lead and eats with his hands. The vegetables are soft and bland, and the meat, although greasy, is tasty just the same. This prompts Planke to ask about the main ingredient.

"Tamarin . . . small monkey. Delicacy," say Ramos, already gnawing on a bone.

Planke glances at Luís Moreno, who, unaffected by the revelation, is busily shoveling stew into his gullet. "*Gostoso*," says the captain, with a full mouth.

Planke spends the remainder of the day wandering around, observing the locals. The village is small. Perhaps fifty adults, in all. He has only seen Willy so has no idea how many children live there. Some of the women tend to a teeming garden, gathering mandioquinha roots, acorn squash, and butter beans. Others haul water in leathery gourds. The men strike him as less industrious, spending much of their time engaged in what appear to be games. A favorite is one in which they chase one another around in a kind of rambunctious rally of tag that finally ends in a flailing scrum of simulated homoerotic sex. To be caught at the bottom of the pile, it seems certain, is to lose the game and to be indiscriminately prodded by a dozen scarcely contained male members.

That evening, Ramos tells Planke he has something to show him. The white hog leads him out of the village to a narrow silver stream flanked by moss-covered rocks and sheltered by attending shrubs and ferns. There is something undeniably Edenic in the air. A kind or vivifying animism illuminates the whole place. Planke guesses that this haven is somehow integrally linked to the elixir of life Ramos claims to have found, which presents Planke with the opportunity he has been waiting for—broaching the topic of Ramos's research again.

"I have to ask you . . . what happened? I mean, in your last correspondence with Arthur you said you'd found it. You were raving about *Hēbē* and ambrosia and the nectar of *Bufo*. What was it you discovered?"

"It's all in my field notes. I assume you found them or you wouldn't be here."

"To be honest, I haven't had a chance to really look at them yet."

"Well then, let me give you the abbreviated version. We found nothing by way of universal cures. Oh, there was the odd herbal remedy that might cure a particularly nasty case of hemorrhoids, but nothing substantial . . . nothing that could be considered a bona fide pharmacological breakthrough. And the rainforest took its toll on the others . . . the isolation, the humidity and heat, the sickness. One by one, they abandoned the project until there was only me and Jerome. If you found my field notes then you must also have found what is left of Jerome."

"That was Jerome? What happened to him?"

"All in good time. You see, one day Jerome and I discovered a psychoactive drug that is a strong hallucinogen. We decided to experiment with the drug, thinking it may be useful as a painkiller for those with terminal diseases or even as a strong sedative. We had no idea what to expect. All I can say is it was euphoric. A mind-altering soma . . . essentially, a backdoor to Nirvana. After weeks of experimenting with the drug, I came to the realization that it was *this* drug that we had been looking for all along. It was the elixir of life. I came to realize with startling clarity that there is no cure-all for sickness and disease. To search for one is as preposterous as the search for the Holy Grail. No, there is no miraculous cure, but there is escape. Escape is the answer. One can leave the world of pain, sorrow, and ignorance, and travel to a perfect place . . . a place of immaculate stillness in the core of one's very being. It is there in all of us. We simply have to locate it. Jerome and I discovered the drug that leads directly to that place of bliss and rapture."

"And what is this drug, this elixir of life?"

"Look around you." He makes a sweeping gesture with two flabby arms. "What do you see?"

Planke opts for the obvious. "Trees?"

"Look closer."

He does, noting the preponderance of toads in and around the stream. "Toads?"

"Exactly—toads. The cane toad. *Bufo marinus.*" Ramos bends his sizable girth with some difficulty, taking up a toad in his pudgy hand. It looks like a normal toad to Planke; nothing sinister or saintly, either way.

"The parotid glands of this little creature secrete a toxin . . . a milky white toxin that is lethal in large enough doses. But in small doses it is heavenly, I assure you. That's what brought us here. That's why we left our research headquarters in Pauini."

The white hog holds the toad close to his lips, pokes out his pink tongue, and flicks it along the toad in a much too sexual way. "The glands are located here, on its back."

This last remark catches Planke off guard, surprises him like a proverbial wet pinkie in the ear. "Did you say on the back of the toad?" Suddenly a big piece of the puzzle falls into place. "That's what you meant in your letter to Hendry. 'Served on the back of *Hēbē* herself.' *Hēbē* is the cane toad. Like the Greek *Hēbē* who serves the gods ambrosia, the draught of immortality. And it also explains the toad-slash-penis lollipops in the anatomically incorrect yet amusing doodles you scribbled in the margins of your last field book."

"I have no recollection of those, but it seems plausible enough." Ramos holds up the toad in his chubby palm. "Go ahead. Try it and you'll see what I mean."

Planke has never been one to indulge in intoxicants of any sort. He has the occasional glass of wine and the odd beer, but that is the extent of his dalliance with toxins. Despite this, he suddenly feels himself drawn to the harmless looking toad. A backdoor to Nirvana. He wonders if it can be true. Maybe just one little lick, he thinks, what can it hurt? Planke closes his eyes and pokes out his tongue like a snake tasting the air. He feels the reptilian bumps, savors the bitter toxin on his taste buds. His mouth fills with saliva and he swallows. It fills again and he swallows again. And again. Until finally it stops filling and he is able to speak.

"What about these people . . . the *caceteiros*?"

"What about them?"

"They worship you."

"That happened quite by accident. One day I was out gathering toad specimens. When I returned to the cabin, I found it swarming with *caceteiros.* To my horror, I also found Jerome dead at their hands. They had clubbed him to death in my absence. When it looked like they were about to dispense with me in a similar fashion, I held up a frog and licked it. They were aghast. So I licked another one. Again they reacted with horror. You see, in that do-or-die moment, I had gambled on the fact that the *caceteiros* knew of the cane toad. Not only that, it seemed likely to me that they or their ancestral kin would have at some point tried to eat one. Only it would have killed whoever ate it. Ingesting a whole toad would result in certain death. I would later learn that the cane toad plays a prominent role in the mythology of the *caceteiros.* They believe it to be a feared and deadly embodiment of a particularly ill-tempered forest god. The fact that I appeared to be immune to its powers meant I myself must be powerful. That is how I was able to save my own life."

"The sign, then, that was yours?"

"*HELP!!!?* Yes, that was mine. An act of desperation. Although in the beginning I'd managed to save myself from an immediate bludgeoning, I wasn't convinced I could fool them indefinitely. So I made the sign on the off chance that an explorer or adventurer might see it, and I might be able to escape this place. But it wasn't long before I was able to convince some of the *caceteiro* men to try licking the toad themselves. Eventually they were all licking it. And it changed everything. Everything. As you have yourself been witness to, it has transformed them from a fierce and murderous people into a harmless and laughter-loving people."

Planke assumes the drug has also transformed Ramos into a mad, corpulent version of himself. "I was witness to that. But why are they dressed as mice?"

"Yes, I suppose they do look like mice. Actually, they're dressed as coatis, a relative of our raccoon. They like to dress as animals when under the influence of the toad toxin. It's a kind of game with them. They are greatly amused by it."

"Yes, I was witness to some of their games, too." Planke notices that he is beginning to slur his words. Then moments later, he catches himself staring intently at an insect on the forest floor, convinced that it is the most exquisite creature he has ever laid eyes on. Then he begins to giggle.

"The toxin is starting to make its way into your system, I see," says Ramos. "Come—quickly. We'd better get back to the village before it really kicks in."

The boy Willy is staring at him when he awakes. Planke recalls little of the previous night, except that it was filled with dreams—the most spectacular, kaleidoscopic dreams. In truth, Planke is not certain they were dreams at all, which unnerves him slightly. They may have been wakeful hallucinations, although he can't be sure, having never had a hallucination before. At least, none that he is aware of. Then he looks down and sees his loins folded neatly into a loin cloth, which alarms him greatly.

Willy points at him and snickers. Searching for the source of the boy's amusement, Planke finds that he is wearing coati ears. A disconcerting memory of him being buried under a throng of sweaty *caceteiro* men flashes in his head, just as his stomach sinks, gurgles into his bowels and sloshes through his gut, causing his rectum to retract deep into the fleshy fissure of his buttocks. Perhaps the toad is not so harmless after all, thinks Planke.

He raises himself onto two elbows and shoos the boy away with a lazy wave of his hand. Willy retreats from the shadows of the longhouse into daylight. Planke needs time to think, to sort things out in his head. The only thing he recalls clearly is his conversation with Ramos by the toad-infested stream. "There is no cure, but there is escape," the professor said. Planke didn't object at the time, but now he wonders how Ramos can believe such a thing. Can it be that the great John Ramos has simply given up? Or perhaps he has become so hooked on his own escapist notion of Nirvana that he's traded his white lab coat and Bunsen burner for a handful of magic beans—mailed in his PhD and got a one-way discount ticket to Wacko-town in Kingdom La-La Land. And what about his following, the *caceteiros*? As far as Planke can tell, Ramos has become a little too accustomed to them groveling at his feet: the cult of the white hog, complete with pig nose and boar tusks.

Just then, Maya appears in the longhouse. "Friend." She says, pointing. "Friend." Planke scans the area for signs of Luís, but he is nowhere to be found. A wave of panic hits Planke. Surely Luís would not have left him stranded here. He jumps to his feet and bolts from of the longhouse. Daylight sears his eyeballs. The veins pounding in his temples threaten to burst. He calls out "Luís! Luís!" in a gravelly voice and then curls over and coughs. "So this is the nirvana hangover," he grumbles. "Enlightenment, the morning after. Ruthlessly cast back into samsara's endless cycle of suffering. Just great."

Maya steps in front of him. She's holding up a gnawed on, badly mutilated mandioquinha root and pointing to the garden. Planke forces himself to stand upright.

"The garden? He's at the garden?" he asks.

Maya nods, and Planke trots away, whimpering in pain, tears streaming from his eyes.

The garden is a heap of green mulch, and Planke wonders if a twister set down there sometime during the night. He finds Luís Moreno is the center of a large and deep excavation—a hole the size of a backyard swimming pool. With some effort, Planke revives the captain, who has also donned coati ears and the loin cloth.

"What in God's name happened out here?"

"Oh, *senhor*. Things got *muito louco* . . . how you say . . . "

"Yes, crazy. I see that. But who did this? Did they try to bury you alive?"

"No, no, nothing like that. I dug the hole with my own two hands. Somehow, I got it in my head that I was *um rato*."

"Not a rat—a coati, actually." Planke pulls the ears from Luís Moreno's head.

"Oh. Makes sense."

Planke is not sure exactly how this makes sense, but he ignores the comment and helps the captain to his feet. "Look, I think we should leave here, as soon as possible. We can slip out unnoticed tomorrow at first light."

"Whatever you say, *senhor* Planke. But what about John Ramos? Will he be coming with us?"

"No. I'd have to drag him back to civilization kicking and screaming all the way. Besides, I found out what I wanted to know. His elixir of life is nothing more than a strong intoxicant. The only thing it could cure is a bout of normalcy."

"Tomorrow it is, then."

"And a word of advice, Luís. Don't lick any more toads, whatever you do."

"Good advice, *senhor*."

That night, *o porco branco* throws a celebration in honor of his guests. As far as Planke can tell, the white hog quite clearly enjoys his company—the "civilized outsider." The hunt earlier that day produced a wild boar, which, slaughtered for the occasion, now hung skewered and glazed over a fire, dripping fat and causing crackling flare ups. The *caceteiro* men, who have just returned from licking toads at the stream, adjust their coati ears and whiskers between pulls from a bottle gourd. When the gourd reaches Planke, he sniffs it and takes a sip of the fermented herbal beverage. He passes it to Luís Moreno, who takes a heroic draught of the brew.

Soon the drums begin to pound out a buoyant jungle rhythm that echoes through the trees, into the night, across the millennia. The sky is a milky slurp of ancient starlight. Planke scans the area, but the white hog is nowhere to be found. He assumes that Ramos plans to make a grand entrance. Planke wags his head, not so much in disgust as disappointment. Even out here, in the heart of the rainforest, hell-and-gone away from the nearest neon sign, still the show must go on.

Planke glances over at Luís Moreno, who has insinuated himself among the *caceteiro* men and is again being fitted with ears and whiskers. Meanwhile, the drum beat swells and the women begin to dance, moving fluidly in a slow viscous dance, their brown bodies glistening with a cherry glow. Then, from out of the darkness, comes the white hog, tumbling into the firelight, end-over-end, in a kind of floundering handspring that defies the angular momentum of his rotund shape. Landing soundly, he snaps and snarls, froths at the mouth then raises his pig snout high and bellows his immoderate arrival.

O porco branco takes three lumbering, exaggerated steps toward the *caceteiro* women and begins to dance. The *caceteiro* men surround them, yipping and howling with every convulsive jerk, every spasmodic twitch the white hog makes. The outlandish scene sets a giggle gurgling forth from Planke's pharynx, a sound which turns to an incredulous gasp when the white hog latches on to one of the dancing women, bends her over, and promptly inserts himself. He pumps his gluteus maximus, medius, and minimus to the pulsating rhythm. When he is finished, he ejaculates on the fire and bites an ear off the scorched boar, chewing it to a rubbery cud.

Planke looks on—perturbed, appalled, even sickened by this animalistic display. It is beyond comprehension. It is sub-human. It is barbaric. Yet it sets something astir in him—some primeval fever that lights a fuse in the deepest, darkest precinct of his primate heart. It sizzles and snaps up his spine, explodes in his head. And in that explosive moment, Planke wonders if maybe John Ramos has indeed found something. Certainly not the balm to soothe all that ails humanity. And not the ethereal Nirvana of Buddhism. But maybe something like it. Something closer to true human nature, something orgiastic yet oddly sublime. Something that civilization gave up on millennia ago. With this thought in mind, Planke surrenders to the beat. He steps into the circle and lets his lanky figure wigwag and flap, flounce and jiggle. In the sopping Amazonian air, Planke joins in the celebration. He dances, he eats, he fucks.

The following morning is nothing more than a painful reprise of the previous one. Planke's head is thick and his limbs heavy. Again, his memory of the night before is cloudy—compromised by an immoderate intake of *caceteiros* moonshine. Planke also seems to recall licking the toad again, a recollection that causes a purple curse to burst upon his lips. He shakes Luís Moreno awake then goes in search of the pants he traded for a loin cloth at some point during the celebration. At the other end of the longhouse, he spies *o porco branco* slumbering upright in some impossibly contorted position upon his throne, looking more dead than alive, more foolish than crazy. Even in his lunatic state there is something sane—something worn but measured in the look that lights upon the curled lips of John Ramos, half smiling below the ridiculous pig's nose. In that moment, Planke imagines himself in the same blissful state, happily unconscious on a leopard-skin throne with the blunted horns and antlers of forest creatures pressing hard into his existence. But this not unpleasant vision passes as quickly as the snap of a twig beneath his heel. Planke turns and leaves the longhouse, rushing to relieve the pressing tightness that has now overtaken his bladder.

It is there at the edge of the village that he sees Maya and the boy Willy—her son. This final detail is apparent in the way that she scoops water onto the brown skin of the boy's back. And in the way she eases the boy's head into the milky waters of the stream. Only when Maya looks up and sees him does Planke turn his unabashed gaze away and retreat from the scene.

They leave the village just as the first rays of sunlight filter down to the forest floor. Neither of the men has spoken of the previous night. The truth is Planke wouldn't know where to begin. How to explain what happened seems impossible. A once-in-a-lifetime occurrence, he assures himself.

As they step briskly down the trail, a rising sense of urgency overtakes him. It dampens the clamor of ache that seems to afflict his entire being, a sickness of the soul. Planke knows he has to get away from this place. And from John Ramos.

As they push through the gray fog, a voice calls out, causing him to pull up in-stride and listen. Planke turns to see Maya rushing through the bush. Willy scurries along at her side, his mongrel mutt in tow. When she reaches them, she thrusts the boy at Planke. "Take," she says. "Take."

Planke is not sure what he has just heard. Or that he has heard correctly.

"Take," she repeats. "Take."

"What? No . . . no . . . he is your son. He is the son of o *porco branco*."

She recoils. "O *porco branco. . . louco . . . louco*." The word, bitter on her lips, needs no explanation. "Take," she commands with a finality that Planke knows he cannot counter—a finality without recourse. She takes his hand and joins it with Willy's. "Take," she says, softly this time. Try as he might, Planke cannot break away from the snare of her eyes. Perhaps he is looking for a tear, a twitch of uncertainty or a shudder of doubt, but there is nothing but resolve—silent and strong. Before Planke can say another word, Maya retreats into the forest, the way she has come, without even a glance over her shoulder.

Willy sniffles and whines almost inaudibly but does not cry out to her. The boy watches his mother go but does not follow. Planke wonders what she has told him, the boy, her son: "It's only for a while? You're going to a better place? A better life?" Perhaps, he thinks.

"We must go quickly, now," says Luís Moreno. "Before o *porco branco* finds out *o filho dele* is gone."

Planke grips Willy's hand tightly. "Yes, we must go," he says. "Back to civilization—back home."

They reach *Começo e Final* before the Sun has clawed its way above the trees. Luís Moreno takes his place at the helm and wastes no time grinding the ship's motor to a rusty start and jamming it into gear.

Planke is still holding the boy Willy's hand, standing at the ship's gunwale as he watches the shoreline shrink into the deep brown tide of the Purus River. He can just see the sign that Ramos painted when the professor still believed his life was in peril. *HELP!!!*

Planke squints at the hastily drawn letters of that single word. Until he is overcome by the feeling that it somehow represents the last vestiges of a fading hope. And then it strikes him, too, that here is a final plea from the civilized world. A last gasp. How loud and long it comes, thinks Planke.

The Unexamined Life

Gallery Modena is the shit. The big leagues, the show, whatever you want to call it. It just doesn't get any bigger than Gallery Modena. Not in L.A., anyway. And that's where I'm headed, Gallery Modena. In less than a week, the news will be out: Vic Ray, artist extraordinaire.

"I'm on my way to the top—" I say, "and this is what you bring me." Tearing the cigarette from my mouth, I put on my disgusted face. "Didn't I explicitly say nothing with fucking fur? People love—"

"—furry animals. I know," says Gillian. "But badgers are furry and people don't love them. They're mean and fat."

That's Gillian for you. Thinking on her own again.

"You want me to put a fucking badger in a blender in front of two hundred art patrons drunk on Dom Pérignon and an army of ass-puckered art critics and purée the poor little bastard? I mean, do you know what fur does to a blender. It's a bloody mess. Pun intended." I take a loud slurp of my Black Russian and chase it with a Marlboro filtered drag.

"Alright," says Gillian. "I get the point. Something ugly—without fur."

"Welcome aboard, babe! Now find me something that people will be outwardly appalled at seeing stuffed into a blender yet inwardly delighted to watch die in a manner befitting the horrible little creature. Some kind of snake or iguana or something like that. Got it?"

Gillian came to me with impeccable qualifications and a glowing recommendation from a former professor. In the beginning, things worked out well. She was fine. Until she started thinking on her own. Now, I fire her once a week, typically Friday, sleep with her on the weekend, and re-hire her Monday morning. It's our routine and the bedrock of our working relationship. Despite her being canned by me on a weekly basis, and my admittedly sometimes less-than-gentlemanly behavior, Gillian has only quit once, walked out on me. That was early on, when I first dreamed up the idea of blending an animal in a performance art piece. She objected to the idea, thought it went too far, thought it was barbaric. *Barbaric*, she actually said. But I was looking for something that would really grab people by the throat. You know, shake them from their safe, middle-upper-class stupor. So I stuck a dead catfish into a blender and made what I referred to at the time as "an aquatic shake." That got the undivided attention of the art world for a day or two. But even back then, I knew I needed something more sensationalistic than that if I was going to float to the top of the turd bowl that is the L.A. art scene.

So I decided to start using live animals in my performance art—turn up the shock value to ten. And it was pure gold. I blended up fish, mollusks, frogs, scorpions, giant centipedes, sea cucumbers—which was a real crowd pleaser, given that a sea cucumber is a dead ringer for a dog's dick. And, oh yes, octopi. How could I forget my first octopus? An inspired performance which, arguably, put me on the artsy-fartsy map. I still remember picking up the gelatinous mass, like some giant curdled amoeba. It was writhing like a son-of-a-bitch. I swear it knew the end was near. (Gillian has since made a point of telling me that octopi are highly intelligent, as far as sea creatures go—she also told me they have three hearts and autotomizing limbs. "Auto-what?" I protested. "Self-amputating," she said, smugly.) It was all I could do to get the brobdingnagian loogie off my hand and in to the blender. Then came the deafening rasp of whirring blades; the whole thing swirled into black and inky paste. When I shut it off you could've heard a heart attack in heaven. I knew I'd done something special. And I knew what I had to do next. It just came to me, like some twisted revelation from some morbid muse. In that spontaneous moment, I poured the foul brew into a glass and tipped it down my unwilling gullet. The dry-retching gag that followed only served to heighten the drama. Then I served it up all over the front row. A projectile vomit, nothing short of a howitzer—a real puke cannon. My code-red exorcism ended up on the front page of every art rag in the greater Los Angeles area. "The Woof Heard 'Round the Art World," one headline screamed. Without a doubt, the proudest moment of my life, thus far. I had T-shirts made up: Have you been *VIC*timized today? And that became my trademark, my shtick: blend, drink, vomit. Vic Ray, *VIC*timizer.

Some of the theoretical interpretations of that performance were priceless. "An anarchist's blend of disrespect, disdain, and death," said L.A. Art Magazine. "Mr. Ray's meaning was clear," wrote another critic. "Our lives no longer mean anything, outside of what we consume and retch up and consume again. Shame on us all! And Bravo, Mr. Ray, for so poignantly, if bleakly, bringing this to our collective attention." I wanted to believe them. I wanted to think I did something spectacular yet something grave and poignant, too. But even back then, in the very beginning, before the bloody parade really got rolling, I knew it was all a steaming crock of shit.

oh yes ringo   good place ringo   scratch scratch scratch
oh yes ringo   ringo poophole itchy   scratch scratch scratch
ringo finger smell   oh yes bad smell   bad bad smell ringo
ringo poophole scratch   ringo finger taste   oh yes bad taste ringo
bad bad poophole taste   trevor not like ringo poophole taste
trevor ringo handslap   handslap handslap handslap
disgusting trevor say   no ringo say   dirty trevor say
no dirty ringo say   smell say ringo   trevor ringo handslap
handslap handslap handslap   ringo trevor kiss   trevor no ringo kiss
kiss kiss kiss   trevor handtalk   trevor handtalk   trevor more handtalk
handtalk handtalk handtalk   ringo no like handtalk
ringo like poophole scratch   ringo like peetrunk play
peetrunk play play play   trevor not like ringo peetrunk play
trevor ringo handslap   handslap handslap handslap
trevor no peetrunk play   rena trevor peetrunk play
rena trevor peetrunk taste   rena trevor peetrunk taste taste taste
ringo see rena play   play play play   rena taste taste taste
trevor like rena play   play play play   taste taste taste   ringo like rena
rena female trevor say f e m a l e trevor handtalk
rena nice rack trevor say   ringo like rena nice rack
ringo rena nice rack play   play play play   rena ringo handslap
trevor laugh   laugh laugh laugh   trevor rena nice rack play
play play play   rena trevor no handslap   ringo no like trevor
trevor handtalk   handtalk handtalk handtalk
trevor ringo banana give   handtalk handtalk   ringo how old trevor say
ringo nine finger old   good trevor say   trevor ringo banana give
what ringo name trevor say r i n g o ringo say
trevor ringo banana give   rena clap clap clap   rena trevor kiss
rena trevor peetrunk play   play play play   taste taste taste
trevor rena nice rack play play play
ringo no like trevor

Gillian calls my cell and tells me I need to get down to the studio right away. Some sort of emergency. "Art or otherwise?" I ask, needing to gage my present level of my intoxication, which always requires a social context.

"Just get down here, now."

"I don't think I should be driving."

"Jesus, Vic. I'll be there in thirty minutes."

"Make it forty and you got yourself a deal. I'm in the middle of something important." I tip a glass to my mouth.

"Just be ready when I get there."

I decide not to fire Gillian this week, as the emergency in question actually turns out to be a bit of one. Two policemen waiting for me at my studio rates as an emergency in my books. But Gillian tells me there's another far more pressing emergency, which is what has brought the police to my studio in the first place—a letter from an animal rights group. The cops are taking it all very seriously. They've even gone so far as to call it a death threat. I've had intimidating letters before, but taken as a whole, they've really amounted to nothing more than blustery name calling. "Murderer!" "Rapist!" "Artist!" No further explanation needed.

The thing I don't get about animal rights groups is who are they to save the dolphins, whales, baby seals, panda bears, giant Palouse earthworms, Abbott's boobies and all the rest of them. Really, who do these people think they are? Who are we—humans—to even want to save the animals? It goes against our true nature. Does being self-aware magically negate all our other predatory instincts? After all, humans put the *ape* in apex predator. We are the best of the best. Top drawer. Our only natural enemy is, well, God, and he's really quite wishy-washy when it comes to predation. The whole mercy and forgiveness thing weakens his predatory resolve. And as far as I can tell, instinct was never meant to withstand such mitigating factors. But that's not all. I hesitate to even mention the fact that we can scarcely save ourselves from each other, so how can we possibly expect to save the animals? But that's a whole other can of worms. Anyway the point is I've had my run-in with animal rights groups, yes. Do they frighten me? No, not really.

A policeman hands me the letter in question. He is so stereotypically a cop that I almost laugh out loud. I want to make him the star of his own reality TV show: *The Cop Who Would Be God.* He must sense my disdain, as he grunts out his displeasure in true cop-like fashion. "There a problem?" he asks. I want to ask him where they keep all the pencil-necked geek cops locked up. Of course, I do no such thing. He pokes his twitchy trigger finger at the letter.

"Any idea who may be behind this?"

I glance over the flimsy piece of yellow scratch paper.

Vic Ray be warned!

If we see you anywhere near Gallery Medona, you're a D-E-A-D man.

NFAS

(P.S. That's National Front for Animal Supremacy, the new guys in town!)

"I'm just guessing," I say, "but I'm gonna go with the NFAS."

"Oh a funny guy. We got ourselves a funny guy here, Jimbo! Well funny guy, you might want to think twice before showing your face around Gallery Modena this weekend."

"Gallery Modena . . . don't go," I pause, scrunching up my left eye. Got it! I have committed that to memory," I say. "Now, if there's nothing else, I'll leave you officers to find your own way out."

What I should've said to the cops, I didn't. That is this: I have endured a battery of chic gallery soirees at Gallery Modena, all in the hope of one day being invited to VICtimize the place. And now that that chance has finally come, no pock-faced, skin-headed, neo-hippie, tree-humping animal rights group is going to intimidate me into canceling. You only get one shot at Gallery Modena, one shot at greatness. Rupert Fairmont will see to that. And nobody fucks with Rupert.

Rupert Fairmont is the only straight gallery owner in the east downtown area. Much to his chagrin. His lack of gay-ness has in the past been a black mark against him, diminishing his credibility as a curator and patron, and seriously limiting what garish wardrobe ensembles he can hope to pull off, without coming off as a wanna-gay-be. There was a time when Rupert Fairmont lived the gay lifestyle and fostered his then gay reputation. He was widely hailed as the blue flame of all flamers in the art scene. But he couldn't sustain it, couldn't keep up the façade of queerness. Rumors began to spread that Rupert may not actually be gay but only seem gay.

It was said that he talked the talk but never walked the walk. In short, he never did it: hiney-love. Oh, he'd grope a few asses, smack a few lips, maybe even tickle a few cocks, but when it came time to put out or get out, he got out. Needless to say, the gay community was outraged. "Rupert is a pretender not a rear-ender," they said. A pretender, they called him. And that, I imagine, hurt most of all.

Surprisingly, once Rupert was forced back into the closet, things turned out okay for him, gallery wise—better than okay, swimmingly, actually—mainly due to his business acumen. He made a few good deals, got himself a reputation for business, and shed his earlier self-perpetuated reputation for cocaine and blow jobs. Today, everyone who's anyone will tell you that, straight or gay, Rupert Fairbanks runs the hottest gallery in the Warehouse District.

trevor ringo leash on   ringo no like leash   ringo no like trevor
sorry trevor say   new roommate trevor say
ringo don't kiss your new roommate trevor say   ringo like kiss
ringo rena like kiss   kiss kiss kiss   newroommate   no handtalk
no handtalk handtalk handtalk   trevor newroomate leash on
newroomate fight fight fight   newroomate big noise make
big big big noise   newroomate noise noise noise
shut up fuckwad trevor say   fuckwad no like trevor
fuckwad fight fight fight   fuckwad no like leash   fuckwad trevor foothit
trevor fuckwad handhit foothit handhit   hit hit hit   fuckwad quiet
rena loud noise make   rena noise noise noise   stop rena say
ringo no like trevor   ringo no like leash   ringo no like handtalk
trevor handtalk   handtalk handtalk handtalk   trevor rena play play play
taste taste taste   rena loud noise make
ah ah ah   play play play   ah ah ah   play play play   ah ah ah
fuckwad sleep   fuckwad no see rena ah ah ah
fuckwad no see trevor ah ah ah   trevor rena nice rack play
play play play   rena trevor peetrunk play play play
trevor peetrunk rena in   in in in   rena ah ah ah   fuckwad sleep
trevor fuckwad wake   trevor water throw   water water water
fuckwad wake fuckwad no like trevor   trevor fuckwad clothes take
fuckwad no clothes   ringo fuckwad poophole see

*ringo fuckwad peetrunk see   ringo poophole scratch
scratch scratch scratch   ringo like peetrunk play
fuckwad no peetrunk play fuckwad no poophole scratch
rena fuckwad peetrunk no play   no play play play   no ah ah ah
trevor say fuckwad cage go in   trevor ringo banana give
trevor say byebye trevor   rena say byebye   ringo rena kiss
ringo rena nice rack play   play play play   no rena say
no no no ringo rena say*

It's only Tuesday, but I invite Gillian to stay the night at the studio anyway. I bought the red-brick warehouse space for a song, before gentrification drove all the other artists out of the Warehouse District, now known as the Arts District. Ironic, that. Gillian calls her boyfriend to tell him she has to work all night. I can't help but chuckle. I've met Josh a couple times before. He sells copy machines. And he's totally oblivious to his girlfriend's ongoing fling with her boss. Tonight when I say something remotely disparaging about her beau, Gillian sighs and tells me Josh is a kind and decent person. "Kind and decent," I say, "are the trappings of mediocrity." Which begs the question, if he's so kind and decent, why is she fucking him over? By that I mean fucking me. Of course, I don't ask her because I would hate for an unexpected attack of guilt to mess up a good thing. Our good thing, hers and mine. And it's good, believe me. It is a handcuffed-to-the-bed-post, sex-beads-up-the-ass kind of good. I mean, Josh seems like a nice enough guy, and Gillian does seem to love him on some level. I just can't make myself feel bad about something so fucking good. Vic Ray, sexual liberator.

I'm running dangerously low on alcohol, so I send Gillian out to pick up supplies. By that I mean Nemiroff and Kahlúa. As usual, she comes back with Chinese take-out along with my booze, in an attempt to get me to eat. "Eat something," she says. She may have a point. My clothes do seem to be hanging off me like the sails of a ghost ship these days. I've chalked it up to nervousness about the big show. Gillian likes to remind me that there was a time when my clothes fit me right. She likes to remind me of a lot of things, which, in all fairness, is part of her job description. But she likes to remind me of things I'd just as soon forget. Like that I was once a talented painter ("Semi-talented painter," I correct her), something

I no longer waste my time on. "Who the fuck paints anymore?" I rant. "Art schools these days are crammed full of dimwitted neo-this's and neo-that's who don't want to hear that painting has become the missionary position of the Fine Arts. The wham-bam-thank-you-ma'am of the creative process."

She also reminds me that I didn't always feel the need to liquefy living things and then drink them. That much is true. I didn't always do that. But I also didn't always get written up in *LA Art* or *Cutting Edge* magazine. And I do now. "You do the math," I say.

"Touché!" says Gillian, stuffing a mess of egg noodles in her mouth. "I'm curious, though," she says. "Don't you ever feel bad about, you know, blending up animals. I mean, were you one of those kids who burns up ants with a magnifying glass or something?"

"No, I don't feel bad. It's show business, babe. People get hurt," I say. "Or in this case, animals get hurt." I stop to top up my drink with Nemiroff. "And no, I wasn't one of those kids who sets cats on fire in the garage or who nails guinea pigs to the wall of the tree house or microwaves baby birds in Tupperware containers." What I don't say is that by rights I could have been one of those kids. After all, my parents did divorce when I was three years old, essentially abandoning me after that.

When you're a kid, you don't care if the people who brought you into this world are unfit parents. It doesn't matter because they're still your parents, no matter how flawed. And, in my case, flawed they were—although it wasn't until I was much older that I realized just how badly flawed. My father was a hanger-on and a hanger-'round the Beat scene in San Francisco, something that caused a deep rift between him and his adoptive father. At twenty-one, jobless and without prospects, he got seventeen-year-old Magnolia Keener pregnant and married her, only to divorce her two years later, at which time she virtually disappeared off the face of the earth. Being neither capable nor willing to single-handedly bring up a child, my father passed the responsibility on to his adoptive mother, Anitia, my grandmother and acting-mother and her husband Tom. Anitia and Tom were never able to have kids of their own, so they put all their parental energies into raising their adopted son William, my father. What they couldn't have known then was years later they would be yoked with the responsibility of raising their only grandson, too.

I have an early childhood memory of Anitia, in which she hovers over me with her cacao brown eyes and creased bronze skin; the ends of her glossy hair tickling my eyelids and nose. From her, I learned only kindness, for animals and humans alike. My black yearning to "annihilate living things," as Gillian puts it, is less sadistic childhood instinct than devious adult calculation. To be honest, in the beginning it was little more than sensationalistic posturing. Vic Ray, art fraud extraordinaire. I admit it, have freely admitted it. Oddly enough, admitting I'm a fraud only seems to affirm my legitimacy—my "artistic honesty" in the eyes of the art world. Ironic, that. I've never hidden the fact that I'm the biggest fraud going; second only to art itself, capital A. The house that Michelangelo built is falling, rotten to the core, and the façade is just that—a façade. Nothing more. There is nothing behind it. Propped up by self-serving critics, there is no substance left. It only seems real from a safe, highly conceptual distance.

trevor ringo camera point   ringo like camera   ringo face funny
facefunny facefunny facefunny   camera laugh   laugh laugh laugh
trevor handtalk handtalk handtalk   ringo handtalk
handtalk handtalk handtalk   ringo see ringo on tv
ringo face funny   funny funny face on tv   ringo clap   ringo dance
ringo banana in nose   ringo banana in poophole
ringo banana squeeze squeeze squeeze   ringo banana throw
ringo noise make   noise noise noise ringo see ringo on tv
no trevor say   be nice for the camera trevor say   ringo camera take
no ringo trevor say   give it back trevor say   ringo peetrunk camera point
camera laugh   laugh laugh laugh   no no no trevor say
fuckwad laugh   laugh laugh laugh   ringo more noise make
noise noise noise   ringo poophole camera point
fuckwad laugh   laugh laugh laugh   trevor cage foothit
foothit foothit foothit   fuckwad quiet   fuckwad smile
fuckwad no like trevor   fuckwad no like cage   ringo like fuckwad
trevor camera take   trevor ringo handhit   trevor camera in box
trevor lab go out   ringo fuckwad handtalk   handtalk handtalk handtalk
fuckwad no handtalk   ringo poophole scratch
fuckwad no poophole scratch   ringo peetrunk play
fuckwad no peetrunk play ringo poophole scratch   fuckwad laugh
laugh laugh laugh   fuckwad poophole scratch
fuckwad more laugh   laugh laugh laugh   ringo make noise
ringo make more noise   noise noise noise   fuckwad peetrunk play
ringo peetrunk play   fuckwad more laugh   laugh laugh laugh
trevor lab come in   trevor cage foothit   foothit foothit foothit

*you sick fuck trevor say   fuck you fuckwad say   trevor cage foothit
foothit foothit foothit   trevor lab go out   fuckwad smile   fuckwad laugh
laugh laugh laugh   ringo ringo cage open   ringo ringo cage go out
ringo camera take   ringo fuckwad camera point   fuckwad finger up
fuck you all fuckwad say   ringo fuckwad poophole camera point
fuckwad poophole scratch   scratch scratch scratch   fuckwad laugh
laugh laugh laugh   fuckwad more noise make   noise noise noise
ringo more noise make   noise noise noise
ringo like fuckwad*

I wake up as Gillian takes my cock in her mouth. Thirty seconds later and it's all over. Head makes me crazy. There's no holding back. A physical impossibility for me. Gillian knows this. I guess it's her way of exercising some measure of control over me. She slips into her panties and fastens her bra. Stooping, peering into an antique mirror, she crumples her auburn highlighted hair into a fist and balls it behind her head, pulling a few strands loose and twirling them around her fingers. Details. For me perfection is always in the details. Somehow this one hits me, this detail, and makes me more talkative than normal. I glance at Retro Rocket Boy on the wall: 11:43 a.m. Truly an ungodly hour.

"I don't get you," I say.

"Don't know what you mean."

"Yeah, you do. I don't get this."

"This?"

"What we're doing here."

"We're fucking. That's what we're doing here. Fucking and working. The two go hand-in-hand. Isn't that what you always say? And now I'm going to drive south of the border and find some kind of exotic reptile for you to blend up in your next show. The big show, don't forget."

"Yeah, the big show." It sounds so ridiculous in the light of day, sober in the light of day. "Listen, what I mean is how can you fuck me then go home to Josh. It's so, I don't know, Machiavellian or Giovannian or something Italian like that. I mean I know you're using the hell out me. But what can you possibly want from him?"

"My God, Vic! I never thought I'd say this but I like you better when you're drunk. I mean, you almost sound serious."

"Serious? How pathetic of me. And how very unbecoming, when you put it that way." I rise from bed and go in search of the Nemiroff. I splash some into a cup and pour it back. "What is it that you find so attractive about Josh? I mean, he's a salesman who struggles to pull down 30K a year."

"You wouldn't understand, and that's exactly what makes you Vic Ray, VICtimizer, and him Josh Johnson, ordinary guy. That's my best explanation. The only explanation you're going to get, Vic Ray."

"Oh yeah, Vic Ray, the VICtimizer. What shit that is. I'd fire the dipshit who came up with that moniker if it hadn't been yours truly." I slide a Lucky Strike from its pack and light it.

"It must be terrible when you only have yourself to blame. I mean, particularly for you."

"Jesus! Thanks for that sure and swift kick to the ego." I'm about to begin my angry pouting routine, which will end with me firing Gillian, but I'm interrupted by the door buzzer. "See who that is, will ya? Jesus! Who is up and actually out of the house at this time of day?" In the meantime, I try to locate some tomato juice.

I'm sitting naked on a barstool drinking a red-eye when Gillian returns with a suit. By that I mean a man in a suit—fifty something, a perfect head of hair that looks to be fighting the good fight against all things gray and aged, teeth whiter than a man of his years ought to have, eyes that creak side-to-side, as if perpetually trying to keep up with what is happening all around them.

"Vic, this is Allan Goldman, an attorney," says Gillian.

"Victor Planke?" he says. I nod. "I represent the estate of your father, William Ramos Planke.

"Victor Planke?" Gillian's confusion wrinkles her almost perfect brow. "Who's that?"

"Vic Ray is my stage name. Legally, I go by Victor Planke." I say, sounding strangely apologetic.

"Since we didn't see you at the funeral, I can only assume you are unaware that your father passed away two weeks ago. I sent a notice to you in the mail, regarding funeral arrangements."

"I got the notice," I say. "Turns out you caught me at a bad time. I couldn't get away from work." My sardonic tone is clearly lost on Allan Goldman. Either that or he's a very good attorney. *Seasoned*, I think, taking another sip.

"Be that as it may, you are in the will. As you may or may not know, your father's accumulated assets are quite substantial."

"You don't say," I say.

"And you are legally entitled to a large portion of those assets."

"I don't want them. Find someone else to give them to."

"Vic, you're not serious," says Gillian.

"I am. It's all money from his book—his precious fucking book. I don't want it."

"I'll give you some time to consider it. But if you really don't want the money then other arrangements will have to be made. There will be paperwork involved."

"I don't need time to consider it. Send over whatever has to be signed and I'll sign it. And now, Mr. Goldman, if that is all, I've got some serious business to take care of, so I will bid you good day, sir." I swivel around on the Naugahyde stool, my bare buttocks squawking out its complaint, and down my red-eye. Then I wait for that sweet numbing sensation to wash over me—the morning ablution of every good and true alcoholic.

*trevor lab go out   rena lab go out   yellow light bright   ringo in cage
fuckwad in cage   fuckwad sleep   ringo   fuckwad poophole see
ringo fuckwad peetrunk see   ringo ringo cage open   ringo trevor desk go
 ringo trevor cigs take   ringo trevor cigs light   ringo smoke
smoke smoke smoke   fuckwad wake   ringo fuckwad trevor cigs give
fuckwad laugh   laugh laugh laugh   thanks fuckwad say
fuckwad trevor cigs smoke   smoke smoke smoke   water fuckwad say
ringo handtalk   fuckwad no handtalk   water fuckwad say
ringo trevor cup take   ringo trevor cup water in
ringo fuckwad water give   fuckwad water drink   drink drink drink
ringo coldbox go   ringo trevor beer take   ringo trevor beer open
ringo drink drink drink   beer fuckwad say   ringo fuckwad trevor beer give
fuckwad beer open   fuckwad drink drink drink   more fuckwad say
ringo coldbox go   ringo trevor beer take   ringo fuckwad trevor beer give
fuckwad trevor beer open   fuckwad drink drink drink
ringo drink drink drink   food fuckwad say   ringo fuckwad banana give
ringo apple fuckwad give   fuckwad eat eat eat   more more more eat
fuckwad trevor beer drink drink drink   fuckwad burp   ringo burp
burp burp burp   open the cage fuckwad say   fuckwad cage shake
ringo cage no cage open   ringo no key   ringo handtalk
handtalk handtalk handtalk   I don't understand fuckwad say*

open the cage fuckwad say   ringo cage no open   ringo no key
ringo cage no open   camera fuckwad say
give me the camera fuckwad say   ringo camera box open
ringo fuckwad camera give   fuckwad camera take
plug this in to the tv fuckwad say   ringo wire plug in
ringo no ringo tv see   ringo fuckwad tv see
fuckwad lab no   fuckwad poophole no
fuckwad peetrunk no   fuckwad bright light   bright bright light
people ringo fuckwad see   people people people
fuckwad black hand big glass in   black hand   black black black hand
ringo hand   big glass make noise   big big big noise   more more more noise
fuckwad black hand drink   drink drink drink   fuckwad black hand spit
spit spit spit   people noise noise noise make   more more more noise
people hands clap   clap clap clap   fuck fuck fuck fuckwad say
fuckwad camera button push   point this at me fuckwad say
ringo fuckwad tv see   ringo fuckwad poophole see
ringo fuckwad peetrunk see   give me his cigarettes fuckwad say
ringo trevor cigs fuckwad give   fuckwad trevor cigs smoke
fuckwad trevor cigs poophole in   in in in
more more more cigs poophole in   fuckwad trevor cigs ringo give
put them back fuckwad say   back in the desk fuckwad say
ringo trevor cigs take   ringo trevor cigs desk in
see how he likes those smokes fuckwad say   fuckwad laugh
laugh laugh laugh   give me the coffee mug fuckwad say
ringo fuckwad trevor cup give   fuckwad trevor cup peetrunk pee
pee pee pee   fuckwad laugh laugh laugh   here fuckwad say
put this on the desk say fuckwad   ringo trevor cup take
ringo trevor desk cup put   fuckwad laugh   laugh laugh laugh
give me the camera back fuckwad say   ringo fuckwad camera give
fuckwad camera button push   tv black   black black black
put this back in the case fuckwad say   fuckwad laugh   laugh laugh laugh
ringo like fuckwad

A warm breeze sweeps over the polished hood of Gillian's convertible Mustang, arching over the tinted windshield in a long gush of sea air. I'm slumped down in the seat, Ray-bans perched on the tip of my nose, a go-cup full of corporate beer, and a head still full of law speak. I've invited myself along on Gillian's trip south of the border. It is, after all, undertaken on my behalf. The problem is Gillian hasn't spoken a word since the lawyer Goldman's surprise visit, unless you count "buckle up" when we left L.A. I know she's angry, but I'm convinced she has no right to be. As her boss, I'm under no obligation to fill her in on my past, go into the details of my family history. If only that were all I was—her boss. As drunk as I already am, I recognize that being her sexual partner may complicate matters some (strangely, this has never occurred to me before). By that I mean, perhaps I should have at least told her my name—my real name. Not that it would make any difference. Vic Ray is who I am. Victor Planke is who I was. It's that simple, really. But then, that's probably not the point. Not entirely the point, anyway.

So I attempt an explanation, but it's a botched one. Gillian isn't buying it. So I get frustrated and fire her. She maneuvers the car to the shoulder of the freeway, bringing it to an abrupt halt on the gummy asphalt.

"Then I guess you'll be getting out."

"Gillian, come on, for Chrissake. It's a hundred and ten degrees out and I'm about to go up in a rouge flambé. I can't think straight. Can you just cut me a little fucking slack here?"

"Just tell me one thing. Who have I been fucking for the last three years, Vic Ray or Victor Planke?"

"What difference does it make? You've been fucking me. Well, me and Josh, if you want to get all nitpicky about it."

"You may not understand this, but it matters to me. It matters that I know who I've been sleeping with. Tell me about Victor Planke. I think I deserve that much, not as a faithful employee but as a semi-faithful fuck."

So cruising down the Santa Ana Freeway, headed for Tijuana, I tell her everything. Starting with my grandfather, John Ramos, extreme pharmacologist and drug fiend of the first order. The truth is I didn't know much about Professor Ramos until I read my father's book. Yes, I read his precious book, his thirty-seven-weeks-on-the-New-York-Times-best-sellers-list book, and the source of his abounding wealth. John Ramos's entire history was right there at my father's fingertips—FBI files, academic records, encyclopedic field notes—all he had to do was put them together into a coherent narrative. Maybe make a quick trip to the Amazon basin and voilà—his father's life story. And a small fortune, to boot.

I tell her how Tom Planke escaped from the rainforest with my father in tow, stopping just long enough to woo his future wife into leaving her home in Manaus and travel to California with him. There, they lived with Planke's aunt in Northern California until Tom took a teaching position and they eventually set up a home of their own. Tom and Anitia Planke legally adopted William Ramos Planke in May of 1941, just weeks before Operation Barbarossa touched off yet another Great War. Willy was five years old.

Gillian asks why my father and I were estranged at the time of his death and what he had done that was so bad it would make me refuse to attend his funeral.

"Nothing," I say. "That's what he did my whole life. Nothing. Except for write his book. It was his obsession . . . what he lived for. He did nothing else. Certainly nothing for me . . . and nothing to me. I didn't know him. He was always gone. Just gone. He abandoned me in order to write his book and to stay true to the Beat code of non-interaction with society. And that, it seemed, meant non-interaction with me. Going to his funeral would have been like going to the funeral of a stranger. And why the fuck would I do that?"

Gillian grunted in a way that suggested my response was not entirely a satisfactory one. And maybe it wasn't—entirely. The truth is my father did contact me once. He called around the time he was first diagnosed with liver cancer. At the time, he was mum as a mussel about the cancer. I wouldn't learn about that until much later from a well-meaning literary agent. And I only talked to him the one time. I recall it being five painful minutes of *ums* and *ahs* and other monosyllabic renderings of what we might have actually been feeling. I'd be lying if I said I haven't thought a lot about that phone call. I guess he was testing the waters, seeing if he dare lay that heavy mortality shit on the son he abandoned twenty years earlier. In the end, I guess he came to the conclusion that I couldn't be counted on for sponge baths, diaper changes, and a tearful bedside vigil. Go figure.

"How did he die?" asked Gillian.

"Cancer ate him from the inside out. Fifty-two years old. Slightly more than the average life span of an English nobleman during the Renaissance. Whatever that means."

"What about his adoptive parents? What happened to them?"

"The establishment happened to them. They became firmly ensconced in middle-class America. And then, after they finished playing the role of proxy-parent to me, they both grew old and died in their sleep, within months of each other—Tom in his E-Z chair watching the Nature Channel and Anitia on the sofa watching soaps with Spanish subtitles. Dying the good death, American style. It wasn't long after that that I moved to Southern California."

This was a part of my past that Gillian did know about—my moving here. At nineteen, I relocated to the City of Angels with one goal in mind: to become famous. Original, I know. I didn't care what it was; I just wanted to be famous. Rock star, movie star, media mogul, athlete, porn star. Didn't matter. The idea of artist never occurred to me until I happened upon a Rothko—*White Center (1957)*, in the Los Angeles County Museum of Art. I think it's fair to say that my reaction was a mixed one. On one hand, I was wholly enchanted by the furry floating boxes—transfixed, transformed, transported, all those past participles art critics are so fond of bandying about. On the other hand, I was convinced that anyone could paint furry floating boxes, or more to the point, that I could paint furry floating boxes. As best I could tell, this Rothko character was a famous painter. By that I mean a wealthy painter. Standing there, mesmerized in front of his beloved meditation on color, I audaciously decided that if Rothko could do it, I could do it. In that moment, I believed I had stumbled upon the path to fame and fortune. So, I enrolled in the Art Institute of California and learned to paint furry floating boxes.

I turned out to be a good painter—pedestrian but good. For five years, I churned out unexceptional works reminiscent (read derivative) of turn-of-the-century expressionists. I even undertook a series of self-portraits, in which I look only slightly more cadaverous than Egon Schiele in his self-portraits. In fact, I still refer to that time, only half-jokingly, as "the carrion years." Aside from the odd student exhibition and later, group shows with the artist collective I joined, I was an anonymous and unknown artist trying to claw my way up, same as the rest of them. And I remained anonymous and unknown, until I discovered the narrow but dazzling appeal of the common, everyday blender. Now, at thirty-three-years old, my star is shining in an otherwise lackluster sky. The only question that remains, according to Gillian, is when I became such an undisputed, king-of-the-hill asshole. That, I tell her, is my magnum opus. An ongoing and continuous unraveling of the knotted ontological skein that binds my human heart and sickens my mortal soul.

"When the masterpiece is completed," I say, "the nuclear spot that remains will be the bare ego, the pure and unadulterated asshole core of my being."

Thankfully, that shuts her up for a while. All the talk about family history has left me with a hankering for something stronger than the lukewarm beer I've been guzzling.

trevor lab come   trevor people come   people people people
trevor cage foothit   foothit foothit foothit   fuckwad wake
fuckwad cage shake   shake shake shake   cocksuckers fuckwad say
 people noise noise noise   trevor cage open   trevor fuckwad handhit
handhit handhit handhit   trevor fuckwad sit   push push push   sit sit sit
trevor fuckwad handhit   handhit handhit handhit   trevor cig light
smoke smoke smoke   people cig light   smoke smoke smoke
trevor smoke smoke smoke   people smoke smoke smoke
fuckwad laugh laugh laugh   trevor fuckwad handhit
handhit handhit handhit   people noise noise noise   trevor wires hold
trevor box hold   black black black box   what are you doing fuckwad say
trevor fuckwad peetrunk wire   on on on   fuck fuckwad say
trevor fuckwad ballsack wire   on on on   fuck fuckwad say
shut up trevor say   people noise noise noise   trevor box wire   on on on
fuckwad jump   fuckwad kick   fuck fuckwad say
fuckwad noise noise noise   trevor fuckwad hurt   fuckwad peetrunk hurt
fuckwad ballsack hurt   hurt hurt hurt   trevor box wire   on on on
fuckwad jump   fuckwad noise noise noise   noise noise noise
i'll kill you motherfuckers fuckwad say
like you killed all those animals trevor say   trevor box wire   on on on
on on on   fuckwad jump jump jump   fuckwad kick kick kick
fuckwad noise noise noise   fuckwad stop   fuckwad no scream
fuckwad no move   fuckwad soft   soft soft soft
ringo like fuckwad

Tijuana is a city ill at ease in its own skin. Although forward looking in some ways, it has failed to shed its past reputation for lawlessness and depravity. So be it. And all the better for me, I think, as we pull away from the border crossing. In my hedonistic travels, I believe I've spent a night or two in Tijuana, if only in spirit. Gillian's travels bring her here for very different reasons. She has connections, a dealer. Apparently, the black market for exotic animals is exploding in Mexico. According to her, big cats, venomous snakes, and endangered monkeys are on virtually every drug dealer's wish list these days. Slicing up rival cartel leaders and feeding them to one's Bengal tiger or Asiatic lion is popular sport down here. It's all the rage. I look at Gillian with something resembling respect. That she knows this macabre fact is impressive enough. But that she would rub shoulders with the likes of black marketeers in order to find new and exciting animals for me to stick in my canary yellow, five-speed Kitchenaid blender is nothing short of heartwarming.

Gillian pulls up to a fish taco stand in Tijuana Centro. She tells me to wait in the car and disappears somewhere behind the crudely if brightly painted particle board structure. Ordinarily, I would object to being treated so much like the way I treat her. But we're on her turf now, so I decide to do as I'm told. I open a can of warm beer and choke it back. I spark up the joint that I have stashed away on the nether regions of my person. The herbaceous calm makes everything better, including the beer. The fish tacos even look remotely appetizing. As I'm rooting through the glove compartment, looking for spare change, Gillian suddenly appears and, with a breathy whistle and a flip of her hand, waves me in.

The meeting place behind the particle board taco stand is nothing more than a poorly configured shack of corrugated steel. Inside are two rows of cages, most of them empty, except for one containing some odd looking feline creature with Dumbo ears. A tall, fit Mexican steps out of the shadows. He doesn't look like a criminal, which surprises me. He looks like an Olympic soccer coach or a splendidly aging airline pilot whose secret to staying young is plenty of R&R. I was expecting the gut-bugling fat guy in a pit-stained bowling shirt, with long wispy whiskers, and flashing a small gold mine's worth of dental crowns. A hyacinth macaw is perched on the Mexican's shoulder. He sees me looking at the bird: "Thirty thousand U.S. dollars," he says, as if I might try and pay with Honk Kong or Zimbabwe dollars.

"No birds" says Gillian. "We're looking for an iguana. Not too big, but ugly."

"Real ugly," I add.

"They're all ugly, Señor. Come back in a couple of days."

Just as we are about to leave, a small monkey scampers into the shack and up the Mexican's leg. The little fella hangs from the black marketeer's sinewy shoulder and begins to chirp the way that monkeys do. Maybe it's the dope, but suddenly the remarkable little creature looks incredibly menacing, which gives me a crazy idea.

"How much for the menacing monkey?"

"Woolly monkey," the marketeer corrects me. "He's sold to a mayor in Columbia."

"Vic, what are you thinking? You can't blend up a monkey, for God's sake."

"No, you're right. It's too cute. But what about just a part of it? Like say . . . maybe the foot . . . or no . . . the hand. Yeah, how about the hand. That would be outrageous."

"Outrageous, no. Nuts, yes. First of all, you'd probably get thrown in jail. And second, you said so yourself, they're too cute."

"But their hands aren't. Look at them. They're creepy, especially the big-ass ones, all black and shriveled up like that. What about the hand of a gorilla or something."

"You're asking for trouble. You'll have the cops coming down on you," says Gillian.

"But no one will know for sure if it's real. They'll wonder if it's real, but they'll think it couldn't be real, so it must be a fake. The point is they'll never know for sure. Nothing like keeping them guessing. It's perfect. And just imagine the critical shit-storm blending up a gorilla's hand will cause. You know, primates . . . our cousins. It's getting a little too close to home for comfort. It'll hit a raw nerve. Guaranteed. Forget the iguana. Bring me the hand of a gorilla."

The Mexican scrunches up one eye, as if calculating the square root of some insanely large and ungainly number. "That will cost you."

"How much?"

"Twenty thousand U.S. dollars."

"Done. Twenty grand it is."

ringo two five   ringo two five show   shit fuckwad say
do you have any sevens fuckwad say   ringo no seven   ringo tongue poke
poke poke poke   fuckwad laugh laugh laugh   ringo three fingers up
go fish fuckwad say   ringo card take   ringo two three
ringo two three show   fuck me fuckwad say
you got horseshoes up your ass fuckwad say   ringo poophole scratch
ringo finger smell   fuckwad laugh laugh laugh   I give up fuckwad say
fuckwad cards throw   fuckwad cig light   smoke smoke smoke

ringo cigs light   smoke smoke smoke
I need a pen and piece of paper fuckwad say
you understand fuckwad say   pen and paper fuckwad say
ringo desk go   ringo paper   ringo pen   ringo fuckwad paper give
ringo fuckwad pen give   fuckwad paper write   write write write
fuckwad ringo paper give
go outside and give this to someone fuckwad say   go fuckwad say
ringo paper take   ringo lab door go out   lab door lock   lock lock lock
ringo no key   fuck fuckwad say   where's the key fuckwad say
ringo no key   no no key   trevor lab come   trevor fuckwad paper take
take take take   trevor paper read   trevor paper break   break break break
trevor cage foothit   foothit foothit foothit   nice try fuckwad trevor say
trevor ringo leash   ringo no like leash
you both just bought yourselves a little hard time trevor say   trevor phone
people lab come   people noise noise noise   trevor fuckwad chair
push push push   trevor fuckwad rope   pull pull pull   trevor cig light
people cig light   smoke smoke smoke   trevor cig blow   Trevor cig red
red red red   hot hot hot   trevor fuckwad eye burn
eyeburn eyeburn eyeburn   fuckwad noise noise noise
eyeburn eyeburn eyeburn   bad smell   bad bad bad smell
people fuckwad eye burn   more more more   eyeburn eyeburn eyeburn
bad bad bad smell   trevor fuckwad peetrunk burn
peetrunkburn peetrunkburn peetrunkburn   trevor fuckwad ballsack burn
ballsackburn ballsackburn ballsackburn   trevor fuckwad nose cig put
in in in   fuckwad noise noise noise   noseburn noseburn noseburn
people noise noise noise   trevor laugh laugh laugh
ringo no like trevor
ringo like fuckwad

When we roll back into L.A., I order Gillian to stop at a liquor store, where I stock up on supplies. Then I tell her to call Goldman and inform him that I'll need the blood money after all. At least some of it. Gillian snaps open her cell phone and arranges a meeting. She tosses the cell on the dash. I assume that she is still disgruntled about me wanting to buy the severed hand of a gorilla. But I'm too drunk at the moment to make a run at defending myself and my insane plan. At this juncture, she's just going to have to grant me some artistic license. So I sip wordlessly from my go cup and smoke cigarettes in the passenger seat, while hurling imaginary hand grenades at every passing Starbucks.

Goldman's practice is located in one of those nondescript glass sky-scrapers, the kind that somehow snuck by the arbiters of refinement and good taste. I decide that said arbiters must have been punch-drunk after nine years of the wankish furor that was the 80s. We park underground and take an elevator to the forty-third floor. Goldman's manner hasn't alter-ed one iota since this morning. By that I mean he must have some hidden cyborg branch tucked away in his ancestral tree. He addresses me in the same stilted parlance as before.

"Am I to presume you have reconsidered?"

"You are to presume that I need twenty grand. You can give the rest of it away for all I care."

"I see. I suppose that can be arranged. There will be paperwork to sign."

"Of course there will."

"A check will be waiting for you at the front desk by tomorrow noon. Does that suit you?"

"That suits me fine."

"And the remainder of your inheritance? Shall I donate it to some worthy cause?"

"A worthy cause. Yes, that's a good idea. Let me see. Any ideas Gillian?"

Gillian, still fuming, refuses to look up from the magazine she's flip-ping through. "Something in the arts," I say. "No. Too predictable. Gay rights? Public breastfeeding? Guns Across America? Cosmic Ray Deflec-tion Society? Xenotransplantation Committee?" Then it comes to me. "I've got it. Make a donation to the NFAS." I pause to savor the irony in this gesture.

"NFAS, Mr. Planke?"

"National Front for Animal Supremacy, the new guys in town," I say. "And make it anonymous. I wouldn't want something like that to get out."

rena fuckwad eye cloth   cloth cloth cloth   fuckwad jump   fuckwad eye red
fuckwad eye big   bigred bigred bigred   rena fuckwad peetrunk cloth
cloth cloth cloth   fuckwad jump   rena no play play play peetrunk
rena fuckwad ballsack cloth   cloth cloth cloth
rena no play play play ballsack   fuckwad jump   those assholes rena say

it wasn't supposed be like this rena say
just sending out a message rena say   just scare you rena say
ringo rena kiss   ringo rena nice rack play   no ringo say rena   no no no
you know they're going to kill me don't you fuckwad say
ringo fuckwad kiss   no ringo say rena   you'll hurt him rena say
rena fuckwad cage close   rena cage lock   rena ringo key give
put this in the desk ringo rena say   ringo desk key go
i'm sorry rena say   there's nothing i can do rena say
call the cops fuckwad say   no rena say   what you did was wrong rena say
you have to pay rena say   i'm sorry rena say   trevor lab come
people lab come   hey sugar trevor say   rena lab go   rena no like trevor
women trevor say   no resolve trevor say   trevor fuckwad handhit
handhit handhit handhit   lucky for you i do have resolve trevor say
trevor cage open   people fuckwad hold   hold hold hold
people fuckwad face push   facepush facepush facepush
people fuckwad face floor   facepushfloor facepushfloor facepushfloor
fuckwad floor kiss   fuckwad leg kick   legkick legkick legkick
fuckwad noise noise noise   trevor fuckwad poophole hose in
hosein hosein hosein   fuckwad noise noise noise   trevor push push push
pushin pushin pushin   hosein hosein hosein   people noise noise noise
people fuckwad hold   hold hold hold   trevor fuckwad water in
waterin waterin waterin   trevor fuckwad poophole stop   stop stop stop
fuckwad small noise   fuckwad hurt noise   hurtnoise hurtnoise hurtnoise
fuckwad tummy big big big   fuckwad poophole stop   stop stop stop
trevor fuckwad tummy jump   tummyjump tummyjump tummyjump
fuckwad poophole boom   boom boom boom   fuckwad poophole water
waterboom waterboom waterboom   fuckwad poophole blood
waterblood waterblood waterblood   poopblood poopblood poopblood
fuckwad breathe loud   breathe breathe breathe   people fuckwad hold
hold hold hold   fuckwad ground kiss   fuckwad noise noise noise
trevor fuckwad poophole hose in   hosein hosein hosein
trevor push push push   pushin pushin pushin   trevor fuckwad water in
waterin waterin waterin   trevor fuckwad poophole stop   stop stop stop
how you feel trevor say
we're gonna clean you right out fuckwad trevor say
by the way trevor say   i saw the video you and ringo made trevor say
you're gonna pay for that fuckwad trevor say   all in good time trevor say
trevor fuckwad tummy jump   tummyjump tummyjump tummyjump
fuckwad poophole boom   boom boom boom   fuckwad poophole water

waterboom waterboom waterboom   fuckwad poophole blood
waterblood waterblood waterblood   poopblood poopblood poopblood
ringo no like trevor
ringo like fuckwad

I'm in the habit of sleeping with Gillian the night before a show, whether or not that happens to fall on a weekend, which it usually does. Gillian has finally calmed down, although it took more groveling than I'm accustomed to doling out. We drink some wine, cheap stuff. For some unfathomable reason, I've never come around to the good stuff, despite the fact that I can afford to drink it. Ironic, that. It drives Gillian crazy. I'll spend two hundred bucks on a bottle of imported vodka and ten bucks on a jug of Dancing Bear wine. Getting in touch with my inner hobo, I tell her. She sips the faux merlot and winces.

"There's your problem right there," I say, slugging back a snifter full of the stuff. "Don't bother trying to savor the flavor, simply wallow in the chemical aftertaste."

Fueled by the oracular fumes of the decomposing bear, we engage in some experimental sex in bed that night. Experimental, but nothing too dangerous. I wake at three a.m.—a preliminary case of the jitters, I decide. Because no matter how I try to avoid it, the thought that tomorrow represents a milestone in my career meets me at every turn. I crawl out onto the metal fire escape and light a Lucky Strike. I used to sit here and dream of this day, as if it would change everything. As if I would be transformed from hack pretender and art fraud to bona fide creative genius in the wink of an eye. Now, sitting on the cusp of the long-imagined moment, it almost seems the other way around. I'm about to get my fifteen minutes—or five minutes, whichever it is—and yet somehow I seem farther away from where I want to be. The thought naturally brings my father to mind. He'd had his fifteen minutes. Was it worth it? I can't help but wonder how he would respond to that question. Was it worth giving up everything? And by everything, I mean me. Didn't he ever wonder about me? About who I was? Who I'd grown up to be?

I go in search of his book and find it fallen behind some others in my bookcase. I blow the dust from it and return to my window stoop, where I open it to a random page and begin to read.

There were to be no children in the village, except for those sired by my father. This was his autocratic decree, his tyrannical pronouncement. Thus, the caceteiro women were all his concubines and the caceteiro men his court jesters. At the time of my clandestine egression from the jungle, I was the only child in the village. The sole heir to the throne. Next in line to lead the cult of John Ramos. The only child, whose only friend was a mongrel mutt with no name.

Sex among the caceteiros was not forbidden. Not even discouraged. When a woman became pregnant by a caceteiro man, she drank the bitter tea of golden sundrops (Oenothera hookeri) and aborted the unwanted fetus. If that didn't work, she beat it out with her fists. It is not surprising that the forest floor around the village teems with death still—the multitudes of tiny corpses silently carried off by bush dogs and opportunistic pumas.

My mother was the favored concubine, the one into whom father would finally deposit his seed. This sanctioned pregnancy had the effect of rendering mother sacrosanct among the caceteiros. The men worshiped her and the women adorned her with the red dye of roucou fruit and the scent of orchid flowers. They rubbed the oil of andiroba nuts on her skin to protect her from the sting of insects, and they waited for the blessed child of o porco branco to arrive.

When I left the caceteiros as a young child, it was not clear to me that the others regarded my mother and father with what can only be described as deistic adoration. Only in the course of my research, when I returned to Boca do Acre fifteen years later, did I discover this. My father was long dead by then, and my mother yet remained in a vegetative state after being beaten severely by o porco branco for having allowed—that is, facilitated—my return to civilization.

I learned that my father was killed by one of the caceteiros men, a member of his drug cult who, in a bid for power, staged a bloody coup. The power-hungry would-be leader had secretly forgone toad licking in order to get his mental edge back, a not-so-minor infraction of the cult code which, had it been discovered, would have cost him his life. As I would later learn firsthand, the drug excreted by the cane toad is so incapacitating that it handily reduces even those boasting a sturdy constitution to the life-sustaining functions of blinking, breathing, eating, defecating, and sleeping. And, of course, laughing. Always laughing. Some ex-perienced toad lickers were capable of certain meta-functions: drinking local hooch, procreating, and defecating in an upright position. All other functions requiring even the most meager degree of mental wherewithal were quite simply impossible. Thus, staging a coup would be well beyond the cerebral grasp of a practicing toad licker. Any caceteiros man with designs on leadership would have to stay straight in order to even wrap his head around the idea of seizing power. In this sense, the cane toad was truly an opiate of the masses.

The sole instigator of the coup was a caceteiro man named Kuin, the white hog's brother-in-law. Kuin cut my father down shortly after the broken-hearted professor beat his caceteiros wife into a coma. When he discovered that my mother had allowed me to be carried off to civilization by the interloper Tom Planke, he flew into a rage. Beating and kicking her senseless, o porco branco then retreated to the mystical stream inhabited by the cane toad, where for several weeks he licked every toad he could lay his tongue to. Kuin, who had witnessed the near-lethal beating of his sister, finding Ramos face-down in three inches of stream water, unconscious but still alive, clubbed him with one mighty death blow.

A rustle inside startles me. Gillian, wrapped in a satin sheet, places her lips on the back of my neck. Clearly, I have some unfinished business to attend to. I close the book and crawl back inside, where I slip into bed, waiting. Wondering what possible sexual permutation, what marvelously sick variation, she can come up with next.

Fashion wise, Rupert Fairmont has really outdone himself. Although he has sworn off the gay lifestyle, apparently he has yet to swear off the gay wardrobe. His ensemble looks to be an uneasy truce for the combined efforts of Dame Edna Everage and Maria von Trapp. Rupert flutters about Gallery Modena—flamboyant, impish and vivacious at once. It's painfully obvious that he is in his element. He glances my way and gives me a wink. The gallery walls are sparsely marred by paintings of clowns riding flying dildos, the work of a young lesbian artist from San Francisco. The music of Philip Glass crashes mutely in the corners.

I scan the crowd, looking for Gillian, annoyed that tonight I feel vulnerable without her there. Instead I spot Jacob Heath, art critic. Top dog at the *Times*. Which is unfortunate, since he has a history of hating me and my work. Perhaps *hate* is too strong. He's indifferent, which is much worse. My only hope on that front is Rupert's intercession on my behalf. That's the kind of sway the formerly gay gallery owner has in this town. And from what I hear, he's been talking up a storm about me. This becomes clear when Heath, spying me, weaves his way through the crowd for a brief tête-ê-tête. He's never spoken to me before tonight. Sure, it's just small talk. But the gesture alone is telling enough. By that I mean he has announced my arrival—to everyone at Gallery Modena and everyone else across the artistic wasteland that is L.A. And to everyone beyond, as well.

Gillian finally appears. She approaches easily, leading me to believe everything is going according to plan. She hands me a Black Russian.

"Not a moment too soon," I say. "You get it?"

"It's on ice," she says, smiling as if the joke is on me.

ringo sleep   sleep sleep sleep   fuckwad sad noise   sad sad sad
ringo wake   fuckwad noise noise noise   ringo sad   sad sad sad
ringo like fuckwad   fuckwad poophole out   out out out
fuckwad poophole push   pushin pushin pushin   fuckwad poophole no in
noin noin noin   fuckwad sad sad sad   sadnoise sadnoise sadnoise
they're gonna kill me ringo fuckwad say   you understand fuckwad say
kill me fuckwad say   trevor lab come   people lab come
get away from him ringo trevor say   trevor ringo leash on
it's the big finale today trevor say   fuckwad noise noise noise
no more fuckwad say   please fuckwad say   too late for that trevor say
trevor big knife hold   trevor shiny knife hold
shinyknife shinyknife shinyknife   people fuckwad hold
fuckwad noise noise noise   no no no fuckwad say
trevor fuckwad hand cut   handcut handcut handcut   blood blood blood
handcut handcut handcut   blood blood blood
fuckwad noise noise noise   hurtnoise hurtnoise hurtnoise
handcut handcut handcut   blood blood blood
fuckwad hurtnoise hurtnoise hurtnoise   fuckwad eye close
fuckwad sleep   trevor fuckwad water   throw throw throw
fuckwad cough   cough cough cough   fuckwad noise noise noise
cry cry cry   people noise   noise noise noise
you don't wanna miss this trevor say   trevor fuckwad hand big glass in
in in in   big glass big sound   sound sound sound   big big big sound
sound sound sound   big big sound stop   trevor big glass hold
trevor fuckwad big glass drink   fuckwad noise make
fuckwad kick kick kick   people fuckwad hold   fuckwad big glass drink
drink drink drink   fuckwad spit   spit spit spit   blood blood blood
spitblood spitblood spitblood   fuckwad breathe
breathe breathe breathe   fuckwad fuckwad arm hold
armhold armhold armhold   fuckwad no hand
fuckwad fuckwad arm hold   armhold armhold armhold
blood blood blood   fuckwad laugh cry laugh cry
laughcry laughcry laughcry   you stupid fucks fuckwad say
it wasn't even a real fucking hand fuckwad say
what trevor say   you stupid fucks fuckwad say
the hand was rubber fuckwad say   couldn't get a real one fuckwad say

fuckwad laugh   fuckwad cry   laughcry laughcry laughcry
trevor fuckwad hit   trevor fuckwad kick   hitkick hitkick hitkick
fuckwad noise   noise noise noise   hurtnoise hurtnoise hurtnoise
do you think that matters now trevor say
ringo no like trevor
ringo like fuckwad

"Mind blowing," says Rupert Fairmont. "You absolutely blew my mind."

I don't know quite how to respond, so I smile and press my drink to my lips, in an attempt to suppress a shit-eating grin. Gillian slips her arm into mine, an act that somehow strikes me as far more intimate than anything we did last night. There's something proprietary in this gesture, which should trouble me deeply but doesn't. Not tonight. Not anymore.

"I mean, the hand was *D-I-S* disgusting. So primitive, yet so sexual in a primal way. And the vomit. Oh my God! Don't get me started on the vomit. Can you vomit at will, Vic? Not that you'd need to. That puree looked *R-E*-volting. I almost had my own private little hurl."

Rupert's banter is going in one ear and out the other. I've got one eye trained coolly on Jacob Heath. He's standing close to the lesbian artist, talking as if they're already well-acquainted. He turns and catches me looking. Excusing himself, Heath strides with fitting regal pomposity over to our circle.

"Jake, wasn't it C-R-A kerazy? I swear it was crazier than a crack whore with a hundred bucks," says Rupert.

"Definitely food for thought." He takes my hand in a limp handshake. "Welcome to the big time."

Only a few stragglers remain, and I go in search of more drink. After all, it's a night to celebrate. Things couldn't have gone better. I lean in and kiss Gillian, tell her I'll be right back. She smiles an honest smile, one I'm not sure I've seen before. I detour to the men's room, fill the sink with cold water, and splash it on my face. I gaze at myself in the mirror. "So that's it then," I say to no one. "Welcome to the big time, Vic Ray."

I take no notice of the three figures slipping into the room behind me. Until one of them speaks. "Nice show, fuckwad."

fuckwad sleep   sleep sleep sleep   fuckwad no move
fuckwad red red arm   fuckwad white white tummy
fuckwad white white peetrunk   white white face   red red blood
fuckwad no move   fuckwad no noise   nonoise nonoise nonoise
ringo sad   sad sad sad   fuckwad no wake   ringo cage go out
ringo fuckwad cage shake   ringo noise make   noise noise noise
fuckwad no move   ringo desk go   ringo rena key take   key key key
ringo fuckwad cage open   ringo fuckwad shake   shake shake shake
fuckwad no move   nomove nomove nomove   red red blood
white white face   fuckwad red red no hand   nohand nohand nohand
ringo black black hand   blackhand blackhand blackhand
ringo fuckwad shake   shake shake shake   fuckwad sleep
sleep sleep sleep   ringo fuckwad pull   pull pull pull   pull pull pull
ringo rena key door in   keyin keyin keyin   ringo door open
open open open   fuckwad no wake   ringo fuckwad shake
shake shake shake   fuckwad no move   ringo fuckwad lab go out
go go go   out out out   ringo fuckwad shake   shake shake shake
ringo blackhand shake   shake shake shake   fuckwad white face
whiteface whiteface whiteface   fuckwad white white face
fuckwad no wake   nowake nowake nowake
fuckwad no sleep   nosleep nosleep nosleep
ringo like fuckwad

My head chatters painfully on the van floor. I hear three different voices, but one of them is clearly in charge. I should be scared, but I'm not. Mostly because I can't stop wondering how this impromptu drama is going to play out in the papers. And how it's going to catapult me to instant stardom. I couldn't have planned a more fitting end than this. In fact, lying there with a black hood over my head, I can't help kicking myself for not having planned this—for not having thought of it myself. I can see the headlines: *Vic Ray, VICtimizer, Abducted by Militant Animal Rights Group.*

It's perfect. The perfect end to a perfect evening—and by that I mean a perfect performance. Top-notch. I've really outdone myself this time, I think.

The van skids to a halt on loose gravel. One of the goons sits me up and rips off the hood. It's dark, except for the cracked plastic globe of the van's light overhead. I'm just about to ask for a black Russian in order to quell the peasant forces of sobriety that are busy rallying in my head when one of them—the leader, I decide—drops me with a rabbit punch to the gut. It burns for a minute and I think I might puke up the random slices of sashimi and the half-dozen cocktails I've consumed over the course of the evening. The goon sits me back up and for the first time I look into the face my abductor. In the low light, his eyes spark and crackle with rage. It's clear to me that this is *his* show, all his, and that I am a part of it. And it occurs to me for the first time that I may have misjudged my situation and that I may be in real danger.

He drops me with another rabbit punch and the goons guffaw and snort. But the leader just stares, meets my eyes with a cold hatred that strikes me as impersonal—impersonal, yes, I think, but all the more dangerous for it. I know then that I am going to pay for what I've done, for all of it, everything. He will see to it—him, my abductor. Of this, I now feel certain.

Finally he speaks in a low trembling tone. "Your blending days are over, fuckwad."

And I believe him. And I know that he's right.

Big MOFO's Specting You

Jerry Chung lowered himself into the office chair and reclined. To be clear, it was not his office, nor was it his office chair. However, Jerry preferred to think of it—them—that way, despite the four other graduate students who paraded in and out of the cramped space and also preferred to think of it—them—that way.

"Mindcast on," said Jerry. He was aware that the others laughed at him for saying it out loud; it was, after all, entirely unnecessary. One had only to think the words in order to activate the Big MOFO remote nestled into his brain stem and neurally "wired" to the cerebral cortex. "Use or lose it," Jerry would say to them. But what he really meant was this: "Speech is what makes us human. It sets us apart from every other species." Of course, he would quickly concede, Reggie was the notable exception to that. The real truth was speaking out loud made it seem more real for Jerry. Sometimes he grew weary of everything taking place inside his head, in that boundless sphere where the imaginary and the real, the perceived and the cognitive, happened side-by-side and one on top of the other.

"Archives. Popular Culture. Jeopardy." A translucent image of Alex Trebek blinked then floated before his eyes like a glowing mirage superimposed over the double-helix poster that one of his officemates had tacked to the wall. In the corner of the image, the ever-present Big MOFO logo—a stylized gray and red telescope—warned him that his present Mindcast was being *spected*.

St. Louis Missouri was named for King Louis XIV of France, who led the seventh and eighth of these military debacles.

"What was the Crusades?" said Jerry.

What was the Crusades? [applause]

That's right. Choose again, Barbara.

I'll take the World at War for six hundred, Alex.

The answer is: In 1619, Rene Descartes went to join the army of the Duke of Bavaria during this decades-long war.

"What was the Thirty Years' War?" said Jerry.

What was the Thirty Years' War? [applause]

Right again. Still your turn.

I'll take the World at War for one thousand.

Okay, here is the answer: The first British recipient of the Victoria Cross, a sailor, received it for action in the Baltic Sea during this war.

"What was the Crimean War?" said Jerry.

What was the Crimean War? [applause]

That's correct. Nice job, Barbara. You made quick work of that category. Choose another.

Jerry was bored and tired of waiting. He'd waited all morning in the ECEG, the Enclosed Climatically Engineered Garden, on the roof of his apartment building before deciding to kill some time in the lab. He checked his watch. The '46 Science Convention should've wrapped up by now. Again, Jerry wondered why he hadn't been invited along in the first place. After all, Reggie was his best friend and roommate, not Professor Shore's. But, then, Jerry was never invited along. It was true the young PhD candidate had been a late-comer to Project Logos. But the Professor had begun the project before he, Jerry, was even born. Jerry felt certain he could not be blamed for that.

Mindcast transmission incoming. The words formed like a thought in his head.

"Jeopardy off," said Jerry. The image imploded into a tiny white dot before his eyes and then vanished. "Transmit."

"So sorry to be late in contacting you, Jerry. *The familiar voice of Professor Shore arose in his head.* Some self-proclaimed bigwig from the Ministry wouldn't sit down and shut up. His closing remarks were worse than water torture."

Jerry cringed. He really wished the Professor would censor that kind of inflammatory thought. What made it especially frustrating for the PhD candidate was Professor Shore knew full well that Big MOFO spected all Mindcast transmissions of Combined Sectors East and West, or simply *Earth*, as the Professor insisted on calling them. And that was the kind of thought that could get them and their projects blacklisted by the Ministry of Science. Why didn't he transmit it as an encrypted thought-o-gram when he felt compelled to communicate such ideas, instead of blurting them out into the ether of Mindcast? The one time Jerry had actually mentioned this to the Professor, he was derided by the venerable fellow. "It's so clandestine," Professor Shore had railed. "Besides, I've got nothing to hide."

Some citizens still doubted whether the Party's main frame, colloquially known by the acronymic moniker Big MOFO, had the capacity to spect every Mindcast transmission communicated in the Combined

Sectors. Professor Shore was not one of these citizens. He knew that Big MOFO had the capacity, and then some. What he did doubt was the Party's purposiveness in ruthlessly cracking down on "unpatriotic" citizens accused of communicating "unpatriotic" thoughts through Mindcast ether. It was true that there had not been a single terrorist act perpetrated against the Party in more than a quarter century—ever since the creation of the Ministry of Specto (or the Ministry of Eavesdropping, as it was unofficially known), whose first official act was the implementation of Project Big Ears, a project with the mandate of implanting Big MOFO remotes in every man, woman, and child in the Combined Sectors. Along with being communication devices and Mindcast portals, the remotes could also be used by the Party for surveillance. By tapping into the visual cortex of its citizens, the Ministry of Specto could see whatever citizens were seeing or had seen; even things they may not have been consciously aware of seeing. Likewise with hearing. Quite literally, the Party had eyes and ears in every nook and cranny of the State. The success of Project Big Ears in effectively ending terrorism could not be denied. The Combined Sectors was a safer place because of it. Correction, the Combined Sectors was a *safe* place because of it—period. But when faced with this particular argument, Professor Shore was known to angrily rebut with one simple question: "At what cost?"

"So, how did it go then?" asked Jerry. "Any bites."

"Well, yes and no. The new home sex-change kit garnered some cautious attention."

"And Reggie?"

"Not so much interest, I'm afraid. No one seems to care about a talking chimp with a 130 IQ. 'Talking apes,' they said, 'as if we don't have enough of those at this convention.' No one is interested in real animal experiments anymore. All I heard for three days was 'virtual animals this, virtual animals that, virtual animals is the way to go. No mess, no fuss, no surprises.' I don't know. Maybe they're right. Maybe we should all be doing studies on virtual animals."

"How's Reggie taking it?"

"Same as always. Not so good. I had to keep him from making some of these morons look like monkeys. They seem to have a real problem with being less intelligent than a chimp."

Jerry bit his tongue at this comment. "So, when are you coming home?"

"Just stepping into the subcoaster. Should be there in a couple of minutes."

Mindcast transmission ended.

That was another thing about the Professor that perplexed—no, irritated—Jerry. Professor Shore never said—thought—*goodbye* at the end of a transmission. Jerry realized that a Mindcast transmission wasn't a phone call—how could it be; after all, phones hadn't been around for almost two decades—but still, he had to wonder if it would kill the good Professor to say "goodbye," "farewell," or even "catch you later" before ending a transmission, just as a token courtesy.

Reggie was spiraling down to one of his angry depressions. Returning to the apartment, the first thing the chimp did was dispense with his clothing, a symbolic act of de-evolution meant to aptly display his disdain for humans and their so-called civilization.

"What's the matter Jerry, do you find seeing a lower primate *sans* clothing a disconcerting sight?" he taunted his friend. After which, he hauled out an antique TV and watched pre-recorded episodes of Mutual of Omaha's Wild Kingdom, something he only did when he wanted to air his primate grievances.

"That Marlin Perkins is a real dick," he said. "How can you humans lionize such a pompous know-it-all? I mean, the truth is the guy knew zero about the animal kingdom. All his anthropomorphizing crap."

To make matters worse, Reggie had his speech transposer set on Sylvester Stallone as Rocky Balboa, something he knew annoyed Jerry terribly. Why Professor Shore had ever decided to include a range of nostalgic movie-voice modes in the speech transposer remained a mystery to Jerry and everyone else associated with Project Logos. Most of the time, Reggie would leave it set on Orson Welles' as the Shadow, a solid if at times over-the-top voice rendering. But there were occasions when he would use the movie-voice modes for effect—or abuse them for effect, as Jerry often accused his chimp roommate of doing. Talking to attractive females, Reggie would switch to Ricardo Montalbán as Mr. Roarke to give him that Latino flair. Approaching the Professor's colleagues, he would set the voice transposer to Laurence Olivier as Henry V in order to sound more intelligent. If he wanted to sound moderately intelligent but dead drunk, he would switch to Sean Connery in any of his roles. If he wanted to sound irritatingly earnest or just wickedly ironic, he would use the Charlton Heston as Colonel George Taylor setting. If he wanted to sound silly, he would set the voice transposer to Elmer Fudd as Elmer Fudd in any of his cartoon appearances. But if he wanted to sound just plain dumb, he would invariably fall back on the Rocky Balboa setting.

"And another thing," said Rocky Balboa. "Marlin Perkins wouldn't know an endangered species if it bit him on the ass."

"Come on, Reggie. Don't take it out on me," said Jerry. "I'm part of the project, too. Remember? I don't want to see it fail."

Reggie sighed, shook his head. "I know," said Orson Welles. "Sorry."

"So, what do you say?" said Jerry hopefully. "How about at least putting on some underwear?"

Reggie bounced with great hominid agility onto the cushions then back of the sofa, springing up to the titanium chandelier, where he hung by one hand and retrieved a pair of black briefs with the other. He dropped to the floor.

"You know, it's just that I'm twenty-three years old and I feel like my life hasn't started yet." His big chimp eyes looked sad and faraway. "I'm tired of being part of Professor Shore's dog and pony show. I want to do something normal, something real." He slipped into the briefs.

"You will, Reg. You will. I know it," said Jerry. "But in the meantime, how about I whip you up a banana shake?" Jerry rose to his feet and strode for the kitchen before stopping abruptly.

Incoming ciphertext thought-o-gram.

"Show thought-o-gram."

Showing thought-o-gram: <youve turned into such a beautiful girl and we were making love again and i tasted the desire in such an wild child so think of me and happy birthday my baby the bad blood just stops when i love you pictures in my head come on baby lets start again cause she was born to lie we spun around we couldnt tell looking through my fears kissing faces far off places wasnt worth the price we couldn't pay my sweet tomboy now wears silk and loves taking you for a ride oo how i love those softly breathing days and i kiss her eyes breaking up is so hard the games no good such a wild child and my fields feel like fire time to turn the page we loved so fast we couldnt tell nostalgia goes running to the one i love> *End of ciphertext.*

"Search for key," said Jerry.

Key located.

"Apply key."

Applying key: <youve turned **into** such a beautiful girl and we **were** making love again and i ta**sted** the desire **in** such an wild **chi**ld so think

of me and happy birthday my baby the bad blood just stops when i love you pictures in my head come on baby lets start again cause she was born to lie we spun around we couldnt tell looking through my fears kissing faces far off places wasnt worth the price we couldn't pay my sweet tomboy now wears silk and loves taking you for a ride oo how i love those softly breathing days and i kiss her eyes breaking up is so hard the games no good such a wild child and my fields feel like fire time to turn the page we loved so fast we couldnt tell nostalgia goes running to the one i love>

"Compress thought-o-gram."

Compressing:

<interestedinchimpprojectcometosectorofficetomorrowbringthechimptellnoone>

"Space and punctuate."

Spacing and punctuating:

<Interested in chimp project. Come to Specto office tomorrow. Bring the chimp. Tell no one.>

Jerry resumed walking, still reviewing the thought-o-gram hovering before his eyes. "Wow, here's something."

"What is it?" said Reggie.

"An encrypted thought-o-gram from the Ministry of Specto." Why the Party insisted on encrypting thought-o-grams in scrambled ballad lyrics from the previous century was a mystery to Jerry, and most everyone else in the Combined Sectors. Professor Shore viewed it as a humiliation tactic on the part of the Party and a way to affirm the new cultural superiority. But Jerry wasn't so sure.

"So what does it say?"

"They're interested in the project. By that I mean they're interested in you, Reggie."

"Don't mess around with me, Jerry. You're kidding, right?"

"I'm not kidding. They're interested! This is fantastic! I told you, Reggie. This is our big chance. Your big chance."

Reverend Billy Layman slammed his fist into the pulpit. At the corner of the soundstage, a soundman tore the headphones from his head and held his ears, whimpering.

"Repent! I say repent, ye sinners!" The reverend spread his arms dramatically, as if taking flight, and lowered his voice to a whisper, at which point the soundman responded by cautiously slipping the headphones back onto his head. "For the Party is merciful. And the Party wants you to be happy."

With what can only be described as well-rehearsed, saintly grace, the magnetic reverend strode to the side of the stage and flaunted his handsome made-for-TV looks before the devoted studio-audience flock.

"Adam and Eve were expelled from the Garden of Eden for eating the apple from the Tree of Knowledge of Good and Evil. Knowledge can be a dangerous thing. Oh yes, we know this to be true, now. But the generations before us squandered their collective existence in search of knowledge. They wanted to know everything and anything. They wanted to know how heaven and the Combined Sectors were formed, how life came to be on the Combined Sectors, how humans came to be talking animals. But what they did not realize then, but we do now, is such things don't matter to people like you and I. Rest assured, brothers and sisters, the Party knows all the answers to all of the questions. And what does this mean to you? To us? It means that we need not concern ourselves with such weighty matters. The Party will take care of them for us. The Party will take care of us. For who are we if not all children of the Party?"

The Reverend wandered back to the center of the stage, where he produced an encyclopedia from beneath the pulpit and slammed it down. The soundman dropped to his knees.

"Divest yourselves of this evil, this quest for knowledge," he bellowed. "Take a good look at this book. This dinosaur and relic of sinful desires. Thanks to the good Party, we can scarcely find them anymore—books. And good riddance to them, I say. Our minds can be purposefully and righteously appeased by Mindcast. Mindcast is all we need, brothers and sisters." He lowered his voice again. "Search no more for knowledge, I beseech you. It is all in vain, I assure you. It will not make you happy, I promise you."

With this final, precisely understated proclamation, Reverend Billy Layman exited stage left and marched straight for his dressing room, oblivious to the booming applause behind him. Two young men who had been preselected from the studio audience according to the Reverend's strict specifications—one blond, one brunette; one thin, one plump; over eighteen but under twenty; high school dropouts; no criminal record, save misdemeanors of a sexual nature; no pimples; and above all, no braces— waited for him, having already been briefed on the situation and knew precisely what was expected of them—from them. Reverend Layman plopped down on a sofa and kicked off his shoes like two fish flopping from the Apostle Peter's fishing boat, at which time the young men rushed to him. One of them, the blond, greedily unzipped the reverend's fly.

"My God," screamed the boy, shrinking in fear.

"Just shut up and start sucking," said Reverend Layman.

"Mindcast on. Archives. Popular culture. Jeopardy."

Jerry sunk his head into a pillow and stared at the ceiling. Alex Trebek hung like a fluffy-haired cloud above him.

This German shepherd was often cast as a wolf or wolf hybrid during its ten-year film career.

"Who was Rin Tin Tin?" said Jerry.

Who was Rin Tin Tin? [applause]

Correct. Choose again.

I'll take Famous Animals for eight hundred.

The answer is: This goat reached the rank of lance corporal in the 1st Battalion of the British Army in 2001.

"Who was William Windsor?" said Jerry.

BEEP BEEP! William Windsor, sometimes known simply as Billy, was the answer we were looking for there. Terry, still your turn. Choose a category.

I'll take Famous Animals for one thousand.

The answer is: This primate shot to fame in 1989 after attempting to save a controversial performance artist from a militant animal rights group.

"Ahh . . . who was . . ."

Who was Ringo the Chimp?

"Huh?" Jerry sat up.

Right again, Terry. The artist that Ringo the Chimp was trying to save was L.A.-based performance artist Vic Ray.

"Stop. Replay."

The artist that Ringo the Chimp was trying to save was L.A.-based performance artist Vic Ray.

Jerry wondered if it were possible. Could this Ringo the Chimp be the same chimp whose DNA Professor Shore had used for Project Logos?

"Search News Media archives. Keywords: Ringo the Chimp and Vic Ray."

Two articles found: Los Angeles Times, August 24, 1989; LA Living Magazine, August 24, 1991.

"Show *L.A. Times* article." A fuzzy column of words fluttered before his eyes before coming cleanly into focus.

Artist Vic Ray Found Slain in NFAS Lab – Five days after being abducted by the militant animal rights group National Front for Animal Supremacy (NFAS), artist Vic Ray has been found dead, near a make-shift laboratory in Seal Beach. In a bizarre turn of events, Ray was discovered after witnesses spotted a chimpanzee named Ringo dragging the lifeless body from a nondescript warehouse near the waterfront in an apparent attempt to save the artist. Witnesses stated that the chimp was highly agitated, and when police finally arrived on the scene, the animal had to be tranquilized before the body could be recovered. Ray, best known for his controversial performance art, died at the hands of his captors from a fatal wound sustained during the abduction. The ring leader, Trevor Lords, is being held without bail, pending trial on first-degree murder charges.

Interesting," said Jerry. But it still didn't answer his question: was this Ringo the Chimp the same Ringo from Project Logos? For all he knew, Ringo was a popular name among primates in the twentieth century. Pondering this, Jerry walked to the kitchen, opened the fridge, and poured himself a tall glass of milk.

What he did know was this: Genetically speaking, Reggie's father was a chimp named Ringo. Professor Shore had extracted DNA from the chimp Ringo shortly after it died in the San Diego Zoo. The Professor had tricked up the DNA with a HAR (human accelerated region) RNA cocktail, loaded it into a stripped skin cell, and grew Reggie in the lab. Thus began Project Logos, a long-term study to see if man's closest relative could be genetically hardwired to acquire the advanced cognitive functions normally associated with humans, foremost among those being speech. In a word, Reggie was the proposed, presumed, and hoped for outcome of a scientific experiment.

"Show *L.A. Living article*." Jerry swigged milk and waited.

PERFORM! is Back and Founder Gillian Hill is Looking for an Encore Performance
by Susan Glum

For Gillian Hill, founder of the annual charity event PERFORM!, the yearly fundraising drive is a labor of love. "I've put my heart and soul into this," said the thirty-four year old widow of the late Vic Ray, whom she married only hours before his final, fateful performance two years ago. "Today is not only a day to remember Vic and the art medium that he so loved, it's a day to do something that I know he would have wanted me to do." That something is raise money for a new primate exhibit at the San Diego Zoo, the same which is now home to Ringo the Chimp, the unlikely hero in the whole Vic Ray tragedy.

Last year, PERFORM! raised a whopping $25,000 in the single-day marathon event for the Zoological Foundation of San Diego. This year they hope to double that number. "At this rate," said Hill, "we'll be able to break ground for construction within five years."

Those spectators who venture out to Exposition Park to take in the performance art extravaganza are invariably astounded by the diversity of the performances and the creativity of the performers. Not to mention their stamina. "I've been climbing and jumping off my homemade corporate ladder here for nearly eight hours now," said performance artist Jason Schlitz. "I've sprained both ankles and twisted a knee. But it's for a good cause, you know. So I'm going to keep on doing it for another eight hours." Not all performances are so rigorous. Esther Ha is knitting a three-piece suit from pink yarn. "I hope to be done my 'pinko suit,' as I call it, before the day is over," says Ha, who drove from Phoenix, Arizona, to be here to-day. "I wouldn't have missed this for anything. I was too young to really appreciate the art of Dick Ray, but I do remember something about him being saved by the chimp Ringo. So, I think we've got to do something, you know, to help. Chimps are people, too."

"Holy crap! You think you know a guy." And by guy, what Jerry actually meant was chimp. The two Ringos had to be the same chimp. Both at the San Diego Zoo—what were the chances? And that meant Reggie's genetic father was a hero. Jerry couldn't help but wonder why Professor Shore had never mentioned this juicy bit of information to Reggie. After all, it might do wonders for the chimp's self-esteem.

But the truth was Jerry wasn't at all surprised that little had been revealed to him about Reggie the chimp. Jerry had joined Project Logos in his junior year at Caltech. By then, Reggie was already twenty-one and the project was winding down to a rather dubious end. Professor Shore had been unable to attract the attention he'd hoped for in the beginning. Practical applications seemed to be lacking, and Project Logos came to be viewed largely as a novelty act within the science community. Furthermore, with the rise of the Party and the establishment of the Ministry of Science, Project Logos was forced even further afield by the ministry's ultraconservative policies. Eventually, it was all but forgotten. Professor shore continued to take Reggie along to various science conventions more as a matter of routine than anything else. To make matters worse, Reggie had begun to grow weary of living in the lab; he wanted a place of his own. And that's where Jerry Chung came into the picture. At Professor Shore's bidding, Jerry found an apartment for the chimp. His role in Project Logos was more babysitter-cum-roommate than actual lab assistant. Jerry knew that, had always known that. But it meant rent-free living for him, so he happily went along with it. He would never have guessed back then that he and Reggie the talking chimp would become fast friends. But they had.

Jerry strolled back into the bedroom and flopped down onto the bed, wondering if he should mention anything about Ringo the Chimp to Reggie. "Mindcast on," he sighed. "Archives. Popular culture. Jeopardy."

Jerry and Reggie took their places on the Subcoaster. It irked Reggie that he had to strap himself into a children's G-force station just because his lower primate stature was such that his head fell below the seemingly random red line which, apparently, separated children from adults.

"Don't worry about it, Reg," said Jerry. "Come on. We're on our way. New York is a mere fifteen minutes away." It was true; New York was a mere fifteen minutes away, thanks to the hybrid steam/water/methane/electric/magnetic powered engine of the Subcoaster system. In truth, virtually all the energy needed to suck the transporter through a four-thousand-kilometer-long tunnel at a ridiculously high speed was leached from the enormous dynamo that is the Combined Sectors' core. It was magnetic energy—clean, safe, and powerful, a point that seemed lost on vestigial environmental groups. Thus, in order to appease these groups, the Party and its Ministry of Nature simply fabricated a hybrid alternative and threw it into the mix.

"Yeah, fifteen minutes all right," said Reggie. Fifteen minutes of shame and humiliation." He pushed his monkey lips into a pliant pout, just as the Subcoaster shot from the station.

The two friends stood before a giant revolver with its giant barrel tied into a giant black knot. Neither of them had ever seen a real gun before. Those days were long gone, part of a violent past that had been shed like an old skin. Gun control was a thing of the past. Quite simply, there were no guns anymore and hadn't been for some time. The Party had seen to that. Not that the giant gun in question was a real gun. But it was close enough to the real thing for Reggie and Jerry.

Reggie recalled from one of his history lessons that the concrete and glass building looming large behind the giant gun had once been the headquarters for the United Nations. Of course, that was before the Party came to power, rendering the organization obsolete, and the Ministry of Specto moved in.

Inside the complex, they were quickly ushered into the office of the Managing Director of Specting in Quadrant One, formerly known as North America. A middle-aged woman with disturbingly red lips and a powdery complexion rose from behind a sprawling desk revealing a set of hips both wide and deep.

"Gentlemen, please come in. My name is Jill Chinaski." She shook Jerry's hand. "You must be Jerry Chung." Dropping her gaze to Reggie, she then cocked her head to one side as if she wasn't sure what she was seeing. "And this is the talking chimp I've heard so much about. Doesn't he look charming in his little outfit? Can you make him say something, Jerry?"

"Uh, you don't have to make him say anything. He thinks and talks on his own, just like you and me."

"Terrific!" The Managing Director of Specting in Quadrant One stooped down eye-level to Reggie. "Hello, Reggie. How are you today?"

At that moment, Reggie contemplated chomping down on Chinaski's nose and liberating the sizable nozzle from her face. But he really wanted this job, so he decided against it. "I'm fine thank you," he said in his Laurence Olivier voice. "How are you?"

"My God! He even sounds smart." Chinaski straightened up, addressing Jerry again. "So tell me, then, how you've managed to accomplish this feat of genetic voodoo."

"Well, Reggie knows more about that than I do. You'd better ask him."

Reggie half-expected this and was now glad he'd chosen to wear his matching brown corduroy slacks and jacket with a professorial-looking turtleneck beneath, shunning the patched jacket, bow tie, and funny hat outfit that was forever the crowd-pleaser.

"In theory, it's quite simple. About half a century ago, geneticists isolated a human gene that had evolved at a highly accelerated rate. In the course of five to seven million years, from about the time humans and chimpanzees diverged, this gene had mutated in significant ways. But these scientists really had no idea how the gene expressed itself or what it really did. It was a big mystery. That's where Professor Shore and his Caltech team come into the story. Just over two decades ago, Professor Shore finally cracked the code and discovered how the gene worked. More importantly, he discovered that, basically, the non-coding gene was responsible for the development of the characteristically large and complex brain of *Homo sapiens*, humans. So, he inserted the gene into chimpanzee DNA, and brought a chimp to term in vitro. That chimp was me."

"My, my. He is a smart monkey!" said Chinaski.

"Why, thank you kindly," said Reggie with his Orson Welles voice.

"My God! And how do you do that?"

"Voice transposer, or more crudely, a voice box." Reggie switched back to Laurence Olivier. "You see, chimpanzees are physically incapable of producing the sounds of human speech because we lack the biological machinery. But a voice transposer gives me the necessary machinery. The choice of nostalgic movie-voice renderings was Professor Shore's idea. He thought it would be amusing."

"Well, he was right. It certainly is amusing, and quite amazing, too. Which brings me to the point of this meeting." Jill Chinaski laid one ponderous buttock on the corner of her desk and perched there in an impossibly uncomfortable position. "You see, some of my colleagues in the Ministry of Science are intrigued by Professor Shore's project and, of course, with Reggie. So much so, that they want to see if Reggie is capable of working for the Party. I'm sure you're well aware that the Party has always got an eye out for its stalwart members, even if they happen to be monkeys. Anyway, it just so happens that we have a position that needs to be filled. Does that interest you at all, Reggie?"

"Well, yes, it does. Absolutely."

"What, exactly, is this position, and what does it entail?" said Jerry.

"Ah, I see you've brought your manager along," chortled Chinaski. "The position is Special Events Coordinator."

It was Jerry's turn to chortle. "The Ministry of Specto has special events?" But the humor in this notion was lost on Chinaski. So Jerry rephrased: "I mean, I wasn't aware that the ministry hosted special events."

"Actually, it doesn't, but it's about to start. Do you think you could handle a coordinator position, Reggie?"

"Well, I—"

"Before you answer, let me show you around. I think you'll like what you see around here."

The tour started in the atrium, which was manifestly void of life. Not that there weren't people there—there were. A lot of them. But they lacked a spark; there was no vivifying germ, no animating pith of humanness somewhere deep within.

"To your left is our most popular attraction, the Party Coffee Shop," said Chinaski. "Should you choose to join our team you'll receive a buy-three-get-one-free card for any size of Big MOFO premium blend coffee."

"Nice," said Reggie.

"To your right is Big MOFO's health and fitness center. Should you choose to join our team, it will be at your disposal, no charge, except for a modest towel fee."

"Nice," said Reggie.

They walked on, finally stopping outside a hulking metal door. "Open door," said Chinaski—it responded by sliding sluggishly. "And this, gentlemen, is where it all happens: the War Room, if you'll allow an archaic and wildly inappropriate analogy."

Reggie recognized the General Assembly Hall from a photograph he had once seen in a book from Professor Shore's lab. The lights were dim and the air in the vaulting hall was stale—no longer alive with the blustery bellows of failed diplomacy. They strolled up the aisle, passing row upon row of men and women sitting in complete silence.

"They're specting every Quadrant of the Combined Sectors East and West right here," said Chinaski. "A special remote has been implanted in the head of every person here. With it, each of them is seeing and hearing what over a million citizens are seeing and hearing at any given moment, twenty-four hours a day. Not to mention the hundreds of millions of Mindcast transmissions and thought-o-grams they are specting in real time. It is an omnipresence that can only be likened unto being God."

"Wow," said Jerry.

"Wow, indeed," said Chinaski.

They resumed walking. Up ahead, plastered on the front wall, was the familiar logo of a gray and red telescope. Beneath it on a marble podium sat what appeared to be an upturned bowl of Jell-O, glowing in a chemically hue of electric blue and red. "And this . . . this is the heart and soul, the blood and guts, the mind and will of the Ministry of Specto. This is the ultimate in surveillance technology. This, my young friends, is Big MOFO. Magnetic Outlying Frequency Obstructer."

"That's Big MOFO?" said Jerry. "Wow! Talk about your misnomers."

"Yes, well . . . what it lacks in physical size it makes up for in symbolic presence. The sights, sounds, and thoughts of every man, woman, and child in the Combined Sectors pass through this very spot, through Big MOFO. Big MOFO allows us to do what we do, spect. Which brings us back to the reason why you are here. Reggie, what do you think? Would you like to join the team, work for the Ministry of Specto?"

Reggie's chimp heart skipped a beat and he responded without hesitation. "When do I start?"

Reverend Layman bit into a bratwurst sausage and let the grease trickle down his finely cleft chin. He chased it with a swallow of vodka & orange juice. The young man who had just then been fellating him under the table got off his knees and slid into a seat, looking more sheepish that one might expect, considering the task that he'd just been at.

"Have some sausage," said the Reverend. "It's to die for."

"I really should be getting back to class," said the young man.

"Yes, yes, by all means—get back to class. I know the routine. I was a college student once."

"Really?" The young man's surprise may very well have been the first legitimate emotion he'd felt over the past twenty-four hours. "Were you here at Columbia?"

"No. Caltech." The Reverend pulled a crisp green bill from his wallet, folding it neatly in two. "College didn't really turn out well for me. But that's a whole other story. A sob story. A sob story that made me stronger, made me the person I am today." He handed the money to the young man. "Have my secretary validate your parking on the way out."

When the young fellator bent to kiss him on the cheek, the Reverend turned away. "Run along now. None of that lovey-dovey stuff. I've got business to attend to."

Reverend Layman rose and walked to the twenty-third-floor window. "Mindcast on. Outgoing transmission. Jill Chinaski. Ministry of Specto." There was a brief pause. Then a nasally voice rose like bubbles from the gray suds of his brain.

"Bill. I wasn't expecting to hear from you. Uh . . . do you think this is a good idea?"

Reverend Layman savored the moment. He enjoyed making Chinaski squirm. He knew there was nothing the Managing Director of Specting in Quadrant One could do. There wasn't a damn thing she could do, except sit there and take it, same as everyone else. For what the reverend and Jill Chinaski both knew was Billy Layman's ministry was a veritable goldmine from which funds flowed freely to the Ministry of Specto. Not only that, the Reverend Billy Layman was one the Party's staunchest supporters and regularly propagandized on its behalf.

"You worry too much," said Layman. "Just a courtesy call to let you know I've donated three million to your Ministry. You should be seeing it sometime today. This afternoon, perhaps."

"That's very . . . very generous of you, Reverend."

"Yes, well, I feel certain that it will be returned in-kind. Don't you?"

"Uh, yes, yes I do. But we shouldn't . . . I mean, I can't talk about that now . . . here. You understand?"

"Of course, I understand. Do you think I'm some kind of dipshit moron?" The reverend didn't wait for a response. "End transmission. Mindcast off."

Reggie arrived to work early, swinging his briefcase and whistling a happy tune. He wanted to get moved into his office, get organized, get a feel for things. Someone had abandoned an old briefcase in the Caltech lab, so he'd appropriated it and stuffed it with a few loose pages in order to avoid so obviously being the new guy on the job. As if being a chimpanzee and showing up for work in a miniature business suit wasn't going to attract much attention at all.

"This is your office," said Chinaski.

Reggie looked visibly disappointed. His big chimp ears drooped and his big chimp grin dissolved into a null and void look. He was expecting something more in line with the grandeur of the Big MOFO Control Room. As it turned out, his "office" was no bigger than a closet. And in fact, it was a closet, or had been a closet, as attested to by the half dozen storage shelves still hanging high on a overhead.

"And this is your computer. It took me a while to lay my hands on this dinosaur, but it's yours to use now."

Reggie stared at the ancient portable computer. "Oh, okay."

"It's called a laptop, although I'm not exactly sure why. You do know how to use one don't you?"

"Yes," said Reggie. Of course, he knew no such thing, but he figured it couldn't be too hard to operate.

"Since you don't have a remote implant, all your work will be done manually. The laptop is actually hardwired right into Big MOFO. Thrilling isn't it?"

"Yes, I guess it is."

The Managing Director of Specting in Quadrant One handed him a piece of paper on official ministry letterhead. "So, here's a list of the guests who are invited to our first Meet Big MOFO Dinner Event. All you have to do is send out the invitations in a non-encrypted Mindcast thought-o-gram. Of course, as I said, you don't have an implant, so you can't actually send a thought-o-gram. That's where the laptop comes into it. The thought-o-grams will have to be sent manually."

Reggie glanced at the paper. There were a few dozen names on the list. "Okay. I think I can handle that."

"Oh, and be sure to type the invitation exactly as it's written on the paper. We're real sticklers for detail around here. And I don't have to remind you that this is top, top secret work, do I? You are strictly forbidden to talk about this with anyone, even your friend Jerry."

"Got it."

"Welcome aboard, Reggie," said Chinaski. "See you around."

It took Reggie most of the morning to figure out the laptop, but by early afternoon he was set to begin sending out invitations. He began to type.

Dear Mr. Shakti,

Big MOFO's specting you! To come to a special dinner event.

When: November 12, 2046

Where: The Ministry of Specto Building

Time: 7:00 p.m.

"Big MOFO's specting you." Reggie chuckled to himself. "And they call themselves intelligent," said Charlton Heston. "Ooh-ooh, aah-aah."

Dear Ms. Freemont,

Big MOFO's specting you! To come to a special dinner event.

When: November 12, 2046

Where: The Ministry of Specto Building

Time: 7:00 p.m.

By 4:00, he'd finished all the invitations, so Reggie decided to go looking for Chinaski to see what other mindless tasks might fall under his job description. That's when he realized that the Managing Director of Specting in Quadrant One's rote farewell, "see you around," was not meant to be taken too literally, as there seemed to be no trace of her anywhere for him to see. When Reggie swung by Chinaski's office, a tolerably cute redhead told him the Director wasn't in. Reggie strolled down to the coffee shop but didn't see Chinaski there either. Then he crossed the atrium to the gym. But the Director was nowhere to be found. That's when Reggie made his first executive decision as coordinator of special events at the Ministry of Specto—his first call, as it were, according to the dictates of his own conscience. Reggie decided to go for a steam, with a towel. "No, two towels," said Reggie to no one.

"Brothers and sisters, I have sinned." The Reverend dropped to his knees with rehearsed remorse and pulled a clean white handkerchief from his jacket pocket. He dabbed at the tears stinging his eyes. The studio audience mooed "no" in unison. The cameraman and soundman smiled yes in unison.

"It's true. I have sinned. For I have desired mammon . . . money. You see, yesterday, I passed a toy store and saw all the beautiful toys. With Giftday just around the corner, I thought to myself, 'Oh Billy! Wouldn't you love to give those toys to the orphans of Layman's Orphan Foundation on Giftday?' And then I thought to myself, 'But I need money to do that. Only money will allow me to buy those toys.' And in that moment, brothers and sisters, I wanted money. More than anything else in the Combined Sectors East and West I desired money so I could buy those toys. But it was a sin. A sin in the eyes of the Party. For money is the root of all evil, says the Good Partybook."

The Reverend rose slowly, as if laboring under the weight of his sin, and shuffled across the stage. "Money has been the cause of all our problems. Money has started wars. When Sector West attacked Sector East in Mighty War I, the war to annihilate all previous wars, it was all about money. And when Sector East attacked Sector West in Mighty War II, again, money was at the root of it. Money has caused mayhem. Remember the Great Bank Riots of '09. People cut each other down in the streets, trying to break into the banks, literally dying to get their grubby hands on their grubby money. Money leads to more serious vices, too. It is a gateway vice. History has shown that those who have money, those who succumb to the vice of money, soon turn to harder vices. They smoke marleybombs. They shoot goats-head-soup into their veins. They snort rubbersoul into their noses.

"But the Party has done away with all of that. There are no wars, no banks, no vices, anymore. No Party-less dictators. No greedy bank managers. No evil vice dealers. There is only the Ministry of Money. And make no mistake, the Ministry of Money wants money. They desire money—your money. 'But, Billy, isn't it a sin to want money?' I hear you ask. 'Didn't you just say that money is the root of all evil?' Oh yes, brothers and sisters, it is the root of all evil. Yes, money is the root of all evil. And that is why the Ministry of Money wants it, your money. They want to save you from the evil that very nearly destroyed the Combined Sectors."

Strolling purposefully now, the Reverend halted at the pulpit, just as a videogram began to roll, hovering beneath the ceiling and soon filling the studio. The audience let out a collective gasp at the sight of it, not because the technological miracle of fourth-generation volumetric video-grams was new to them, but because of the images so vividly, so promi-nently, displayed therein were shocking to them.

"This, brothers and sisters, is how I paid for my sin. This is how I begged the Party's forgiveness." Above the crowd, the hologramatic rev-erend, wrapped loosely in a poorly fastened loin cloth, shoveled green-backs into a blazing inferno. Sweat glistened on his smooth chest and soot smudged his brow. With each shovelful of money he unloaded, the flames growled, snapped, and snarled with Cerberean ferocity. As they nipped at his scorched heels, the faint odor of burning flesh became detectable in the studio. And suddenly the room felt warm—just kept getting warmer. Until it was sweltering.

The reverend allowed a few moments for the sights, sounds, and smells of the videogram to sear into the collective memory of his audience before resuming. "This, brothers and sisters, is the Ministry of Money. This is what the Party does with evil mammon. This is the eventual end, the deserving end, of all money. Yes, I paid dearly for my sin. But you, you, brothers and sisters, need not feed the everlasting fires. The Party is your intercessor, your mediator, your savior. You need only put your faith in the Party. Believe that it can save you from the sin of money. Demon-strate your belief by sending your money to the Party. Demonstrate your belief today, here and now! And the Party will cast the evil mammon into the fiery pit that is the Ministry of Money. Send it now! Divest yourselves, I say unto you, brothers and sisters, of all your money! And be free! Be free from sin!"

The lights dropped low, and the audience gasped again, with renewed surprise, as the words *Demonstrate your belief!* blazed brightly above their heads. In unison, they bowed down before the luminous decree, vowing one-and-all to divest themselves of mammon and abandon the sin of money.

The Reverend took this opportune moment to exit stage right, where an elated producer grasped his hand and shook it forcefully. "That was amazing. I've never seen anything like it before."

"Save it," said the Reverend, spying two young men standing doe-eyed in the shadows. "I've got business to attend to."

Reggie sipped and sucked his free Big MOFO's premium blend cappuccino from the edge of an extra-large mug with the Big MOFO logo emblazoned across it. As he did, he contemplated a quick workout at the gym —just long enough to flirt with some of the specto girls using his Ricardo Montalbán voice. It had worked like a charm yesterday, and the day before yesterday. And the day before that. Yes siree, Reggie was starting to feel right at home in the Ministry of Specto.

He'd already sent out half of today's invitations to the Meet Big MOFO Dinner Event, and it was only 11:00 a.m. When he arrived at his office this morning there was another list waiting for him on his desk, just as there had been every other morning since he'd started. And since he remained incommunicado, as far as Jill Chinaski went, there was nothing else to do but pace himself. In an obligatory nod to the polycelaphic sisters, balance, harmony, and proportion, he was now in the habit of doing half the list in the morning and half in the afternoon. The rest of his time was spent drinking Big MOFO's premium blend coffee and steaming in Big MOFO's health and fitness center.

Reggie took a final gulp of his cappuccino. Jabbing his long primate tongue into the mug, he lapped at the cinnamon-flecked film of steamed-milk foam. He checked his watch—a Curious George Timex that had been a gift from Professor Shore on his thirteenth birthday. Despite its considerable age and growing keepsake value, the watch kept time perfectly. Deciding to forego a steam this morning, Reggie strolled back to his office in a characteristic semi-upright gait, careful not let his knuckles drag too noticeably. Along the way, he delighted his colleagues by greeting them with a variety of voice settings. "Morning," said Orson Welles. "Heya," said Sylvester Stallone. "Hi there," said Sean Connery. "Salutations," said Laurence Olivier. "Nice to see you," said Charlton Heston. "Hewwo," said Elmer Fudd.

He climbed into his office chair. Although reluctant to mess with his routine, he picked up the letterhead and scanned the second half of the list. Names and more names. This is going to be some event, thought Reggie. He did a rough calculation in his head, concluding that he must have sent out two hundred invitations in the past four-point-five days. If even half of them show up, it will be quite the production. It was then, as he imagined the guests sucking up electric blue Jell-O and chit-chatting politics around Big MOFO, that something on the page jumped out at him. A name. A familiar name. "Wow!" said Reggie to no one. "Is Professor Shore ever going to be surprised." And then he had an idea. A great idea. To his amazement, it popped with great ease into his oversized chimp's brain. And so it was that vibrating with excitement, and tingling from too much Big MOFO premium blend coffee, Reggie opened the laptop and began to type.

"Mindcast on. News media. Current news. Los Angeles" Jerry broke three eggs into a frying pan and scrambled them. The PNN newscaster materialized there among the broken yolks.

. . . with the Mayor vowing to crack down on wilderness radicals who insist on keeping canines and felines, euphemistically called pets, in their homes. Humans -first groups have applauded the Mayor's tough stance but say it just doesn't go far enough.

The door behind him wheezed and slid open. "Hey," said Reggie.

"Just in time. You want some scrambled eggs?"

"Yeah, sure. I'm starving." Reggie pulled a stool up to the stainless steel island marooned in the center of the kitchen.

"Professor Shore was asking about you at the lab today."

"Oh man. What did you tell him?"

"The truth, sort of. I told him you got a job, which is true . . . in a grocery store, which is not true. But he'd flip out if he knew you were working for the Ministry of Specto." Jerry worked the eggs back and forth with a spatula. "How is the coordinator position going anyway? What kind of special events are you planning?"

"Can't say. Top secret," said Sean Connery as 007.

"What can be so top secret about special events?"

"You'd be surprised."

"Hang on," said Jerry.

In other breaking news, Party officials have confirmed that eighteen people in the greater Los Angeles area have died from an ether-born virus sent to them from an unknown and apparently untraceable source. Specto agents are feverishly searching for clues but so far have come up empty-handed.

"What is it?"

Jerry raised a halting hand.

Among the dead is Rajiv Shakti, a geneticist at the California Institute of Technology, whose controversial work on the prolongation of human life was blacklisted by the Ministry of Science last year after he exhibited a lab rat, Methuselah, which allegedly had been genetically programmed to live four hundred years. Officials were quick to point out that Shakti's prediction of a four-century life span for the rodent turned out to be highly erroneous when the rat Methuselah was only days later euthanized by Ministry of Nature officials.

"Holy cow! Rajiv Shakti is dead. I wonder if Professor Shore has heard the news yet. They go way back."

Reggie took a moment to process this information. He knew that Rajiv Shakti he was a professor at Caltech. But he had the oddest feeling, a nagging suspicion, that the name Shakti should mean something more to him than that.

The Ministry of Health says it has never seen such a virus before. Experts claim that the virus causes a neural overload, leading to acute encephalitis and ending dramatically with brain detonation.

"So what happened to him?" said Reggie.

"Some ether-born virus. Probably embedded in a Mindcast thought-o-gram. Sounds like the virus causes the brain to explode."

That's when it hit Reggie—the name, *Shakti*. It had been the first name on his list. He'd sent out an invitation to Rajiv Shakti in a Mindcast thought -o-gram on his first day. And now, five days later, the Professor was dead.

Reggie felt sick. His stomach gurgled, went from simmer to boil in the space of a moment. His breathing became sharp and labored, and his head felt light and tingly. Just when it seemed he might succumb to this un-expected malaise, Reggie snapped out of it. Shook his head and gathered his wits. He knew what he had to do.

"Eat up," said Jerry, sliding a plate of scrambled eggs in front of him.

"Sorry, lost my appetite," said Reggie. Then he sprang from the stool, landing with impressive primate agility, and sprinted for the door.

"Where you going?"

"New York," said Reggie. "To see a woman about a monkey."

Fifteen minutes later, Reggie was scampering up the aisle of the Big MOFO Control Room with his laptop pressed tightly to his bare and hairy chest. He had opted for a back-to-the-wild look, partly as a primate protest and partly because things could, and in all likelihood would get a little wild—Mutual-of-Omaha wild. The row of spectors, who sat silently specting every man, woman, and child in the Combined Sectors, took no notice of him. That is until he jumped up onto the marble podium.

"You maniacs!" screamed Charlton Heston. "Goddamn you all to hell." A few heads raised and a few sets of eyes then focused beyond the faraway sights and sounds in their heads to front-and-center of the control room. Reggie raised the laptop over his head. "Clear out or Big MOFO here gets an unexpected upgrade." He made to smash the glowing, overturned punch bowl but stayed his hand at the last moment. It was dramatic but effective, and the spectors suddenly jumped to their feet and scrambled for the door.

"Tell Chinaski to get in here, pronto. And I'm not monkeying around."

Reverend Billy Layman's black limousine conveyance dropped to street level and sidled up to the curb. The tinted window whirred open and a shirtless young man sporting a black cowboy hat and a mind-numbing web of tattoos stepped up to it. "Nice conveyance," said the goateed young cowboy, clearly impressed.

"Get in."

"You got it, pops." The cowboy pulled off his hat and jumped in. "What do you want today? Felch? Fuck?" His wide grin had been chipped by the lusty, sometimes hard-hitting demands of the job. "I know. I bet you wanna ring my bell with your ten kilo hammer. Am I right?"

"Shut up," said the reverend. "Let's keep this simple. I do the talking and you do the sucking. Nothing fancy, twisted, or unnatural. Just a good, old-fashioned, down-on-the-farm, face-fuck. Got it?" With this, the reverend dropped the zipper of his pants and waited.

"Holy shit, pops! What the hell happened to you?" The cowboy's outburst was cut short by Billy Layman's small but ringed fist crashing into his jaw.

"What did I say about shutting up? Now, start sucking."

The young cowboy regained his senses and dropped his head down to the reverend's lap.

Incoming ciphertext thoughtogram.

"Show thought-o-gram."

Showing thought-o-gram: <i ask for more i swear i think of two they fall in love when the feeling is gone away my hopes were gone too this one is you are tryin the feeling for real and im ready to change for you know i cant love anymore when im there even now> end of ciphertext.

"Search for key."

Key located.

"Apply key."

*Applying key: <i ask for **more** i swear i **think** of two **they** fall in love when the feeling is **gone** away my **hopes** were gone too **this** one is you are **tryin** the feeling for real and im **ready** to change for **you** know i cant love anymore when im **there** even **now**>*

"Compress."

Compressing: <monkeygoneapeshitneedyouherenow>

"Space and punctuate."

Spacing and punctuating: <Monkey gone apeshit. Need you here now!>

"Extirpate thought-o-gram."

Thought-o-gram extirpated.

Reverend Layman's eyes fluttered and rolled back in his head, the only discernible sign that he had right then reached climax. "Okay. That will do."

The young cowboy sat up, wiped his mouth along his tattooed arm.

"Fifty bucks, pops."

"Here's a hundred. Now get out. I got somewhere to be."

The Control Room door opened and in walked Jill Chinaski. "It's about time," said Reggie, half to himself, half to his boss. As Chinaski approached the podium, a man stepped from behind her.

"Who's that?" Reggie raised the laptop and waggled it over his head.

"Let's just say he's an interested party."

"I'm Reverend Billy Layman, Reggie. I understand you're doing top-notch work around here."

"Until I found out they're using me to send out a head-exploding virus."

"Calm down, Reggie. What are you talking about?" The words swished soothingly from Chinaski's crimson lips. "What virus?"

"Don't mess around with me. I know about Rajiv Shakti. Did I do that? Tell me now or I'm going to lobotomize Big MOFO big time.

"Okay, okay. Technically, you didn't do it. It's like this. In a truly astounding, almost poetic way, in a way that would have Saussure rolling in his grave, the word actually is the thing, in this case. The phrase Big MOFO's specting you is the programmed virus. When written out manually and sent as a Mindcast thought-o-gram, the otherwise harmless phrase becomes a lethal virus. Clever, don't you think?"

Reggie's shoulders drooped perceptibly, as the full force of this painful realization right then hit him, landed like a sucker punch. He was a killer. A murderer. "But why me? I mean, anyone could have manually typed that phrase and sent it out in a Mindcast thought-o-gram."

"But anyone else would've been tracked down by our own spectors. Don't forget, Reggie, that you are a chimp. You have no Big MOFO remote implant. Even if the spectors were able to track the thought-o-gram back to your laptop, there's no one there, no one to identify. You see what I mean? They would've written it off as some kind of technological glitch. But you were smarter than I thought and you figured it out, smart little monkey that you are. That was my mistake."

"Yeah it was." Reggie felt his throat tighten. He thought he might cry. But he stiffened his normally elastic upper lip. "So, how do you stop the virus? I want you to save Professor Shore. I only sent his invitation yesterday."

Chinaski rotated her head toward her companion, who had remained silent up till now. The Reverend took a measured step forward, slipping easily into character. "There's no way to stop it. Your professor will be dead by morning. In fact, he may be dead now, even as we speak"

"Goddamn you!" cried Charlton Heston. Reggie blinked out a tear. "Why, why do you want Professor Shore dead? Is it because of me? Because he made a talking chimp? Because he messed with your precious natural order of things?

The Reverend chuckled, as if gauging the utter absurdity of the question. "Reggie, Reggie. It really has nothing to do with you. You are a pawn in an extravagant, albeit deadly game. Oh yes, a talking, intelligent monkey is fascinating and all. But really, what does it matter if monkeys do or don't talk? There are so few of you left anyway—monkeys, I mean." The Reverend took another step closer. He unfastened his belt, unzipped his zipper then dropped his pants.

"Oh, Bill! Is that really necessary?"

"Shut up, Chinaski!" He spun around and raised a hand, as if to strike at the Managing Director of Specting in Quadrant One, but he didn't. "You work for me. Don't forget it." Then turning back to Reggie, the reverend spoke calmly: "Look at this Reggie. Come closer. Look at this."

Reggie's round chinless jaw dropped. There between the Reverend's legs, sprouting from his pelvis was a horribly bent penis. It looked like some giant mutant worm skewered on a giant mutant fish hook. The tip was flat, as if at some makeshift moment in the past it had been used to nail white pickets to a fence. It was hideous, truly hideous. There was no getting around that. But the real problem, as far as Reggie could see, was it appeared that the horribly bent penis with a flattened tip wasn't the only sex organ in that general and private region of the reverend's person. Below it, a splayed mollusk-like vagina, gray and swollen, sucked air in a bewildering way. For the second time tonight, Reggie thought he might be sick. He gagged back a rallying force of spittle.

"Yes, that's right. I'm a hermaphrodite . . . in the very worst way, thanks to Professor Shakti and your Professor Shore."

"But I don't understand. How could they possibly be responsible for that . . . for those?

The Reverend pulled up his pants and fastened them. Then he slid his wallet from a back pocket and removed a photograph, flicking it to Reggie.

"Your daughter?"

"No that's me. Belinda Layman. It was taken when I was an eighteen-year-old coed at Caltech. You see, I was enrolled in a course in elementary genetics with a young, charming, and particularly brilliant professor. Yes, that's right, it was Professor Leo Shore. You see, about the time Leo started Project Logos, he was also working with a senior colleague of his, Professor Rajiv Shakti, whom you know of, developing an easy-to-use, two-step home sex-change kit. The first day of classes, they asked for volunteers who would be willing to try the test. I had never really considered a sex change before that point, yet I had always felt that my feet were too big for a girl, and I had a fair harvest of peach fuzz on my upper lip. At the time, it seemed I was halfway there already. Anyway, I wanted to get close to Professor Shore, so I volunteered, thinking that if the sex change actually did work, then I would also be able to change back the other way if I didn't like being a man. What I didn't know at the time was the kit was in the earliest stages of development and had never been tried on humans before. Oh, I think they may've turned a cock into a hen, a goose into and gander, and maybe even a hog into a sow, but nothing more than that. To make a long story short, this is what happened. As you can see, it didn't work. And there was no going back. I dropped out of college, humiliated, confused, and worst of all a virgin."

"But I thought the sex change kit was Professor Shore's project." said Reggie. "Professor Shakti has never come with us to any science conventions."

"It was Professor Shakti's idea in the first place. But he dropped out of the project while it was still in the early stages, sometime after my unfortunate incident. That left Professor Shore. He refused to give up and took over the project himself. Twenty-five years and he still hasn't given up, developing new and improved home sex-change kits every few years. Talk about your perseverance, talk about your patience! But he's not the only one who's patient. Twenty-five years I've been waiting to take my revenge. It took a quarter of a century for me to become wealthy enough and powerful enough to finally exorcise those old demons. And I couldn't have done it without you, Reggie."

"But what about all the others? What did they do?"

Chinaski stepped forward. "Nothing. At least nothing to me.

"Then why did you make me kill them?"

"Reggie, Reggie. Such a naïve monkey," said Chinaski. "Why did I do it? For money, of course. What else? You'd be surprised how many rich people will pay to see the heads of their enemies explode. It wasn't hard to find—"

But before the Managing Director of Specting in Quadrant One could finish that thought, Reggie was down from the podium, up the aisle, and out the door.

"Should I send someone after him?"

"Let him go," said Reverend Layman. "Who's going to believe anything a talking monkey has to say?"

The apartment was unlocked and the lights were on but no one was around. He wondered if Jerry had rushed off somewhere. Reggie scuttled from room to room, alternating hands and feet, in a frantic search for his roommate, his friend. He tried every voice setting he had. "Jerry?" said Orson Welles. "Hey, Jerr," mumbled Sly Stallone. "I say, Jerry. Are you at home?" intoned Laurence Olivier. "Come on, Jerry," slurred Sean Connery. "Jerry, my friend," purred Ricardo Montalbán. 'For God's sake, Jerry," bellowed Charlton Heston. "Jerwwy?" lisped Elmer Fudd. But none of them got a response. That's when Reggie began to really panic.

His present consternation stemmed from the fact that he, Reggie, had made two executive decisions, according to the dictates of his own conscience, as coordinator of special events: the first was to take a long steam his first day on the job; the second was to invite his friend Jerry to the Meet Big MOFO Dinner Event. The idea had come to him when he saw Professor Shore's name on the list. No one from the ministry would know if he added one more name to the list, he'd thought. It was going to be such a wonderful surprise, maybe even make up for not being invited to the '46 Science Fair. And the cruel, really twisted irony of it all was he'd thought Jerry would be excited, so excited to accompany Professor Shore to the special event.

Finding no sign of Jerry in the apartment, Reggie decided to look around outside. He hurried to the floor transporter. To say time was of the essence was the understatement of his life. But then, even if he did find Jerry alive, he didn't know what he would do. There was nothing Reggie could do to save him. He knew that. Still, he had to see him, to talk to his best—only—friend.

There was no sign of Jerry in the ECEG or the apartment lobby. That left the conveyance lot. Even from a distance, in the heatless light of techsave green bulbs, he could see Jerry, hanging half-in and half-out of his economy conveyance. Reggie rushed to him, blubbering already.

"Jerry, Jerry!" The frightened chimp pulled his friend out onto the ground and placed the dying man's head in his truncated lap. It was immediately clear that Jerry wasn't doing well, not well at all. His nose and ears were bleeding and his eyes were the size and color of genetically engineered beets.

"I'm so sorry, Jerry. So sorry," sobbed Reggie. "It was me. I did this to you. I did it to all of them."

"Prof . . . Profess . . . Shakti?"

"Yes, I killed Professor Shakti. I killed Professor Shore. I sent the thought-o-grams."

"Prof . . . Profess . . . Professor Shore?"

"Yes, he's dead, Jerry. I killed him." Reggie spoke frantically now, as it was clear the end was near. "Can you forgive me, Jerry? Please Jerry! Can you forgive me?"

Jerry pulled him close. "Du . . . Dumb mon . . . monkey." A smile trickled from his lips. Then his eyes opened wide and he went stiff. There came a voiceless shriek and shutter, and a moment later it was over. Jerry went limp, suddenly limp, deathly limp. Reggie watched his friend's brain leak like a dark caramel sap onto the pavement.

And Reggie wept.

Closed his eyes and really wept. Long and loud it came, with heaving gasps and moans, a sound that needed no voice transposer to render it intelligible. For it was an unbridled jungle sound that echoed through the hollow chambers of Reggie the talking chimp's housebroken heart.

More than anything else, he'd wanted to tell Jerry about the job, about his first job, only job. And that the past five days had been the best days of his life (except for the brain-exploding virus part). It goes without saying that he hadn't meant to kill anyone. Least of all, his friends. He'd only wanted a chance to prove himself. To Professor Shore, to Jerry, and most of all, to himself. How desperately he wanted to prove that he was more than just some lab experiment that was no longer relevant, no longer of interest to anyone.

Reggie held his dead friend close. He thought he might never let him go, might drag him through the streets screeching and howling: "My friend, my friend, I have killed my friend."

Reggie felt his own brain swell and feared it too might explode, as if it were too big for his chimp skull, as if the weight of it were more than he could bear, as if five to seven million years had passed in the wink of an eye and left him feeling suddenly tired, so tired.

The events of the past week looped through his head, over and over, crowding him closer and closer to the edge, where even to fall was no release. For what lay below was but a rocky landing of hard questions.

Why? Why had Professor Shore done it?

Why had he so profoundly messed with natural order of things?

Why had he, Reggie, been born—made—at all?

Was it only to bring death to those who cared about him? Loved him?

A tear trembled at the edge of the chimp's eye. It was painful to see how naïve he had been, really painful.

But Reggie saw it all so clearly now, like a fog lifting over the treetops or a mist blowing off the water. What the chimp now knew was this—he'd been a monkey and not a man. Or maybe it was the other way around—he'd been a man and not a monkey.

He wasn't sure which.

Acknowledgements

Thanks to Kent Wolf and Didier Imbot for shaping early versions of the novel. Thanks to Vincent Ponka for first publishing the book. Thanks to fellow authors David Lentz and Terry Richard Bazes for championing it. Thanks to Jack O'Keefe for recent revisions, and to Alan Shaw for making me look prettier than I really am. And last but not least, a special thanks to Jinhee, for her patience and understanding.

About the Author

Gary Anderson lives with his wife and three children in central New Jersey. *Animal Magnet* is his first novel.